WOULD I LIE TO YOU?

Also available by Nicole Blades

Have You Met Nora?

The Thunder Beneath Us

Earth's Waters

WOULD I LIE TO YOU?

A Novel

NICOLE BLADES

NEW YORK

Published in the United States by Crooked Lane Books, an imprint of The Quick Brown Fox & Company LLC.

Crooked Lane Books and its logo are trademarks of The Quick Brown Fox & Company LLC.

Library of Congress Catalog-in-Publication data available upon request.

ISBN (hardcover): 979-8-89242-493-6
ISBN (paperback): 979-8-89242-494-3
ISBN (ebook): 979-8-89242-495-0

Cover design by Heedayah Lockman

Printed in the United States.

www.crookedlanebooks.com

Crooked Lane Books
34 West 27th St., 10th Floor
New York, NY 10001]

First Edition: April 2026

The authorized representative in the EU for product safety and compliance is eucomply OÜPärnu mnt 139b-14, 11317 Tallinn, Estonia, hello@eucompliancepartner.com, +33757690241

10 9 8 7 6 5 4 3 2 1

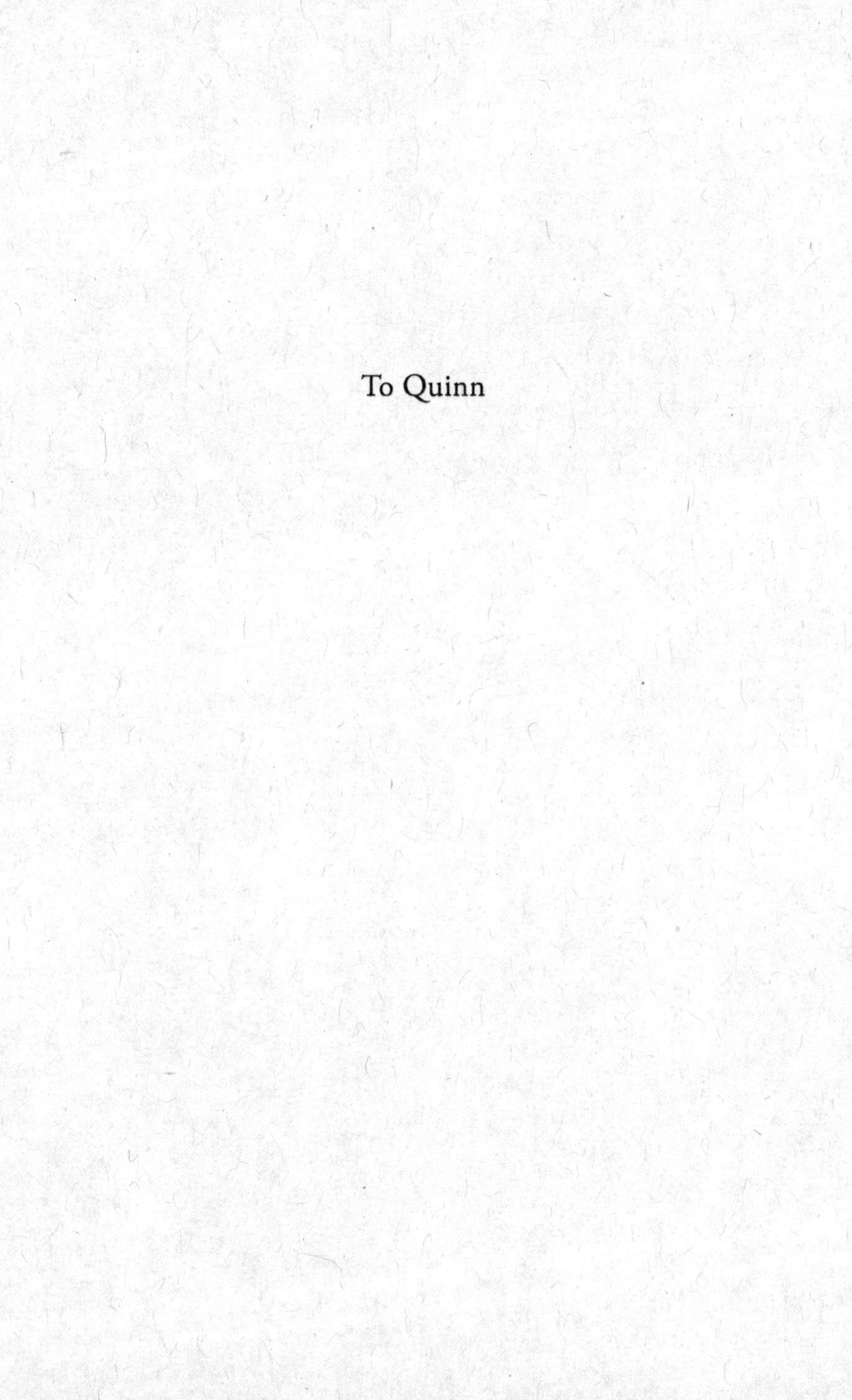

To Quinn

"In order to rise
From its own ashes
A phoenix
First
Must
Burn."

—Octavia Butler, *Parable of the Talents*

CHAPTER ONE

I'm too old for this shit.

Lu has whispered these six words at least three times in the last ten minutes. She is crouching against a thick, open door to a subterranean vault, sweaty and panting, making the mouthpiece of her sleek ski mask damp and gross. The red light strobing above her intensifies. Soundless alarms—so sly and smug—have always annoyed her more than the blaring box standard sirens. She glances up at the flashing light, snarling at the loathsome thing, then quickly snaps out of the one-way stare down. She knows that the sound of shuffling boots on the ground is imminent.

This is the absolute last place Lu wants to be right now. She would trade anything to be somewhere else. Truly, *anywhere* else. Even getting cornered by Lizette, her maudlin downstairs neighbor with the unfortunate veneers, and having to listen for far too long as the woman unloads one of her classic, disjointed stories—again!—about the time some badly aging celebrity tried *to get some of her cookie* at a long-defunct nightclub feels like a good time compared to this mess. But Lu knows that no amount of wishful thinking or low-chanted mantras will change the facts, which are: One, she is trapped like a feral night creature in this camouflaged jewelry vault, and two, she is the only person skilled enough to find a way out.

When the coded message arrived about this job, Lu accepted because it was close to home and seemed straightforward enough. Plus, if she had declined, it would have elevated in status in the system and would surely mean a trip to Antwerp for her to complete a bigger job with a more complicated everything—strategy, target, delivery, degree of risk. And, most important to Lu, a more intricate cover story. Coming up with a plausible, clean story had been the hardest part of her last job. Hardest part of her last seven jobs, if she's being honest. It's as if, even in his young years, her sweet Solomon can see through the pilling woven knits, find the frayed yarn ends poking out clear enough to pull them and unravel the whole thing. Perhaps, after lying to him for most of his little life, the boy can just smell it on her, the forced fiction.

If she could have it her way, this would be Lu's very last job. She would make the necessary sacrifices, throw herself on the fire, and beg to be released from this work, from this sideways life. If she could write it, she would have asked for leniency the moment she found out she was pregnant. Every job since her son's birth has had an added thick layer of risk lobbed on top. The thought of getting pinched, not being able to see her sweet boy grow up, wakes her randomly at night, sweaty and panicked. If she could write it, she would have found some obscure reason to be rendered *not viable*. Put on medical leave, as if that were a thing in this very particular line of business. This, the compunction, her morality rearing up to bite her in the center of her lukewarm heart, this is what is driving Lu to want out.

Out. Lu scoffs at the thought. The first rule of The Atlas was simple: the only way out was in a pine box, with your identity released to the authorities and your real name besmirched, posthumously. Lu shakes her head with tuts of disapproval for pinning hope to the impossible and wasting critical minutes doing so right now on what was supposed to be a cakewalk.

She shakes her head again at the reality of the situation. It wasn't even hubris that landed her here. She had studied the blueprint with her usual careful calculation. Gaining entry to the nondescript warehouse in Hell's Kitchen was indeed a cakewalk. That is, until Security Guard Number Three.

"They're definitely not paying that asshole enough for all that," Lu says, remembering the spinning, bucking ride she had taken on the man's broad, slimy back moments ago. "Where'd he even get that dowel? A fucking metal *dowel*," she hisses.

The sharp sting to her left side quickly reminds her that she cannot afford to stay put. She draws a deep breath. The dank of the basement crawls up her nostrils like weakened smelling salts. Lu stifles the cough it brings, but this only causes her lower abdomen to tighten, which in turn expands the pressing pain beneath her ribs. Hand-to-hand was never truly her thing. She can hold her own in a relatively fair matchup, but this was not that. SG-3 was the size of a full-grown grizzly bear.

Lu looks down, trying to assess the wound, but of course her skintight black coverall makes it impossible to see anything. At least there's no blood. She nods. This is either going to be a horrendous bruise or her spleen has ruptured.

"Do or die," she says, clutching her now-throbbing left side and peeling herself off the floor. She slides her feet forward a single pace and peeks around the corner. Nothing but a long, dark hallway in front of her. Lu pulls herself back to the wall and listens. There's been a shift in the quiet, and it's not just her quickened breath. In the distance, she can hear music. Or is it talking? She injected SG-3 with a near-lethal amount of dirty ketamine. "How is he awake," she mumbles, a slight panic beginning to flutter in her chest. The fact that she is worried is creating its own new, acute class of anxiousness. More proof that Lu needs out of this life.

The talking is a bit louder now. Speedy, anxious talking. Maybe it's the radio, she thinks. Comms base. Lu holds her breath, closes her eyes, and plugs one ear, straining to listen deeper.

Nothing clear comes through and waiting to decipher anything more is a mistake.

Lu strips off the ski mask like a husk and pushes back the sweaty attached hood, gripping the pooled fabric behind her neck and lightly pressing the back of her head into the rough, scratchy surface. "Failure is fatal," she says and takes two more breaths, each one slow and even. She checks her vintage pilot watch. The red sweep-second hand strikes twelve.

"Do or die," Lu says again, louder this time, and scoops up a small duffle bag resting at her feet. There's a glimpse of something dazzling, diamonds shimmering as she zips the bag fully shut. Lu yanks the sweaty mask down over her head again and pulls up the hood along with her posture, straps the bag to her chest, and sprints at full speed toward the hallway. As she reaches its opening, Lu drops to her knees, bends her body flat backward—like the ultimate limbo move—and slides beneath a laser beam sensor alarm. Then, without even a heavy exhale, she disappears into the dark void.

Lu stands on a bustling sidewalk in Times Square, the warehouse and its airless basement in the far distance. She looks like a wholly different version of herself. Reimagined. To anyone watching, Lu appears composed and stylish, her clammy ski mask replaced by an auburn bobbed wig and her fitted jumpsuit mostly covered by a black, belted-waist, high-neck trench. Despite the pain in her side radiating and reaching up along her rib cage, Lu appears unwrinkled as she practically glides in a pair of strappy, brushed-leather heels toward a waiting black SUV with tinted-out windows. She gets into the back of the car like a royal: bum first, a swing of her legs up and into the vehicle, knees and feet pressed together. It's all smooth and unrushed. No attention paid to the blaring sirens from police cars—many unmarked—as they race west toward Hell's Kitchen.

With the shallow echoed *click* of the car door closed, Lu flops back onto the leather seats and tosses the duffle beside her. She nods at the driver through his rearview—only catching the very top part of his face, as usual—and slides the seat belt on, wincing as she connects it on her left side. She is hurting, but decided: This needs to be one of the last jobs. Needs. The vehicle takes off, cruising into the stretched-out traffic and blending into the lights, cabs, cars, and chase of the New York night.

True, she may be too old for it, but Lucille Barlow is still *the shit*.

CHAPTER TWO

Harry always likes when his wife is on top. He especially enjoys Lu on top during morning sex. Seeing her in control, her firm breasts, sculpted arms, trim waist, and impressively flat stomach, all in their smooth, glistening glory, so exposed and inviting, gives him an indescribable thrill. Put plainly, over their decade together, he's had to work on his stamina. In the beginning, those first couple of months after they got together, Harry would often find himself *leaving the party early*, as he used to put it, hoping his willingness to poke fun at his own shortcomings (literally) coupled with his natural charm would quell the utter mortification of this unfortunate prematurity. That's why, even all these years later, on the off day when Lu tells him that she's tired and would rather just give him a hand job instead of the whole avocado—his term—it translates to a point of pride for Harry.

But this morning, for reasons unknown to him, Lu seems ready for all of it. The whole avocado and the toast too! Harry refuses to question or even have a second's thought about it. His wife wants him. Ravishingly. And Harrison Barlow is no dolt.

Lu is meeting Harry at every stroke. It's all so energetic and free, and a little smutty. Lu seems unconcerned about the thinness of the walls in their brownstone or potentially waking their eight-year-old son, Solomon, asleep in the bedroom a few steps away from theirs. It feels like the old days, Harry thinks, as he glides his hands from cupping her breasts down along her sides where the sheets are bunched around her like a hoop skirt. He had noticed that Lu is covering up more this morning and she keeps moving his hands away from her waist. But he's quickly distracted from pondering this when she leans down, wrapping his hand loose around her neck, and whispers steamy filth directly into his ear. All of it shifts Harry into another gear and right now he wants nothing more than to plunge himself deeper inside of this woman—as deep as humanly possible. A single purred *more* from Lu against his cheek and Harry is about to implode. He roughly presses his fingers into Lu's skin, just above her waist, beneath the sheet, as if she were something he could use to ground himself.

As Harry pushes Lu down further on his thrusting pelvis, he grips her side, hard. Lu lets out a yelp that sounds like a wounded barn animal.

"Christ! You all right?" Harry squawks. He scrambles to sit up without pitching his already folded-up wife off the side of the bed. "Did I do something?" He doesn't know where to put his hand first, as the two are still connected at the sex bits.

Lu, bent into a trembling ball, rolls off her husband and gathers herself onto her knees, her head buried in the short stack of decorative pillows the two didn't bother removing from the bed last night. She doesn't want to whimper but also doesn't want to move even an inch. The doctor told Lu yesterday that a bruised spleen will feel like this—along with left shoulder pain, potential lightheadedness, blurred vision, and confusion—for two to four weeks.

"You need to be much more careful, Lucille," Dr. Sherbrooke had said, stating the obvious while writing out a script for pain meds that they both knew Lu would never use. "Yes, you're in fantastic shape for your age—obviously—but next time let one of those strapping UPS guys help you move the heavy equipment around the studio, OK?"

For your age. The backhanded slap of a compliment barely gets a brow raise from Lu anymore. She has been told how much younger she looks her whole adult life. Melanin, she used to demur with an easy smile back in her thirties. Genetics, she would say in her early forties, despite growing up in foster care and having no clues about who her birth parents were. But now, at forty-eight, receiving this worthless bouquet is akin to telling this woman that she has curly hair or size eight feet. It brings no reaction from her at all. That said, Lu's youthful appearance has been an incredible (and free) marketing tool for the Pilates studio she owns. And that small business has helped to keep her largely injury-free for her *other,* much bigger business. Well, not counting SG-3 and the Mystery Dowel, as Lu has dubbed the warehouse incident that went down five days ago.

"No . . . you didn't do anything," Lu whispers through clenched teeth. "I—hurt myself at the studio. It's nothing."

"Woman, what are you doing to yourself . . . let me see," Harry says, carefully trying to unfurl his crumpled wife.

"It's fine, it's fine." Lu pulls the sheets up, covering herself. She knows how concerning the purple contusion looks, and the pain is beginning to cloud her thoughts. She cannot afford to trip up on any key details to her story while trying to manage Harry's distress. "I'll be fine."

"I just"—he nervously runs his hovering hand along Lu's torso, unsure of where to set it down—"don't like seeing you broken like this. It's weird."

"Weird?" Lu says with a grimace. "H, don't start with the strong Black queen diatribe. Please. I beg."

His eyes narrow and his face begins to pucker. "Strong Black—Jesus, I'm not saying that!" Harry pulls himself up in a rush, ready to defend his virtues, when he catches a glimpse of Lu's subtle smirk. He relaxes back against the headboard. "Ah . . . you're havin' a laugh, heh?"

"Yes, my Black king, I am having a laugh," Lu says, and flattens out the curve of her back, still wincing. "We're good, I'm good. Let me just catch myself for a minute and then—"

"Round two?" Harry says, with alacrity. "I did have all those blackberries yesterday." He wags his brow at her.

"God—you have to stop listening to that podcast."

"Sometimes they have good advice," Harry says, with a deep shrug.

"Like the whale testicle thing?" Lu eases onto a pillow, making sure to maintain her I'm-totally-fine disposition.

Harry cringes. "Yeah, that wasn't the best episode from my boys."

"Exactly. Show some pride, if not as a scientist, at least as an adult male with a developed frontal lobe, babe," Lu says. "Anyway, the movers are going to be here in less than two hours, and Lizette said that company is oddly punctual."

"Doesn't matter, really. We're not footing that bill, right?"

"Still, I don't want a bunch of sweaty dudes cracking their knuckles, annoyed and waiting on us to be ready."

"We'll be ready, Loubie," Harry says.

"You still have to finish up your man hobby box under the stairs."

"*Man hobby?* Can you make me sound more ridiculous?"

Lu adopts Harry's wry look from a moment ago. "We could also let the movers just rifle through it, free of context . . ."

"Fine," Harry says, moving to get out of bed. "But I'm keeping my Sir Bobby Charlton mug. Don't mind that it's cracked; it's commemorative." He scoops up his pajama pants bunched at the bottom of the bed, slings them over his shoulder, and strides naked toward the door of their cramped en suite bathroom. Thanks to a big win at the genetic lottery, at fifty-four, Harry looks at least a decade younger. Trim and sinewy, the man is debonair defined. And a fine example of what it means to be a gentle man.

"I'll pop in the shower," Harry says. "Get it started for you." He blows Lu a light kiss and makes his way through the mostly empty room. It's just their bed—which is being left behind—and stacked-high moving boxes waiting to be carted off.

"You do your thing. I'll make us some tea." Lu stretches for her ratty robe at the foot of the bed, gnashing her teeth behind a tight smile. "Last time in the ol' scullery, innit?"

"Well, be on with it, then," Harry says through a chuckle. Her cheap takes on his accent always brings at least half of a grin.

Lu waits, listening for the sound of the shower turning on. Once the familiar squeak reaches its pitch, she pads over to the small walk-in closet. She checks over her shoulder to make sure the bathroom door is still closed before hustling to a corner of the closet and pulls out a shoebox—her burn box—stashed in a loose baseboard. The box is filled with money stacks; passports

for Germany, Italy, France, Sweden, Belgium, Canada, and the United States; a collection of flip phones; and a worn leather tool roll. She glances over her shoulder once more before slipping a black, unembellished device—several grades up from a burner—into her robe pocket and then removing the roll from the box and spreading it out. Inside sits a hefty necklace in gold, silver, and sparkling gemstones, including the flawless, heart-shaped, one-hundred-and-three-carat Eternal Nova diamond in a tamper-evident bag on top of a lineup of lockpicks and bump keys, along with an angle grinder, miniature cordless Sawzall, and a dismantled thermic lance.

She holds the necklace up to her face, peering at the twinkling jewelry in the baggie. "Bitch, you weren't even worth it," Lu says before clutching at her bruised side with her free hand. She shakes her head while stuffing everything back into the shoebox and returning the baseboard to its place. Lu turns to the phone next, an extremely secured line she uses to communicate with The Atlas. After a few quick screen taps, a pleasant-sounding automated female voice begins:

"Welcome to Atlas Ventures International. Please state your ID number."

"Twenty-two," Lu says.

"Voice match verified," the automation says. "You are now being connected to the help desk, Twenty-two. Thank you, and have a productive day." There's a *ping* and then silence.

"Proceed," says a new voice. A human one. Male.

"Hey, uh . . . I need to talk . . . well, actually, first I have to—"

The man interrupts. "Are you compromised?"

"No—no!" Lu shakes her head. "I need to connect with my principal."

After a heavy pause, he responds, flatly, "Your request to connect to Seven is approved."

"Great," she says. "I'll fill him in and then—"

"You've been approved to leave a *message* for your principal. Connecting to voicemail for Seven. Stand by."

There's a *click* and another *ping* all before Lu can even object. A *voicemail*? Telling—and not asking—Mr. V about her New England move in a curt voicemail just doesn't seem right. There's no room for subtlety or grace in a voicemail. She disconnects without leaving a message and pulls herself up to standing.

The distant whoosh of the shower continues, but Lu hurries her movements anyway. She grabs her crumpled black duffle and stuffs the shoebox inside it as she walks quickly back into the bedroom and over to the moving box marked LU'S PILATES. She tucks the bag in it, beneath an assortment of resistance bands, deflated exercise balls, Pilates rings, and deconstructed parts of a springboard, then yanks the burner phone from her pocket, tossing it into her nearby yawning black canvas tote.

"Loubie?" Harry calls out to her from the shower, and she clambers across the bed to the closed bathroom door, racing to right herself. "Let's skip the tea," Harry says. "Coffee feels more like it."

Lu drops her head back, releasing her hard puff to the ceiling, then replies through the door. "Sure . . . no problem," she says.

"I need to be done with this," she whispers to herself, and tightens her robe sash as best she can without adding further pressure to her wounded side. She makes her way to the creaky hallway. It's time to wake him anyway. The boy. Lu's full beating heart, and her biggest motivation for desperately needing out.

* * *

AS LU ROUNDS the corner to the kitchen, she can hardly contain her smile. Part of the reason for this melted-butter grin is the bright, warm space itself. It was the main area into which she and Harry poured their money when it came to renovating the well-preserved late-nineteenth-century brownstone. They could tolerate a cramped bathroom with dated plumbing in their bedroom, and they silently agreed to ignore the random, wonky hisses and cracks the house would utter at any given moment. But for the kitchen, the command center, the Barlows refused to skimp. The bigger cause for Lu's early morning giddiness is parked at the eight-foot, white granite island, on his favorite of the four counter stools, eyes glued to his iPad propped up against a turned-over Cheerios box, watching the latest findings from the James Webb Space Telescope.

"Good morning, pumpkin," Lu says, softly, as she moves toward the boy, leaning in.

"It's having sensor issues again, Mom. Can you even believe this?" he says, not daring to look away from the video. "Why so many sensor issues? This is NASA!" He makes a face while reaching for a short mug to his left, his attention still fixed on the screen, and takes a careful sip.

"Wait. Young Barlow, you just gonna leave me hangin', bruv?" Lu says, playfully tossing her hands up in a deep shrug.

"Oh, sorry," Solomon says, giggling. "Good morning, Mom." He tilts his face up to hers, flashing a toothy smile as he waits for their usual AM greeting: an air high-five followed by a fist bump with the butt of the hand, a two-cheeked kiss, double finger guns fired simultaneously, and a wink—which until very recently used to be a blink from Solomon. As soon as it's over, the boy is back to the happenings of NASA.

Lu reaches out for the crown of his head and gently tousles the curly top of his faux-hawk. She scans the counter. Spilled dry cereal; milk dribbles and splash circles; a small, dingy-white, balled-up Nike sock; a patterned paper plate with crusted-over mac and cheese; a messy pile of old newspapers and torn-out catalogue pages; and four moving boxes, most of which contain a few kitchen and dining items that were tossed in at random.

She glances over Solomon's shoulder, narrowing her eyes at his screen. "Wait. How are you even on that thing this early? Did you bypass the parental controls again?"

"Mom. Please. Calling what you've set up *controls* is generous," Solomon says, taking a slurpy sip from his mug and ending it with a loud gulp. He presses and swipes at his iPad with the easiest flick of his finger. "A toddler can figure out how to bypass it. But we can work on improving your"—he makes exaggerated air quotes—"*parental controls* later, if you want."

"Doesn't that defeat the purpose?"

"I don't have all the answers!" Solomon says.

Lu palms his head, lightly wiggling her fingers against his scalp. "Good thing you're cute." She peeks into his mug as he reaches for it again. He's made himself some milk with a splash of tea in it. "Did you already figure out some breakfast? There should be a box with snacks for the road trip—" Lu looks around at the prized kitchen in disarray. "At least, I think there is . . . maybe there is?"

"Uh, I was thinking about maybe some toast or those peanut butter cracker sandwich thingies or the bagel chips or the granola bar or the—"

"But you couldn't decide."

"I couldn't decide," Solomon says, his shoulders dropping slightly as he looks down at his hands now gathered in his lap. He begins picking at the ragged skin around his cuticles.

Lu reaches out for the top of the boy's head once more before pulling out her own seat beside him. "Can we talk for a second?" she says. The boy nods but keeps his eyes on his fidgeting fingers in his lap while the YouTube video continues. Lu taps the screen to lower the volume, then latches on to the bottom edge of Solomon's stool and drags him into her even closer. She wants him to physically feel her steady, calm presence. "You know that it's OK to just choose something—anything—because you want it, right? Because it feels like the right thing for you. Even if *no one* else thinks so, it only matters how you feel about it, hon. And if that changes—if you decide in the middle of all of it that it's not what you want anymore—it's OK for you to choose something else."

"You mean if I make a mistake and choose wrong?" he says, slowly looking over at his mother at last.

"That's the thing, sweet pea. It's not a mistake. It's not wrong. It's just . . . one way instead of the other. You understand?"

Solomon turns back to staring down at his lap, his puckered lips twisted to the side as he chews the corner of his cheek, processing. He takes a breath as if to speak but nods a few times instead. Then, after a few more breaths, "OK," he says, plainly, and then again with more heart. He's smiling now and looking right into Lu's eyes. "I understand."

She pinches his chin. "Now, brekkie. I think I know what I can make that'll hit the spot."

"Thanks, Mom," he says, his soft voice squeezing Lu's heart, as always.

Solomon returns to his iPad as Lu heads over to the fridge. She pulls the door knowing that it's practically empty, but ventures in anyway. Two eggs, down-to-the-rind Parmigiano-Reggiano, chives, a swallow of apple juice, a handful of Alpine strawberries, and whatever milk hadn't already flooded Solomon's tea. With a plan to make the boy a quick but delicious omelet, Lu digs up a small frying pan from a half-packed moving box. She winces with each hinge at the waist but tries to breathe through it, stiffly checking over her shoulder, making sure Solomon is still focused on anything but her. There's something about the boy's deeply brown eyes, when they are locked in on Lu, that makes it hard for her to keep her lies as tightly stitched together as usual. Pangs of conscience will somehow manifest as a random nose-twitch or scalp itch when explaining to Solomon where she's been for the last two nights or answering his follow-up query on why she destroyed that cell phone in the backyard with a hammer.

Lu takes her time flipping the omelet just so before neatly folding it and sliding it onto a paper plate, then shaving off some flakes of cheese for the top. She rinses and cuts up the strawberries, the small, sharp knife moving with quickness and precision in her hands, then she adds the juicy red wedges to the side of the omelet—making doubly sure that the two things do not touch. She pours the bit of the apple juice into another squat mug, topping it off with water from the tap—a move she also must carry out stealthily—and positions it all so she's carrying it in one hand like a veteran server at a diner. She keeps the other hand gripping at the robe gathered to her left side. As she sets the plate, mug, ragged sheet of paper towel, and fork in front of Solomon, Lu stumbles, knocking his iPad over face down and splashing some of the juice on the counter. There's a fine dew of sweat collecting along her forehead and temples as a fresh stabbing pain between her rib cage assumes control of her whole body. She holds her breath, almost afraid to release it, and squeezes her eyes shut.

"Mom?" Solomon squawks as he leaps from his seat, grabbing at her. His clammy hand feels good against Lu's heated, prickly forearm. "What's wrong?"

"Ugh, God . . ." Lu mumbles and groans, exhaling through her gritted teeth. She drags her belly button toward her spine, tightening her core and trying to stay still. More than maintaining a slow and steady breath to ease the pain, Lu is concentrating on doing it for Solomon. He needs to see her whole, unscathed, standing upright and fine. "I—I—stubbed my toe just now."

"Your *toe*?"

"Yeah, I'm fine," she blurts out and quickly hobbles off toward the powder room down the hall. Short of shouting "Look over there!" and running away, the stubbed toe is the best Lu can do. She knows she cannot give this child even the slimmest chance to apply his keen observational skills and inductive reasoning to the moment.

Just as she hits the top of the hallway, Harry is swooping into the kitchen, his salt-and-pepper fade haircut so sharp it could slice bread, with a trim beard to match. He's wearing a pair of slim-fit black chinos and an untucked navy-blue oxford shirt with the sleeves rolled and only the middle three buttons fastened. His head is down as he runs his belt through the front loop, and so the two collide.

Lu's tears are already pooling; there's nothing she can do to stop them.

"Hey . . ." Harry grabs hold of Lu at the shoulders, easing her out of her hunch. "You all right?" he says, craning his neck, trying to meet her eyes..

"I . . . hit my toe on the island," she says, tossing her head back toward the kitchen. Her voice returned to its regular poise. "I'm good, though." She leans back and away, slightly, so that Harry can see her face. "I'm good."

"Yeah?"

"Yeah," Lu says, with a firmness that makes her almost believe it too.

CHAPTER THREE

A fourteen-year-old Lucille is sat in the back of a cramped, junky station wagon parked in front of a small multifamily with a dated façade in Flatbush, Brooklyn. Beside her, a single shabby rucksack with a small pair of men's tactical boots tied to it. The social worker, a white woman with muddy-brown, overgrown, frizzy layers, a weak chin, and a prominent bosom, is on the sidewalk at the tail end of a stilted conversation with an unsmiling Black man standing like a soldier at attention by the top of the concrete steps. He is tall, with a taut belly, broad shoulders, and a sharp jaw. Lucille leans, easy and slow, toward the window, keeping her movements smooth while straining to hear the details of the discussion without turning to look directly at them. "Don't be obvious," she whispers to herself through gnashed teeth and tight lips. A refrain she had learned from the same stoic man talking to the social worker. Recalling yet another lesson the man, her latest foster parent, had taught her—this one about *the art of listening*—Lucille holds her breath, closes her eyes, and casually plugs the ear on her left. She can hear, but the voices are muffled. She slides her hand over to the handle of the manual window crank to ease it open a crack.

"Again, like I said on the phone last week, and the weeks before that, this wasn't my call. If it were up to me, she would stay put. But it's not up to me. I feel like I need you to know that I've always been in your corner, Vincent," the social worker says, before the man interrupts.

"It's Mr. King," he says. His voice deep and tone even, with his crisp Jamaican accent floating on the surface. "Although it may seem as if we are familiar, Miss Jacobs, we are not. I suggest we maintain the level of respect required even as our dealings have come to an end."

Lucille steals a quick glance at the scene, a scant grin peeling up the side of her face. She can't help it. Watching Vincent King put someone in their place had become one of her favorite things in these three years of living with him.

"Oh, uh, sorry . . . I—I apologize, Mr. King," Miss Jacobs stutters. "I guess I just didn't want to leave things without letting you know where I stood . . . at least. I've said many times that Lucille really thrived here with you, but she could benefit even more in a different environment."

"You mean, in a white neighborhood."

"No! I—I—that's not—no. No one is saying that." Miss Jacobs's voice is high in her chest. "I believe I've mentioned that our new agency director is African American. And it's not—I'm not saying that because she's African Ameri—wait, I—uh . . . look, you yourself agreed that Lucille could do well in a two-parent household, especially with a female influence in the home. And other children. You know that Lucille has been an only in the past three foster homes. She needs to be around other children, peers who are not just her classmates. You agreed with all of that in the meetings."

After a long beat, Mr. King, still staring down at the woman frozen on the cracked sidewalk, speaks. "Yes, and nothing's changed," he says. "Do not mistake my question now for some eleventh-hour plea to reverse something set in motion months ago, Miss Jacobs. I'm simply trying to confirm with *you* that the new home is safe."

"I understand that. However, like I said, I'm not allowed to share that information with you, Mr. King. I'm sorry," Miss Jacobs says, quickly adding, "But, as I've assured you, the welfare of these young people is always our top priority." Her words decanted into the wide gap between them, as if this time it might ease his foot from her neck.

"Right," he says, flatly.

"Uh . . . good . . . OK," she says. "Well, we should get going, then. Would you like to say one last goodbye to her before we leave? I know these things can be tender. I could wait here if you wanted to have a few minutes alone by the car . . . ?"

"Not necessary," Mr. King says. "We're good."

"Oh, OK . . . um, so . . . take care and . . . thank you, again," she says.

Lucille sneaks another glance through the corner of her eye as she eases the window back up. She can see him, hands in his pockets, statue-still, watching as the social worker scampers over to the car.

Once inside, Miss Jacobs turns to the back seat and gives Lucille a tense smile. The woman's droopy face is flushed and her already rheumy eyes seem even soggier. She gestures at the front steps with a tilt of her sloped chin. "Wave goodbye to Mr. Vin—King, Lucille. I know he will miss you as much as you will miss him." The smile begins to slide off Miss Jacobs's face despite the clear effort to keep it plastered there.

Lucille turns her head fully now and looks up at Mr. King, while the woman returns her gaze to the front and starts the car.

"I think this next home will be good for you too," Miss Jacobs says. "I mean, once we get you placed. In the meantime, you'll be at the group facility for a week or so. Then we'll get you placed . . ." The rest of her words get buried in a whisper. This is not what she told Mr. King mere seconds ago, not what she assured him. "Just a couple of weeks. You'll see."

But Lucille isn't listening to the woman's lies; she's already drifting. She can hear the social worker talking, though not really. It's as if the master volume on the world is gradually being turned down. She doesn't respond to the social worker, nor does she break her stare through the window. Her eyes are locked on Mr. V, the name she has called this man from day one of being under his care, and his eyes are locked on Lu, the name that he gave her.

Just as the car is about to pull away, she puts her open hand to the window, a wordless farewell to the stone-faced, quietly kind man and the old and creaky, safe, warm home he provided her. It's when Lu begins to move her hand away that Mr. V at last returns the goodbye with a stiff wave and a sad face. He stays like that, his hand held up in the air in front of him, watching, stock-still and doleful, until the car drives off.

Lu shifts around in the seat, pulling the safety belt around her, and it tumbles out of her ratty coat pocket: a sleek, vintage men's pilot watch. She lightly squeezes it in her palm, relieved to have it in hand, grateful to have it at all, then glances up to check that Miss Jacobs is fully focused on the road ahead. Furtively, she leans down to examine the watch closely for probably the fiftieth time since it was given to her this morning. She smiles while her eyes follow the red sweep-second hand from the six all the way up to the twelve. Lu strokes its face and slides the treasure back deep inside her pocket.

CHAPTER FOUR

She can feel Harry's eyes on her. He wants to say something, clearly, but isn't sure how to start. He's always been a little afraid of Lu, and she knows it. She keeps her head turned away from him, staring out the window at nothing, pretending it is the most engrossing vista this side of the Atlantic. Her mind is loud and busy with how she might begin to tell Mr. V about the unsanctioned cross-state move, wondering if he might actually see it as she does: a chance at a real reboot and the end of this cleaved life. But then, once again, the image of the incredibly priceless pilfered necklace stuffed into what amounts to a sturdy Ziploc baggie sitting in the bottom of a box in the Jeep's cargo pushes its way to the center of her thoughts and all bright visions of her reinvented Connecticut housewife life disappear. Besides the fact that she willfully flouted protocol by not reporting her relocation to The Atlas, it's the other matter of the necklace drop being overdue that brings the twitch in Lu's left brow to a steady rhythm.

"Welcome to Connecticut!" Solomon bellows from the back seat, and points out the window at the sign he just read.

The outburst brings Lu's attention back to the car with her two favorite people. "Yes, welcome," she says, dryly, and gives her husband a wry smile before adding, with a sinister whisper, "Or did it say *get out*? You know . . . like Jordan Peele."

"Beyond hilarious," Harry says, with a snarky half grin.

Thirty-five minutes later, another road sign, this one smaller and understated, alerts the Barlows that they have finally arrived at their destination.

PARTRIDGE HOLLOW
Founded 1749

Solomon slides his headphones off the back of his head, securing them around his neck before sending his window down and jutting his face out to get a better look at his new neighborhood. Lu follows suit, surveying the environs through her downed passenger side window. She is bowled over by what stands before her.

When Harry came home with the big and shocking news about the big and shocking job offer from biotech giant Kastille and announced an impending move, Lu did a quick search on Partridge Hollow. She learned that this coastal town of just under eleven square miles is the second wealthiest in the country's northeast region. She scanned high-definition pictures of palatial homes sat on acres, with lush landscaping, circular Belgian block courtyards, and winding paver driveways all conveniently set against clear blue skies. It was a cursory search and nothing more, because not that deep down, Lu didn't believe any of this would come to fruition. There had been other job offers over the span of Harry's impressive career, but none of them from the likes of Kastille. Also, Lu knows Harry to be a man of safety and routines. He sticks to what works, sticks to the rules, *risk* being a heavy four-letter word in his mind. So sure that the new job and move wouldn't happen, Lu didn't even entertain what it might mean for her or her *job*. And so, she let Harry connect with the Realtor alone and barely glanced at any of the property listings he had shared with her.

Being here now, seeing the town in its full dimensions, prismatic and pristine, everything astoundingly large and exquisite, Lu's eyes cannot get wide enough to fully absorb the details of this impossibly affluent enclave. Harry keeps his speed below twenty, cruising along their new street as the little family tries to grab hold of their collective suspended breath.

The car turns up a sloping driveway. Lu can see a light-gray Nantucket-style colonial spread out at the very top of the hill with the familiar moving van parked out front, the men busy unloading boxes. As they draw closer to the manor, the smell of the waterfront hits Lu's nose before the unobstructed view of the historic ocean inlet in the short distance registers with her eyes. She takes in the wide slip of green off to the side—a preview of the three acres of open park-like grounds leading to the water's edge that constitute their new backyard. Finally, Lu pierces the quiet bubble. "*Jesus.*"

"But you said you didn't need to see it before I signed the papers," Harry blurts out.

"I know," Lu says, still gawking out the window, "but this . . . this is . . . Jesus."

"Exactly," Solomon says.

Lu is about to turn to give the boy a smile when she notices a big-body, gunmetal gray, luxury sedan parked by the four-car garage.

"Is someone here?" Lu asks Harry, without taking her eyes off the car. Her already heightened senses prickle and a chill runs the length of her spine. *What if they know that I'm here? What if they tracked me down to get the necklace? What if the file has been escalated to Level 5 and inside that car is the counteraction team?* She is perched on the seat's edge, her brain scrambling for quick ways she might be able to protect her family from the pending threat within the sedan. Although she has had hand-to-hand training, she has never used firearms or knives or any true lethal weapon. Not her style. Plus, it's broad daylight, a quiet suburban neighborhood. Bringing violence in the open air is not how The Atlas operates. Not usually, anyway. Still, Lu begins to run a mental inventory on the tools tucked inside her Pilates equipment box in the back that might serve as protection. Just as she moves to wrestle her Atlas phone from the tote on the car floor and unbuckle her seat belt to ready herself, Harry speaks up.

"Right . . . erm, that's my car," he says, meekly.

Lu slinks back in her seat to look at him, her fists still clenched. "What—what are you talking about?"

"That"—Harry points over at the car—"is my new car. Kastille provides top-line executives with their own vehicle. And that is mine."

Lu falls back in her seat fully now with a loud exhale. "Why is this the first time I'm hearing about this?"

"I don't know . . . it just . . . slipped my mind, I guess."

"Slipped your—this is not a welcome-to-your-new-home fruit basket, H. It's a goddamn luxury car!"

"They told me it would be parked at the house for when we arrived. Honestly, I thought they would lease me some Lexus or something . . ." Harry looks over at the car now, shaking his head. ". . . not a fucking Lucid Air," he says, elation taking over.

Lu glowers at him. Ninety seconds ago, she was about to blow her cover and defend her family all in one fell swoop, only to have it be some slipped-my-mind bullshit and the man mooning over an overpriced electric car.

Solomon is already opening the door, readying to jump out of the Jeep. "Hang on! Let me put it in park first, Boxer!" Harry says, scrambling to move the gear shift.

An older white woman with a precise, layered platinum bob, heavy spray tan, and a face with far too much filler begins to slowly approach their car. She is dressed in cream—from her peak lapel double-breasted wool blazer down to her three-and-a-half-inch stilettos—and carrying a bottle of wine with a large white bow around its neck.

"Welcome to Partridge Hollowwww!" the woman says with a honeyed drawl and a throaty chuckle.

Solomon bounds past the lady and races up to the house. Several paces in, he realizes his misstep and turns, now barreling back toward them. "I forgot," he says, breathing heavily. "Can I go ahead . . . without you?"

Harry turns to the woman, his brows pushed together and his teeth exposed in a cringe. "So sorry, Annabelle. Is it all right if he goes in?"

"Of course you can, young man! It's your house too, darlin'. You go straight on ahead." She reaches out and tries to touch Solomon's hair, but he arches away and gives her hard look. As does Lu.

"Yes, sweet pea," Lu says, touching his shoulder. "Go on. We'll be in right behind you."

Annabelle Dupree, luxury Realtor and self-proclaimed "powerhouse," is partially frozen in place with a pinched smile, bouncing a nervous glance back and forth between Lu and Harry. After letting the awkward pause hang heavy in the air, Lu attempts to smooth it over, gesturing at the bottle in Annabelle's hand and smiling at her sweetly. Upon closer look, Lu sees that it's not wine, but champagne. The very good kind.

"Is that for us?" Lu says.

Annabelle nods and proudly presents the bottle . . . to Harry. Lu narrows her eyes ever so slightly at the woman's profile.

"Annabelle, you shouldn't have," Harry says, accepting it, his aw-shucks appeal dialed up. "This is incredibly kind of you. Thank you. Lovely, cheers." Catching himself, Harry quickly turns to Lu, stepping closer to her and floating an arm behind her lower back. "I don't believe you've met my best half in person. This is Lu."

"Oh, right, of course. I think she and I have only spoken via email and maybe once on the phone," Annabelle says, sliding her eyes over at Lu at the word *she*. Lu, on the other hand, keeps her stare set on Annabelle, unfazed. She's accustomed to this reaction when meeting a woman who has met Harry first. His posh accent, disarming demeanor, gentleman's charm, and those smiling eyes—plus the goddamn off-the-charts hotness—have been winning women's hearts for as long as Lu has known him. They see him and his bespoke suits and envision everything from Black James Bond to their handsome hall pass. This harmless (mostly) obsession-possession bubble is burst the minute these women—especially white women of a certain age—are introduced to Harry's actual wife. "For half a blink, I almost forgot this dapper devil is married," Annabelle says, her grin stretched much too wide.

"Maybe I should've stayed in the trunk a little longer. *Jump out*"—Lu shouts, flashing her palms by her face for jump-scare effect—"just as your shoulders relaxed." Annabelle's hazel eyes go wide and the corners of her smile begin to twitch as she fidgets with the crown-engraved buttons on her blazer while Harry shoots Lu one of his classic *be nice* looks. Lu nods back at him with a barely noticeable eye roll. "Just teasing," she says, smirking. "The price one pays for being married to Idris Elba, right?"

"Oh, you are so *funny*—and absolutely stunning!" Annabelle chortles, her Georgia twang spreading like boiled syrup. "Let's be honest, honey, Harry lucked out too, didn't he? I mean, pretty as a peach does not even cut it," she says, the wind returned to her sails.

"Well, thank you. You're just as lovely," Lu says, smiling. "Happy I get to finally meet the famous Annabelle Dupree—*the powerhouse that gets the house* . . . wait, what was it?" She turns to Harry, playing up her feigned confusion around the Realtor's uninspired slogan. Harry, practically cracking his tooth enamel from clenching, tries to roll off another subtle glare at his wife. But her attention is already off him and back on Annabelle. Like a sneeze she can't contain, Lu proceeds with her quiet party trick: clocking the woman's jewelry, the market prices of each piece flashing before her like a game show. The weird talent—a sort of photographic memory but for precious gems and fine jewelry—developed naturally and early, and made Lu a rare commodity with the shady thieves and cat burglary set. With the scan complete and the *basic older-white-lady-of-means fine jewelry* assessment rendered, Lu drags a genuine-*ish* smile out from the smirk and rejoins the conversation, committed to playing nice. "Honestly, Annabelle, you've outdone yourself here," she says with extra energy. "I mean, this house, the neighborhood—just gorgeous." The home truly is spectacular. Grand on a scale that Lu can't quite fathom.

Annabelle, shimmying her shoulders, melts into a proud smile before remembering herself, her baked-in manners, and waves her hand, fanning away the praise. "Oh, you're kind to say that, dear." Annabelle gestures for the couple to walk with her toward the house. "I don't want to spoil anything, but I have to tell you, y'all are in for a real treat." She slows to a stop, her expression stiffening dramatically before her smile explodes again, blindingly white veneers taking over the lower half of her face. "The Group is coming!"

"The group?" Harry says.

"PH2 . . . the Partridge Hollow Hospitality Group." Annabelle says it as if the couple should already know this. "Most of the neighborhood—I'd say a good eighty-five percent—is made up of people who work at Kastille, of course. However, PH2 comprises mainly the wives of Kastille's top-tier executives. The C-suite wives. The ladies are charged with welcoming new neighbors. They have their own golf cart and deliver a delightful gift basket. All sponsored by Kastille. You'll see, Harry, this company takes good care of their people."

"With a golf cart," Lu mutters.

"Ha! There you go again, gorgeous *and* funny. I love it!" Annabelle squawks, adding her shoulder shimmy behind it. "But in all seriousness, these ladies are going to be your nearest and dearest, Lu. Trust me. They'll give you top recommendations for florists, nannies, landscapers, holiday display designers, housekeepers—they call them *household managers* now. My point is—and there is one, *ha!*—anything to make this new home feel like home, PH2 has got you covered. You should see how they showered the Greys with warmth and welcoming. They were the most recent family to relocate here, a little over a year ago. Well, I should say, the mom made the move, *solo*, if you could believe that. The husband works for a financial services company in Asia somewhere, but I know for certain he's thrilled about their wonderful house."

"You could work your magic from Mars, Annabelle," Harry says.

"You're too kind," she says, beaming, then turns to Lu in a snap, as if suddenly remembering an item to add to the grocery list. "Oh, the mom, Finola"—Annabelle grabs ahold of Lu's forearm, slightly conspiratorial—"cute as a button. Even though she's not a Kastille wife, she fit right in immediately. She's just one of the gang now. And I know they're going to *adore* you with . . ." Annabelle flits her hand around Lu's hair. ". . . all of this Brooklyn charm."

Brooklyn charm? Jesus. I was rooting for you, lady. Lu cracks her mouth, forcing her scowl into a believable half grin.

Harry can practically hear his wife's inner hiss and jumps in with the quick segue before Annabelle has a chance to let off another clueless gaffe. "Annabelle, would you mind giving Solomon and me a little walkthrough of the game room?"

Annabelle's face lights up anew. "Of course, honey!" she says. "And, Lu, Harry tells me you're going to be looking for studio space for your little Pilates business as soon as you get settled. I hope you'll consider me to help you find that studio space when you're ready."

Lu only has time to flicker her slightly narrowed eyes at a sheepish Harry before responding in kind. "Of course!" she chirps. "You're just what my little business needs."

"Should we get going then, on the tour?" Harry says, the corners of his mouth twitching.

"I just need to say again. Lu, not only are you drop-dead gorgeous, but also—"

Harry's nervous grin morphs into a cringe as he locks eyes with Lu, bracing for what he and his wife know is surely coming next.

Don't do it, lady . . .

Annabelle reaches out, grasps Lu's forearm, and wags it. "—just so well-spoken!"

There it is.

Harry gently bows his head and lets out a soft sigh.

"Well, at least there's that," Lu says and swallows the other sharpened words gathering on her smooth tongue.

Solomon reaches them before Annabelle tosses off another gem, or what Lu had long ago dubbed a BBC—Black Backhanded Compliment. "Dad, can we see the—"

"Game room? Already on it, Boxer." Harry offers a clearly delighted Annabelle his arm as Solomon trots ahead of them up the steps and into the home's wide front door.

CHAPTER FIVE

Pacing is a waste. As Lu saw it, marching along a short stretch, effectively spinning in a circle, offers nothing constructive, no kind of advancement to a situation. Yet here she is, surrounded by mostly opened moving boxes in her capacious dressing room, doing exactly that. In one hand, the baggie with the diamond necklace dangles, swinging with each of her footsteps, and in the other, a cell phone. Not hers; that is sitting on the wide, mauve, tufted upholstered bench in the middle of the room nested into the closet island. The screen on her personal phone is still lit up and zoomed in on a story with the words "Breaking News Update" in bold, extra-large font across the top (Lu still refuses to cave and get readers).

More details emerge about the major jewelry heist that occurred three weeks ago here in the city at a Hell's Kitchen warehouse. A team of thieves made off with the centerpiece of the rarely seen Neapolitan collection, a necklace featuring *the flawless, heart-shaped, one-hundred-and-three-carat Eternal Nova diamond. The necklace is valued at $115 million. Investigators are looking into . . .*

Lu grips the special Atlas mobile tighter and takes another lap up and down the length of the white, warmly lit room. In between heavy sighs she continues muttering, trying out different ways to explain, succinctly, to the nameless, faceless central agent why she is more than two weeks late on following closeout procedure. There's also the part about informing her employer about the move. She's beyond tardy on this too, with no plausible excuse.

She stops moving long enough to look at herself in the largest of the four mirrors in the room. A deliberate onceover taking in her faded black Janet Jackson Rhythm Nation T-shirt, leopard print pajama shorts, and decades-old, threadbare satin bonnet. She steps in closer, studying her sunken eyes and dark circles in the mirror for a breath. The reflection reminds her of the way-back days, when Mr. V first brought her into the game as a fresh nineteen-year-old. Unable to sleep—the vestiges of her conscience drained away, leaving insomnia in its place—and too afraid to spend any of the money she earned on anything that might draw unwanted attention her way, Lu spent her time reading and practicing her made-up choreography in the mirror while listening to music on her clunky yellow Sony Sports Walkman—a gift from Mr. V for cracking her first safe with ease and speed after only practicing on a tiny replica for a half day.

Lu shakes her head and moves along from the mirror and those memories. It's time, she tells herself with a firm nod. She digs her fingernails into the cold sides of the phone and repeats the phrase *cook and curry* to herself. Something Mr. V would often say whenever Lu would find herself at the edge of panic. *Everyt'ing cook and curry, yout.* She relaxes her seized fingers and raises the device to her eyeline again and stops the pacing. She can almost see Mr. V's face, looking at her with his slow blinking and clenched jaw, disappointment emanating from his every pore as she attempts pitch him on her larger plan for her future.

"Just get to him," Lu says, loud and gruff, as if instructing someone else to make the request to speak with Mr. V. She plops down on the bench, letting her tired eyes sweep around the elaborate walk-in. Bigger than her entire bedroom in Brooklyn, Lu doesn't even have enough clothes and shoes to take up a quarter of the space in this luxury closet, with its sparking chrome racks, pristine white drawers and floating shelves, valet rods, soft lighting built into the walls, and elegant vanity. It's in one of this vanity's drawers that she had to stash the hot necklace. A quick fix after Solomon had barged into the dressing room while she was unpacking her secret shoebox in the dead of night. Harry was fast asleep, already unpacked and settled into his own smaller, but still luxurious, walk-in closet across the narrow hall; his offer to help Lu with hers had been gently refused. Solomon awoke and, bypassing his snoring father in the king-size bed, followed the dim lights directly to Lu in the belly of her closet. He told her that his throat felt dry and scratchy and there was a dull drumming in his head keeping him awake. Lu figured it was nerves; the boy was starting school the next morning, a full week after it had officially begun for everyone else. It also didn't help that he'll be the youngest fourth-grader in the class on account of his late birthday and skipping first grade. She shoved the baggie and burn box into the nearest drawer and walked with Solomon down to their impressive new kitchen where she administered her very own perfected can't-sleep remedy: warm milk.

Back to the light of this day, phone in hand, Lu takes a slow inhale and pushes the breath out before quickly dialing the numbers.

The phone line rings three times, then a pause, followed by the modulated double beep tone heard on calls in the UK. Lu holds her breath as the usual prompts begin.

Voicemail again? This is the fourth time. Lu is ready to toss the phone through the window, but knows she has no choice at this point. She clears her throat, preparing to leave a message. Though she knew it was coming, the shrill beep on the line still startles her. She quickly drops to the floor to steady herself, hoping to add some bass to her voice. "Hello, sir, it's Twenty-two sending a yellow flag. I'll check the help desk in a couple hours for how to proceed. I can even come into the shop in the city or Brooklyn with the external drive; I think it's fried."

As short as the message was, Lu still feels like she's just run a half marathon. Her shirt is damp by the armpits and around the back collar. She tucks the necklace baggie and her phone back into the vanity under a basket holding a dusty gym bag with different black swimwear pieces poking out the broken zipper. A better hiding spot later, Lu thinks, because right now a shower is required and the new and glorious spa-like en suite bathroom is hollering her full government name.

* * *

LISTENING TO HARRY'S light snoring used to bring Lu a sense of comfort. Now it only serves as an annoying reminder that sleep is a stranger to her. Brief, bothered, uneven bouts of shut-eye are all that has come Lu's way since moving here, and it's beginning to make her skin itch from the inside. While Harry can sleep next to a rocket launch without so much as an eyelid twitch, Lu's longtime battle with insomnia has only intensified in the last several months. She never bothers with soporific drugs. Allowing a pill to dull her acuity is simply not an option.

With so many sleepless nights stacked up on themselves since moving to Partridge Hollow, she no longer does the toss and turn thing, nor does she bother futzing around with pillows and refolding the covers just so. Lu just naturally assumes the position: still and flattened on the bed, squinting through the blue darkness, begging for sleep to come. A humble couple hours' worth is not too much to ask. She strains her eyes trying to make out the elaborate light fixture high up in the ceiling. "Too big, too fussy" was what she had said when she first saw it on move-in day. But Annabelle—who was weirdly still lingering after the initial grand tour—assured her that the chandelier was *very elegant, honey.*

Lu rolls her head to the side, looking over at Harry's naked back, watching as it gently expands and releases with the slow rhythm of his breathing. She is tempted to reach over to caress him, even moving her arm out from beneath the quilt to maybe rouse him awake for a middle of the night pet and play session. But she shakes away the thought and pulls her hand back in. Rolling around with him in the sheets won't solve anything. The last time she initiated sex—just two nights ago—Lu could not quiet her mind enough to truly tap in, and their usually creative dirty-talk devolved into a cringey spewing of porn schlock. The number of times Lu let out a listless "work this pussy" is wholly unforgiveable. Instead, she slips out of the wide bed to go try a different and perhaps more effective cure to her stress-induced insomnia. Warm milk with a shot of dark rum on the side.

After her usual quick peek in on a snoozing Solomon, Lu, still taking soft steps throughout the large house, makes her way to the kitchen next. She gets the milk from the fridge to warm before padding over to the bar for the booze. She forgoes turning on lights and uses whatever the moon is offering through the tall windows. She grabs her favorite mug from the pantry—a sturdy porcelain cup covered in daintily painted flowers with her initial calligraphed in purple on both sides—and rests it on the counter next to the quart of milk. She's about to move to the center island cabinets to get a small saucepan to warm the milk the old-fashioned way, low and slow, but stops in her tracks. Frozen. Not even a slip of a breath through her parted lips. Despite her exhaustion, Lu's basic senses are keen as ever. There is a shift in the usual fragrance of this room and an added thickness to the particular low-current buzzing that happens in here this late at night. All of this tells Lu that she is not alone. Someone—someone who does not belong—is in the kitchen too. She resumes her movements, keeping her back steady as she pours a splash of milk into the mug. Her eyes dart right, to the magnetic knife block glinting by the canisters. It's too many paces away for her to get there fast enough, and her knife skills are pitiful at best. She clears her throat and tilts her head back, slight and easy, toward the breakfast nook. That's where the intruder is; she can hear the light wheeze of their slow breath. Lu takes another smooth step toward the knives anyway, heavy mug in hand like a weapon, but stops again when she gets a whiff of something oddly familiar, though in her quiet panic is unable to place it.

Her eyes are adjusting to the dim. Without moving her body, she scans deeper, along the countertop that stretches to the stoves. There is a teaspoon resting next to an uncovered sugar bowl. This is when Lu notices that the coffee machine's touch screen is on. Harry never drinks coffee in the evening. *Is this home invader that bold?* Another step to her right; this time she raises the mug with her hand wrapped around it to her lips, pretending to sip from it as she slowly angles her body toward where she believes the prowler may be lying in wait, ready to pounce. Lu prepares to pelt the mug at the intruder as a distraction so she can dive over to the magnetic block for the eight-inch chef's knife and do what she can to stand her ground.

"It's too far," a man's voice says, flatly.

Lu's arm holding up the mug drops, spilling the milk to the floor by her feet. For this is not just any man's voice. This one belongs to Mr. V. It takes two full heartbeats for it to register. He is in her kitchen. He is in her home.

"What the fu—"

"Easy now," Mr. V says, his Jamaican accent pouring out slightly thicker than Lu remembers. "You can find better words."

There were rules that came with being under Mr. V's care. A code of behavior that Lu was expected to adopt and maintain from the moment she set foot in the man's home right through to now, when he had somehow found his way into hers. Nothing was explicitly outlined for her back then. His rules were mainly expressed by proverbs and loose edicts. *Profanity is the product of a weak mind*, for example. This is what he had told her upon hearing Lu mutter the word "shit" after she had burned a finger on his old kettle.

"You serious right now?" Lu hisses. "My family's upstairs. How did you get in here?"

"That's a question for your so-called alarm company, my yout," he says, and casually tosses his head back to pop something into his mouth.

His loud crunching takes over the room, the smug sound of it skittering up into Lu's ears like a stubborn beetle. She takes a few long steps toward him, closing in the space between them. The last thing she needs now is for Harry or Solomon to wake at the sound of her vexed voice and stumble downstairs to catch this man—a common stranger to them and the only parent Lu has ever really known—sitting relaxed in their kitchen as if he owns it. Lu is livid, but at the same time relieved to see him, unharmed and regular, his unbothered set point intact. Unsure of what might surface on her face next, a scowl or a smile, Lu clears her throat and looks away from him for a few blinks. When she returns her attention to him, the building ire is moving quickly to the surface. The clenching of her fist still around the mug's handle helps to slow it a little. She takes a breath and focuses on keeping her voice just above a whisper. "You broke in?"

"More *walked* in," he says, and rattles something in his hand before popping it into his mouth. "Guardian Alert Systems? Please." He makes a sneering face. It's all so arrogant.

Lu shakes her head, irked by the absolute gall of this man, but also at her inability to tell him to go straight to hell. Still, thirty years later, their power dynamic has stalled out and remains stuck in the past. She will always be his *yout*, a child forever under his tutelage, and he will always be her savior, the first person in this world who gave a shit about her. At their first meeting, Lu assumed he would be like the other foster parents, in it for the money and maybe a modicum of the self-satisfaction that came with *helping these poor, broken, tossed-away kids*. But he was immediately different. He was interested in her, as a person. He had asked her questions about what books she had read and whether she had any hobbies. The opposite of talkative,

Vincent King seemed to speak only when it was necessary and chose his words wisely. He didn't smile freely either, but his stern demeanor somehow made sense to young Lucille. *The world is a serious place*, he had told her on that first feel-out day they had spent together in the social worker's cramped office, *and it's the smart man who meets it in kind*. "Every skin teeth ain't a laugh" were the exact words he had used that late morning. It was the first of countless colorful Caribbean proverbs that the man would bestow on her.

As she takes a few more steps toward the nook in the shadowy corner, she sees his coffee cup and beside that, an opened tin of pricey gourmet spiced nuts—Harry's favorite—and the macarons that Lu planned to surprise Solomon with after school later today.

Mr. V leans into the wide beam of light coming through the large picture windows beside him. His close-cropped hair is entirely gray now, like a dusting of snow atop his round head. Even his thick, hard-angled eyebrows are silvered over. But that face, his dark, tempered complexion, looks as it did two years ago when she last saw him. Truth told, he looks exactly as he did even a decade ago. As hard and unsmiling as he is, there is nothing wizened about his features. Not a wrinkle or line, and smooth as glass. But there is something different that Lu catches in between his slow blinking. Something in his eyes that was not there two years ago. Not rheumy or tired, but a definite sadness is cresting the surface of his deep-set, inky eyes. Her anger and annoyance at him are now pushed aside by genuine concern for him. He's still Vincent King, the Mighty Number Seven, a true maverick. But different. Diminished.

With a slight tilt of his head, he gestures at the ripped-open cellophane wrapping of French pastry cookies. "Care for?"

Lu grips the mug dangling by her leg. "Why are you here?"

He gently slides out one of the cookies. "Didn't you call me? Repeatedly . . ."

"How did you find me?"

"These are not real questions," he says and bites into the mint-green confection. "A real question would be, how were you ever going to reach these cookies all the way at the top of that cupboard?" Another bite, finishing the whole thing. "I do enjoy macaroons every now and then."

"Those are macarons. French macarons," Lu says, her tone slightly softened. "Macaroons are made of shredded coconut. You hate coconut. Upsets your stomach."

"Good thing you know me better than I do, ain't it," he says, a tiny smile winking at Lu in the dim. There was a time when he would flash that same grin—quick and charming as it was—at a young Lu. Stoic being the man's baseline, Lu believed that he reserved this hard-won smile just for her, in those moments when she made him proud. This glimmer of looseness and warmth faded as she got older and more embedded at The Atlas. But after her marriage to Harry and more so the birth of Solomon, it dwindled even further to the mere figment it is now. Mr. V lightly pushes away the snacks from beside him to the middle of the table. "Why don't you put that cup down and have a seat. Ask me what you really want to know." He reaches under the table and nudges the corner of the adjacent bench out toward where Lu is standing. "You can clean up that spilled milk later. Unless you're hoping I'll do it . . . clean up your mess."

His usual spell takes over and without a second's thought Lu does as told, taking the seat and resting her empty mug on the table. She takes a slow, quiet inhale next, hoping it will help to gather her thoughts. "You can't pop up on me like this," Lu says.

It takes a few seconds but she pulls her eyes up to meet his. "This isn't Brooklyn. It's different here."

At first, the idea of moving and leaving Brooklyn felt impossible. The mere mention of looking at houses—in Connecticut, of all places—set Lu's stomach to a steady churn. Then, once the move became real, offers and contracts signed, Lu's skepticism around change and refinement suddenly abated. The storm in her tummy settled, and she finally allowed herself space to dream about a recast life, envisioning a healthier version of herself. She could at last see a path away from all of the dark and diabolic. Instead, she could try being normal. She could rest back in the regular, or at least figure out what exactly that means for someone like her. Maybe the new Lu would find hobbies that are not sneakily linked to her criminal activity. She could dig into those things that had long enticed her, like photography and learning to play the violin. She could even tackle Italian—properly, not just learning her way around directions, threats, and curse words. She could make Halloween costumes from scratch and bake elaborate cakes for family celebrations and start a local foreign film club and join the soccer carpool roster, *and, and, and* . . . Lu could do all of this, pour into herself, into her most important roles of mom and wife, without a big box of secrets and lies tethered to her ankle like a rusted anchor.

In a matter of four weeks, Lu went from being irritated, at best, to being inspired by and invested in this move to rechart the course of the rest of her life.

"That so?" Mr. V says. "It's *different* here?"

She takes another measured breath. "Yes . . . and I need to be different here. That's why I called you."

Mr. V releases a fatigued sigh. "Wha'ppen to yuh, Twenty-two?"

Lu bristles and responds in a gritty growl. "Don't call me that offline . . . please."

He tilts his chin down and peers into Lu's eyes. "All right, then . . . *Lucille*, what do you need from me?"

The last time Lu was under his glare like this, trying not to mince her words and just spill out the untreated truth, was a little over eight years ago. The two were sitting in a booth at a dingy diner in Queens, Mr. V slicing into a bloody New York strip with two runny sunny-side up eggs and crispy rye bread on the side, while Lu nursed a cup of mint tea and dry toast. She could barely look at his messy, soupy plate, sure that her stomach would empty right there on the damp table. Lu needed to tell him, then, that she was pregnant and wanting to keep it. Wanting to keep Solomon. To Lu's utter surprise, Mr. V, on behalf of The Atlas, granted her this permission. She had been approved to use her own womb as she wanted. "It lends weight to your cover," Mr. V had told her, and returned to his plate. Not even a feigned look of warmth or whispered felicitations from her mentor and de facto father. Lu was annoyed at herself right then for being so foolish as to expect anything more from him. By that point, their already unusual father-daughter/mentor-protégé dynamic had grown strange and strained. The fabric between her and Mr. V began to pill and thin after Lu announced—*ask for forgiveness, not permission*—that she was getting married. Adding a baby to the mix only widened the rift. She took his perfunctory remark for what it was and just returned to nibbling on the corner of her toast, keeping her joy-filled grin at bay. Despite Mr. V's indifference, the silver lining was shining bright for Lu. She was going to be a mother. And it was real; nothing to do with her cover.

Mr. V arches a single brow and lowers his chin further, just an inch. Slight as the move is, it pulls Lu away from the sticky diner from years past and back to the current tension rising in her kitchen right now. Lu knows all of his cues like the back of her hand. She knows that she needs to force the words stuck in her throat up to the tip of her tongue and ready herself to speak. Because she also knows that this man will not be repeating his question.

"I want to apologize. I know that I fuc—that I messed up protocol. Twice. I was planning to make that recent drop right after the job, but I got hurt and then time got away and everything got jumbled with the move. But I will get it done before it lapses. I *will*."

"I know that," Mr. V says, his gaze locked on Lu.

"And then the move . . . I should have reported the relocation right away. But I needed time . . . I needed to talk to you about why we decided to do this. Why this move is important."

He sniffs. Or maybe it's a faint snort, Lu is not sure. The sadness that she noticed earlier returns, clear and present. She is almost tempted to ask if he's all right. Perhaps the reason he's been a ghost has nothing to do with her or any of her recent failings. Maybe he's dying, Lu thinks, then quickly dismisses the leap after taking in the man's barrel chest, his taut belly even as he sits, and an overall sturdiness that belies his seven-plus decades. Hale and hearty defined. He's not dying, but he's not well, she tells herself. Something is wrong.

Either way, she presses on. Lu cannot afford to back down now. "I need it to be different here," she says, willing herself to maintain eye contact. "*I* need to be different here."

"And how does that work?"

"I . . . I need out."

Mr. V raises a brow, so slight it would be imperceptible to most. Most, not Lu. And she knows exactly what it means. He's displeased; more hurt and insulted than angry. He plays it off well, as usual, without a trace of the dismay and affront visible. "Out?" he says, toneless.

"Yes, out!" Lu snaps. "I want out. I want to be done with all of this. Free."

"This is not like you, simple and absurd. What you do, how this system operates, there is no switch from on to off. You know that."

"What I know is that I have done everything that has ever been asked of me, for thirty years. I have handed over my life to them . . . to you." Lu finally releases the grip on the mug, but her fists remain clenched, the fleshy side of her hands pressing into the table. She wants to let her raging words roar out, obliterating the fire walls erected over too many years, and let the brunt of this blaze—the head, flanks, heel, all of it—vent at last. But she keeps her voice low, seething. Waking her family to join this nightmare is not an option. She lets out a heated sigh. "Through some impossible luck, I finally have a chance to change all that. To be different. To be whole. That boy—my boy, my little family—they deserve more than fragmented pieces of me, they deserve a whole person, at the very least . . . they deserve a real and honest person devoted to only them. I need to give that to them. I need to just be normal."

"*Normal* . . . pssh," he scoffs.

"Don't do that. Don't mock me, please."

"Lucille," he says, his voice stern but quiet. "I am not mocking you. I am reminding you; you are not normal or standard or ordinary. You can never be that."

"One of one—I know. I know! But I don't want to be extraordinary . . . not like this. Not doing *this*. I just don't want this life anymore. I don't want to do—"

"Enough," he hisses, and leans back in his chair. "This is not the time."

Lu recoils at first, her spine reflexively straightening, shoulders pulling back, chin up, and eyes forward to the window in a snap. She can hear her quickened pulse, feel the loud thump in her neck, along her temples. Lu parts her lips to let free a low, trembling breath. She slides her eyes to the side to look at him once again and continues despite everything that could happen next. "Then tell me when? When does my life become *my* life?" Her voice catches and Lu can feel the heat beginning to stir in her face. The tears are moving in quickly, but she clenches her fists in her lap to stave them off and continues the forward march. She turns to look at him directly now. "Mr. V, sir . . . I am coming to you as me. Not Twenty-two. *Me.* Lu. Your star who's pushing fifty, and pushing it hard. I don't have it in me to keep this up. Physically, the bounce back ain't there like before." Lu brings her hand up to her opposite side and rubs beneath her ribs by her still-pained spleen. "And that boy, my son, he's sharp, observant, his senses are keen. He's the very best thing I've ever done, and I don't want him anywhere around this. I'm asking you to listen, hear what I'm actually saying, and help me, this last time. Help me get out."

He reaches for his cup, swirling around whatever is left in it as he takes in the spacious kitchen with a slow sweep. He brings the squat teacup to his mouth for a shallow sip before gently placing it back on the table. He looks over at Lu next. Somehow the sorrow that had earlier glazed over his vision is gone. Dried up and blinked away. "I listened and I heard you . . .

Twenty-two. Now you must hear me. Listen to me as if this is the most important thing I will ever say." Mr. V brings his head out of its reproachful tilt. "This house, we put you in it. The move that you failed to report was orchestrated by us two years ago." Lu's face falls. His words hit like an anvil to her chest and she feels instantly flattened, trapped in an airless state between terror and oblivion. Despite her obvious dazed disposition, the man continues speaking, phlegmatic and unhurried. "Your husband's *opportunity of a lifetime* was created and put into play by the very organization at which you are turning down your nose. You say you want to be free of us, of this work, this life . . . very well. But to even entertain this idea, we would first need something from you."

"Wh-what? This . . . this isn't real?" Lu stutters. "You set him up. You set Harry up. Why would you do this? Why would you drag him into this? He's done nothing. What even is this?"

"This is the job. That's what this is. All part of the job they pay you to do."

"*Part of the job?*" she spits. "How the hell is this part of the job? Harry is not part of this job," she says, still numb, hardly able to hear her next thought.

"It's not about him," he says, pausing to peer at Lu, as if checking on her, making sure she's still breathing, still listening. "It's about the company. Kastille. Your fella"—a slight frown begins to drift over his features like a cloud, dragging that now-familiar gloominess in behind it—"he's just an unfortunate consequence, a smaller piece in a larger game."

She cannot process Mr. V's words fast enough. Lu's brain flattens as a blanket of static covers it, end to end. She looks over at Mr. V, staring right into his eyes. The doleful look was not imagined. It is stretching across the man's face like nylon. What was once tacit is now loud and clear to Lu. He doesn't want to say what he's about to say, yet he has no choice. "Tell me," Lu says, in an arctic whisper.

"The telomeres restructuring project," he says. "We need the nanocode."

"That's Harry's project," Lu says, incredulous, the words barely skating over her dry lips. Harry had made it clear to Lu years ago that he doesn't enjoy talking about his work—he doesn't enjoy talking about anyone's work. *How a person makes a living, pays the bills, is the most boring thing about them*, he often said. But Lu had gleaned enough to know that the nanocode was more than that. It was more than how he paid their bills, more than a simple project. It was revolutionary, a development that would literally change lives, change how long those lives could last, and it was shaping up to be the pinnacle of Harry's career. It was, after all, why Kastille brought him on board. Or so they were led to believe.

Mr. V gives her a firm nod.

"And . . . you want me to steal it. You want me to *steal* from my own husband."

"It might do you well to think of it as Kastille's project."

She shakes her head hard. "I can't believe this is happening."

"A client in Germany needs it. Kastille's competition," he says. "Paying handsomely for the leg up too." Mr. V nods again, this time quicker, before lowering his chin as if observing a brief moment of silence while the weight of what he just said sinks Lu deeper into the ground.

"I can't do this. You can't ask me to do this."

"But we are . . . and you must," he says. "There's a plan in place. When the time comes, you'll be clearly instructed. And your part will be complete. Then we may talk about your being done. Or *out*, as you say."

Lu turns her glance to the window before her, looking out into the darkness of the expansive yard, squinting as if that might bring any of this madness into a finer focus. Then, after a deep-rooted sigh, she breaks the clumsy silence with one word, spat out like venom. "*Fuck.*"

CHAPTER SIX

Although Mr. V didn't exactly give Lu a deadline to complete this mission, she has enough common sense to know that there is, indeed, a clock on her and it is very much ticking. In the two days since her world was utterly rocked, Lu has found herself crouched in the deep corner of her closet any free moment she can scrape together, scouring the web—the regular and the dark—for everything she can find about Kastille.

One thing that's immediately clear: This job requires an advanced level of computer hacking that stretches beyond her capabilities. While cracking the code to the Belgian viscount's elaborate jewelry safe proved slightly challenging for Lu, hacking into a military-grade mainframe feels virtually impossible.

With everything else stirring in her life, Lu has only seen Kastille's offices in person once, from the outside and in passing on move-in day over two weeks ago. Harry had happily driven his little family around on a quickie tour of their new town—the best coffee shop, the post office, Solomon's new school, the library, and finally the very impressive Kastille campus.

Lu's recent research gives her a little bit more to go on. The four ultramodern buildings cover about sixty percent of the sprawling grounds. The remaining property is already spoken for, according to classified company paperwork Lu stumbled upon. Kastille's heavyweight board recently approved an expansion project that would break ground next summer and end with a futuristic Bioengineering and Rehabilitation Center with an AI-Driven Genomics and Data Analytics Wing a decade later. Reading over the company's plans for interactive walls and subterranean data vaults and glass-dome pavilions, Lu wondered if Harry would even still be working at Kastille by the time this highly innovative creation is completed. Would she—in her reclaimed life—and her family still be living in Partridge Hollow? Or would she and Harry, newly christened empty nesters, be decamped somewhere else, like London or Lisbon?

The brief fantasy comes to a rough halt when Lu remembers why she now knows all of this about Kastille. She continues combing through the intel she dug up online, like the company's old blueprints that she found on the initial architectural firm's simplistic semi-defunct website. She notes that the R&D department and production labs are located on the third floor of the larger building in the partially tucked-away northwest corner of the campus.

That's her target.

The vial containing the nanocode sits inside a locked case inside a small vault inside a secured suite near one of the main labs. Getting to it will mean hustling to that far end of the property on foot, with an essentials-only backpack, and then rewiring an elevator or, better for her purposes, unlocking the emergency back stairs. From there, to gain access to the suite she—

Crap!

Lu enlarges the screen to re-read, slowly, what is now the most critical part of her entire plan. "*Of course* it's fucking fingerprint-protected," she hisses, and slams the laptop shut, shoving it away like it's a plate of rotting meat put before her on a dare.

This, her final job, is asking Lu to stretch every skill to its maximum and pull out all the stops. But the one thing she is determined not to do is involve Harry in any of it. She'll have to find someone else's fingerprint to dupe.

Lu moves her stiff upper body out of its hunch and rolls her neck clockwise and then counter. On the last sweep 'round, she catches the tang of something unpleasant. She rips the slack collar of her shirt forward and back twice, quick enough for the odor to waft up her nose. It's her; she stinks. Sweaty and stale. Lu makes a face, then pops up to standing to rectify the reeky situation immediately.

Showers used be about pure function for Lu, but this luxurious bathroom has swiftly transformed body-washing into a sublime experience, a necessary moment of bliss. She slips off the pajama bottoms and flings them toward the most stylish bin for dirty clothes she's seen to date. As she starts toward the dressing room's threshold, heading for the bathroom, she hears what sounds like squeaking wheels from a car in the driveway. Lu's heart is pounding as she reaches for a pair of black joggers from the nearest moving box and hustles over to check the security panel in the bedroom. "No fucking way," she whispers, her eyes going wide, taking in what she sees on the sharp video screen. A group of women, four in total, are huddling by Lu's front doorstep, their golf cart parked not too far behind them in the driveway. One of the women—a petite blond—is holding an ostentatious, cellophane-wrapped gift basket in both hands. Lu is about to head downstairs to greet them when the video panel's sound picks up their voices . . . and their conversation. "Genie, do I still get two more wishes?" Lu snorts.

"This looks bad," the gift-bearer says, staring down at the tinselly thing, grimacing.

A redhead with her hair slicked back into a thick ponytail and lathered in shiny jewelry turns and glares at the side of her. "That basket is perfection. I put a lot of time into it," she says, sharply. "There's even that coconut Bundt in there, the one that Tom Cruise sends to everyone for the holidays."

"You ordered cake from *California*?" a gorgeous, statuesque brunette says, her voice a little whiny and covetous. "When did we start ordering cakes all the way from Hollywood to welcome people to Partridge Hollow?"

"Relax, OK?" Red says, turning to scowl now at the glamazon beside her. "We didn't order anything; I made it from a recipe on Instagram, and Cormie said it's fucking delicious."

"Of course he did. Graybeard loves everything you put out," Glamazon says, snickering, then adding, "Just ask those six kids."

"*Ooh*, he's old and horny. So fucking original. I'm cracking up over here. Really," Red drones, glowering at Glamazon. "*Anyway*, like I said, this basket is perfection," she says, adding a snotty jiggle of her shoulders.

"I don't mean the basket; it looks fantastic," Gift Basket says. "I'm talking about the fact that these people moved in three weeks ago and we're just showing up today. I'm talking about the optics here."

"Oh, for God's sake . . ." Red groans, shaking her head.

The bickering women suddenly turn to look at their friend with a shiny mane of jet-black hair, standing slightly toward the back of the group. She lifts her sunglasses just to her brows and holds them there with a pinched set of fingers. "Did you just say *optics*?"

"Yeah . . . I'm saying it looks bad," Gift Basket says, leaning toward her.

"I know what optics means," Black Stallion says, her eyes still locked on the woman. "I just can't believe you're trying to bring *that* into this."

"Oh, no, no, I wasn't implying—"

"Yeah," Black Stallion says, lowering her sunglasses back down onto her celestial nose, "you definitely were, and it's absurd. This isn't some deliberate slight or coded message, OK? This is the first morning we're all available, and you know that. Nothing more to it." She reaches into her black, quilted Chanel waist bag, slung over her bony shoulder, for a lip gloss and smooths the wand over her tight pout. "The only downside is, at this hour we won't meet the reportedly hot husband."

"Oh, he is definitely hot," Red says.

"Wait, you've met him?" Black Stallion says, sounding vaguely intrigued.

"Not in the flesh," Red says. "When Cormie told me that this new guy—*Harrison Barlow*—would be joining the ranks and pretty goddamn high up, I got curious, so . . . I hit Google, and let me tell you, I was not disappointed. The man is a fucking smoke show. The definition of tall, dark, and handsome. And I heard he has a thick British accent. Can you say Idris El—"

"Um, this basket—beautiful as it may be—is not light," Gift Basket says, shifting her weight from one foot to the next.

"Maybe she's not even home. Wait . . . did anyone actually ring the doorbell?"

"You can't be serious!" Red says.

"Ladies, I gotta bow out," Glamazon says, her voice soft and sweetened. "*Sorry*, I've got a sweater shipment coming in and I really do need to be there. Tell her I'm so sorry and welcome to PH"—she starts to trot off toward the golf cart—"and that she'll love it here!" Glamazon says, the slightly hollered words tossed over her shoulder.

"Better get this going before you two disappear next," Red says, reaching over in a rush to press the doorbell.

The fancy chime bounces through the house. "*Front doorbell activated. Person detected*," an automated voice pipes in through a speaker neatly embedded in the video monitor that Lu has been watching this whole time.

Lu lets out a long exhale as she presses the button to stop the security system's voice from repeating the notification. She scans the three women again for good measure, as each of them seems to be fidgeting, adjusting something at once—hair, sweater, gift basket—and prepping to power on their perfectly white, wide smiles.

"Let's see what we get out of this," Lu mutters to the screen, "the grand welcome by the Real Housewives of Partridge Hollow." She emits another long, low sigh. "Brace for bullshit."

The brushed nickel chime box on the wall sounds off once more just as Lu lands in front of the thick double doors, readying to open the left side. Before reaching for the handle, she backtracks to the large standing mirror artfully hanging in the grand foyer for a last glance and to quickly tuck away any loose curls or body parts, for that matter—she did not have time to throw on a bra.

She smiles at herself, a practice run, but it comes across as more pained than anything remotely pleasant. Lu fans her hand at the reflection, waving away any further effort, and slips over to the door again. She forces her shoulders down and back, takes a breath, and pulls the handle with vigor.

The sharpness of the morning light hits Lu's eyes, but she makes a point of not squinting. She doesn't want to do anything that might get her written off as angry or unmannerly from first meet. As her eyes adjust, she does a quick scan of her company's jewelry. It's involuntary at this stage, an occupational hazard. Some nice pieces in the mix, but of course Lu will take a closer look in a moment—one by one—under her built-in loupe to be sure. She then glances at each woman's face, taking in the larger details of their countenance along with any obvious distinguishing marks and anything that even the HD screen of the security panel didn't fully convey. It also helps that yesterday, while dropping off an info flyer with important town hall numbers, the trash/recycling schedule, and the school bus map, Annabelle gave Lu an extensive, bordering on gossipy, rundown of the five women. Now it's time to connect the actual names and faces with their respective backstories. For three of them, anyway.

"Good morning!" Red says. The other two ladies chime in a half-note late. "Welcome to Partridge Hollow, Lucille!"

Lu smiles, wondering if this is the self-proclaimed leader, Didi DuBois. But something about the red-haired woman doesn't present as the ex–public relations heavyweight Annabelle described. Her greeting, the timbre of her voice, her shrugged posture, it's wanting in natural confidence. Although attractive, she doesn't have the killer-curvy physique of a former plus-size supermodel, Lu reasons, so she's probably not Calista

Caudwell either. Those va-va-voom attributes definitely fall in line with Glamazon.

"She owns a local boutique now," Annabelle had said about Calista, sounding disappointed. "But if I had her looks and that body? Honey, you wouldn't find me standing around refolding cashmere sweaters and dusting hangers. I'd be upside down hanging from a chandelier in a bikini. And the bikini's a *maybe.*"

"Good morning to you too," Lu says, calmly. She reconnects with her body and realizes that the way she is standing—her hips parallel to the floor, feet shoulder-width apart and at an angle, dominant foot slightly back with the heel raised, and her body filling the space of the open door—might be read as aggressive or at least defensive. She tries to relax her posture into something more at ease and congenial, but her body hardly moves or changes. Old habits, like fighting stances, die hard. "And please, call me Lu."

"Well, then, welcome to the neighborhood, *Lu*," Black Stallion says, roughly nudging her way in front of the other two women, landing her standing uncomfortably close to Lu. She pushes her sunglasses to the top of her head, unleashing her piercing eyes. Blue-green, flecked with gold, and dark rings around the edges of the iris that make her gaze even more captivating—and probably other times chilling. Her oval-shaped emerald-and-diamond stud earrings are just as captivating, in Lu's professional opinion. "We're the little welcome wagon here in PH," Black Stallion says.

Lu nods. *Bingo.* The poise and self-assurance. This is their leader, Didi DuBois.

Gift Basket peeks out from behind the package. "Yes, welcome!" she says. "We had planned to be here when you moved in, but scheduling conflicts, so . . ." She shoots a nervous side look to Didi. "You know what? This shit's heavy. I should probably just rest it in the kitchen," Gift Basket says, a tense grin still pulled across her lips. "Yeah, I'm gonna rest this in the kitchen." With a move that is somehow gentle and pushy at once, she shoulders her way past Didi and barges in, forcing Lu to step aside. The two other ladies file in, following Gift Basket's unexpected lead, with Lu left to close the door and tread on their heels.

Lu unconsciously smiles watching Gift Basket as she moves along. Something about her petite frame, pixie cut, and a wide path of fine freckles stretching from one cheekbone over her button nose to the other side of her face makes her downright adorable. She isn't wearing any major pieces. No layered necklaces, no sparkling ring stacks, no glaring tennis bracelets, not even a weighty engagement diamond spinning around her bony finger. Just a simple wedding band, gold with round diamonds. Her gold stud earrings are quite darling, too, shaped like a curled-up serpent. The Nāga dragon, to be more precise, with the tiniest emerald for an eye.

Gift Basket finds her way directly to the vast kitchen without a single direction given and sets the basket on the closest of the two marble-top islands. She pulls out one of the stools nesting beneath the counter and sits on it with a relieved exhale. The two others gather behind the cute woman like seasoned backup singers. "Better, right?" Gift Basket says to no one in particular, then answers herself. "Yes. Much better."

Lu looks on, making every effort to keep her grin warm. She pegs the basket-bearer as either Margot Pearson, the old-money (who married even older money), New England–bred, spirited stay-at-home-mom of six with the much older husband, or, as Annabelle put it, "very May-December, but glamorous, not trashy." Or it's the former executive recruiter and newest member to the group, Finola Grey, about whom Annabelle knew only the basics.

"My God. Where are our manners?" Didi says, removing her sunglasses from atop her head and stashing them in her purse. "We haven't even properly introduced ourselves and we're already deep into your kitchen. I'm Amandine DuBois, but everyone calls me Didi. We've lived in the neighborhood going on ten years, right next door to one of my very *best* friends, Evangeline Bloom—who is still trapped in the south of France. Lab research; poor girl. She's a wellness guru slash lifestyle brand maven slash entrepreneur slash cutting-edge innovator."

Slash my throat, because what the fuck is this? "Wow . . . she's a busy boss, huh?"

"Yes, very," Didi says. "She's been traveling for work for, like, three, four months now."

"Ooh . . ." Lu widens her eyes, trying her best to at least feign interest in what these women have to say, but she can feel her smile already deflating like a balloon in the sun. All she can think is which one of these women she will have to fake fuck to gain access to Kastille's inner sanctum.

Didi inhales loudly through her nose and parts her lips, readying to continue eulogizing Evangeline, Lu assumes, when Red interrupts, earning a slow burn cut-eye from Didi.

Red receives the look of censure like a light blow to the chin and presses on, sounding almost giddy as she begins her spiel.

In the bright light of the kitchen, Red's sizeable gold hoops dazzle almost as much as her round-cut engagement ring. Vintage. Possibly one of a kind. There's also a chunky gold bracelet on her right wrist and a short stack of thinner ones jangling together on her left, all clearly Cartier, as is her large-model watch. Her neck is adorned with more twinkling yellow gold, a layering of six necklaces ranging from link chains to a long, hefty statement piece featuring a cow-jumping-over-the-moon pendant resting right at the base of her breastbone.

"You're going to love it here," Red says. "Like our lovely president already stated"—she makes a flitting gesture toward Didi, while Lu's eyebrow pitches at the *president* sobriquet—"the level of community is unmatched. Our kids play together; the neighborhood hosts themed festivals—you just missed the end-of-summer barbecue. What a fuckin' blast, right?" She looks to her two friends for backup, but they only offer modest smiles and hard stares.

Clearly, Red has gone off book, Lu notes, and decides to throw her a life ring. "Sorry we missed it," she says. "A barbecue is a good time, every time."

"Every goddamn time!" Red says, laughing harder than necessary. "So, I'm Margot, leader of the Pearson tribe—honestly, I'm gonna start saying the Pearson Dynasty! With eighty-four kids, can you blame me?" She sticks out her tongue partially and makes a goofy, panting face as she lurches forward toward Lu. "It's just six kids, but still! Jesus Christ . . . of Latter Days Saints, right? JK; we're not Mormons, just horny Irish Catholics." Margot lets out that overdone laugh again. It echoes around the hushed kitchen. "Anyway, we live a little farther out than the others. We're kinda stranded in the ghetto—" Margot's head whips around as if called—or pinched beneath the counter—and her full smile instantly dims. She then sweeps her already perfect auburn bangs across her forehead and straightens her back as she looks at Didi for a beat. "Uh . . . I-I mean, well . . . it's not a *ghetto* ghetto. It's still really nice there, obviously. I just mean it's not as close in . . . it's near the golf course entrance. So . . ."

Again Lu decides to save her. There's something kind of endearing about Margot. Or maybe it's the fact that the stench of her desperation—to say the right thing, to get a kind look from Didi, to be considered delightful, to be considered at all—is practically coming through her pores. "Nothing wrong with being ghetto adjace, right? Besides, it sounds like you've got a good setup there so close to the green and all. I'm sure you can break eighty," Lu says.

"Ha! Yeah, right. If that were the case, I'd be in the Pros, friend!" Margot says, chuckling, her face relaxed again. "My thing is pickleball anyway. Do you play—"

"Oh, goodness, where are *my* manners?" Lu says. She had sworn way back in 2020 that she would not entertain any talk of the sham sport no matter how effusive the instigator. As she put it quite succinctly to her chatty downstairs neighbor Lizette, who had often raved about her pickleball obsession: *Fuck that shit.* "I'm so engrossed in hearing about all of you that I haven't even offered you a cup of coffee or glass of water or anything. My apologies!"

"No apologies needed," Gift Basket says. "Seriously, you don't need to offer us anything. We're the ones interrupting your morning."

And of course, you must be Finola. Lu raises her brows, waiting for Gift Basket to start her portion of the presentation.

"By the way, I'm Finola Grey." She reaches to the side of the gift basket, stretching a little across the island top to extend for a handshake—the only one of the women to do so. Lu appreciates that it is firm and not the overcooked noodle she was expecting.

"Good to meet you," Lu says, returning the sturdy handshake.

"We're basically around the corner from you, and are also members of Margot's Horny Catholics Club," she says, giggling, then saluting Margot. "I mean, we only have two, though. Twin girls. Told Matty we're done. *He* can be the boy of the family. Anyway, he got the big snip, basically the day after the girls came home, so we're all set!" Didi clears her throat and places a gentle hand on Finola's shoulder. Like a pulled puppet's string, this makes Finola straighten her posture, tighten her jaw. "But that's a story for another day . . . with wine."

"Sure, that sounds good. I only have one kid, so . . ."

"Solomon, right? He's eight?" Finola says.

"Yeah," Lu says, sounding suspicious at first, but softening it the second time around. "Yeah. Solomon. He's eight going on twenty-eight. Wise, that kid. Too wise sometimes."

"Wait until he hits the mean tween stage," Margot says with a laugh. "Is he liking the new school? Making lots of new friends, I'm sure. I only have my littlest two still at Maple Grove. But I'll tell them to look out for him."

"That's nice of you," Lu says. "I think he likes it . . . so far. He's slow to warm, but—"

"Well, anyway, we just wanted to welcome you and"—Finola roughly pushes the basket toward Lu—"offer this small token from us . . . from the neighborhood, really. But mainly us." She moves her eyes from the basket to Lu a few times, a mix of squints and weird winks as if attempting to send her a message via Morse code.

"You could let Lu finish her thought, Finola. Honestly," Didi scoffs. "Someone is super excited about no longer being the low man on the totem pole, huh?"

"Actually, that's not OK to say anymore—totem pole," Finola says, the words easing out of her clenched teeth. Both Didi and Margot roll their eyes dramatically. "It's offensive, and it's also misappropriation and, like, kind of trivializing the traditions of—"

"*Wowww,*" Didi says. "Optics, misappropriation, trivializing traditions . . . gosh, looks like we have our own DEI manager now."

Finola catches herself. She quickly tries to fill the awkward silence with choppy clarifications. "I . . . sorry, I didn't . . . I wasn't trying to imply—"

Lu again jumps in, this time to save herself from this ridiculous, sinking showboat. "Don't worry about it," she whispers, looking over at a red-faced Finola. But pauses for a blink when she notices that Finola looks more indignant than embarrassed. *Hmm . . . a renegade.* "I don't mind getting some coffee going. Harry has this outrageously fancy machine. It's fussy but fast if you just want something strong and black," Lu says, so tempted to add *like me* to the end of that just to see if it pulls Finola's cord again and sends Didi's head spinning.

"Thanks, but we're going have to rain check," Didi says. "We've already taken up enough of your morning, and I'm sure you still have so much to do to . . ." Didi, with undeniable deprecation streaking her face, looks around at the missing furniture, empty corners, and overall dishevelment of the adjoined spaces. ". . . get settled." She makes the first move, stepping away from the kitchen island, setting off a chain reaction as the other women fall in line behind her.

"Oh, yeah, there are still a few things to do before we're fully settled," Lu says, as she slowly guides the three women out of the kitchen to the foyer. "But, this is very kind of you. The basket is . . . outstanding."

"It's nothing," Finola says.

"Well, I wouldn't say that it's nothing, Grey," Margot says. "I—uh—*we* put time and careful thought into these baskets. Each one is different. We want people, like Lu, to feel truly welcomed, you know?"

"Oh, I didn't mean it like that. The baskets are amazing," Finola says. She turns to Lu now as they round the corner into the foyer. "I don't know why I said that . . . I wasn't thinking."

Didi, standing right by Lu's shoulder, snickers in her ear. "That part's obvious." Once again that hand is on Finola's shoulder, almost like a leash tug. "We'll get out of your hair," Didi sings as they head to the door.

The women bid their new friend adieu, each spouting off some banal line that melds together as one blah-blah blob to Lu: *So good meeting you we'll have to do coffee soon enjoy the basket welcome to the neighborhood again!*

Lu grips the handle tight as she closes the door behind them. She wants to race upstairs to get back to her Kastille research, but first needs a shot of something to settle the freshly plucked nerves. By the time she arrives in the kitchen, her choice has changed from espresso to vodka. She decides to forego the glassware. A swig from that ice-cold bottle in the freezer drawer is a much better call.

With the warm-cold liquid burning its fast path down her throat and the bottle resting against her chest, Lu debates taking another deep sip. She turns to look out the back window and notices a forgotten pair of sunglasses on the counter. Lu starts taking a step over to the dark, square frames when she hears the *clack-clack* of sandals slapping against the tile. Finola appears in the kitchen archway. They both point at the sunnies, with Lu's other fingers still hugging the bottle's neck. Finola notices the vodka. And Lu notices her noticing. She opens her mouth, taking a breath to spout off a random excuse for the morning spirits, but Finola holds up a hand.

"No explanation needed," Finola says, smiling in earnest.

Lu turns the bottle toward Finola and raises a brow.

"Thought you'd never ask." Finola takes quick, light steps over to meet Lu by the fridge where she takes possession of the vodka bottle and tilts it back into her mouth. It's a strong shot, and Lu is impressed. She returns the bottle and wipes her lips gently with the back of her hand. Then, after checking over her shoulder, Finola leans in to Lu and whispers, "In the basket. Slipped a little something extra in there, from me to you."

Lu cocks her head, squinting as she looks over at the woman, waiting for the reveal.

"The small, orange-and-white metal round: Cindy's Fun Gumms," Finola says. A wry smile peels across her lips, changing not only the shape of her face but also her demeanor. No longer a meek mouse, Finola transforms into an artful fox, and Lu is once again impressed, even a bit dazzled, by what she didn't see coming from this diminutive woman. "Each gummy is just two migs. But it'll work."

It's the most natural and relaxed this woman has been since she first barged into the house, Lu notes, resting the vodka on the countertop near the gift basket.

"Well, OK, then. Thanks."

"Oh, you're welcome," she says. "If nothing else, it'll help you to prepare for the brunch circus show this weekend."

"The what now?"

She chuckles, shaking her head. "Oh, yes . . . the gift basket is just the beginning. There's also a brunch to welcome you. It's at Didi's."

Lu gives her a sharp look and stays on pause, unblinking and frozen, for a solid fifteen seconds. "I'm waiting for the part where you say *just kidding*. Please tell me you're joking."

"Ah, but there are no jokes here, my dear. Didi hosts a welcome brunch for all the new families. For ours last year, it was a tropical luau theme—pig on the spit and everything. My girls still have nightmares and refuse to eat bacon."

"Stop it."

"Exactly." Finola smirks as she pulls a pen and a slip of paper from her small shoulder bag. "Full transparency, we were supposed to be here with this basket weeks ago. That's usually when the brunch invite happens too." She jots something down on the paper. "But everything's been completely backwards with you guys."

"Lucky us."

"I don't mean it like—I think there's just a lot going on with everyone. But we're still glad you're here. Seriously." Finola hands Lu the paper—an old restaurant receipt with a hefty tab. "Here's my number. Call me! I'll give the quick rundown on all the Partridge Hollow lore."

"Good lookin' out."

She gives Lu a firm nod and scoops up the sunglasses. "Cool, then I guess it's bye for now, neighbor," Finola says, and turns to leave.

"In a while, crocodile."

Lu listens closely for the sound of the heavy front door closing before pushing aside the booze to get a better look at the basket. She doesn't reach for it. Lu remains there for a few breaths before closing her eyes, listening until she hears the golf cart pulling away and rolling back down the driveway. With that, Lu grabs a paring knife, snatches up the basket and pokes a hole into the bottom side of the cellophane, carefully slicing it open just enough to fish out the round tin with the edibles. She shoves it into the yawning pocket of her joggers, then marches the relatively undisturbed gift basket to the backyard and over to the horizontal refuse storage shed, opens the lid to the recycling section, and rests it on top of a neat pile of collapsed moving boxes.

On her way back inside, an idea leaps to Lu's mind. It's so obvious now, it pulls a slow, sure smile across her face. It's the PH2. These exasperating, solipsistic women are the key to pulling off her final heist. They will be her Trojan horse.

CHAPTER SEVEN

"You have to go *today*?" Harry asks through the large mirror as he adjusts his four-in-hand tie knot for the second time this morning.

Lu, perched on the slim edge of their freestanding tub, stares into the linear electric fireplace, her eyes dry and irritated. Sleep has been ever more elusive since the devasting tête-à-tête with Mr. V just days ago. Visions of her mentor's face—vacillating between cloaked anguish and his typical austerity—continue to haunt her whenever she tries to close her eyes for more than five minutes. She is being held together by coffee grinds and unfiltered angst, her thoughts scattered and nerves shot. How is she going to access any of Harry's secured files? While he has always been rather tight-lipped about what goes down in his laboratories, Lu has managed to cull some basic information over the years about what Harry's work entails. Gene therapy. Or maybe it was gene editing. Or both. Most important, Lu knows that her husband doesn't work on the Island of Doctor Moreau. He hardly ever talks shop outside of the lab, adhering to his long-held belief that bringing work home is what corrodes intimacy between couples. Now she'll have to find a way to pierce this bubble and desecrate Harry's canon. How could The Atlas do this to her? Put her in this grim position to choose between them and him, as if determined to see her fail? Why would Mr. V not try to nix this on her behalf? Over the years, Lu could rest assured that Mr. V was always on the case, ironing out wrinkles for her, mending fences, salting over grease fires. He was her fixer or, as Mr. V put it a few times too many for Lu's taste, her sin-eater. Where does betrayal fit into that?

And with all this on her chest, how can she possibly make the necklace drop today? It is past due and creeping up on being filed as delinquent. The Atlas takes a hard line on most things, but even a suggestion of duplicity bumps matters to another level. Double-dealing is high on the list of infractions and the consequences of failing the client are swift and severe. Lu knows that a contract will be put on her head before she even has a chance to plead her case. Maybe Mr. V told them, assured the powers behind the powers that be that she would deliver. Lu shakes her head at her slide backward into foolish gullibility. The ship has long sailed on Mr. V acting as her protector. Sailed, leaving her drowning in the oil spill left behind.

"Lu . . . did you hear me?" Harry says, turning to look right at her. "Can you push it a day or two? Does it have to be today?"

She snaps to attention, as does her timbre. "Yes! Today. It must be today!" Lu tries to dial it back, but everything about her comportment has a saw-edge to it. She slows her breath, collecting herself with a quick, silent chant. *Cook and curry.* "Sorry . . . it's my certification stuff. I need to get it straightened out before everything lapses and I get jammed up trying to open the new studio. Today's the last day I can do it. And I'm pissed at myself for waiting this long." Lu spits out a few curse words, her hands balled.

Of course Harry notices the fists and her frustration beginning to edge toward anger. Although he knows Lu to be relatively even-keeled, there have been a handful of times when whatever wrath she has kept contained over the years boils over into an inferno, the flames never reaching far enough to harm anyone else but Lu. Mirrors smashed by tossed objects. Appliances dented by barefooted kicks. Welts on her long limbs by her own punches. Harry always tries to catch her before she crosses that bridge between understandable annoyance and unreasonable rage, the latter too often ending with some brand of self-inflicted injury. "It's all right, it's all right . . . we'll figure it out. Not helpful to punish yourself," Harry says, dipping his head to attempt eye contact with Lu. It doesn't work; her eyes are trained on the fireplace. But at least her fists are unfurled. Harry spins back around to check his knot and collars once more before sliding into his suit jacket that was carefully folded in half and propped on the vanity top far enough away from the sink to avoid catching an errant splash or dribble of water. "What did the pediatrician say?" Moving her attention to Solomon is a trick from the bottom of Harry's small, shallow bag. He noticed from early on how this diversion tactic seems to work, without fail, when it comes to talking his wife down from her ledge.

Lu nods. She knows, too, when she's being worked, especially by her own husband. But she also knows that Solomon is her one true kryptonite. "We can't get in to see her until tomorrow, twelve forty-five, at the earliest," Lu says. "And the other doctor at the practice is off today."

She watches as Harry fusses with his attire some more. As much as she enjoys seeing her man always impeccably dressed for work, this time Lu's irritation ticks up a level with each layer Harry has put on. She pops up as if pulled and starts pacing, almost against her will. Harry, fully dressed and leaned on the counter now, lets his eyes follow her as she moves back and forth like a slow pendulum. "I've run the battery, all the tests. It's not strep or COVID or RSV or any fucking thing that can be named. It's like Random Kid Virus Number Eighty-Four!" Lu shakes her head at her most horrible luck. The day she needs to slip into her other skin for a quick trip to the city is also the day that Solomon, one of the most resilient kids any pediatrician has ever seen, wakes in the middle of night with a high fever. "After-hours nurse said to just watch him, keep him hydrated."

She looks over at Harry, locking eyes with him, trying to silently feed him his next line. But the thing that she most wants Harry to say right now is not what comes out of his mouth.

"Maybe you can have one of your new mates from the golf cart gang watch after him while you go to New York."

Lu narrows her eyes at him. This wouldn't have been a problem back in Brooklyn. Lizette was always happy to keep an eye on Solomon if Lu had to tip out on the spur. There was also the babysitter, Sasha, who adored the boy and even stayed overnight on the off times that Harry worked late and Lu was otherwise occupied. But now, in this new house, new state, new life on the bizarre new planet on which they've landed, Lu has no options. No small but trusted village. No easy covers.

"First, they are not my *mates*. I don't know them," she tells Harry. "Second, do you honestly think our guy will be at ease being left with people he barely met a couple weeks ago?"

Harry concedes with a quick nod.

She stops pacing and looks to him. It's a second chance for Harry to say the right thing.

"Have him tag along with you, then?"

That was not it.

Lu stares at him, her face fixed on irked. All she wanted was for the man to peel out of his navy bespoke suit and volunteer to skip work—for once—and stay home with their febrile child. She would have even been fine with a work-from-home concession. Because the absurdity and egregious impropriety of taking a kid, moreover *her* kid, on a ride-along to a highly illegal product drop arranged by her covert, illicit organization has Lu on the verge of curling into a trembling ball with a blanket tossed over her head. That, or breaking into raucous laughter, the unhinged kind. *This is not going to work*, Lu tells herself, shaking her head as she lets her worried gaze rest on Harry for a breath. He looks so sharp and smart in his suit, getting ready to happily head into Kastille, his dream job fashioned from lies and deception. She shakes her head more, her shoulders dropping forward under the heft of what she now knows, the sickening truth that Mr. V dropped on her lap the other night.

Off her look, Harry's brow furrows. "What?" he says, tilting his head as his worried expression deepens.

"Nothing . . . I guess I'll try Finola, ask if she can watch him for a few. She's got the time. Her twins go to a fancy boarding school in New Hampshire basically year-round, I'm told—"

"By Annabelle?"

"Of course by *Annabelle*," Lu says with a *duh* wince and an eye roll. "That woman runs on gossip and chardonnay." Harry chuckles at this. "I'll see what Finola says. Just don't know how Solomon will do alone in a house with this stranger."

"Ah, give him some Motrin and an iPad and go with God. What's wrong with that?" He shrugs, his arms poking out to the sides. "Look, if I could stay behind with him, I would . . ."

But?

". . . but I have a series of big meets on the top floor today," Harry says. "And I'll be in the lab for hours after that. You know that place is not kid-friendly. Even for a kid like ours."

"OK . . . I'll work it out," she says, and mutters, "I always do." While normally this might be the case, Lu in control and on top of things, nothing feels further from that truth right now. The rug not just ripped out from under her, but also set ablaze right before her eyes.

"Hey," Harry says, gently grabbing Lu's hand. He stepped up to catch her before she clears the bathroom. "We're teammates. Remember."

She nods and lets him off the hook with a sincere smile.

"I'm serious," he says, pulling her into him and softly kissing both corners of her mouth. "We're teammates, Loubie. Right?" He pinches her chin and pulls it up to kiss her squarely now. "I need to hear you say it," he whispers between more kisses. "We're teammates who . . . ?"

"We're teammates who . . . shag," Lu says, and somehow pushes out a small, crooked grin.

"*Loubie.*"

She capitulates, sinking into his chest and accepting his tenderness in full. "Fine," Lu says. "We're teammates who win *because* we're teammates." Hearing herself recite their cute mantra, knowing what she knows now, makes Lu want to vomit.

"There we go," Harry says, and delivers one more kiss, this one deeper and longer. He makes a show of pushing her away from him, but lets his hands linger on her shoulders. "How about I get Boxer up and dressed, give him a bit of breakfast—or at least some milky tea—and then before I leave for work, I'll fashion the back of your Jeep into a little nook."

"He does love a nook," Lu says, with a weary grin.

"Indeed," Harry says, smiling broadly. "And you can use that time to get sorted and ready for your little adventure . . . *Loubie and Boxer Take On the City.* Don't stress; it will be good. Fun. What's the line from that book he loves . . . ? *Never do anything by halves if you want to get away with it. Be outrageous. Go the full mile.*"

Lu sighs. "It's *go the whole hog.* P.S. Quoting Roald Dahl at me? Immediately no," she says, with a sarcastic pat to the man's shoulder before slipping out of his hold and starting to her dressing room. "Also? He hated that book . . . and so did you, Forgetful Jones."

"Hang on, is that the cowboy Muppet? Give me points for remembering *that* at least!" Harry calls out to her back, with a playful chuckle. "Dove, before you move on . . . don't forget, not a word about all the dog business, right? Believe it or not, I'm still waiting for them to approve our application. It's a dog, for fuck's sake! Anyway, mum's, yeah?"

She stops to turn and give him an exaggerated salute, then back around to continue walking away. The minute she clears the bathroom door, her building panic crawls back into her chest. She races into her closet, scrolling through the phone for Finola's contact—still listed as Gift Basket—and sends off a quick text.

Hey, it's Lu. Crazy ask . . . any chance you can watch my feverish kid for a couple hrs today? Appt in the city I can't miss. I'd owe you a kidney if you can help me out—lmk

Finola's response comes back just as fast:

GB: Wish I could, so sorry!! I'm on my way to Westport to meet the others. We're helping out at Didi & Jonathan's foundation event. Sorry neighbor, next time for sure!

Lu lets the phone drop along with her shoulders as the reality of her circumstances settle in. Even a dehydrated, feverish, under-the-weather Solomon is as curious, astute, and observant as a seasoned journalist. She will have to be perfect in her answers, crafty with her creative spins, and hypervigilant in preempting anything that could go awry with the drop. This might be Lu's most precarious charge in the thirty years she's been doing the clandestine work. Although she knows it's as good as cotton candy in the rain, Lu still says a silent prayer and prepares to walk the finest of tightropes.

CHAPTER EIGHT

The thin, stretched-out clouds streak the blue sky like chalk marks as the sunlight pours through the windshield, toasting the air in the car. Traffic is moving along as expected for a Thursday, late morning. Normally, driving anywhere with Solomon, Lu would be playing easy R&B, something from the '90s to introduce her son to arguably the genre's best decade. No explicit lyrics, just soulful, singable, inspired music. But today, nothing is normal.

Lu grips the steering wheel with her uncharacteristically clammy hands. Her jaw is clenched so tight it feels wired that way as she experiences something she has not felt in more than thirty years: mortal dread. The cold sweat, the persistent headache, the unbridled fear causing her stomach to churn, the ragged heartbeat—all of it stuffed beneath a thin cloak of counterfeit calm. As much as she tries to focus on the road ahead and what she's going to do to regain control of the problematic situation at hand, she keeps revisiting the kitchen from the other night. How could she not? The knife is still wedged between her shoulder blades and the vision of Mr. V's sad, darkened comportment is etched into her marrow.

"True say, you have much to consider," he had said before pushing back his chair and slowly rising from the breakfast table. "But a pound of fretting cannot pay an ounce of debt. Trust your gut, my yout. It ca'an send you wrong." And with that, Mr. V returned to the dim corners of Lu's kitchen and eased out the back door. He had moved so smooth and quick, Lu was left to wondering if it had been real. Perhaps her insomnia and frayed nerves conjured it, and this unimaginable muddle is simply a very bad dream. That used to happen when Lu was younger and feeling anxious; she'd lie in bed with her mind racing too far ahead, devising inflated, impossible scenarios. On the nights when she felt exceedingly uneasy, the one fantasy that would reliably take hold of her wits, flood her senses with warmth and hope, playing in her head like a perfect lullaby over and again: Mr. V adopts her; she becomes a King. No longer would she carry the transposed name of the woman who delivered her—Dr. Lucille Pearline. And Mr. V becomes her father outright. Not mentor or handler, not wily mastermind or maneuvering puller of strings, just her dad who loves her fully and protects her because she's his family.

Lu shakes her head and grips the wheel tighter, an attempt to shoo away the useless throwbacks. She needs to focus on the now, eyes on the road ahead, readying for a feasible plan to spring forth and guide her on what to do when they arrive in New York City within the hour. Despite the clear directive, her obstinate brain falls back in the past and pulls yet another memory to center stage.

She can see it playing out clearly against the horizon:

Mr. V—or Mr. Vincent back then—is walking with her to his car, the house of horrors group home behind them. Lu—or Lucille Doctor back then—is carrying the same rucksack he had given her four years earlier, that is until the older man wordlessly relieves the weight of it from her shoulder, slinging it instead over his. She is eighteen here, and Mr. Vincent is about to lead her out of a cruel and broken childhood, and usher her into The Atlas—or a *life-changing opportunity* back then—and a brand of adulthood that will eventually rob Lu of her agency.

The news radio station's "updates on the tens" chime brings Lu's attention back to the Jeep and, more importantly, to controlling it on the highway. She glances at the dashboard clock. There are still forty minutes before they reach the Garment District in the city, and almost a full hour before the scheduled drop. Early is on time. On time is late. Lu had heard that old chestnut more times than she would care to count, even before joining The Atlas. From the organization, she had picked up a different gem to add to it: *Never let time become your enemy.*

Lu doesn't have the time or space for rueful reminiscing. One brick at a time is the only way for her to break out of this walled-off corner she's in. How to recover from the kiss of Judas will have to wait. As does her Kastille-Harry predicament. The only thing that matters now is pulling off this drop with an inquisitive eight-year-old in tow.

Improvisation is the worst ingredient to add to a job. A theory proven to Lu more than a few times. But she has no choice this time. There is no rock, no hard place, it's just bad. All of it. She glances back at her son through the rearview to help maybe regulate her nervous system. The mere sight of him like a blanket of oxytocin. Lu's breath begins to even out, but her hands and temples remain sweaty.

Solomon, fast asleep, is sat buckled into his booster seat beneath the canopy shade from a beach chair jury-rigged to provide the roof to his cozy car fort. Two thick throws and a pillow create the rest of the fort's frame. There is a book on top of an iPad in his lap, and his jacket zipped up to his chin along with a knit scarf wrapped around his neck just so renders him into a cocoon. His lips are a little chapped, but the rest of his face looks bright and sweet, as always.

Lu fiddles with the radio button on the dashboard's screen, trying to find a station with more local news. Although this isn't the first time (it's the second) that the feds have investigated one of her jobs, Lu needs to stay alert and ahead of all it. She lands on an AM station right as the latest NYC headlines are being read. Lu bumps up the volume by two increments.

Federal authorities have narrowed down the list of suspects in last month's Hell's Kitchen jewelry heist. Although the stolen piece, a priceless necklace from the Neapolitan collection reportedly valued at more than $115 million, has not yet been recovered, investigators are making progress and focusing their attention on new details in the robbery. NYPD is not yet releasing any names, but sources close to the case say that a warrant for the arrest of forty-eight-year-old Lucille D. Barlow of Brooklyn, New York, a career criminal, is expected within the week.

This is, of course, not happening. The actual news headlines do mention the robbery along with a rare storm in Europe causing extreme flooding, a controversial former US senator releasing his tepid memoir, the vice president's plans to attend a summit on artificial intelligence in the UK, a dismal box office opening for the latest World War II epic, and a bombshell celebrity divorce after seventeen years. But Lu is still convinced that with the very next news headline, she will be implicated. The next update might very well be the one that ends it all for her.

"Mom?"

Lu sits up, turning her head to smile quickly at the boy squirming in the back seat. "You OK, bubba? Do you want some water? I have your NASA cup up here with me."

"No . . . I'm OK right now," Solomon says. He stretches with his whole body just like Lu used to do as child. This brings her another smile.

"How you feeling?"

"I feel a little weird. Kind of dry and a little dizzy. Or maybe it's groggy."

"Yeah, it's probably that. Having a fever is never fun. But some water can help with the dry part?"

"OK . . . I'll take some now," he says, holding out a hand and wiggling his fingers.

Lu hands it back and listens as he takes loud gulps. "Better?"

"Mm-hmm," he says, nodding and smiling at her through the mirror. "Mom, I was going to tell you something before but then I fell asleep by surprise."

"Yeah, naps can sneak up on you like that. What did you want to tell me, sweet pea?"

"Your necklace, I like it. It's shiny; looks like a giant star."

Lu takes her foot off the gas pedal, and the car snaps back. She swallows hard, sure she misheard him. "What do you mean, jelly bean? What necklace?"

"The one that you had in a Ziploc baggie when you were in your big closet," Solomon says before taking another deep sip of water. "Did Dad give that to you as a gift for moving here?"

She keeps her head very still and the car cruising along smoothly, only moving her eyes to take easy glimpses at Solomon as he speaks. "How did you see what I was doing in my closet? Have you looked in there before, looked in the closet in Mom and Dad's room?" Lu makes sure to keep her eyes gentle and her smile warm as she talks to him.

"No," he says, with a loose shrug. "I only saw you holding the necklace baggie because of the spider."

"Ah . . . say more."

"I was in the nook in Dad's closet—"

"There's a nook in there?"

"*Technically*, it's just a shelf on the bottom part in the closet where Dad keeps those itchy sweaters he got from when he went to visit Grandpa. The *jumpers*. The way he has them stacked all together, it looks like a building made of clouds, but it's not as soft as it looks."

"Oh, yeah. They're made of Irish wool, sweets," Lu says. "But I still don't understand how you went from his closet to mine."

"I was getting to that," Solomon says, giving his mom a sarcastic look before taking another long sip of water. "I like lying down in the shelf-nook. It's dark, but not too dark. I can see things through my mini microscope better. And it's warm in there too. The other rooms aren't as warm yet."

"Makes sense," Lu says, calmly, despite her heartbeat sounding like a drum in her ears. "Keep going. What happened next?"

"What happened was, while I was lying down, I turned over so I could be on my tummy, like I always do, and that's when I saw a spider! And you know how I feel about spiders, Mom!"

"Oh, I do . . . indeed. What did you do?"

"I jumped out of the nook, that's what I did. I was going to go find Dad to capture it and get it out. Like, *right out* of the house. But then I remembered that book you read to me about courage the night before I started at Maple Grove. Remember? With Clarkey the scarecrow?"

"Of course I remember, sweet pea. That's a good book, right?"

"Yeah, it *is*. So, I told myself that I could be courageous too, just like Clarkey. That's when I went back to face that spider." Solomon pauses here and looks out the window at a passing flatbed hauling scraped metal.

"Don't keep me in suspense, hon," Lu says. "This story just got to the good part!"

"Oh, yeah . . . so the spider? It wasn't even a spider, Mom! It was some curls from my hair!"

"Goodness me!"

"I know. I got all jumpy for nothing. I felt so stupid." He stops himself short. "I know, I know—*don't say that about myself.* But this brain . . ." Solomon taps at his temple hard with the pads of his fingers. "It made me really believe that it was a spider. And I got all scared. Like some dumb baby."

Lu eases up on the accelerator again so she can linger on the boy in the rearview and still maintain control of the car. "*Hey* . . . you're not a baby or dumb or stupid or any of that."

"Yeah, I know." He keeps his head down, fiddling with flip straw on his cup.

"No, I want you to hear me for real, bean," Lu says. "Look at me." Solomon does as told and rests his eyes on Lu through the rearview mirror. "Your brain was doing what brains do. It was actually doing you a favor when you thought you saw that spider."

"A favor?" Solomon's voice lifts as his spirit seems to reinflate, his curiosity returned.

"Yes. There's a part of your brain called the amygdala. *Amygdala.* It's kind of like a threat detector, and it's always working hard, scanning your surroundings, assessing how safe you are, and ready to alert you at the first sign of trouble."

"Oh . . . so my brain was just letting me know that the black fuzzy thing over there might be a spider? Like . . . like a notification on my iPad?"

"Exactly." Lu sends him a toothy grin. "It's a survival mechanism, and it's super important. Its whole purpose is keeping you safe. Nothing dumb about that, right?"

"Right," he nods. "Amygdala. . . . *Amygdalahhhh.*"

"Yeah, it's fun to say too!"

Solomon laughs and nods again. The hunch in his shoulders is released and he relaxes, bringing his fluffy blanket up to his chin. "Thanks, Mom. You always have the answers," he says, and reaches for his tablet, nestling it into his lap again.

A swell of something fills Lu's chest and quickly rushes up her throat, blocking the air for a few split seconds and adding immediate pressure behind her sinuses. Her eyes want to water, they want to spill over and let go. The sob, it's right there at the edge. *Not now*, she chides herself. This somehow works and Lu blinks back the tears beginning to pool. She reaches for the dash screen, tapping it to raise the volume on this latest set of local headlines, increasingly concerned that her own threat detector might be malfunctioning.

"Oh!" Solomon says, leaning forward as if startled awake. "You forgot to answer my question. Is your new necklace a gift from Dad? And if it is, does this mean that I might get a moving gift too . . . as in a furry one with four legs?" The boy is grinning so wide all his tiny, white teeth are showing.

Lu takes a beat as she completes her lane change, readying to take the upcoming exit. She has not eased her intense clench of the steering wheel for the last forty-five minutes but makes sure to maintain an airy tone each time she opens her mouth to speak to Solomon. "And *you* forgot to tell me how you even saw the necklace, mister."

"Oh . . . yeah . . . so, I saw you put a plastic baggie in your backpack with your hat just when I was about to go look for Dad to help me with the spider-not-spider," Solomon says. "I thought it was maybe snacks for this car ride. Like, some Annie's packs or Zbars or that sweet popcorn or those teeny cheese and crackers things—I would have even settled for those frozen grapes you're always talking about. So, when you got out at the gas station before we got on the highway, I checked the bag to get the snacks. But, just like the spider, it was not what it seemed. And before you say it, I'm sorry that I was being nosy with your private stuff. I know I'm not supposed to, so, I'm sorry, Mom."

"That's all right, hon. I appreciate your honesty and the apology." Lu glances back at him, checking that he's not beating himself up for *doing a wrong thing.* He seems fine, but looks over at her expectantly. She knows that he's waiting for an answer about the necklace. She decides to go with the truth—or a version of it. "That necklace isn't a gift from your dad. It's not even mine. I borrowed it from someone without properly asking. And I need to return it before I get in trouble for having it."

"Trouble?" he says, an obvious disquiet leaking through.

"Nothing for you to worry about. Even though this friend is kind of upset with me for being late in handing it over, what matters is, I'm doing it now. I'm doing what I was told to do, what I'm supposed to do."

"Are you sad about your friend being mad at you?"

"Um . . ." Her voice catches unexpectedly. "A little."

"Maybe after you give it back to your friend and tell her you're sorry, she'll tell you that she appreciates your honesty and your apology. Then you won't feel bad about it. That always helps me when you tell me that."

"Could be, sweet pea . . ." His face is so open and wholesome. It's too much for Lu, and she turns her eyes to the highway. A rough lump soon lodges in her throat. She must swallow hard before trying to drag out the next string of words. Words that are not the right thing. "You know what might also help me not feel bad? Us not talking about it anymore . . . or not talking about the necklace with anyone else, even Dad."

"But you said secrets are not safe. Especially for kids."

The good parenting pride Lu feels is fleeting in this moment, replaced in a split second by unchecked shame. Since this boy was old enough to comprehend layered sentences and ideas, Lu has taught him that secrets are ultimately destructive. She reinforced the notion that adults telling children to keep secrets were rarely ever leaning toward something benevolent. She takes a moment now to rethink and rephrase. "Still true," she tells him. "Maybe we can just talk about it when we're in the Jeep together right now and leave it behind us once we hop out of here. What do you say? Think you can leave it in here?"

"Definitely!" Solomon sings. "Can I say one more thing?"

"Honeydew, maybe let's not—"

"It's not about the Jeep thing. Not really."

"OK. What's the one thing?"

"I don't think anyone could ever stay mad at you. And if they do, they gotta be losers with a boulder for a brain. Because you are a good person, maybe even the best person they'll ever meet."

Lu looks back at him now—she must—forgoing the rear-view reflection and turning around for a swift, but fuller glance at this darling boy. His face is flushed, smile still bright, and he's practically teetering with joy. Something fresh washes over her as she returns her attention to the road ahead. A resolve. The distress from a moment ago dissolves and Lu can settle her shoulders, unclench her fists and sweating palms wrapped around the steering wheel. She can hear her thoughts again, but they are centered on one clear goal. She doesn't need to glance back at him again; she's sure.

"Protect him." Lu says this under her breath. The whispered declaration underscores what she is now certain will come to pass. She will do the unthinkable and betray her husband to complete the complicated Kastille job, and this will be her final heist. It's the only way to protect Solomon. Earn her freedom, walk away from The Atlas, leaving this degenerate shadow self far behind. She will not ask them for permission or forgiveness. She has given her whole life to this unscrupulous entity. It is time, at last, for her to take it right back.

CHAPTER NINE

Solomon is fast asleep, snuggled in his makeshift nook. Lu can only hope that he stays that way as they will soon arrive at their destination. Sixth Avenue in the city is bustling as always with cars and cabs and bikes and people. Lu keeps her eyes peeled for any sudden moves from the same cars and cabs and bikes and people, her foot balanced and hovering, moving between the gas and brake pedals.

She checks on the boy through the rearview yet again. Solomon is snoring, lightly, and Lu is quietly grateful. The Children's Motrin has finally caught up with him. As her eyes return to the busy streets, another lucky break: a parking spot right in front of Saint Anthony's Basilica.

The first time Lu had to do a drop at this nearly two-hundred-year-old Catholic church, she balked, even triple-checking the coded message from comms while parked in a nearby open-air garage to make sure she had not misread something. The irony of skullduggery in the sacred space—one dedicated to St. Anthony of Padua, patron saint of lost things, no less—was jarring. And now, even thirty years later, the nerve of her, traipsing through these hallowed grounds, dragging her brand of grime along the brick floors, it still doesn't sit all the way right with Lu. But what choice does she have? Lu is convinced that making this drop happen—be it in a church or right outside the gates of hell—is the first step in her plot to get out for good.

True, there are irrefutable pieces of evidence that make Lu's quiet-quitting scheme seem basically impossible.

Exhibit A: The Atlas does not have a viable retirement plan.

Exhibit B: No one has successfully just *walked away.*

But then there is the approach-the-bench tidbit about the unconfirmed tale of Number Fourteen, a.k.a. Maxwell Trotter, the alleged lead in the 2003 Waldon Security Deposit robbery in Chicago, where $109 million in cash and valuables were stolen. Days after the heist, Trotter allegedly sent word back to The Atlas, via the coded central agent system, notifying the organization that he would be taking his leave after the drop was done and the mission was filed as completed. And that was the last anyone ever heard from Number Fourteen. Allegedly. Although the details around both this infamous job and Trotter himself have always existed in a foggy space between myth and reality, to the handful of his counterparts privy to upper mantle intel, the generally accepted ending to his story is that, somehow, he did it. He made it out of the darkness, into the plain and natural light, and is now living an ordinary, bona fide life somewhere on this globe. Allegedly.

More than getting out, what Lu truly desires is a Maxwell Trotter ordinary ending, where her story becomes the new legend for what could be once free—allegedly.

Lu parallel parks the Jeep in one easy reversing swoop and then puts on the rest of her uniform. A dark-beige bucket hat, pulled down far on her head, the coiled ends of her hair in four large twists tucked inside of it. She gently wrestles her beige light wool coat over her shoulders. Nothing to zip or button, just an open front—making it easy to wiggle out of, if needed—and large patch pockets with flaps to conceal any small tools of her trade. The clothes beneath are also some variation of beige or neutral. Nondescript. One of Lu's first lessons after joining The Atlas was that going unnoticed was an essential part of success in the business, especially when doing any proximity work. To that end, she made sure to sharpen her observational skills to a fine point by people-watching and clocking the details of their attire down the smallest accessory. There's a lot of story behind the clothes people choose to wear. However, Lu had learned long before she even landed in this game that as a Black woman moving through largely white, affluent spaces, she will always be noticed. A contrast. For her, the next best thing is to be dull, flat, forgettable. Her small brown backpack is the last piece of her outfit, but perhaps the most important, with the heavy necklace inside practically burning a hole through its fine Italian leather. Out of the car, she walks around to the back passenger door, opens it, and carefully lifts Solomon out of the Jeep. He feels a lot heavier than he should and the twinge at her side from the bruised spleen reminds her that she's not operating at a hundred percent either. She locks the door with a push of the remote key fob before sliding it into one of the coat pockets and adjusting Solomon's resting body on her right side, then moves, as smoothly as the extra weight would allow, along the narrow pathway and up the staircase of the Midtown church.

Inside the vestibule, the heavy thud of the outside door behind her that would normally wake her son doesn't seem to stir him in the slightest. His light snoring continues, unbroken, with his face peacefully nestled in the crook of Lu's neck. She takes a deep breath into her diaphragm, trying to make as little movement as possible while stepping inside the ornate entryway. She does a sweep of the pin-drop-quiet space. It's empty. Confession hours will soon be over for the day. The only eyes on them are coming from the Divine Tapestry, the mosaic art piece covering the entire surface of the sanctuary featuring Madonna and Child, angelic hosts, and other Biblical scenes whose context stretches far beyond Lu's agnostic heart.

Although she has not been to this church in almost four years, she falls into action mode without a blink, each choreographed step of the method grafted on to her bones. She scans for a safe spot to lay her son down before preparing to take her own place in the second pew from the front, right side. Solomon has always been a good sleeper, even as a newborn. The constant screams of sirens, the honking and holler of Brooklyn served as a built-in sound machine, leaving the boy capable of sleeping through a sonic boom. Still, Lu needs to play it smart, attuned to the insidiousness of optimism and the recklessness of relying on things going according to plan. Last thing she needs is to be foiled before she even gets started by the hardness of the wooden church pews rousing the kid. There's no time for what-ifs or playing out scenarios in full. That is the only certainty.

She shakes her head and adjusts Solomon's resting on her shoulder. As Lu goes to take another step forward, she hears a familiar shuffling behind her, more specifically coming from the gallery above the narthex where the organ is. Her breath settles and she is tempted to laugh loudly at her unusual and startling luck further unfolding. The prime parking spot directly in front of the church was one thing. A mere fluke. Then the empty chapel, plus the ever curious, hyper-observant child rendered practically unconscious behind a random virus, fever, and ibuprofen. And now, if her ears do not mistake her, that chipping, sandpaper sound is emanating from the uneven, dragging gait of the church's longtime organist in her weathered, black, 1940s oxford shoes.

An easy quarter turn to the right, and there she is.

"Miss Goodwin," Lu says, barely above a whisper, smiling as she watches the older Black woman make her way down the stairs.

"Is someone there?" Miss Goodwin says, padding toward Lu and Solomon. "I mean, I see you there . . . your shadow." She squints, her milky eyes behind the heavy amber tint of her oversize glasses, and draws closer and closer still, until Lu can feel Miss Goodwin's warmed, peppermint-sweetened breath near her hand resting on Solomon's back.

"It's me, Miss Goodwin," Lu says, purposely moving her quiet voice into her nose.

"Celeste?" Miss Goodwin says, and her face blooms into something honeyed and bright. "Oh, dear me, is that really you?"

"Mm-hmm," Lu says. The nondescript edict expands beyond the clothes. Even Lu's cover name and the jumbled, general details of her life must be an amalgam of neutral and featurelessness. Ordinary enough to simply fade into an easy fog of a memory.

The fact that the old woman, a live witness, is legally blind appeared to be a godsend back when Lu first encountered her. However, that box was roundly unchecked ten minutes into chatting with Miss Goodwin.

Though the cataracts have all but destroyed her vision, the octogenarian's sense of hearing remains in fine fettle, perhaps even stronger all these years later. A naturally gifted organist, Miss Birdie Goodwin can play anything perfectly hearing it only once, and when it comes to voices, she will always remember yours. As she told Lu when they first met here decades ago, "I hold tight to my memories. Scripture says, 'The memory of the righteous is a blessing, but the name of the wicked will rot.' I always remember good people's names."

"Celeste Davis, as I live!" she says now. "I haven't heard you around here in must be a good five years, maybe more . . . or was it four years, now? No, no—four. Definitely four years."

"It's good to see that you're still here, taking care of that ol' pipe organ up there."

"Oh, please, that dusty thing takes care of *me*," Miss Goodwin says. "How have you been, dear? All the years without coming by . . . did you find another church family up in . . . now where were you again? Harlem, right?"

"Right," Lu says, unsurprised by the woman's sharp recall.

"Which church did you land at up there—oh, hold on, now. Who is this you got with you?" She leans in, within sniffing distance of Solomon's shoulder. "You got a little one? What's this young lamb's name?"

"No, this is my nephew," Lu says, the corner of her mouth twitching. "His name's Ali."

"Ollie, like Oliver?"

"Ali," Lu says, just a hair louder. "Like the boxer."

"OK, that's nice. Over there, sleeping like a log, sounds like!"

"Yeah . . . he's got the flu."

"Aw. You came to pray over him?" Miss Goodwin says, her voice like a soft melody.

"Something like that." Lu shifts in place, the weight of both Solomon and her own dishonesty beginning to set in. "I was going to go to confession, actually."

"You want to put him to lie down for a bit? There's a little bench, it's just over there by my robes. I can watch over him while you go atone for your sins, reconcile with our God."

If only that were possible. "Uh . . . I don't want to put you out—"

"Celeste, that's nonsense." Miss Goodwin swats away the mere idea of her inconvenience. "It's right there. You can even see it from the altar."

"Thank you. Truly. Don't worry; I won't be too long, Miss Goodwin," Lu says. "I really appreciate you." That last part being completely true. If blessings are real, she is indeed one.

"And if he stirs?" Miss Goodwin says, leading Lu toward the small coat area to the side.

"Yes . . . he might be a little loopy. The medicine has him a bit delirious."

"Oh, that cherry syrup will do it to you, honey," the woman says, with a stiff nod.

"If he wakes up . . ." The twitching returns to the corners of Lu's mouth. "He might be confused, like I said, and he might ask for his mom. My sister and I look a lot alike, so . . ."

"Say no more," Miss Goodwin says. She gestures to the bench for Lu to lay the boy down and pulls a short stool next to his feet and sits there. "I have a small box of tea biscuits right under that little side table, if he stirs . . ."

"Oh, perfect," Lu says, resting her hand on Solomon's lukewarm forehead for a breath before urging herself to take a large step away from him and Miss Goodwin. "I won't be long. Thank you, again."

"Don't even mention it, dear," Miss Goodwin says. "It's important for you talk to your God. It is good to praise Him. Praise the Father, the Son, and the Holy Spirit." She crosses herself. "Let us bless and exalt God above all forever!"

The twitch spreads from Lu's mouth to her nose, and soon moves into her eyes. She is fighting for control of her own face. "Amen," she says through gritted teeth, the only way she can keep her pained expression at bay.

Lu nods and takes another step back from the bench before she turns away completely and starts toward the pews. From the minute Lu locks in on the pulpit in the distance, her entire comportment shifts into something sharp and chilled. Her jaw tightens. Posture, rod straight. And her eyes have gone steely. She is transformed into her shadow self and can see nothing that falls outside of the clear commandments for finishing this job.

Lu follows each forensically detailed step of the program, her heartbeat slow and even, moving as if in a trance. She walks to the specified pew, enters, kneels, then makes the sign of the cross, pretending for a breath to pray. She remains there, head bowed, for exactly forty seconds, slowly counting out each Mississippi in her head. She then rises, exits the pew, making sure to genuflect like a proper Catholic as she leaves. Lu bends the knee once more as directed and begins a solemn, measured walk toward the confessional, first stall. Although the church is practically empty, no one there to witness this performance, Lu knows that at these covert drops, somehow they find a way to keep watch, ensuring that nothing goes sideways, that there are no attempts to hoodwink from either side. She moves into the confessional, gliding on conviction and calm. Once seated, the shrouded, alleged priest clears his throat.

This is Lu's cue.

She raises her bowed head and, with an unhurried blink, speaks her line: "Bless me, Father, for I have sinned. It has been twenty-two days and one hour since my last confession."

From behind the screen comes Lu's next prompt: a loud sniff.

She follows through and confesses her sole sin. "I have been dishonest to my brother and deliberately broken a promise to him. I'm sorry for these and all my sins."

There's a second, softer throat clearing, then a line delivered quietly by the supposed ecclesiastic. "The breadth of charity widens the narrow heart of the sinner," the man says, his light Irish accent sounding flimsy and forced.

Lu leaves the carefully wrapped product by her feet, then rises and leaves the stall. She continues her steady stride down the aisle toward the vestibule, following through on the final steps in this routine: no lingering, no looking back.

CHAPTER TEN

It's been a little over a week since the necklace drop, but Lu can still feel it. Shame. It's resting heavy on her chest. She feels the crush of it most anytime she catches a glimpse of Solomon in the rearview mirror, a reminder that she did the thing she swore never to do: She involved the boy in her dirt. True, he was asleep through all of it and arrived back home from New York like nothing happened, but the sting and stench of it is real for Lu. Even now, looking back at him on this otherwise bright Saturday morning, she's consumed by fresh guilt. The compunction making her stomach feel spoiled, a sour taste lingers on her tongue.

She forces herself to glance at him anyway, because not only is he wide awake, but he's sulking. Has been for the last fifteen minutes. "I like your cut, G!" she says, playfully.

"*Mom . . .*" he grumbles.

"Sorry. Are the youths not saying that anymore?"

"Did they ever?" he says, clearly exasperated.

"Well, I do like it. Looks really good. Frames your face," she says of his new haircut. Neat and tidy with a bit of big-kid swagger. "I was a little skeptical. Old white guy barber and all. Plus his own haircut was not at all flattering. I was kinda bracing for disaster."

"*Mom!*"

"I know, I know. Book by the cover," she concedes. "It's just that, historically, white barbers and stylists don't always fully grasp the intricacies of Black hair."

"What does that mean—*into the seas*?"

Lu stifles a chuckle. "Wait, it's *intricacies*. It comes from the word intricate, which means detailed or complicated. And Black hair is that, but in the best way. The range is wide, you know? So, I was surprised, pleasantly, that a guy named Flynn knew his way around your hair. It also means I don't have to drive you back to Brooklyn to go to Phil's like your dad does."

"OK, I understand," Solomon says, and continues staring out his window.

"Above all that, though," she says, "the question is, do *you* like your haircut?"

"It's fine," he says, flatly.

"OK, what's going on, Grumpy McDaniels? You've been a total wet blankie all morning. You didn't crack a single smile while eating those chocolate chip pancakes at Sunny Side Spot either. Show me someone who sulks while eating fluffy, delish pancakes—again, with chocolate chips—and I'll show you an AI robot."

This causes the tiniest twitch of a grin from Solomon, but he maintains his staring contest with the world outside his window. Lu is about to make another joke but doesn't want to push it.

Solomon's always required some space to process his upset feeling and bad moods. Even as a baby, barely two years old, he would ask—with that adorable toddler lisp—to have "a time-in," which meant he would sit in his bedroom with a light blanket over his head while he dealt with his personal prickles and ruffled feathers.

"You know, the hot chocolate place is coming up . . . at least I think so."

"No, thanks, Mom. I'm not in the mood for hot chocolate."

"See? That's what I'm trying understand here, sweet pea. What's up with your mood? You seem off your usual happy vibe . . . anything you want to talk about?"

Solomon, at last, turns away from the window to look at his mom through her rearview mirror. "Why do we have to go to this brunch?"

"Oh, pumpkin. I know this is not what you want to be doing with your Saturday afternoon, but I doubt it's going to be horrible," Lu says. "If anything, it'll give you chance to get to know some of the neighbor kids outside of school. See them in their natural habitat."

"I don't know . . . all of those kids are . . ." He shakes his head.

"Tell me. It's OK . . ."

"They're not nice kids. I mean, they're not nice to me."

"Oh? Is this something I need to step into? Is someone bullying you?"

"No, no . . . it's not like that. No one's punching me or anything. Most of those kids that live near us kind of act like I'm not even there."

"I thought you were getting along well with Miss Margot's son . . . uh—"

"Declan. Yeah, he's good. I have like two friends. *Two.* Declan Pearson and Asher Avery. And they're not in my class. Both of them are in the fifth grade. They're the only ones who treat me normal and, like, *like* me. The other ones—*especially* Miss Didi's kids—are . . . like what you called that guy on the motorcycle that cut us off by Mr. Flynn's shop . . ."

"A little shit?" Lu says, and the boy nods timidly. "The Killigrew kids are little shits?"

"Yes, like, really, really *that.*"

Not far the from the goddam tree. "Ah, I see. OK, well, I'm glad you told me. Also, here's the thing, you're going to meet a lot of people, especially as you're coming up in school, who are not nice, who treat you unfairly, and who are—if we're being honest—shitty human beings. But it's super important that you never let how they treat you affect how you see you. Does that make sense, hon?"

"Yeah, it does, Mom. Thanks." His little face begins to brighten. "So . . . does this mean we don't have to go to the brunch?"

"Not so fast." Lu chuckles. "Tell you what; we'll go, show them how cool we are, then when we're ready to leave, we'll just leave. In fact, we can create a little hand signal right now. Once you flash it at me, I'll hop into action and get us outta there. How's that sound?"

"Like a good plan," Solomon says, and gives her a firm, committed nod.

LU QUICKLY GLANCES at herself in the closet's jumbo mirror one last time. She is wearing the first of the three outfits she had pulled from her closet and modeled for Harry yesterday. The one that earned instant applause from him. Loose, straight-leg denim, a corset-waist black wool blazer with a top edge of a lacey bra peeking out, and her favorite white with black patent leather Mary Janes.

"Edgy," Harry had said. "Love it."

"Chilled indifference, that's the vibe I'm going for. Is that what you're getting—relaxed but chic 'I don't give a shit'?"

"Dove, you've got nothing to worry about. You're fit!" Harry had said while giving his wife a steamy up-down. "Anyway it's just brunch. Nothing truly important ever happens at brunch." It was not lost on him—or Lu—how the mean-girl ethos of the golf cart crew had sprouted some of the weeds of her long-buried group-home insecurities. As much as she is trying to act unbothered by these women and their glaring affluence and privilege, and view them instead as convenient pawns in her larger scheme, the truth is, Lu is indeed rattled by them, slight as it might be.

He comes around the corner of her closet now, dressed for the brunch, gently tugging at his shirt's cuff beneath his cashmere sweater. Even Harry's casual weekend looks are impeccable. "You about ready, darling? Don't want to be tardy, especially for something in our honor," he says, still fussing with his own outfit before looking up at Lu. "Oh, my . . . you're looking very, *very* good." He licks his lips; it's subtle, but the message behind it is clear.

Harry puts his hands in his pocket and leans back on the doorjamb. His smirk is filthy, and it drags a stubborn grin out of Lu in response.

"*No*," she tells him through the reflection of the mirror. "Wipe that thing off your mug this minute, sir. We have a child downstairs waiting for us."

"Trust me, Boxer would be all too pleased if we got held up in here and skip out on going to this whole brunch affair."

"I don't really blame him, though. Honestly, I'm not hyped about going either."

"It'll be fine, dove. Promise. Of course . . . there is . . . one thing I suppose I should warn you about." Harry makes a face.

"Oh, God. Hit me."

"Jonathan, he's a bit of a—"

"Little shit?"

"What?"

"Nothing . . ." Lu smirks. "Continue."

"A blowhard, I guess you'd call it," Harry says. "He talks a lot, brags a lot, and laughs very loud, often at his own very mediocre jokes. He's like that character in the movie you watch anytime it's on . . . *Glengarry Glen Ross.* You know"—Harry tries his still-horrible New York accent—"'Yeah, these are my brass balls. And this watch costs more than your car.' That guy."

"Ugh, he's a Blake? Really?"

Harry laughs. "He's not exactly as bad as that Blake character, but he definitely gives that energy. You're good at ignoring that kind of thing, though."

"Any other scoop on these guys that I should know?"

He walks past Lu to attend to her back, massaging her shoulders through the blazer's stiff padding. "A cheat sheet on these geezers? Where's the fun in that? Let's just go and get it over with, yeah?"

"I suppose I should let you in on the agreed upon exit-stage-left hand signal, then, huh?"

"What in the world . . . ?" Harry says, through a hearty chuckle.

"The boy will fill you in."

THE BARLOWS' LIVELY car debate ranking the top ten Sesame Street characters comes to an abrupt end the minute they reach the top of Didi and Jonathan's driveway. The trio step out of the car next and walk toward the house in silence, with Harry gently swinging his leather booze tote carting two of his faves: a pinot noir from France and Hennessy Black cognac. Meanwhile Solomon's sulk is back and threatening to set in for the day, and Lu is scanning the compound, outlining it with her squinting eyes.

She can't help but scoff at the exceedingly obnoxious size of the house. Even compared to her own overdone mansion, the DuBois-Killigrew home is simply insufferable at a little over seven thousand square feet with six bedrooms and eight baths on two acres, according to the listing from Annabelle's high-end realty group, Prestige Properties. Lu had looked up Didi's home a few hours after that first ambush meeting of the PH2 gang. She did the same for the other women, studying the blueprints and room layouts of their respective Partridge Hollow homes in case a stealthy snoop-around is in order.

Once inside the grand two-story entrance, Lu continues eyeballing every corner and curve of the house, unsurprised by any of the high-end furniture and elegant art on display in the well-appointed rooms they walk through en route to the breezy patio in the back where the brunch is being held.

There's a low cheer from the small crowd gathered when the Barlows are ushered in by a neatly dressed real-deal butler. Lu counts about fifteen people, not including the many children spilled about the massive backyard. Margot is up first, rushing over to them.

"Welcome, welcome!" she sings, grabbing Lu's forearm. The room's attention swings toward the Barlows. "Actually, there was a secret bet going that you might not show," she whispers loudly to Lu. "I'm kidding of course," she adds, as she spies Didi approaching with a broad-smiling Jonathan trailing far behind her. "This outfit, mama—*love*! Just fabulous. Hey, Harry"—she wiggles her fingers at him—"and Mr. Cutie Pie Solomon! Declan has been asking when you're going to get here every five minutes. He's super excited."

Solomon's expression softens immediately. "Oh, cool," he says, and looks to his mom.

Lu is about to nod and set the boy free when Didi and Jonathan step over to them. "Let's say hello first," she mouths to Solomon.

"Welcome to your welcome brunch," Didi says. Her tone is pleasant and her arms are open but not in a way that indicates she's looking for an actual hug. In fact, it seems she's using them more to covertly elbow Margot out from crowding her space.

"Thank you for doing all of this," Lu says. "This is beyond generous." Through the corner of her eye she can see the other women from the PH2 moving in. She braces for the swell of annoying chitchat and stagy compliments.

"Yes, very kind of you," Harry adds. "All of you. Wonderful community here. We're lucky to be a part of it."

"Thank you, Miss Didi," Solomon says, quietly, and again looks to his mother.

"Oh, my goodness! *Miss Didi*. So formal. Aren't you a little gentleman. And so handsome," Didi says with a grin that looks decently warm and authentic.

Lu gives the boy a whispered "you're good" and a wink, and he races off to find Margot's son while she and Harry move deeper into the half-in-half-outdoor space perfectly adorned with flowers and autumnal decor.

The other woman from the gift basket delivery, the one whom Lu had dubbed Glamazon, waits her turn to greet the guests of honor. She, too, is put together, but less tailored business chic and more flowing stylish elegance. She smooths out her mauve feather-print midi dress while looking down at her white pointed-toe ankle boots, posed just so, as if she knows Lu is taking her in. Her jewelry is simple and dainty—rose gold fleurette necklace; gold signet ring; Classic Winston round diamond engagement ring; and dangle pearl earrings. After the initial PH2 storming of the doors, Lu had done her online scans on each of the women and their respective Kastille husbands. This is Calista Caudwell, the forty-three-year-old mom of two and former supermodel turned fledging local boutique owner. She is married to Ashley Avery, EVP of R&D, who's been bouncing between Switzerland and Belgium for the last two months, according to a press release that Lu had read on Kastille's website.

Except for Finola, all of the golf cart women are married to members of the company's top-level alphabet gang. Didi's husband, Jonathan Killigrew, is the CEO. Margot's literal old man, Cormac Pearson, is the COO. And Ward Bloom, Kastille's CFO—"Carbon copy of a 1970s Paul Newman; I'm talking with the scruffy beard and all," Annabelle had said, back when she was first giving Lu the download on the Kastille notables—is married to PH2 member-at-large Evangeline Bloom, a fresh-faced blond, longtime socialite, and daughter of real estate magnate Bernard St. Clair. "She basically looks like Charlize

Theron but with the blue blood of the Rockefellers and the business sense of Kim Kardashian," Annabelle had said, dizzy with delight. "She now heads up the luxury wellness brand Bliss Bloom. So savvy."

Lu gives Calista a furtive up-down sweep. It's quick as a blink but manages to catch every bend and sway of her voluptuous form. Annabelle was right, that woman's body is fire.

Calista shakes out of her stance and struts over to Lu. Once close enough, she tickles the air with her fingers in a cute, easy wave. "Hi there." Her voice is mellow and warm, almost inviting. "We didn't get a chance to meet before. I'm Calista—Caudwell. But around town I go by Calista Avery. My husband, who's still in western Europe"—she throws a pleased glance toward Didi—"he gets a weird kick out of people calling me by my married name," she says, barely stifling an eye roll. "Anyway, whatever with all that . . . it's so nice to meet you." She stretches her hand to shake Lu's, and tousles her thick, wavy, auburn hair as she does.

"Good to meet you," Lu says, inhaling the woman's alluring scent, fresh as a spring breeze, a gust of roses and irises with a touch of something warm and sweet. She sniffs again. It's magnolia and something sweeter, like apricot drizzled with vanilla. The inviting aroma is strong but not overpowering. Lu is almost tempted to close her eyes and take another deep hit of it, but instead pulls back from the elegant bouquet enveloping the woman.

"H-man!" Jonathan bellows, abruptly interrupting Lu's olfactory trance. He makes a production out of shaking Harry's hand excitedly, punctuating it with a double slap to the side of his arm.

The whole overdone thing seems to serve as a kind of bird call, as the other men, Harry's main colleagues, flock over now too. Lu nods along mindlessly to whatever Didi, Margot, and Calista are talking about while keeping her attention trained on the husbands beginning to gather. These men are the blue bloods of Kastille, a company with a staggering market cap of nearly six hundred billion dollars, and Lu needs to discern which one of them—other than Harry—will help her complete her mission.

Jonathan breaks from loving up on Harry and turns to Lu. "Ah, so you're the much talked-about Lu. Good to meet you, finally." He moves in closer, his hand extended. She shakes it, making sure to be extra firm with her end of things. His narrow, icy-blue, deep-set eyes feel like they might just pierce hers straight through to the back of her head. In all of the pictures Lu's seen of him so far, his textured, barely graying curtain hairstyle looks long, floppy, permanently rumpled, but right now the tresses are tamed, with a crisp side part and slicked back, seemingly still wet, as if he just walked out of the shower. He's attractive, no doubt, but there's something sinister bubbling beneath that, a noxious stench that hits Lu square in the face like a mean jab. More than not trusting him, immediately Lu does not like him. "I gotta tell ya, Harry is *the* man. If there were awards at Kastille, your husband's got MVP locked down."

"Aw, he's a good man, indeed," Lu says, joining in beaming at Harry.

"*Enough*," Harry says, demurely.

"Actually, is it OK if I whisk this all-star away for a minute?" Jonathan asks Lu, but doesn't care to wait for her reply. Instead, he turns to speak directly to Harry. "Carter Huxley, you know, that guy from Legal with the really old, really rich boyfriend . . . he's got that dumb cabbage haircut and always looks hungover . . . anyway, he handed me a box of Padrón 1964s yesterday. High-level, anniversary series."

"Carter is a good brother out on the sesh," Harry says.

Out on the sesh? When did he start saying that?

"Oh, for sure. Carter always has the best connects for basically *anything* you might need," says Ward Bloom. Lu takes him in for a breath. His online photos don't quite do him justice. He's undeniably good-looking with the classic movie-star face, the definition of smoldering. Ward greets Harry and then Lu with simple handshakes. "Evangeline sends her regrets," he tells Lu. "I'm sure she'll have the pleasure of meeting you soon."

"You in on this, H-man?" Jonathan hollers, moving toward the steps leading outside.

"You should go, *H-man*," Lu says to Harry, wryly. "Plus, Padrón 1964s . . . ? You gotta."

"Mac! Join in," Jonathan shouts over to Cormac Pearson, who gives him the in-a-minute hand signal.

Cormac, standing beside his wife, whispers something in her ear that causes her to giggle and blush. He appears younger and healthier up close compared to the online photos Lu had scoped of him. A textbook charming gentleman. Handsome too, with his full head of gray hair and thick matching beard. He bears a strong resemblance to actor Gabriel Byrne, except Cormac sports a bulbous belly along with his big beard. There's a warmth emanating from him, a natural magnetism about him. Lu can see what pulled Margot into this man nearly twenty years her senior. His money being old also helps.

Thanks to Annabelle, Lu got a major head start on cybersleuthing this Kastille group. She even gave Lu a detailed backstory on the Pearsons' intergenerational romance. "He's over sixty, but wears it very well," Annabelle had said. "And with six kids, seems like everything *else* is working very well too."

Margot gently pulls the man's arm along, walking him closer to where Lu is standing. "You gotta meet Cormie! The sexiest COO in the nation. Cormie, this is Barlow—*Lucille* Barlow, but everyone calls her Lu."

"Good to meet you, Lu," Cormac says. The whisper of an Irish accent mixed with his throaty voice is soothing. He gently shakes Lu's hand. "Everyone calls me Mac . . . or Graybeard or Old Man Pearson, but those last two are mainly behind my back," he jokes.

"Cormie, stop. No one calls you that!" Margot swats at his shoulder, then gives Lu a quick, waggish look. Cormac glances at Margot adoringly, his sleepy eyes widening as he takes in her every syllable and gesture. He is obviously smitten, still, all the years later.

Mac kisses Margot's cheek, then steps away, off to join the others preparing to pollute the air with Dominican cigars. Margot excuses herself and retreats as well, heading inside to find where her own gang has gone.

"Heyyy," Finola says, stepping up for her turn with Lu. "First, I love everything about this look, head to toe, perfection."

"Oh, you're so kind. Thanks," Lu says.

"How you holding up? I know it's a lot of fuss and muss at these things."

"It's not too bad," Lu says. "Getting to know everyone in one sweep is good." *And pretty damn helpful.*

"I'd like us to get to know each other better. Maybe we can get togeth—"

The brittle clang of a bell interrupts everyone's chatter. The sound is coming from Didi, standing at the patio door with a ridiculous, vintage Bevin bell in hand announcing the official start of the brunch.

Finola makes a wry face—again showing Lu that there's a more authentic person percolating beneath the sycophant shell. "Like I was *about* to say, maybe we can do something together. Just you and me. How does that sound?"

"Like a good plan," Lu says.

CHAPTER ELEVEN

Sipping on too-hot coffee, whereby the singe lingers on her lips a good ten minutes later, is Lu's version of a cold plunge. She takes that first impressive sip from the scalding quad over drip. The punch of heat and caffeine straightens Lu out of her slouch as she leans against the kitchen island. But the grand serenade of the doorbell drives her almost-settled shoulders up to her ears.

Lu rests the cup on the counter and forgoes the security screen. The worst possible intruder has already trespassed on her family's private space. She heads toward the door, tossing a quick scowl at the breakfast nook, aimed at the chair where Mr. V sat over two weeks ago.

The hot liquid still warms her throat and chest as Lu zips up her thin black hoodie and then pulls open the door, ready to feign surprise at whoever is standing behind it.

"*Heyyy*," Finola says, so pleasant it sounds like the first note of a ballad. She is dressed in olive-colored leggings and a matching fitted running jacket with white, thick-soled sneakers. Lu scans the jewelry. Again, no major pieces. Although she's replaced the curled-serpent gold studs with medium-size silver hoops—basic and delicate, but nice. Finola catches Lu's glance lingering by her shoulder. "It's just me this time. No looming golf cart," she tells Lu, winking.

"Oh, I wasn't checking. You're fine." Lu smiles, but it's listless. Covering up her personal hell, the side effects of her Faustian bargain, has become a heavy lift. Still, she stretches her smile while straining to keep it natural, warm. Now more than ever, securing her usual mask is imperative. Plus, it's Finola. The edibles aside—although it did score cool points—Lu deems her the most likeable of the haughty housewives. And despite Lu having a painfully short list of companions to reference, there's something about Finola that feels oddly familiar, maybe even safe. Like, perhaps in another life, a very plain and peaceful one, the two of them could have been real friends.

"Sorry to even to drop in on you unannounced. *Again*," Finola says, fidgeting with the small leather belt bag slung across her chest.

Despite the mix of curiosity and suspicion stirring in her gut, Lu toggles on her affable mode. "Girl, please. Come on in. Is everything OK?"

"Totally! This is in no way an emergency," Finola says.

"Good. Then join me for some coffee," Lu says. "I was just ingesting my usual caffeinated magma. Happy to make you a cup of something suited for human consumption." *Please don't ask for some double pump, no fat, glitter sugar cube, pumpkin dust bullshit.*

"That sounds delightful," Finola says, then quickly stops Lu from walking ahead with a soft grab to the forearm. Lu's eyes pivot to Finola's hand resting on hers. Her reflexes twitching, ready to kick out her elbow like a chicken wing, jabbing the woman in her side hard and slipping out of her hold in self-defense. Perhaps sensing Lu's body tensing up, Finola lets go but doesn't make a moment about it. Instead, she just keeps talking. "Actually, I should come clean . . ." Lu's brow stays arched as Finola continues, "I came over to apologize."

"For . . . ?"

"For leaving behind weed gummies, like some graceless idiot." Finola sighs, her face reddening. "That was presumptuous, and so embarrassing. We had just met."

"Behave. It wasn't like that. If anything, it just shows that you're one of those *vibes only* girlies, making sure everyone feels good and leveled. I appreciate that."

Finola exhales, clearly relieved. "OK, so, we're good?" She nods quickly, answering her own query. Her face remains stuck in cringe-smile. "Now, for the other reason I came by . . . I was hoping you'd maybe want to join me for a walk?"

"A walk?"

"Not far," Finola says. "Just down to the beach entrance and back. Barely two miles, which should be a total breeze for you. I mean, *hello*, Pilates hottie body!" Finola waves her hands around Lu's torso. "We can chat and catch up . . . without the PH2 gals jumping in. Like, I'm dying to know what you thought about that brunch! You all left so quickly after. I was going to pull you aside and get your take *fresh*."

The dots connect quickly for Lu now as Finola moves from tolerable neighbor to inadvertent abettor. The necessary cracked-open door into her impossible Kastille mission. "I'm in," Lu says "*Walking*. I swear it's the thing I already miss most about Brooklyn."

"See? It's like I know what you need before even you do," Finola says cheerfully.

"Cool trick," Lu says. "Let me grab my hat, kicks, and keys, and we can—"

"Keys . . . ?" Finola chuckles. "You sound like me last year. Locking up everything."

"That's changed?" Lu says as she grabs her sneakers from the closet. She slips her hat over her low twist-out bun before squatting and using her thumb as a shoehorn.

"No one really locks anything in Partridge Hollow." Finola shrugs as she pulls out sunglasses from her designer pouch and slides them on. "Somehow we just . . . trust each other."

"No need to covet thy neighbor's house when you already have everything, right?" Lu makes a show of grabbing her keys from the antique metal pedestal bowl on the console table.

"Honestly? Yeah, kind of," Finola says. "It's really safe in Partridge Hollow. Like a little village. Maybe it's the way that Kastille looks out for its people—and by extension anyone else living here." She removes her shades again, her expression soft but with a streak of something serious running through it. "You feel protected in a way that's hard to explain."

"Sounds like something a former NXIVM cult member would say at the start of the true crime doc," Lu says with a wry smile, and pulls the bill of her hat down further. She glances at her wrist for the time. She's wearing the watch. The one that used to be reserved for jobs. The one that used to be a good luck charm worn ironically during those dark pursuits where fluke and fortune were in no way tied to her success. Now it's just a timepiece; the gossamer-like mystic power it once effused has vanished forever. "Ready?"

Finola nods and heads out with Lu following close behind, her key in hand, ready to lock up. "I don't want to sound like one of *those*, but I really do think you're going to find what you're looking for here, Lu," she says. "And I think it's going to be good for everyone."

The two women begin walking down the sloping driveway. Lu's mind is already racing through the myriad ways she might extract useful information from Finola all while maintaining her billed nonchalance. From the corner of her eye, Lu notices Finola fidgeting with her smartwatch. Suddenly, Finola stops walking, her lips mashed together and face beginning to flush.

"I have to come clean . . ." Finola blurts out.

"Again? Wait . . . are we walking into an intervention, because I refuse to give up any of my vices, no matter how many people in that room *love me like crazy*."

This brings a laugh. "No, it's not that. I know I said this was not about the PH2 but Calista just texted me. They're coming to meet us." She floats out a demure smile.

"Ah, the old *walk with me* ruse, huh?"

"No, no," Finola says, laughing once more as she takes the few steps closing the short distance between where each of them had stopped. "I definitely wanted you and me to do the walk. But they tracked my location on my phone—"

"Hold up . . . they track you?"

"Not like that . . . I mean, we just keep tabs. Anyway, they saw that I was at your house, and they're coming to meet us because—well, it's the question we're all wondering."

"All wondering . . . ?" Lu says softly. *Woman, I ain't joining your cult!*

"We would never want to pester and hound. It *is* your first, of course, but time is getting a bit crunchy—three weeks!—and

Didi likes to have RSVPs locked by now, especially from the prime households, like yours. So, they're probably going to ask you if it's going to be a yes."

"Is this a riddle?" Lu says, her expression sliding into something slightly irked.

Finola chuckles. "Sorry, I'm skipping ahead. Didi was planning on reaching out to you about the RSVP, but I mentioned I'd be walking by your place today anyway—"

"RSVP?"

"Yes, to the Secret Garden Gala."

"Wait, what gala?" Again Lu's countenance betrays her and she cannot pull it back.

"The Secret Garden Gala . . . the annual masquerade ball? You received the formal invitation, right? I know it's late, but you did just move in, after all. And Margot triple-checked all the hand-delivered ones," Finola says, nonplussed. "After the gift basket fumble and crazy delayed brunch, we made sure that the Barlows were at the top of the invite list."

"Nope . . . still don't know what language this is."

"Harry didn't mention it?" Finola says and gently brushes away the fringe of her perfect pixie cut from the furrows in her brows.

"Harry?" Lu's head tilts, and now she's the one frowning. Though guilt and nerves have left her avoiding prolonged contact with Harry since the necklace drop and, more distressingly, the Mr. V bomb-drop, hearing another woman speak his name brings a deeper churn to the pit of Lu's already roiling stomach.

"Yeah . . . I assumed when it was hand-delivered to Harry the other day, he would have passed along the envelope right to you."

"You spoke to Harry? When?"

"Oh, God. Did I get Harry in trouble?" Finola says, her tone light but sincere.

"No trouble. It's just weird that Harry didn't mention this party—"

"It's the Secret Garden *Gala*," Finola says through a stilted chuckle.

"Stand corrected."

"Look, I know how silly it all sounds, but it's a major event here. Kastille hosts it, but PH2 puts the whole thing together. Really, it's Didi's baby. And I have to say—having been to it for the first time last year—it's an impressive feat. The who's who of this town, of *Kastille*, shows up and . . ." Finola's coy smile returns, and she moves her mouth as if melting a mint on her tongue. ". . . let's just say the carousing shifts into another gear as the evening unfolds. It's a good time."

Lu nods and gives the woman a limp smile. While she recognizes the intel being served fresh, Lu is unable to pull her attention far enough away from the bigger piece of new information: that H seems to be minding secrets of his own. First the spendy company car he somehow *forgot* to tell her about until it was parked in their new driveway. Then the whole cigar-smoking, H-man, semi-bro persona he's been parading around at work. Now there's this red-carpet-y, glitter ball gala that he—and apparently the whole town—knows about. Why not at least mention it to her? Moreover, what else might he be hiding? Although Lu is self-aware enough to see the audacity in her being rankled by this when she has a full-blown, morally corrupt undercover other life, it's somehow not the same. Because, in Lu's mind, Harry is the good one. He'll always be the good one.

There's buzzing growing louder in Lu's ears. It's Finola; she's still talking about the gala. Lu's lashes flutter and she shakes her head, trying to disrupt the rumbling in her suspicious mind and rejoin the Finola broadcast.

"Anyway, hoping you and Harry can join us!" Finola says.

A range of plausible excuses begin a slow march around Lu's brain when she spies the golf cart approaching in the distance.

Finola sees it too. "Shit! Here they come," she mutters, and freezes in place. She seems legitimately on edge by the mere sight of the white cart chugging along up the modest hill.

As the other women get closer still, Lu watches Finola squaring her body in their direction. She sets her shoulders back and quickly brushes the end of her bangs and adjusts her crossbody pouch. In what appears to be her final recalibration, Finola transitions from gritting her teeth to exposing them in a natural-looking, warm smile. She has a mask too, it would seem.

"Hey, hey, ladieeesss!" Margot shrieks as they approach. She is shimmying her shoulders, the low vibration from the cart providing her a rhythm as it hugs the curb before coming to a stop. "Fancy meeting you here!" She is out of the golf cart in a blink, arms extending, prepping for effusive hugs. Her thick red hair is swept over her right shoulder and she is wearing a brown silk button-down blouse, wide-leg toffee-colored trousers, and leather ballet flats. She looks undeniably chic and sharp, dressed like she's heading into a glass-wall conference room to lead a hostile takeover. That, or a chatty lunch with her interior designer.

Calista hangs back, as if she's accustomed to her friend's immoderate ways, giving Margot the space to run through her usual production. After the hugs are dealt, she tips out of the passenger seat on her own time like a graceful, pretty bird.

"Bated breath over here, Grey," Margot sings. "Do we have the RSVP?"

Margot and Calista turn toward Lu now, both of them beaming and curious.

Lu sputters out a jumble of words amounting to a non-answer. "Oh, uh . . . well, we will have to . . . I think—"

"She should at least talk to her husband, right?" Finola says. "My Matty always hates when I say yes to things for both of us."

Margot curls her lip at the mention of Finola's husband. The soured reaction is quick and slight, but not quick and slight enough to escape Lu's sharp perception. "So, you failed the task, then?" she says, pointing an angry finger at Finola. A brief, awkward pause ensues as it seems none of the other women can tell whether Margot is being serious. That is, until she cracks a toothy grin. "Just fucking with you, Grey. Relax."

"We should get going," Calista says. "Didi's waiting for us at the gala venue."

"Yeah, and she's on a time crunch, running straight to the city after," Margot says, and starts back to the golf cart. "Make sure it's all extra perfect at the suite."

"It's Didi and Jonathan's anniversary. *Lucky* thirteen." Calista tosses the explanation over her shoulder toward Lu as she makes her way to the cart too. "A three-bedroom suite at the Aman is pretty perfect already. Plus, the kids and dogs are with her in-laws at the pied-à-terre on the Upper West Side for the whole week? Heaven."

"True," Margot says. "It's a nice tradition they have, celebrating big like that every year. Even the house staff gets excited for it. They get the time off, sometimes as long as a week. Anyway, I wonder what he'll give her this year."

"A divorce," Calista half-whispers through a wicked smirk.

Margot's head nearly snaps off in turning to glare, eyes wide, at Calista. "*Caudwell!*"

"I'm joking. I'm sure whatever Jonathan gives Didi, it will very shiny, very big, and no doubt very expensive."

"And gorgeous," Margot adds, nodding at Calista, sounding like a mom coaxing her toddler to *say thank-you to the nice lady.*

"Of course," Calista concedes, nodding right back at Margot. "Always gorgeous."

Lu notes all of this—what is being said, but especially what is not. Finola is standing quietly at attention, watching her two friends get ready to leave.

Once settled in the driver's seat, Margot motions at Finola the way a person might rudely summon a waiter. Lu is quietly astonished when Finola goes to her without objection. "Sorry to cut your little hangout short," Margot says. "Maybe we can *all* get together for lunch or something. There's a new hot yoga place with really good collagen smoothies."

"Who doesn't love a collagen smoothie," Lu says, not even trying to cover up the snark.

"Funny you should say that," Calista says, chuckling. "Didi hates smoothies in general."

"Ah, don't let that scare you off, Barlow. That's just Didi being Didi," Margot chirps at Lu, while busily getting the cart ready for a quick takeoff. "We all have our little *things*, right?"

"Oh, I'm sure you do," Lu says under her breath as she sends the trio off with a wave, estimating on which side of her rigid usefulness scale each of them might land.

CHAPTER TWELVE

Scowling. This is how Lu rounds the walk that she and Finola barely got started. After she got jilted, Lu decided to go ahead with the trek anyway, scope out her surroundings and the so-called beach. Her crumpled expression now is owing to a mix of issues, including the fact that this *barely-two-miles*, *easy-for-you* walk was neither of those things. Already moving at a brisk pace, she pushes out even more speed as she approaches yet another incline, pumping her arms and exhaling with energy through her open mouth.

"This is bullshit," she hisses. All of it, bullshit. The ridiculous number of sneaky hills in this neighborhood that are twice as steep on foot. The golf cart gang rolling in like well-dressed marauders and snatching up Finola, who left without a word of apology. The high probability that she'll have to attend some rich people's dress-up party. Bullshit, bullshit, bullshit.

She nears the top of the knoll now, undoubtedly panting and fully vexed. More than the breaking of an unplanned sweat and being deserted by her potential source, what has Lu truly rankled is her husband. Specifically, his apparent new habit of keeping secrets from her. She wants to blast him for the shady moves but knows she needs to stay on his good side if she plans to start casually asking him more often about Kastille. Even though he won't respond well to the line of questions. Harry is not a "this crazy thing happened at the office" type. The man's work can sometimes stir controversy. The uninformed hear *gene therapy* and they think designer babies. They hear *genetic editing* and think GMO humans and Captain America–style super soldiers. And don't even think about mentioning things like telomeres, chromosomal stability, restored cell division. That's the stuff of disturbing dystopian novels and *it-could-happen* sci-fi films directed by Denis Villeneuve.

The few times that Harry has mentioned his telomeres-lengthening work to random folks at chilly cocktail parties, he's been met with long, quizzical looks, as if he's speaking a whole other language, or, more often, wide-eyed patent horror and a swift end to the conversation. Actually, it was after one particularly odd and charged encounter with a youth pastor at a neighborhood Fourth of July block party in Brooklyn ten years ago that Harry decided to nix engaging in work chatter with non-work folks. Harry had started to explain to the younger man how the nanocode that he was helping to develop for a gene editing tool could—with the right kind of ethical support—effectively extend human life expectancy by lengthening telomeres, the structures made from DNA sequences found at the end of a chromosome. This prompted an unexpectedly explosive, unhinged reaction from the pastor, who practically pelted Harry with a literal Bible he had been carrying in a backpack. The barbecue came to a quick end and the Barlows were expressly uninvited from all future outdoor hangouts with the neighbors at that end of the block. From that point on, Harry would simply reply "clinical researcher" when asked the dreaded "So, what do you do?" at social gatherings. Even more recently, he's whittled it further to "lab tech" if pressed for more information. "It's not like the people asking really want to know," he had told Lu after that first time he trimmed his incredible resume down to two words. "Easy enough to swallow," he had said. "Quells their actual suspicion around what a Black man is doing on this side of a groundbreaking laboratory."

His reticence to talk shop even with Lu is more straight ahead. "It's boring, Loubie," he often claimed. "Rather talk about you. A delightful trove in gorgeous packaging."

"H-man being H-man." Lu snorts and shakes her head as her huffs and puffs get louder with each step forward. A clear picture of Jonathan Killigrew's face flashes in Lu's mind and her shoulders pitch toward her ears as the icky feeling that had washed over her upon meeting the man at the brunch returns. That asshole is up to no good; Lu is sure of it.

She stops walking to physically shake her body, hoping the sharp wiggle will jostle Jonathan Killigrew clean from her thoughts. It works, partly, and Lu starts again on her final climb up the last hill, her house now visible on the horizon. A wispy whining floats from over Lu's shoulder and nestles in her ear. She knows the sound well. It's a car, an electric one, driving at a low speed, trailing close behind her. Lu continues walking, making sure not to look back or appear suspicious. The last time she jumped to conclusions—and almost into action—there was a logical explanation for the strange car parked in front of her new house. Maybe this time it's a neighbor slowing down, prepping to turn into their stretched-out driveway. Or maybe it's an older driver, adhering to the twenty-five-miles-per-hour speed limit on the winding hills. Lu reminds herself to breathe as she maintains a casual, easy pace, drawing closer to her house, keenly aware that the car is still tailing her.

Or maybe . . . maybe it's Mr. V, she thinks, driving by with another Molotov cocktail in hand, this time lobbing it directly at her head through the passenger side window. "He wouldn't," she whispers, "not in broad daylight." Just as she begins to turn her chin to meet her shoulder to check who it is, she hears the voice. Harry's.

"Hello, darlin'," he says leaning his torso across the armrest to smile at her through the window. "Now, what on earth are you doin' out here?"

Relief morphs into annoyance as Lu remembers the gala invite that apparently *slipped Harry's mind*. She rolls her eyes at him and his little secrets. "What's it look like I'm doing?"

"Oh, my . . . well, my next question has to be, would you mind giving me the other half of my head back, please. The side without your teeth marks, that is."

Lu scoffs and keeps walking, purposely not looking at him. "What are *you* doing here?"

"Hop in and I'll explain," he says. Lu can hear the smile in his voice along with something a little tense skimming the top. She keeps walking, ignoring him. "I've got something to share with you. A surprise, of sorts. Come on; I'll drive you up the little ways to the house."

"Pass," Lu sniffs. She is too settled into her pout and petty to say anything more.

"Is this real? You're pissy at me?" Harry's tone finally switched to serious. "Look, whatever this is, I don't want to be the only two Black people in the neighborhood arguing in the middle of street. We're not in Brooklyn anymore, Toto. Please, just get in." This brings Lu to a full stop. He knows that *The Wizard of Oz* is number two on her list of top three films of all time. He also knows any reference to it—no matter how garbled—will get a reaction. Lu turns to look at him; of course the devilish grin has returned. "Come *onnn*. Stop fighting it, dove. Just get in."

Lu relents and walks over to the stopped car and slides in. From the moment she closes the door, before her back even touches the slightly reclined seat, she gets a whiff of something different emanating from inside the car. It's not coming from Harry; the sweet, floral notes from his usual Green Irish Tweed fragrance—lemon and sandalwood and verbena—are ever present. She begins to look around the car, letting her nose lead her, when Harry claps his warm hand on her leg, just above her knee.

"Before you say anything . . ." he begins, but is interrupted by a distinct, high-pitched yelp coming from the back seat behind Lu. She whips her head behind her as fast and far as it can go. "Lu, Lu, *Lu*. . . ." Harry continues, saying her name slowly while firmly squeezing her thigh, trying to distract her from checking behind her seat. "Allow me to explain—"

As if prompted, here comes a tiny bark from the back seat. Lu twists her full torso around to find a black-and-tan Cavalier King Charles Spaniel puppy, slightly bigger than a hot dog bun, curled up on a fluffy towel in the corner of the seat.

"Are you kidding me?!"

"I know, I know," Harry says, the contrition overflowing in his tone. "We said that we would decide"—Lu glares at him—"*as a team* about this," he says, putting the car in park properly. "But then I was made aware of this geezer"—Harry turns to join Lu in staring at the cuddly pup—"desperate for a home, and I before I realized it, I was scooping him up into my car."

"Scooping him up and backing *me* into a corner."

"The catch was, it had to be today. So, I figured forgiveness might come easier than permission." Harry turns to look at the dog once more and makes the melted face he made when toddler Solomon tried rooibos tea and loved it. "He was the runt of the litter, dove. Once we made eyes, I couldn't leave him. Plus, he's already backyard potty-trained and calm as a priest, I'm told." Harry rests his eyes on Lu's temples, his teeth clenched as he braces for Lu's response.

"What do they call him?" Lu says, studying the dog, his round eyes locking in on hers.

"They've just called him Puppy so far, which feels a bit hollow, innit?"

Lu scoffs. "Maybe my mother named him. Puppy the Dog."

"Hey . . . knock that off," Harry says, frowning. "We don't talk like that. You're past all that shite about her, yeah?" He stares at Lu, studying her profile. "What's going on with you?"

"I should ask you the same." She turns to face forward, her jaw tight, actively ignoring the adorable whimpers from the puppy.

"Lu. Cut me a break. Let me into whatever's happening here. Please," Harry says.

She looks over at him, her eyes wide. "Straight talk: You are keeping things from me, and I am not down with that."

"Keeping things from you?"

"Yes. This car, for one—"

"Ah, for Christ's sake, we've already been over that, Lu, and I apologized. It was an oversight. That's it," he says, roughly throwing the car back into drive and pulling off toward their house. "What are the other *things*—plural?"

Lu knows how silly she is for fretting over his not telling her about the gala.Probably another case of simple oversight. If only she could tell him what's really underneath all of this angst and irritation, and beg for forgiveness, preemptively, for what she's being forced to do, for what she must do in order to be finally free, maybe then it would feel a little less horrible, less deceitful. Maybe, being the kind heart that Harry is, he might understand her choice, moreover, understand that she really doesn't have one. But she cannot take that chance, and she hates it. She hates that in the end, she will have betrayed Harry—the one man she trusts with almost everything—and he will be none the wiser. Lu looks at him, at his bemused expression, and knows she must proceed with the absurd scene, with her starring as oversensitive hausfrau and Harry playing the role of dutiful, put-upon husband. "You didn't tell me about the garden party masquerade ball bullshit. Everyone knows about it but me." Lu wants to roll her eyes at herself as the next set of words gather in her mouth. "It feels like you're being sneaky."

Harry presses the brakes hard as they pull up to the top of their driveway and whips around to glare at her. "*Sneaky?* What the—is this a prank?"

Lu drags herself further down this inane path. "You know how much I hate feeling like shit is happening around me but without me. I had to hear about the masquerade party—and that you were given the invitation, no less—from the golf cart gang."

"Lu, get off it," he says, his voice back to its lower register. "You're not interested in that posh nonsense and masks and ballgowns and those welcome-wagon ladies and all their dizzy business. As such, I didn't think to tell you about the gala until it was necessary."

"Necessary? It's in a couple weeks."

"Yes, I know . . . look, this is work for me. I need to attend these things, be involved in their culture, join the Kastille *community.* It's part of the job. That might not resonate with you; you don't work a normal job." Lu's brow flies up. Harry closes his eyes and softly taps the side of his fist on the cushy, leather steering wheel, trying to temper his exasperation. "You know what I mean!" Harry snaps. Another tap at the wheel and a shallow sigh. "Of course I understand that your work is worthy and real. Travel agent, Pilates studio—all of it, yes, valid. What I don't think *you* fully understand, though, is about my needing to be a part of that office culture, no matter how silly or annoying some of it may appear. So, yeah, I told some of the men on the team that I'd talk to you about the gala—"

"About it or into it?"

"Lu . . ." Harry hisses, squeezing his closed eyelids tighter.

"OK, OK, fine. I get it. I understand work culture. I do. I just . . ." She glances over at him, at his loose first atop the steering wheel, his clenched jawline, his tired eyes looking a little beyond the dash, and it instantly softens all of Lu's rough edges. The notion that Harry—this man who puts her and Solomon first, always—could ever be sneaky or malicious is ludicrous. She feels like a heel for even thinking it. ". . . I just want to hear these things from you first. That's all," she says, sheepishly. "Also . . . *sneaky* was a bit much. I apologize."

"Accepted," he says, nodding firmly and tossing Lu a wink.

He slides the car into park, jabs his thumb into the seat belt anchor to release it, and presses the ignition's off button in one smooth movement. The couple sits in silence, staring out at the garage doors for a few beats before Lu draws a slow, deep inhale.

"Although . . . you kinda gotta give me this one," Lu says, plainly, gesturing with her thumb at the precious puppy snoozing in the back seat. "I'm well within my rights to be pissy about this. I mean, a whole-ass surprise dog?"

Harry's head bobs, a series of quick, short nods. "Not my finest showing."

They both turn to look at each other for a breath, infectious grins beginning to peel across their respective faces as they continue craning their necks to the glance back at the furry fellow resting, utterly oblivious.

Lu tilts her head to the side and fixes her gaze on the dog. "Solomon's gonna love you forever for this; you know that, right?" she says in a light whisper, her heart warmed and instantly expanding to welcome in this darling little furball.

"Yeah. Too bad about being knocked down to second-favorite parent, mate," Harry says. "You had a good run, though."

"Watch it," Lu says, her smirk going crooked as she moves just her eyes over to Harry. "We're still not all the way friends yet, Sneaky Pete. You owe me big for this."

Harry turns in his seat so he faces Lu squarely and tilts over, resting on the armrest between them. He smoothly leans in toward Lu, his nose mere inches from the top side of her forehead, and with heated, sweetened breath whispers, "I rather like owing you big."

Just as smoothly, Lu tilts her face up and to the right so her lips brush against the sharp edge of his jaw. "And don't be trying to pull the sex wool over my eyes. I know your stunts."

"Stunts? I would never," Harry says, fighting his smirk and losing. He pulls back to take her in, his eyes drawing a slow, appreciative outline of her face. "I should push off, anyway."

"To go where?" Lu says, snapping out of the sultry haze beginning to take over the car.

"Erm . . ." Harry bows his head slightly and closes his eyes. ". . . to meet Annabelle."

"Should I be taking a closer look at the goings-on between you and Annabelle?"

"Leave it out," he says, playfully frowning at Lu. "She's offered to introduce old fluff here to her veterinarian. Apparently, he's a five-star vet and booked up for the next year to new clients. So, Annabelle's going to work her magic and get us in."

"Wait . . . so if you hadn't spied me walking out here, when would I have met Puppy?"

Another timid grimace. "That's the other part . . . I was planning to introduce you and Solomon to the dog at the same time."

"Oh, an ambush. Love those."

"I already admitted it wasn't my best turn. And yes, I figured you probably wouldn't slit my throat in front of our son," Harry says.

"*Probably.*"

"*Probably,*" they say in unison, after a beat.

"You're a delight, you know that, right?" Harry says.

"Indeed, I am." Lu slips out of the car and slowly opens the back seat door, carefully pulling the bunched-up towel—with the dog seemingly glued on top—toward her. "Out you come, Puppy," she whispers over his perfectly round head and draws him into her chest. "He really is a sweetheart."

Harry gets out as well and meets Lu and the dog on the other side of the car. He gently strokes the downy hair between the puppy's burly brows, causing the dog to wrinkle its nose while soundly asleep. Harry moves his loving gaze over to his wife. "Hey. I'm sorry about springing this on you. I just wanted to give Solomon something fresh and wonderful. He's been so gray about the new school and all."

"Yeah . . . I get that," Lu says. "But next time, promise to stick to the plan, H. OK? I just need things to follow the plan."

"Fair," he says, still eyeing Lu as they each continue lightly petting the dog. "Sins properly confessed. Now, do you have anything to tell *me*?"

Lu's hand stops in mid-air, hovering over the dog's small head. She presses the puppy deeper into her chest. "What do you mean?" she says, flatly.

Harry's hand falls away too, and he leans back on the car. He looks suddenly serious as he peers at Lu. "Like . . . *I forgive you, H.* Or, *I can never be mad at you, you dashing bastard.*" By now Harry's wicked grin has taken over his face and Lu's shoulders relax again as he continues. "Or maybe, *I love you so much, you can have your dirty way with me tonight, man.*"

"Mmm . . . I could see myself agreeing with that last one," Lu says. "But I'd want to first check with Annabelle . . . see what she thinks about it—"

"*E-nough.* Gimme the puppy, you little tyrant," Harry says, and playfully retrieves the dog from her grips. "I'll see you later, after the vet. I'll try to be back here when Boxer gets home. We're good, yeah?" Lu nods. ". . . Teammates?"

She stops nodding and looks right at Harry. "Always." Lu says this like she means it because right now—all too aware of how good this man is standing before her—she really does.

CHAPTER THIRTEEN

"Do I have a doctor's appointment or something?" Solomon says as he slides into the back seat of Lu's car. He nudges his bulky backpack, sitting next to him like a slouching toddler, in order to quickly fasten his seat belt. Even though his mother always waits until he's buckled in before driving off, the boy doesn't like the idea of being loose and unsecured even for a half second. A rule follower to a fault. "When Miss Wylie told me to go to the car pickup line instead of the bus line, I got worried. Did you tell me you were coming to get me and I forgot?" Disquiet sets in on his little face like a cloud.

Lu puts the car back into park, pickup line flow be damned, and turns to look at Solomon. "Hon, I didn't tell you that I was coming to get you today, so you didn't forget anything. And there are no appointments. This is a good-news, surprise pickup." She smiles at him and sees the developing fret instantly evaporate and the brightness return to his face. "Now, I cannot tell you what the surprise is because, well, it's a surprise, but it's good. Really good!"

"Wait . . . are we playing that game again?"

"What game, sweets?" Lu says, glancing at him through the rearview before driving off.

"The spy game. You're . . . what was it again? . . . Oh! Code-name Celeste!" he chirps. Lu mashes the brakes, causing them to buck forward and the car behind to hit their horn.

She waves *sorry* at the driver through the rearview and grabs another quick look at her son in the mirror and pulls off again, slowly. Panic is something else, something scaled down from whatever it is that Lu is experiencing right now. "Uh, I—why did you—" She takes a careful breath. "What do you mean, Solomon?"

"The game we played . . . you know, in New York . . . when I was sick and sleepy? You pretended to be your sister—well, a fake sister—Celeste. And my name was . . . ugh! Why can't I remember anything? Can I just do a new name this time? Maybe we just scramble up our real names—like, you can be Sue and I'll be Lolomon, or Lol." He lightly slaps his temple and shakes his head. "No, that's so dumb! I'm not good at this game."

"Honey, that's not—"

"Oh, is that old grandma lady going to be there again?"

Lu's mind replays the necklace drop, start to finish, on triple speed. The boy was soundly snoozing before they even parked the car. She's sure of it. Was sure of it. And at no time during the quick, whispered goodbye did Miss Goodwin mention anything about Solomon waking up. *Not a sigh or whimper from him.* That's what the old woman said as Lu scooped him up and lumbered back to the car with Solomon still asleep in her arms. "No, honey," Lu says, her focus returned to the Jeep now, the interior thick with awkwardness. She slows down further by easing her foot off the gas pedal slightly and gripping the steering wheel with both hands. Stopping the vehicle altogether would mean turning to look her son in the face, and that she cannot do. Not right now. "That woman—she was just a helpful stranger," Lu begins. Clearing her throat so her voice is brighter. "A *confused*, but helpful older lady. I would just forget about all that. It was weeks ago, and you're back to yourself now, right? One hundo percent in good health. We can just leave that whole crazy New York visit in the past."

"Oh, OK . . . did I do something wr—"

"Nope, not all. You did nothing wrong," Lu says, again making sure to sound chipper. She keeps her face steady, too, masking the rank disgust she feels as she prepares to obliterate her own sturdy rules and set boundaries around her special boy. "It was just a busy rush-around and you took all that medicine that can make you a little dizzy—like in a dream state . . ." She fans her hand by an ear. "Who knows what was real or fantasy. Best to leave it all behind. OK?"

"Yeah . . . OK." The boy looks out the window, a frown moving across his little face. "Oh my gosh!" Solomon shouts, snapping to attention. Lu's hands tighten around the wheel. "I think I know what the surprise is!" He pumps his fist in the air as Lu's exhale seeps out slowly. "Mom, is it a dog? It's a dog, right? A new puppy. That's the surprise, isn't it? Just say if it is!"

"I cannot confirm or deny, young sir," Lu says, and fights to keep her chest from folding.

Solomon's stretched grin remains in place for the rest of the ride home. He looks ready to leap out of the car as soon as it comes to a halt in the garage.

"Should I act surprised when we go inside?" he asks with a big cheesy grin.

"I think you *will* be surprised, pumpkin," Lu says, through a strained chuckle. She turns off the car, presses the garage door button to close, and gathers her tote and favorite mug from the cupholder. Her body feels sore from the gripping and gritting and tensing.

Solomon yanks his book bag from the back seat, still beaming. "Wait," he says as they enter the dim mudroom. "Is it a new telescope? The OrionOptic XT8?" He kicks off his shoes, dumps the bag beside them, and starts a little hoppy dance while chanting, "XT8! XT8! XT8!"

Lu walks ahead of him, quickly, into the kitchen and scans the room in full, making sure it is exactly how she left it—no coffee cups by the sink, no dirty spoon with pooled milk beneath it resting on the counter or, more important, no erstwhile mentors tucked in the corner of the breakfast nook. She had done the same baseline scan before heading out to Solomon's school, and expects to do this involuntary double-check forever now, or at least until the dreaded Kastille job is complete and she is free at last.

"Is the telescope already upstairs?" Solomon is racing to his room before the question is all the way out of his mouth. "Let's see that XT8! XT8! XT8!"

Lu can only shake her head and wait for his return downstairs with his face puzzled and looking to her for more information or at least some viable hints. She pulls out her phone next. Harry had said he would be home within the hour. She doesn't know how much longer she can keep this happy secret. She doesn't get the first word of the text to Harry typed before she hears the garage door opening. Solomon heard it too and is barreling back down the stairs. The boy runs over to his mom, jaunty and bouncing in place. "I don't think I can pretend to be surprised, Mom! I'm way too hyped!"

"Be however you want to be, sweet pea," Lu says, trying to catch him in a still enough moment to tenderly stroke his shoulder. Impossible. The kid is a quake of elation.

"Knock, knock," Harry hollers from the mudroom.

"We're in here!" Solomon shouts, clapping his hands and jumping in a circle. "We're in the kitchen!" He is about to take off toward his father when Lu gently grabs him.

"OK, hon. You have to wait here and let your dad come to us. Deal?" she says. "We don't want to make any sudden moves that—"

"Sudden moves—oh, my gosh, it's a doggggg!" Solomon breaks into a rhythmic dance complete with smooth heel-toe footwork, hip bounces, chest rolls, and choppy hand moves.

Watching her son soaked in pure joy fills Lu's heart so fast it feels like it might burst open. She is tempted to pull him into her, this popping kernel, and wrap him in a tight squeeze. Seeing him this happy is one thing, but knowing that he deserves this and more makes the moment even sweeter. He deserves every good thing the world has to offer.

It's the bottom edge of the dog's metal crate that pokes out first as Harry rounds the corner into the kitchen, and the room explodes with Solomon's giddy howl.

"It's a dog! I knew it!" Solomon shouts and runs over to his dad and new best friend.

"It's a dog," Harry says, setting the crate down and opening its door slowly. "It's *your* dog." With his misty eyes, Harry tosses a warm look at Lu and giggles seeing that she too is tearing up. “It’s our family dog. And you, Boxer, get to name him.”

“This is so—I don’t know what word to say! I love this dog already!” Solomon says, and buries his face in the dog’s neck. “I have so many things in my head right now, my brain feels like it could melt!” The puppy’s little tongue and nose connect with the side of Solomon’s face. It’s love overflowing between them, and Lu and Harry are exceedingly happy to soak it all up.

* * *

EVERYONE IS ASLEEP upstairs except Lu and Puppy, the still-nameless dog. The two of them are sitting in Harry’s favorite recliner in the family room, with Lu staring blankly at the television on mute and the dog looking up at his new favorite person with each of her weighty sighs. Although Solomon spent his entire bath time coming up with potential names for Puppy, the boy used his last bit of energy begging for the dog to sleep with him in his bed. A no go. Lu and Harry agreed it wasn’t the best idea. Not yet, anyway.

“Puppies sometimes get up in the middle of the night to go to the toilet,” Harry had told him, which got a big laugh from the kid. The image of their cute dog hoisting itself up on to the commode—hind legs barely draped over the seat—was simply hilarious to his eight-year-old mind. The child went to sleep breathless from uncontrolled giggling.

Lu offered to take first shift with the dog, and Harry did not protest. “It’s been a long day,” he had told Lu between flossing and brushing his teeth. “And Killigrew leaving early did not exactly help. I had to figure out how to cover his end of things in two separate meetings."

"What does that look like, *covering his end of things*?" she asked, knowing the typical non-answer that would surely come next. And it did.

"Ah, dove, it's all boring bits," Harry told her, following a series of yawns, each making the man's eyes increasingly water until he had to throw in the towel. "I need sleep right this minute; got nothing leftover. I'm off to bed to dream about you as always. You're a real star for staying up with the pup, Loubie. I'm indebted."

But his kind words only served to make Lu feel gross about her true plan for the night. The dog's innocent gazing into her strained eyes right now isn't helping either.

Somewhere between the sweaty uphill walk and convincing her own child that he dreamed up Miss Goodwin, Celeste, and the drafty church, Lu devised a new plan of attack. This one involves digging deeper into Kastille's VIPs, moreover their giant, prized homes, seeing what dirt she can find to use not as leverage but more a diversion. A pointed finger far away from Harry should this job somehow go sideways.

Mercenary men like Jonathan and his C-suite cronies always keep secrets, as Lu has seen, and they often keep them in a home safe. Breaking into their houses feels like an easier feat than slithering into the heavily surveilled and secure office. With Didi and Jonathan away for at least tonight, starting at their unattended mansion is obvious.

"I promise it won't always be like this," Lu whispers to the dog snuggled into her lap as she gets mentally ready for this dark work.

She's dressed in all black, including the same sleek hoodie she likes to wear on night jobs and her custom lightweight non-marking-sole boots. Slumped beside her in the chair is a tiny black backpack reserved for smaller single-item heists. Inside the bag are some basics: mini roofing hammer, keystone tip screwdriver, a slim assortment of bump keys and lockpicks, plus a tensioning tool, electrical tape, and hairspray all gathered neatly in a leather roll. In the front zipped section for easy access, she has her compact night vision goggles with thermal imaging and a police force expandable solid steel baton. Just in case. Slid into her right pocket of her fitted track pants is her trusty slimline flashlight. And in her left pocket, something very new to her thievery toolkit: dog treats.

A check of her watch tells Lu that it's time to move. She turns off the TV, picks up the bag and the dog, who, despite the late hour, seems quite alert and compliant. She sets the dog down and attaches his new marine-blue leash to the matching tiny body harness he's already wearing. His eyes are bright and shiny. He's eager, tail wagging, but calm. Not even a whimper as he looks up at Lu, patiently waiting, watching for her lead.

"Let's go," she whispers to him, and he moves when she does. There's a tiny jingle with each step coming from his tags on his collar. Lu bends down to remove it; he licks the top of her hand sweetly before she shoves his collar deep into her jacket pocket. "Now we're ready."

Walking around her old Brooklyn neighborhood at this time of night on a random Wednesday, Lu could never be fully prepared for what she might see. Of course, there was the expected: scattered yellow cabs angling for fares back over the bridge; people stumbling home alone or with *company*; the guy without a helmet speeding down the middle of the street on a rickety messenger bike singing aloud to whatever's playing on his giant headphones; that older woman pushing a shopping cart filled with empty cans, bottles, and sundry quilts; stray cats; bold rats; and dim lights emanating from the back kitchen of the popular bagel shop on the corner. As for the unexpected, Lu would always stay ready, aware but never afraid, prepared to do whatever was needed for her to return home in one piece.

However, strolling now through the quiet of her new environs, the difference is glaring. Out here, there are the hissing sounds of singing insects and tiny frogs and the distant low crash of the slack waves meeting the shore, with a thick hush falling over all of it, like a blanket meant to smother anything trying to leap out of the whispering chorus's range. The stuff of soothing white noise machines, yes, but there's also something a little eerie about it. How still it is. Even the night's darkness feels deeper out here.

The dog trots alongside Lu, his little legs keeping up with her brisk pace as they make their way in stealth mode down the short hills to Didi's house. Once there, Lu surveys the dimly lit mansion, sat in the exact center of the sprawling property, from across the street. She moves her narrowed eyes from left to right, scanning each of the darkened custom windows up above on the second story before taking in whatever details of the main level she can make out in the dark. Of course the last time she was here, it was a sunny, early afternoon, and Lu has always believed that things—rooms, streets, cars, people—look different in the light.

She draws a deep breath. On the slow exhale, all of her random thoughts and fretful inner chatter come to an abrupt end. Her attention is fixed on the job, on getting in and out of this mission easy and unscathed. Even the dog has morphed from cute companion to convenient alibi in her focused mind. She crosses the street and walks right up to the boxwood hedges closest to the driveway. Another sweeping scan of the property, this time to locate the cameras on the front and side of the house, noting their angles and estimating the field of vision for each.

She and the dog jog toward the side of the house with the deeper shadows and fuller coverage. Lu squats in a perfectly hidden spot beneath the large maple trees there. She reaches around for her bag to grab her jamming device and, in a handful of seconds, proceeds to block the cellular signals between the sensors inside and the alarm base station. Lu then pulls her mask, acting as a thin cowl-neck scarf, up beneath her nose and takes out two fat, peanut butter-filled treats from her pocket. She offers the crunchy bits to the dog, and he happily but quietly accepts, wagging his tail as Lu gently secures his leash around the foot of an Adirondack chair. She illuminates her watch, noting the sweep hand moving toward the three. Six minutes. That is all the time she's allowing herself on this job. She knows exactly which rooms to hit and where they are located. Lu drags her skintight gloves over her hands, slides the ski mask up over her head, and, staying low to the ground, zips across the lawn over to the side door, whipping out her tool roll and flashlight as she arrives. The lock to the French doors off the laundry room is picked and Lu is in the house with barely any effort.

Treading swiftly but carefully through the chilly house, Lu hits the stairs two steps at a time. She had not seen this upper-level section of the house at the brunch and stops at the landing for a breath to look at the two large black-and-white portraits mounted over an iron bench upholstered in Prussian blue velvet. In one picture, the Killigrews' four children—three girls, one boy—stand shoulder to shoulder, lined up in descending height order, dressed in their Sunday best, but all of the kids' clothes are bedraggled and their hair disheveled, as if they had been rolled down a springtime grassy knoll the minute before the shutter button was pressed. Their faces are covered in broad smiles and what looks like chocolate syrup. The other portrait is of Didi and Jonathan, but from before, from their younger days. They are seated in candid poses on barstools in a dark space with backlit smoke wafting above them. Didi, sporting a severe angled bob and bangs, is leaned into the side of him, her chin nestled in the crook of Jonathan's neck, and she is gazing up at the top of his ear so doting and smitten that Lu can almost see young Didi's heart beating out of her chest. But then Lu slides her eyes over to Jonathan's face. His expression is smug, irksome, and devoid of anything tender. Lu stares into his steely glare for a beat—one that she really cannot afford—before pulling her attention back to the center and moving on, with haste, to the couple's spacious bedroom.

It's straight to the walk-in closets now. Just like at the Barlow house, each adult has their own capacious closet on opposite sides of the master suite. Lu guesses correctly that Didi's is the larger one the left. Inside with the door closed behind her, Lu moves her goggled head around like a pedestal fan on its lowest setting, slowly circling the immediate vicinity in search of a low-lit lamp to pop on. She finds one on top of a nearby built-in dresser and pushes her night goggles to her forehead just where the ski mask hits her brows. Although Lu knew walking in that this dressing room would reek of opulence, she is still taken aback seeing it live. Every gown, shoe, stole, purse, hat, jacket, even belts and sunglasses, has a precise place in the closet, arranged by hues mainly. Lu's admiring of the space ends the moment her eyes land on an off-center, out-swing French casement window at the back wall. It wasn't in the layout sketch, and she's not certain which way the window faces out. Lu races back over to the lamp and turns it off, returning her goggles snuggly over her eyes and gripping her flashlight tighter in hand, primed. Moving through the darkness is how Lu prefers it on jobs anyway, convinced she can see better, see beyond what's there.

As if called, Lu whips her head around, eyeing the weird, unexpected window once more. She moves over to it, spotting her light along the wall as she draws nearer. There is an odd, old, and out-of-place vanity wedged in the corner there with some perfumes neatly arranged on top of it along with a lineup of sleek bottles and jars with skincare products. Lu makes a beeline to it and discovers that the antique desk is actually a shoddy cover for an electronic in-wall safe, the hind legs of the vanity too skinny and the stained mirror too wobbly to offer a proper cloak.

"Of course," Lu mutters, after stooping down to give the safe a closer examination. She slips the end of the flashlight handle in between her teeth to free up both hands. Although she hardly needs them. This brand of safe is fairly cheap and shamefully easy to crack wide open.

Quick and clean, Lu picks the override lock near the bottom of the keypad, and the safe's door pops opens with a dense *click*. Inside, on the safe's top shelf, are several money stacks. From the currency strap colors, Lu's math puts the stash at three hundred thousand dollars. The British sterling she estimates at fifty thousand pounds. The shelves below that hold neatly stacked felt storage boxes with lids, some containing the family's passports, deeds, and other papers in labeled folders, and a small collection of Didi's more lavish jewelry. Lu's usually steady hand jerks and brushes against the side of the safe, which then pops opens a drawer, a secret compartment with a small, locked, vintage-looking leather Gladstone bag embossed with the initials JPK in gold letters. Tucked just behind the worn, black doctor's bag is a flash drive, haphazard, as if it somehow escaped being added to the bag. Time is running thin. She foregoes picking the bag's lock and instead swipes the more intriguing flash drive, then pushes in the popped-out compartment, closes up the safe, and hustles out of there.

On her way toward the bedroom's double doors, basic nosiness gets the best of her, and Lu does a last-minute spin through the rest of the master suite, homing in on the nightstands, where most crafty secrets are kept. Jonathan's wavers between streamlined and desolate. On top, a built-in, wireless charging station with sleek outlines for which devices go where, along with a scattered pile—at least two weeks' worth—of dried-up, crinkled, discarded contact lenses. Inside, the drawer is practically empty, save for a tube of lube squeezed and contorted out of shape and a beat-up burner phone tucked beneath a flattened jock-itch ointment box.

Didi's drawers are filled with hand lotions, lip balms, fuzzy socks, and sleep masks alongside pens, highlighters, and several dainty, monogrammed canvas pouches. The largest of them has a collection of mini vibrators, batteries, and massage oils. Another pouch, slightly smaller than the first, has seven or eight prescription pill bottles rattling around inside. But hidden beneath the bulk of the pouches is a book, *The Trust Blueprint: Rebuilding Your Relationship Brick by Brick*, littered with color-coded sticky note tabs. Lu is about to rifle around the drawer further but checks her watch—it's been seven minutes and forty seconds. Annoyed at how easily she is distracted, Lu eases the drawer closed and bolts.

* * *

PUPPY IS SLOWER on the walk back home. Lu suspects he had been snoozing while she traipsed through Didi's house. The neighborhood is even quieter now, leaning toward being spooky. For a minute, Lu thinks about scooping up Puppy and running the rest of the way, but it's uphill, so that's a no. "You need to get used to pulling your own weight anyway, good boy," she tells the dog, who is easily keeping up with Lu.

She slips Puppy's collar back around his fluffy neck and they both ease into the house through the side door. She drops her backpack on the bench and toes off her shoes. Lu and the dog are just past the mudroom's threshold when she hears movement coming from the kitchen. She braces, her fists forming reflexively as she stoops down and gathers the dog up in a tight clench by her ribs. Lu holds her breath as she swiftly glides down the hallway toward the kitchen, slowing only as she approaches the corner, preparing herself to round it and find Mr. V in his now usual spot by the breakfast nook.

"Mom?" Solomon calls out, his voice small and timid.

Lu's eyes go wide and she rushes into the kitchen. Solomon is standing near the fridge in the midst of the dimness, his arm tucked behind him as if to hide whatever he's holding. "Pumpkin," Lu says breathily, her heart still racing. "What are you doing up?"

"Where did you go? Where did you just come from right now?"

"Oh, Puppy . . . you know, to the potty," she says, letting the dog rest on her hip while trying to regain full composure.

"But I checked. I looked in the backyard, all the way up to the first trees, and you weren't there," he says. Solomon's arm drops beside him, revealing a flashlight in hand.

Lu creeps over closer to him, noticing his bare feet with a dusting of damp soil. "Honey, did you go outside?"

He nods. "But no one was there."

"Have you done that before, gone outside at night—checking for me?"

He shakes his head. "I never had to. I never had a dog before." The concern on the child's face melts away the minute his eyes connect with the dog's. He moves into the puppy, putting his nose a kiss away from the dog's while scratching under his furry chin.

"That makes sense," Lu says. "Are you OK?" She reaches out and gently takes the flashlight from the boy and brings him into a group snuggle with the puppy.

"Yeah . . . I figured out a name for him." He pulls away from the hug a little so that he can focus on petting the dog.

"Oh, yeah? That's great. Here, why don't we get you back to bed and you can tell me about it while I tuck you in." Lu guides his shoulders and nudges him to begin the forward march.

"The name is actually a—wait, what was that word that you told me again? It happens when you combine two words and it makes a new word? Like, brunch is breakfast and lunch put together? Portomoto?"

"Ah . . . *portmanteau*. It's French; pronouncing it can be tricky. You were really close, though, honey," Lu says, smiling. "Let's do this: You go on up, maybe wipe your feet really well on the bathmat in your bathroom, and then hop into bed. I'll put Puppy—or name to come!—in his bed and then I'll tuck you in. And you can tell me all about this fancy name!"

"OK," he says, and sweetly pats the dog's head one last time. "Good night—oh, my gosh! I almost called him by his new name!" Solomon giggles and practically floats up the stairs.

Lu takes Puppy over to his crate and gently sets him down. She puts her index finger against her lips. "Not a word to anyone," she whispers to the dog, and takes the quick lolling out of his tongue before nestling into his cushy bed pillow as his implied agreement.

Upstairs in his bed, Solomon's eyes brighten watching his mom approach. He flutters his feet under the covers as Lu pulls the thick quilt up to his neck, then folds the top over to rest on his sternum. "Hit me. What's his name? No—tell me the words that make up his name first."

Solomon releases a big yawn, but his lips return to the smiling position when it's over. "OK. So, I was thinking about the dog and how cute he is and everything. I was trying to sleep but I felt so filled up with, like, that excited, hyped feeling, you know what I mean? Then I said out loud, in bed, a promise to the dog. I said, *I'm going to give him all my love*. And then I shortened that to *all my love*. And then, I shortened it even more to *my love*. And those two words combined made Mylo. That's his name, M-y-l-o. Mylo."

"Pumpkin—" Lu's voice catches. "Honey, that's perfect. And beautiful. *Mylo.* I love it."

He nestles into his pillow, not unlike his new dog did a moment ago, and another big yawn falls out of his mouth, this one causing his eyes to get heavy and his blinking to slow. "I love it too. Like, a lot," he says, just above a whisper.

Lu leans in and kisses the top of his forehead. "And I love you . . . like, a lot."

CHAPTER FOURTEEN

Lu almost pushed her little family out the door this morning. So desperate to see what is on the flash drive. She was even tempted to sneak downstairs late last night after tucking in Solomon and Mylo, but did not want to take any more chances with the boy potentially waking, wondering, and wandering. Plus, something tells Lu that this new dog is a light sleeper. More than potty-trained, Mylo needs to be tip-toe-trained.

She pours a second cup of her scalding coffee and heads right upstairs to her ad hoc office—the deepest corner of her walk-in closet. She digs up her work box hidden beneath the chunky winter sweater she had tossed over the thing when Harry padded in unexpectedly this morning to ask which of his ties, the burgundy or the mustard, worked better set against his crisp white shirt and dark-gray windowpane suit. Burgundy won that one, and the man moved on, thankfully. Lu roughly rifles through the tech section of the box, pushing aside the new and shiny pieces like the nano bug with audio and GPS, pen camera with Wi-Fi streaming, and compact EMP generator fashioned as an actual pressed powder makeup compact, searching for the old and faithful: her thumb drive duplicator. The tiny thing has helped Lu on some big jobs. It's a random point of pride for her, having held on to it for this long.

She cocks the lid over one side of the box and pushes it under the sweater again, then bear crawls over to where her handful of gowns hang. Behind them is a small suitcase that temporarily houses her rucksack where the ultra-slim company laptop is stashed. The Russian tea dolls setup makes for a clumsy series, but it works for now. Another reason—a lesser one—that she cannot wait to be done with The Atlas and all its trappings. The hiding of all of it has become increasingly challenging. She is so ready to dash her secret stockpile at last. It feels like Solomon is three days away from stumbling upon her underground reserves.

She worms her way back to her corner with the tiny computer in hand. The laptop powers on in a blink and flashes the prompt for Lu to complete the four-step verification process, then enter her passcode. She does all of this with her eyes practically closed, then cracks her knuckles as the requisite access-granted screens pop up. Hidden among the other official job files on this laptop is her own private folder. She created it back when the device was first shipped to her along with the other "starter pack" items—cash, bank notes, various fake IDs, and a then very old-school, brick-like, untraceable mobile phone. She used to keep a log of her time stats—how long it took her to break in and out on jobs—in this private folder, as well as a running tab of her large payments that she'd socked away in offshore accounts. Over the last decade, though, she's moved this information off of the laptop and into a slim

Moleskine notebook, written in barely legible and heavily coded terms.

Lu simultaneously slides Jonathan's flash drive and her thumb drive duplicator into the waiting ports. She takes a deep breath and holds it, her body stiffened as she waits for the copy transfer to be completed. She doesn't bother trying to guess what Jonathan might be hiding on it. Could be virtually anything—secret second family, grimy snaps of Didi for revenge porn, poorly covered tracks of embezzlement. "Hell, maybe it's a list of his OnlyFans subs," Lu mumbles as the completion percentage bar nears 100 percent.

There is a single folder on his drive. Nothing is password-protected. Lu clicks on it, her heart beginning to race, a weird exhilaration tickling her nerve endings. Picture after picture of a person in a fursuit—a fox, to be sure—fills the screen. In some photos the fox is dancing with drink in hand at a gathering. In others the fox is fondling the breasts of what appears to be a sexy cat furry wearing just the giant head of the costume and a skimpy black bra and matching body harness on the rest of her very female, very human form. Each photo of the fox and the cat lady frolicking is more explicit than the last, despite the two being surrounded by other people. It's an orgy. A furry orgy. Lu swipes through each frame trying to make sense of it. *Is this his voyeur kink?* And then, Lu lands on it: pay dirt. A photo of the fox without his head on doing a line of cocaine. Her eyes go wide and mouth drops open as she leans in, gawking at none other than Kastille's fifty-three-year-old phenom, CEO Jonathan Killigrew, a.k.a. the fox. Videos are next, featuring Jonathan—sans fox head—engaging in various versions of raunchy sex with the cat lady. The camerawork is shaky enough to appear clandestine, undoubtedly shot without the participants' consent, but the videos are visually clear enough to reveal an unmistakable and oblivious Jonathan freely enjoying his secret side. There are two emails following the string of smutty videos. Standard blackmail threats with demands for large sums of money.

"Jesus," Lu hisses, as a pang of sympathy flashes in her chest. Lu's version of sympathy, anyway. "Poor dummy." But this pity is quickly pushed to the side when she realizes this has nothing to do with Kastille. "Should've went for the fucking doctor bag," she snaps. "Who's the dummy now?"

The chime of the door startles Lu. She slaps the laptop shut, pulls out the drives, and tosses everything back into her rucksack before trotting over to the security screen as the automated voice runs through its programmed announcement. It's Finola. Again. She hurries back to the closet to shove her things into their respective hiding spots, but kicks over her cooled coffee in the process. "Shit!" She grabs the first thing at hand from a pile of clothes still sitting unpacked a month later. It's one of her favorites, too: Harry's blue Oxford hoodie from his ancient uni days. With another muttered curse, Lu tosses the sweatshirt, hurriedly, over the spill as the door chime rings out once more. She's down the stairs in a dash just as the bell song comes to an end. Mylo appears at Lu's right side, his collar tags still jangling, exposing his scrambled trot just as she pulls open the door.

"Morning! Sorry to disturb you," Finola says in one rushed breath. She widens her eyes at Lu—a silent message delivered—before making a quarter turn to reveal Didi seated in the passenger seat of the idling golf cart just off the side of them at the top of the driveway, her phone held up to eye level, engaged in an animated video call.

"No, it's all good," Lu says, sending a smile over Finola's shoulder at Didi, who sends back a weak head-nod. A chin-raise, really.

"He's so cute," Finola says, changing into a baby voice and bending down to talk directly to Mylo, which he thoroughly appreciates. "Aren't you adorable?" But then something clicks and she remembers herself, glancing back at Didi. She snaps out of the cutesy puppy-talk. Mylo, not pleased by the abrupt end to the lovefest, moseys over to the base of the staircase and plops down with a loud sigh.

"You good?" Lu asks.

"Yeah . . . totally," Finola says, smiling meekly. "So . . . Didi—well, we all wanted to invite you to the Bliss Bloom event at Sage and Stone Spa on Friday."

"The what-what where and when?"

"Sorry, backing up . . . it's Evangeline's thing. I know you haven't met, but she, I mean, her company, Bliss Bloom, is hosting this wellness event at the big spa in town." Finola again steals a glance over her shoulder at Didi in the short distance, still on her call. She is clearly not tuned in to what's happening on Lu's doorstep, but Finola seems to lower her voice anyway. "Uh, I need to c—"

"Come clean?" Lu says with a smirk.

Finola responds with a cheerful huff and quick nod. "The event's been in the works for months, before Evangeline even left, but Didi felt that it would look bad if we didn't include you. The late basket. The late welcome brunch. The gala invite. She couldn't bear another late thing. No one wants you to feel slighted."

"I don't, but appreciate the concern," Lu says, shrugging.

"See? I told them you wouldn't be offended. Didi insisted we ask you in person . . . and then she got a call from Evangeline, so. . . ."

"Ah, you're the buffer—or maybe the fluffer?" Lu says, causing Finola's laugh to shoot out of her mouth like a trapped cough. "So, what's the event?"

"Ugh . . . this is going to sound so ridic—just hear me out, OK?" Finola says. "It's a rejuvenation thing"—she sighs—"for the vagina. Lunch is included, of course."

"Ah, well, my vagina does appreciate a nice lunch with a side of Kegels."

Finola laughs. "I know, it's Bliss Bloom's whole culture. The company is about the essentials of women's wellness and all the New Agey solutions. Energy work and crystal healing and skin care and supplements and vaginal spas and—"

"Oh, this is a *spa*? So, she's getting a massage along with the lunch?" Lu says with mock enthusiasm, gesturing at her nether region with a raised brow and slight bow of her head.

Finola's face wrinkles with a comical frown. "It's so absurd, but please say you'll do it." She leans in toward Lu, her voice hushed. "You have to come. I need another regular, non-woo-woo person to send secret eye rolls to during the organ release exercise."

"I'm sorry, the what?"

"Oh, my God . . . after the lunch, this energy coach guides us through an exercise where we release energy from different organs specifically in our abdominal and pelvic cavities. We have to repeat after her, in a kind of low chant. It sounds so crazy. Like a sitcom episode."

"*I release anger from my liver,*" Lu says in a facetious, singsong, quiet incantation, with her eyes closed and subtle Om hands. "*I apologize for the Casamigos Blanco.*"

Finola's amused huffs from her nose grow quicker and louder. She checks behind for Didi, who is now pacing beside the golf cart, still talking. "I'm not even joking; that's basically what happens. Only you missed the part where we have to say, 'I love my liver completely and am grateful for all its work,'" she says, no longer trying to contain her laughter. "And we do this while wearing different colored scarves for the different organs. It's color therapy, to reduce anxiety *and unlock our magic*." Finola's chuckle expands to an open-mouth guffaw as she and Lu begin to double over. "Now you totally have to come! Just to witness it."

"What did I miss?" Didi says, sidling up to the two laughing women like an inept ghost.

"You know, just gabbin' about angry livers and peaceful *punnanis*," Lu says. "Oh, punnani is slang, patois, for vagina," she adds, jokingly, off the women's confused looks.

Didi gives Lu a weak nod. Her jaw stiffens. "Vaginal health is actually a really important part of our overall wellness. Evangeline's valuable work has helped us learn to prioritize this."

Finola's smile falls away and her mouth flies open, ready to explain and excuse and atone. Lu cuts in before Finola can start prostrating. "Of course it is. Very important. No one here thinks otherwise," Lu says, her own face gone somber now. "But . . . vaginas can also be funny. I mean, *queefs*?"

Through the corner of her eye, Lu sees the look of shock chased with amusement pulling across Finola's face. Didi, on the other hand, is clearly horrified, though she recovers quickly and manages a tight smile.

"Right . . . I mean, sure," Didi says, the remnants of a blush lingering. "I just think we can all stand to be more"—her head trembles and her eyes go skyward as she searches for the right words—"possessive . . . no, obsessive about our health. About *women's* health. It's one of Evangeline's biggest passions. Modern medicine has pushed women's wellness to the back of the bus forever, and that is just unacceptable to me."

Not the back of the bus. "Oh, I hear you," Lu says. "Especially when it comes to Black women's health, right? Guess if you're at the back of the bus, we're under it."

"No—it's not—I wasn't trying to imply anything like *that*," Didi says, her voice beginning to waver a little. "Like Evangeline always says, we women—all of us—are facing an entire medical community, a whole industry that continues to ignore us, diminish our worth." She sends a charged look over to Finola, a silent indictment.

Finola in turn picks up the ball that was lobbed at her head and runs with it. "Right . . . exactly. It's not about dividing and separating—Black, white, purple with perfect polka dots—it's about women. *All* women, you know?"

"Of course," Lu says, gently, and it's convincing. "I gotta say, all jokes aside, this hoo-ha spa sounds like a fun experience. Text me the details?"

"Oh, definitely. Will do," Finola says, bouncing a pleased look between Lu and Didi. "It's really such an amazing event. The gift bag alone is—"

"That reminds me," Didi interjects, "we need to stop by Calista's on the way to my house. She forgot the Beau Rêves notecards for the gift bags." She turns to include Lu now. "Calista's so generous. She's donating a ton of lingerie. It's overstock from her special line, but it's still appreciated."

"Sounds like the whole crew has a hand in this *vajeen* party," Lu says.

"We support one another in this town," Didi says, with an irked expression.

"Oh, totally," Finola says. "Actually, Didi is basically like a silent partner in Bliss Bloom. Her creativity, business acumen, and PR savvy—unmatched. She's an incredible resource." Finola looks over at Didi as if she's a bronzed saint statue. "You should really think about asking Didi to help with your small business—a Pilates studio, right?"

Jesus, Annabelle. Mouth like a faucet. "Yeah, good idea," Lu says, nodding. "I mean, if you have time one of these days, Didi . . . I know you stay booked and busy."

"Sure." The word seems to come out of Didi's mouth against its will.

"Uh, so you'll join us?" Finola says, her tone, pleading.

"It'll be a small, select group of women who really get it, who want to pour into the community here," Didi says. "We'd understand if that's not your thing."

"It's a soft launch for Bliss Bloom's vaginal jelly beans," Finola chirps. "So, that's why it's a small group. Keeping it intimate."

"Uh . . . she gets lunch *and* jelly beans? Say less." Lu snorts. "Count me all the way in."

"Great," Didi says behind that same strained smile. "We'll see you there." She turns to Finola. "I'll meet you back at the cart. I have a call." Another bratty grin tossed in Lu's general direction and then she's off, moving with haste down the Barlows' front walkway.

"It really is good that you'll be there," Finola says. "There's a lunch first, then the whole sales pitch of it all. The good stuff begins right after that. The whole thing runs a little under three hours," she says, cringing. "I know, that's a big time commitment . . ."

"Nonsense," Lu says. "Anything for my vagina. That's my *gurl.*"

"All right. I'll text you the info," Finola says, chuckling. She waves goodbye, then trots along to meet Didi, already seated in the cart on her alleged phone call.

Mylo rejoins Lu standing on the front step as she watches the golf cart make shaky quarter turns, then glide back down her driveway, her dislike for Didi growing deeper with each meter and mile.

CHAPTER FIFTEEN

Lu blows Harry a kiss from the front step as he prepares to reverse down the driveway. He mimes catching the sweet thing and gobbling it up. This, of course, brings a playful eye roll and hand swat from Lu. But her flapping hand quickly turns into an earnest wave as she stays watching him drive off to work, albeit later than usual after he volunteered to take Mylo to an early morning vet appointment. The fancy company car fades into the distance and so does Lu's warm grin. A bilious wave runs through her full being. This—all of her sneaking and duplicity—had officially reached too much, too far, too despicable weeks ago, but now, having hacked her husband's work phone just an hour ago while he was kindly tending to their dog's health, Lu has hit the bottom beneath the bottom. She's entered hell and deserves to rot there.

Lu knew Harry was different from the moment they met in a café of an art gallery in Italy. She was there on a job: intercepting forty-five pieces of priceless treasure being transported from a vault in Milan Cathedral to a museum in Bologna. After the two of them quite literally bumped into each other, Lu had no plans of doing anything more than *him*—in a coat room at the gallery, no less—and moving on. But when that first meeting spanned into the wee hours of the next day and continued into a second night, all without ever once removing a single piece of her clothing, it left a mark on Lu. She felt good around this man in a way that was destabilizing and exhilarating at once. They talked for long stretches those two-and-a-half days, as if pausing for too long would rattle the easy balance between them, waking them from their blissful dream state. With her specific skill set and talent for stealth and deception, Lu had long been seen as exceptional, but for all the wrong reasons. Harry somehow made her feel truly special, for the right ones.

Back in her closet corner office, Lu is practically folded in half, the weight of her transgressions threatening to break her back. With Harry's phone turning up absolutely nothing, she'll need to look elsewhere, and be especially crafty about it, too.

Her own ringing phone pulls Lu out of her frowning focus. It's a local area code, but it shows up as **Unknown Caller**. Same thing happened two weeks ago. Turned out to be the PTO president at Maple Grove Academy calling from her cell phone asking Lu if she might have time in her schedule to be a volunteer at their library twice a week. It was a nice but immediate no. Lu only really tolerates children who belong to her. She answers the call half expecting it to be the PTO taking another run at Lu to volunteer for classroom parent this time.

"Hello?"

"Good day. Is this Lucille Barlow? I'm calling from Atlas Appliances."

All of the air is dragged out of Lu's lungs as her mouth hangs open. The voice. The timbre. The accent. It's him, but it shouldn't be. This is her personal cell phone. Direct contact like this is not following protocol. Lu presses the phone against her ear, listening intently, hoping she misheard, her nerves somehow conjuring an auditory hallucination.

"Hello? Is this Lucille Barlow on the line?" the man says again, slowly.

"Yes." The word, wispy and light, floats out of her mouth like a soap bubble. Lu checks behind her even though she knows she's alone in the house. Her stomach twists into a tight knot as she tries to focus and think ahead. Anticipate why he's calling her and what it might mean.

"Sorry to bother you, ma'am," he continues, "but your garbage disposal needs that new part after all. I will need you to sign for it."

Sign for it. Shit. Lu's heart is beating loud in her ears; her temple and neck throb like tom drums. *Sign for it.* This always means one thing: He is here. She moves the mouthpiece of the phone away to cover the agitated sound of her quickening breaths. Lu pulls herself together enough to follow the script. "Oh . . . OK . . . can you text me the address to your shop again? I've misplaced it."

"No need. I'll come to you, ma'am," he says. "I'm only seven minutes away. See you soon." And like that, the man on the phone—and it is definitely him—is gone.

Lu dictates a text to Finola as she hustles out of her special corner:

Old friend from NYC is in hospital. Won't be able to join the fun after all. Please give the happy housewives my sincere apologies. Will catch up later

Breathless and baffled, Lu stumbles out of her closet and hustles to change back into her jogger set, bracing for the impact of seeing Mr. V on her front doorstep—or, more likely, already seated in the breakfast nook—once again.

THROUGH THE WINDOW at the top of the landing, Lu can see a white panel van parked not too far from the driveway's end. She forgoes the foyer—he's not ringing any doorbells—and instead beelines to the kitchen. There she finds Mr. V settling into his same seat at the breakfast table, a squat mug in one hand. With the other, he's petting a chilled-out Mylo sat on his lap.

"Since when do you like dogs?" Lu blurts out.

"I don't," he says, stroking the top of Mylo's soft head with his thumb.

"How long have you been here?"

"Again, is that the real question you want to ask me?"

Lu moves toward Mr. V, close enough to give Mylo a dirty look behind his betrayal. "Look, you can't keep doing this. Breaking and entering, it's not even noon. What if one of my neighbors saw you?"

"In all this acreage? Highly doubt," he says.

Lu turns away from him, grimacing, and walks over to the fridge for water, but mostly to grab a brief moment to rein herself back in. She spins back around to face her mentor turned antagonist. "Mylo, get down," she says, adding a loud, crisp finger-snap. The dog bolts from Mr. V's lap over to Lu and lowers his back half, gingerly, to sit at attention, staring up at his favorite human. She bends over to reassure him that he's a good boy and not in trouble with a little tickle beneath the dog's neck. A glance over at Mr. V, the vinegar in her voice restored. "Maybe you can respect my space, my family's space, and not just turn up here whenever you'd like. Them seeing you . . . it messes with my cover."

"I'm not here for tea and biscuits, my yout," he says. "There's always a reason for you to see me. Mind you get ahead of yourself."

"What's the reason this time?" The fact that the man could very well drop yet another bomb on her chest sets her gut on fire, sending a ball of heat radiating up her trunk and out to her limbs. How much more can he ransack her life?

"There's a sizeable bonus being offered to you by the client. Of course this means an additional step in order for the assignment to be considered complete."

"What's the ask?"

"In addition to the take, they feel it necessary that there is also a leave-behind."

"A leave-behind?" she squawks. So sharp, the sound makes Mylo's head pop up from resting by her feet. "Like what, a notecard with hints that their proprietary product is gone?"

"Being snide offers you no help," Mr. V says.

"OK . . . sorry." She hates how sudden the apologies leap from her mouth when it comes to him. The way she instantly reduces the bass in her voice and this instinctual cowering the minute his tone turns sharp—still, after all the years—is mortifying. "What is it they need left behind?"

"A virus."

"For the computers, or are we talking smashing a test tube to the floor?" she says, half smirking. Mr. V lightly clears his throat and continues glaring at her. "Sorry . . ."

"The former."

"A computer virus?" Again her chirp rouses the dog awake. "Does the client know I'm not Ethan Hunt? I deal in jewels and gems, and the occasional prized piece of artwork. I don't do computers and viruses. Why do they even need to do all that?"

"For reasons that are not central to this discussion, the client requires the added piece in order to bring this project to fruition, and, frankly, submit full payment." Mr. V rises from his seat, making sure to gently push the chair back in place. "I have every confidence that you will be able to move forward and close out the assignment as planned."

"Sir, I am not equipped—"

"Are you refusing the request?" He walks right up to the edge of the kitchen island between them, his hands pushed into his pant pockets, calm and collected as ever. He repeats himself yet again—not his regular practice. "Are you refusing the request, Twenty-two?"

Lu bends down and scoops up the snoozing dog, clutching him to her side tight while keeping her eyes trained on the tiled floors. "No . . . I just . . ."

"Is the answer printed on the tops of feet?" Mr. V says, sharply.

Lu snaps her head up straight to look at him. "No. I was . . . no." She nods, sheepishly, knowing he will not budge until there is a verbal acknowledgment. "I will close out the assignment as planned, including the new request."

"Very good." Mr. V spins back to the table to collect his brown tweed flat cap resting topside-down on the breakfast table bench. Lu had not noticed it earlier when she walked in, too distracted by her dog's lack of stranger danger awareness. She also didn't notice the smallish, square gift box wrapped in red paper and finished with metallic gold grosgrain ribbon also on the bench, sitting inside his cap. He slides the hat over his head, covering his close-cropped silver hair completely, and turns back around with the gift box in hand, placing it gently on the counter between them and then pushing it toward Lu. "A necessary gift. The rest of your directives will be delivered through the regular channels. And then you'll have everything you need to proceed."

Lu stays peering down at the red box, the urge to snatch it up and tear it open making her twitch in place. Mr. V has already made his way over to the back kitchen door by the time her attention moves off of the red box. She levels her gaze at him, her thoughts lined up again. "There's one thing," she says, stopping him short. "A condition for all of this."

"Oh? There's something more you could want other than the retirement, the freedom from us you so desire?" Mr. V looks over at her, his normally reserved face showing a glint of curiosity. He takes a few steps back toward her.

Lu rests Mylo down by her feet. He immediately scrambles off to another room, as if he can smell the stiff awkwardness permeating the kitchen and is now desperate to escape it. "I need it to be clean, Vincent . . . sir," Lu says. "This job is the last job and it needs to be the last job. The leash that's been around my neck, it needs to be let go . . . for real. The break from you, from them, it has to be a clean one. Even though they had a hand in us moving here, we're here now because we want to be. And this beautiful house, it needs to be *our* house—mine, my family's."

"What do you mean to say with all of this?"

"You can't just show up here anymore," Lu says. "If we need to meet about this final assignment, we meet through the proper channels."

Mr. V nods, his lips pursing ever slightly. "You don't want the boy to meet me," he says. There's no question in this statement. They both know that it is true. "What would I even be to him, his foster grandpappy?"

"No. You'd be nothing to him," Lu snarls. His face registers a streak of something she doesn't fully recognize. Hurt? Insult? The beginnings of regret? Restitution at last? She forces herself to ignore whatever it is and continues riding her wave of righteous indignation. "He doesn't exist to you. He doesn't exist to them. That's what I mean about it being clean. No thin strings tied to me in any way. After this is done, this is done."

"You've always been one to know exactly how to get this world to bend your way," Mr. V says, his expression a mix of pride and provocation. "I'll leave you to it, then." He continues toward the patio door, then smoothly slips through it like a magician behind a curtain.

Lu waits nearly a full two minutes after he's left, thinking he might just return, if not to issue one of his layered parables for good measure ("*What you need is what you have, my yout.*"), then maybe to wish her success and safety on this her final assignment with one of his old edicts ("*Leave no crumbs.*"). But he's gone for real.

She reaches for the gift box next, tearing it open in a hurry. Inside is a champagne-gold box that has another leather box matching in color within that. Lu recognizes the packaging straight away. On her twenty-first birthday, Mr. V presented her with an identical box. They had been in London, their paths happened to overlap for that one evening in her posh hotel suite. She was headed to Amsterdam the next morning for her first sizeable heist from a private collection and he had been moving through parts of Europe—Copenhagen, Barcelona, Paris, Zurich, and Milan, according to what he had told her—for the last few weeks. He had said that the London stopover was merely a fluke, but Lu knew him to be a man who wholly dismissed nonempirical things like chance and fate as flimsy and useless. No, it was clear to Lu back then that he had made a point to be in London at the same time as her to ensure that they see each other on her big birthday. And that he happened to have a present for her on his person "just in case" only added further proof to this theory. That neatly wrapped box from decades ago had held two thick gold West Indian bangles—one being slightly thinner—with two sets of cocoa pod heads pointing toward each other.

"Those bangles, sometimes we call them bayras, they have a deep and rich history," he had told Lu as she gleefully slid each on to her left wrist one at a time, gently squeezing the cocoa pod heads closer together to secure the bangles as she admired the etchings on the cuffs. "Another time I can tell more about it, but right now what you need to know is that the thinner of the two bayras—the pods can be removed and pushed together to make a key for a lockbox in the secondary hallway adjacent to the main site."

Lu's smile instantly fell apart upon realizing that the bangles were not gifts at all, but rather props, tools required for her to complete the job. "These bangles aren't real?" she had said, unable to mask her disappointment.

"Of course they are real," Mr. V had said. "Better than real; they serve a purpose."

Lu ran her fingers along the sides of the bangles, feeling the texture of each etched line. They were indeed real—eighteen-karat gold, from what she could tell. "Do I get to keep them after the job is done?" she had asked him, expecting a flat no in response.

"I don't see why not," he had said, and cracked a tiny, sweet smile—or at least that is how Lu chooses to remember it, right up to this day. Then he stood up abruptly, reached into the breast pocket of his suit jacket. "There's also this." Mr. V had handed her a padded envelope with her new Danish passport and a prepaid cell phone. And that was the end of it; her birthday celebration was over and they were back to business. After they had exchanged a firm handshake, Mr. V turned and left. Lu was alone in the luxury accommodations and decided to do the only thing she could think of: order sticky toffee pudding for dinner, no candle, no song.

Standing now in her kitchen, her twenty-first birthday tucked clean away beneath a thick wool in her mind, Lu opens the current box without a clue of what she will find inside.

A small gold wrap bracelet with a lock charm dangling from the chain like a key. Lu rolls the charm between her thumb and index finger. The pendant dislodges from the bracelet and reveals that the tiny lock actually expands into a thumb drive—the smallest she has ever seen. She takes a long moment to admire the craftmanship of the covert flash drive and then the beautiful bracelet on its own. She wraps the shimmering thing around her wrist but doesn't fasten it, then tilts her hand this way and that. And in a deep, dour voice parroting her once mentor, Lu answers out loud the same question back in her mind again: "I don't see why not."

CHAPTER SIXTEEN

Use the time that is given. That's something Mr. V taught Lu long ago. Granted, he was talking about the commissioned heists at world-class museums, subterranean vaults, and—on a handful of occasions—multimillion-dollar penthouses, not the mansions of snooty suburban aristocrats in Partridge Hollow, Connecticut. But with the women at Sage and Stone, stuffing their lady bits with quartz eggs and jelly beans, this block of time is a gift. When would these houses be vacant like this again? These women's husbands are the trusted secret-keepers of Kastille and they hold the collective key to unlock all doors, helping Lu to get closer to freedom.

The skulking around their homes now includes a heightened hunt for a VIP fingerprint to copy. With this being breaking and entering in the middle of the afternoon, Mylo has to sit this one out. Even someone passing by in a car would notice a cute dog abandoned, tied up to a tree. It doesn't take a second's thought for someone like that to determine that the puppy is being neglected, or worse, mistreated, and move quickly into calling the authorities.

Lu, wearing all-black leggings and a thin matching hoodie with a small canvas tote slung over her shoulder, keeps her walk toward Evangeline and Ward's house brisk and determined. Her braided-down hair is tucked into a stocking wig cap and her head is covered by a long black ponytail wig with a black fuzzy bucket hat on top of that. Her sunglasses are dark and stylish but oversized, covering the upper third of her face. Tucked neatly beneath her chin is a black flat-fold surgical mask, a holdover from deep in the pandemic days, ready to be pulled up to obscure the balance of her face if need be.

As Lu arrives at the Bloom estate, a recently renovated Nantucket-style colonial sitting on three-and-a-half park-like acres, she scans the grounds from the base of the driveway, figuring her stealthiest approach. As she predicted, they use the same feckless alarm company as the DuBois-Killigrews. Lu tips her head toward the blue logo sticker on one of the windows. A smug, quiet thank-you.

She closes her eyes for a breath next, bringing the blueprint of this home front of mind. Six bedrooms, six bathrooms, and two partials, spread across 8,450 square feet. The heated pool in the back is relatively close to the house. Should anything go awry, Lu can instantly be a town inspector checking after permits or a pool service tech there on an end-of-season visit. She can visualize the French doors leading into the house off the patio; *that's* her entrance.

Lu walks toward the left side of the property with its superb landscaping, moving casually, as if she is supposed to be there, even pulling out her phone, keeping her head down, studying its black screen as she gets closer to the back the house.

The minute she is out of view from the street, she pounces into action, hustling toward the rustic pasture fence, slipping through, barely opening it. Unlike at Didi's, there is not a lot of tree coverage near the house. Lu pops a squat by the pool's humming heat pump, which is large enough to obscure most of her. She pulls out her jamming device from the tote. If Finola is correct, none of the doors are even locked and thus the alarm system would be off, but Lu is not about to put her full trust in someone who can barely stand up to the bullies in her own little friend group.

With the cellular signals between the sensors and the alarm base station blocked—just in case—and all cameras paused, Lu, staying low, scuttles to the closest French door off the patio. She does yet another sweep of the grounds behind her before pulling her mask up and trying the doorknob. It opens with barely a creak. Finola—1, Doubt—0.

Lu checks her infamous watch; she's giving herself no more than twelve minutes to be in and out of the Bloom house. No dawdling. No tangential snooping. If she sticks to her plotted timing, she'll make quick work of it and be back home long before any of the pampered housewives return from the privileged pussy spa.

She steps inside onto a thin welcome mat in the bright dining section of the palatial open kitchen. It's all dove-gray cabinetry and pristine slabs of marble with brushed brass accents. To her left, by the heart of the gourmet kitchen with full, sparkling, luxury appliances, there's yet another dining area, positioned around an impressive island. Nothing is out of place here, not even a couple bowls or mugs turned upside down, drip-drying on a tea towel by the sink. To her right, a den with marshmallow-white cozy chairs and sofa, round wicker tables, and a fireplace with a massive modern art piece above the mantel instead of a TV. Or maybe it's one of those pricey flat-screens in art mode.

"Goddamn model home," Lu grumbles as she slips off her black Vans and drops them in her tote. She skates across the clean, white tiles in her lightweight no-show socks, heading toward the three-story foyer.

It's as massive and magnificent as it sounds, and Lu feels pulled to check out the other rooms and wings on this floor. Like the large living room anchored by the Palladian windows with what looks like an indoor hammock strung up to the high ceiling. Or the formal dining room down the long hall where, craning her neck, Lu can see just the beginnings of it—the end piece of an oval marble table and wallpaper featuring Chinese flowering trees in an ivory silhouette set against a sapphire-blue background. It's so perfect in these spaces, unique and curious. Must be nice to come home to, Lu thinks as she moves through the rooms. Although, on a closer look, is anyone coming home to this? True, Evangeline has been in Europe for weeks, but what about Ward or their kids? Not a thread is out of order on this main level; it doesn't appear lived in at all. No left-out laptops or random chargers in the wall. No kicked-off shoes by the door.

The walls along the main staircase are bare. It's only at the top of the landing that Lu finds a small array of framed photographs starring the family—immediate and extended, it seems—both in color and tattered black and white, artfully displayed on a bronze console along with random ceramic pieces and an old, rusted fishing hook.

Lu doesn't study the photographs for too long beyond noticing that everyone, even the supposed grandmas and grandpas in the pictures, looks like they were ripped from the pages of a fashion magazine. And Evangeline's entire family tree is made of gold leaf, including the former famous movie star mother and insanely rich mogul father.

Lu breezes by the three Bloom kids' bedrooms next. Children and their personal spaces have always been off-limits for Lu. She only takes a beat to note how grand and whimsical each bedroom is and thinks about Solomon's new room and how much more work needs to be done to make it speak to *his* personality as these three surely do.

She remembers from the blueprint that the master suite is somewhat secluded on the third level in a luxe alcove, and pushes on to the staircase at the end of the lengthy hall leading to it. Evangeline and Ward's bedroom is enchanting. Quiet and moody while still being glamorous and well-appointed. Although Lu's digital copy of the home's layout did not show it, she soon discovers that the couple forewent his-and-hers walk-ins and instead knocked down the wall of the bedroom next door and used the entire space as their custom closet. After a careful but quick sweep, she sees there's no safe, not even a craftily hidden one.

Both nightstands have nothing more than lamps on them. No leather catchall or three-in-one charging station. No telltale books—something brawny (the history of Spartans) or dreamy (spicy enemies-to-lovers romance). Lu takes a random guess that Ward sleeps on the right side of the bed and goes there first.

Bingo.

With gloved hands, she pulls the drawer open and a wave of something familiar is released into the air. Lu drags the mask down to expose just the tip of her nose and inhales. It's perfume. She tugs the mask down a little farther and takes another whiff.

Where do I know this from? Lu digs into the deep, tidy drawer, carefully moving around Ward's slim collection of personal effects—weighty classic fountain pens; two pairs of identical sunglasses in matching softshell cases; noise-canceling headphones in a leather case; an iPad with neatly rolled charger; and two wooden watch boxes stacked large on top of the slightly smaller one. Of course Lu pulls out the small box. It's obviously being hidden, though poorly. As she does this a pretty silk scarf is dislodged from its secret spot, and the fragrance billows up even more into Lu's nostrils.

Calista.

She presses the scarf up closer to her face without actually touching her nose to it. This is Calista's perfume—all of the notes are there. Lu unfolds the scarf and examines it. She finds a swirly monogram on one corner.

CC. Calista Caudwell.

Lu folds the scarf and tucks it toward the back of the drawer, then continues with the smaller box. Inside, instead of watches, there are three things: a basic flip phone, a point-and-shoot digital camera, and a pair of black panties folded just so. The tiny label on the lacey underthing catches her eye. *Beaux Rêves.* Lu gives the skimpy underwear a sly look, her pursed lips releasing a quiet tsk-tsk, but leaves them as is. She plucks out both the camera and the phone from the watch case. She removes the camera's memory card and, working smarter this time, reaches for her travel SD card duplicator from her tote. As the transfer gets underway, Lu searches the phone's call history. There are even some text messages that she's able to pull up. It seems to be a code made up of letters and figures, like a cryptic accounting ledger. The transfer is complete and Lu puts the camera back in place, closing the drawer with a judgmental smirk and moving on to the bathroom, searching for a toothbrush or shaver—something that would have Ward's semi-fresh fingerprints.

The bathroom, like the rest of the enormous house, is pristine. Even the ends of the towels folded over the wide rack are perfectly lined up. Lu goes for the large top drawer of the massive two-sink bathroom counter and pulls it. There's a tray of identical black toothbrushes; each looks unused. But the toothpaste! The tube is squished, twisted, and rolled. She's about to reach for it when she hears the distinct sound of a car door—a van—slamming shut.

Oh, fuck. Lu glances at her watch. She's over her time limit by three-and-a-half minutes.

There's an abrupt silence; the vehicle's engine is off. Another van door sliding and loudly slamming shut springs Lu into a bracing, ready position. She impulsively drops the found cell phone into her tote and flies over to the closest window. This angle offers Lu only a partial view of the circular section of the paved driveway. But she can tell, there's definitely a vehicle there.

Visions of her clash with Security Guard Number Three cause a phantom pain to flare up on her side. Lu remembers that, according to Annabelle, the Blooms don't have a household manager or even a nanny. Evangeline is one of those women who seems all too proud to let people know that she has it all, does it all, all by herself.

Lu trains her ear to the window, pressing up as close to it as possible while still hiding off the side of it. There's a light echo of two women—one with a louder, husky voice—speaking a different language. Spanish. No, that's not it; they sound like Antonella, the hilarious Brazilian yogini who rented a cozy storefront three doors down from Lu's studio in Brooklyn. These women are speaking Portuguese. Antonella would often slip into her native tongue when regaling Lu with the bawdy details of her post-divorce entertaining encounters with the men she'd met on the apps.

Doesn't matter what language they're speaking. The two women are here, at the Bloom house, readying to enter. Lu slips out the bedroom and lurks for a breath on the landing, listening and mulling her options. She can either hide and wait it out, hoping this is a brief layover for these two women and that they keep their business on the first floor. Or, more realistically, she'll need to get the hell out of there.

Moving to her tiptoes, Lu takes long, swift strides closer to the top of the stairs. She hears the thud of the front door and the women's voices are louder, but still with a bit of an echo. They're inside, probably organizing themselves in the mudroom by the side door. She takes a deep breath, counting out the long exhale, trying to slow her heartbeat. A thought—an image—jolts Lu out of her breathwork. *There's a back staircase.* She can see the mansion floor plan clearly in her mind. It starts on the level below her; it's there by the hallway near the kids' rooms. Taking those stairs would land her in the back kitchen, the very one that she scoffed at when she saw it in the Realtor photos, so ridiculous and showy. Do they really need a "dirty kitchen" when the main one is essentially a football field, equipped with every high-end design element and top-notch appliance?

"*Focus.*"

Her mind back on track, Lu runs through the possible outcomes before taking another step. What if the Portuguese-speaking duo's reason for being here is in that same back kitchen? Or what if they start whatever work they do here, in the alcove? What if they are on their way up right now? What happens if she makes the wrong rushed choice and ends up meeting the women moving up the main staircase just as she is careening down it? None of these options are good. And without her rappelling equipment on hand, slipping out of a bathroom window isn't in the cards either.

She is well past her time limit on this mission. A decision must be made right *now.* Lu goes with the back stairs plan and trots, still on her toes, down the narrow steps from the alcove, slinking along the hallway, her back flush with the white wall. She pauses by the doorjamb of the first kid's room—the pinkest, frilliest one of the three—for mere seconds, tilting her head a few degrees forward, watching and listening for the women. Their voices—and free laughter—though growing louder, still hang in the distance. She listens deeper, closing her eyes to focus, trying to ascertain the direction of their footsteps. *They're coming up the main stairs.* The forward stomp is clear. This gives Lu some time, not much but enough.

Lu removes her hat first, jamming it into the tote. Then takes the bag off her shoulder, clutching it tight to her chest, and bends down, duck-walking across the hallway runner toward the back stairs. In the span of only a handful of seconds, Lu partially unzips her hoodie, stuffs her tote inside, slips off her socks, and pulls them over her palms. Next, she hops on the wood banister, seated on her socked hands, and leans back to a thirty-degree angle, sliding down the staircase like an unruly frat boy.

It's a fast, rough landing. Lu feels a twinge of something in her right ankle, but there's no time to tend to it. She doesn't bother putting the socks on her feet or digging up her shoes. Definitely no time for that either. Lu scuttles through the back kitchen and into the bright main one. The woman are talking, but it sounds different, separated. The one with the hoarse voice seems to be in motion, getting closer, definitely heading to this kitchen. The ankle, it's sprained, maybe even twisted; either way it's throbbing and heating up. Hobbling and wincing, Lu reaches the back door. She eases it open and practically falls through it onto the patio pavers.

"Goddammit!" she spits, her words hushed but hot. In her tumble, she managed to close the door quietly behind her. She also managed to scrape up her left elbow. It's stinging and surely bleeding. On the one working foot, she hops over to the respite of the pool's heat pump, stopping for barely thirty seconds to check her trail for dropped items or, more important, for picked-up tails.

All clear.

She presses on toward the side edge of the property in a staggering sprint, moving with purpose. Lu makes it to the tree line, collapsing onto the wide trunk of an impressive Japanese maple. Her face mask damp from her hot breath, Lu only gives herself one full minute to ease her heart rate a little and right her clothes, wig, hat, and tote. She squeezes her dewy feet back into her shoes. Her ankle is in bad shape, swelling by the second, already double its normal size. She tosses the ruined socks into her bag and runs her open palm along her hurt elbow. The fabric of the hoodie is shredded; she can feel the crisp breeze kissing her wound. When Lu draws back her hand, she's not surprised to see blood. She looks over at the back of the house, checking each window, top to bottom, hoping she doesn't meet a pair of frantic eyes capturing her, unmasked and barely hidden.

Once again, all clear. Time to shuffle out of here.

Before pushing off, Lu unblocks the alarm signals and resumes all camera function. She's down the side of the knoll, walking along the property line, as far away from the driveway and the women's parked black van as possible.

Hobbling home, Lu pulls her bucket hat down farther over her sweaty temples, shaking her head all the while, annoyed. Not only was she almost busted, she's still in possession of the cell phone from Ward's nightstand too. Add to that these new and gnarly injuries, for which she'll need a plausible cover story, and the fact that she's no closer to getting a fingerprint, and Lu is striking out. Big time. She is down bad and only has herself to blame.

As if following her by GPS tracker, Finola calls just as Lu finishes her wincing crawl into her bathroom, lying flat on her back on the automatic heated tiles. She answers, even though her patience and pretense are all but evaporated.

"Hey, everything OK with your friend?" Finola says, her voice chipper but still getting drowned out by the sounds of women chattering, laughing, and squealing.

Lu moves the phone away from her mouth and, as softly as her body would allow, releases a tight exhale through her clenched teeth. "Well, I gotta come clean . . ."

Finola is laughing before Lu can even get the rest of her fast fiction out. "Oh, no . . . what?"

Mylo slinks into the bathroom, as if he knew his services were needed in the lie, and plops down next to Lu, rolling over into a graceless sprawl, exposing his belly. Lu stretches out her uninjured arm and gives the waiting pup the tummy rubs he deserves.

"So, Mylo . . . took him for a quick walk. He got rather excited about the postal carrier's van and bing, bang, boom—heavy on the *boom*—he got me all tangled in his leash and I went down hard. Ankle and elbow are jacked up."

"Oh, my God! Are you OK?"

"I will be," Lu says, sincerely. "However, my vagina is pissed and actively giving me the silent treatment."

"No matter what gets thrown her way," Finola says through a hearty cackle, "Lu Barlow will always find a way to make it hilarious."

Lu pulls herself up to seated, leaning against the freestanding tub, a soft chuckle tumbling out behind another barely stifled wince. "Hmph . . . yeah . . . I always find a way."

CHAPTER SEVENTEEN

"I have a very special delivery for you," Harry says, and gives Lu a playfully faux stern look from his leaning post by the doorjamb.

In one smooth move, Lu closes her laptop and slides her hidden stash of research notes and secret devices—both of her phones, Ward's mystery cell, the memory card reader, and all the cords and cables—even farther under the pushed-aside mountain of pillows and sits up straighter in the bed. Her face is bright owing partly to the mandatory bed rest she's endured for the last nine days. The ankle is almost back to a hundred percent after the nasty sprain that was more severe than she initially assumed. With this being the final morning of the doctor-mandated intermission, Lu is ready to do cartwheels and summersault—or at least a decent moonwalk—out of this bedroom, finally.

"Is it more flowers from them? Please say it's not more flowers. I beg," she says, shaking her head and waving her arms in front of her like an enthusiastic aircraft marshaller.

In addition to a giant, overdone, get-well gift basket, the PH2 has also showered Lu with elaborate bouquets nearly every day of her recuperation. There were also plenty of calls and texts, mainly from Finola, as well as the heavy hints fishing for an invitation to come see Lu in person. For each crafty request, Lu came up with a plausible excuse to nix any visitors. Except for Annabelle Dupree, who found a loophole (argh, Harry!) and tiptoed into the bedroom that first morning after Lu returned from the hospital still reluctantly high on pain meds.

"Oh, honey. What does the other guy look like?" Annabelle had said after laying eyes on a drained and deflated Lu. She then gently placed a box of pralines and a bottle of Barolo, both with her signature white bow, on the nightstand and asked if it was all right if she sat in the corner chair and "communed for a spell" with Lu before she had to head off to a meeting with a rather eager shared client looking for a new summer home in Nantucket.

The conversation was largely one-sided, with Annabelle talking mostly about the building excitement around the upcoming gala and how fortunate Lu was that she'll back in fighting shape just in time to attend the extravagant event. Toward the end of the cheerful monologue, though, Annabelle moved on from issuing general assurances ("*There are plenty of very stylish, sensible flats that you can get at Nordstrom. Under a gown, nobody can tell what's on your feet anyway.*") and softhearted reminders ("*Always keep the dog's leash high and taut.*") to more pressing warnings.

"I don't mean to stir worry, but you might want to lean into your alarm system and the cameras and such," Annabelle had said. It was the most somber Lu had yet seen the woman's stretched-plastic face appear. Even her eyebrow moved . . . a half inch. "There's been a buzz brewing about strangers lurking around the neighborhood. Just be alert is all I'm saying, dear."

Lu had been sure to layer in the right amount of shock and concern as she listened to Annabelle, adding a well-timed, "It's rough times for a lot of people out there."

She shakes the moment away and turns to Harry now, waiting for him to reveal this very special delivery, really, really hoping it's not more flowers or, worse, the full PH2 crew pushing their way into her bedroom . . . with an even bigger obnoxious gift basket.

"No, it's not more flowers, love," Harry says, swooping in to sit at Lu's bedside. "It's this"—he turns and pulls his wife into a tight bear hug—"directly from Boxer. He told me that the hug needed to be really big and really tight and last at least ten seconds—to commemorate this being your final day of *bed jail*—his term. He felt like the one he gave you this morning was . . . what was it he said? Some new gen word . . . anyway, whatever! Basically your son felt his hug this morning was subpar and made me swear to deliver the improved version. And I did."

"That you did. Thank you." Lu casts her eyes down and then back at her husband while forcing a grin, hoping it lands as authentic. Her heart has felt a distinct and horrible ache each time she's looked into Solomon's concerned eyes over the last nine days. He took her Mylo-induced tangle injury personally, as if her "fall" were somehow his fault. He had not put away the dog's blue leash in the mudroom as the house rule dictates, resulting in his mom having to use the longer black retractable one that easily knots and tangles. Despite Lu's insistence that this incident was all her doing—not paying attention, looking down at her phone, wearing shoddy shoes, and on and on—the boy remained swimming in contrition.

Harry plants a sweet kiss to each corner of the wide smile that Lu's made every effort to pull across her lips. "Still cannot believe it took a cute fluff ball to ground the mighty and ever bendy Lucille Barlow."

"Right . . . Netflix should definitely send Mylo a special plaque. I've watched every episode of everything." She pats the closed laptop to pad the lie. The truth is, Lu's only launched the streamer as a cover for what's actually been on her screen. "I'm ready to defend my dissertation entitled, quote, Hollywood, You Look Like Shit, *colon*, The Enduring Collapse of Creative Courage in the Age of Infinite Sequels, end quote."

"Funny bone did not get sprained, it appears," Harry says, stroking her arm before leaping up from the bed and heading across the room toward his closet to add finishing touches to his dapper-as-usual work ensemble. "Right. Mylo's relaxing in his crate—he loves it in there. And I'm already late, so . . . you're good for being up and moving freely today, yeah?"

"Indeed. Ready to rejoin the world." Lu grips at her churning stomach under the covers. Beyond the stress of the looming deadline—delayed by ten days of being bedbound—there was also the gnawing fear that Mr. V could still pop up just about anywhere with yet another add-on to the already unconscionable job. The angst and physical manifestation of her mounting lies are intensifying, leaving the pangs of conscience festering in different areas of her torso, but primarily her gut.

I release guilt from my stomach. I apologize for . . . everything.

Harry pokes his head out from the closet. "I'll try to make it home on the early side today, but no promises, all right? Dinner is already taken care of, so don't trouble yourself with all that. One of the golf cart ladies had their food service people deliver yet another feast for us. This one looks like it might be good too, seasoned and everything. Think it's a curry. Honestly, it's all quite lovely, innit? They're like actual neighbors here. We're living in a nineties American sitcom! We really must have them all over for dinner as a show of thanks, yeah? Maybe after the costume party—"

"Gahlah, dahling," Lu says in a teasing tone through her hoisted nose. "It's a *gahlah*."

"Yeah, whatever. I'm truly surprised how involved and unreasonably excited the men at work are about this masquerade ball." Harry is back near the bed, adjusting his pocket square peeking out so perfectly from his suit jacket. "It's all they talk about. You would think we don't have an actual major project unveiling in five weeks. Anyway, love, as always, be good, be careful, be beautiful"—he kisses her, this time longer and square on the lips—"and I'll see you this evening."

Lu doesn't even wait until she hears the side door close before she whips the covers off and pulls all of the hidden gadgets and papers into a semi-neat pile in the middle of the bed. She swings her legs over the side next and carefully removes her ankle splint. Although her leg was fit to bear weight since earlier in the week, Lu continued to take the precautions that both the physician at urgent care and Dr. Caleb Weavers—their new, hip, high-top-sneaker-wearing, "just-call-me-C-dub" general practitioner—outlined to ensure a full and optimal recovery. Each morning, after Solomon was off to school and Harry to work, she would slink over to her office corner of the closet only to grab this or that before quickly finding her way back to the bed to work her research from there. Day by day, the slink turned into a light hobble, then an easy limp, into the slight catch she has right now.

The initial anger Lu had felt over her stupidity and carelessness that sidelined her, and at such a critical phase of the main project, magically morphed barely two days into her confinement when the silver lining shone through. Lu realized that she could use the time alone to drill down on her sleuthing. Her fuller plan crystalized. Unearth what exactly these key members of Kastille's C-suite are hiding—because these men are *definitely* hiding something—and how their possible transgressions might be useful should Lu need somewhere to angle the shade of suspicion once she's done with her assignment.

She started with the Blooms. Her curiosity around what was on that camera had taken over her every thought. And though the images had nothing to do with the inner workings of the company, the payoff was still delicious. The first set of nearly fifty images featured Evangeline, Ward, and their three beautiful children on a beach vacation in Barbados for the holidays captured in the usual poses and scenarios. A fish-fry in the evening. Relaxing by the pools at the luxe villa. Catamarans, swimming with giant turtles, private tours, clear oceans, and buckets of fun. But then there was a separate folder containing another photo collection, this one smaller—less than twenty images—and far more interesting. Another beach getaway, but instead of their three children, the duo was joined by Calista and her husband, Ashley. The two couples were all hugged up cozy and tight. Lu had already surmised, from the scarf and panties stashed in his nightstand, that Ward and Calista were having an affair. However, these confidential photos stirred a new key ingredient into the sneaky stew.

"Swingers!" Lu had squealed, after studying the zoomed-in photo. "Well, well, well." But the schadenfreude quickly fizzled when she scrolled through Ward's stolen cell phone—no passcode!—and discovered a larger shifty scheme at play. With Evangeline's lifestyle company, Bliss Bloom, underwater, hemorrhaging money by the week, Ward created Horizon Holdings, a shell company set up specifically to help pull the business out of its sinkhole. The layers of corruption ran deep with this one, and Lu wondered if Ward's slimy tentacles extended into Kastille's financials too. One thing was sure, these bad business dealings leapfrogged Ward over Jonathan for the position of chief scapegoat.

Today, the last official morning of her bed rest stint, Lu is back to searching for a way to nab a fingerprint. Her buzzing phone pulls her out of the ridiculous hunch over her laptop. It's Finola calling. No surprise; the woman has shown true concern throughout Lu's ankle ordeal. *It's called friendship*, Harry told her, teasingly, when Lu wondered aloud about Finola's regular check-ins and visit requests. Margot called too, just once, and Didi issued a text "sending healing vibes" to Lu from "all of us" with a line about how much they were all looking forward to seeing her soon at the Secret Garden Gala. There was an actual ™ next to the event name which caused Lu to toss her head back laughing—a needed thing during her first few days of bed rest.

"Hey," Lu says, in her brightest tone.

"Hey! Free at last, right? Today is the day you break from the shackles?" Finola says.

"Something like that," Lu says, cringing, and wonders if these people ever taste the shoes they regularly lodge in their mouths. She packs up her Kastille files and moves, basically pain-free, from the closet into the bathroom. "Thanks again for all the food deliveries. Very sweet."

"Of course! Anything for my peeps, *gurl*."

Lu grimaces, again. "Right . . . so, how are things with you?"

"Really good. You know, busy with all of the gala prep. You and Harry are still a yes, right? Your ankle should be back to sprinting by then, no?"

"Might be wearing sensible flats, but yeah."

"Please, you've got two weeks, you'll be totally fine. Doing the *Riverdance* at that point, hon, ain't ya?" Finola says, this last bit in a perfect Irish accent.

"OK, Saoirse Ronan," Lu says. "Impressive accent work."

"Please. More like Lucky Charms Leprechaun," Finola scoffs. "Actually, my great-grandmother was from Dublin originally before shipping out to Boston, planting roots there. She handed down my name, but that's the closest I am to the Emerald Isle. But enough of my boring blah-blah-blah. How are you feeling? Any chance you're up for a walk? We'll go slow . . ."

Lu stares at her reflection in the bathroom mirror. So washed out and crusty. She gently drags her fingers through her matted, dry curls. But the fresh air actually sounds good. Plus, Finola likes to talk, an open faucet of hot tea and tattle. Maybe because the others in the group are so quick to dismiss and diminish her, she really lets loose around Lu. A good thing. "You know what? Yeah. Let's do it," Lu says, searching her side of the under-the-sink cabinet for her trusty hair gel. It's a slick-back kind of day, no question.

"Great! I can be there in like, forty minutes?"

"Bet. I'll be set to jet."

"Still hilarious, wonky ankle or no. Gosh, I'm so excited to see you!" Finola's voice is sweet and happy. Her friend is back, and it's clear that she's missed her.

And in a way—one not all the way definable to Lu—she's missed Finola too.

CHAPTER EIGHTEEN

Lu and Mylo are posted up outside their front door waiting for Finola to arrive. Before her ankle mishap, she and Finola had set a challenge to take late morning walks together at least four days a week. "Mobility is super important, especially at our age," Finola had said more than once. "Yes, yes, we all want to look like Jen Aniston in our fifties, but honestly, the real secret sauce is staying limber. We have *got* to stay limber."

The dog is excited to tag along, his tail wagging as he repeatedly looks up at Lu. To his fault, Mylo would follow Lu into a warehouse fire. She likes having him nearby too. He's adorable, for one thing, but also his joining the walks helps her to feel a little less shitty about pumping her new friend for information.

When Finola arrives, it gives both Lu and Mylo pause to see her pulling up not in her own giant SUV but rather the infamous golf cart. She is waving at them from much too far away.

"I can explain!" she shouts from the idling cart. "But you've gotta hop in."

"What's up . . . ?"

"It's not an emergency, per se, but Margot kind of needs us," Finola says, and looks down at Mylo twice, her smile dimming more with each glance. "You can totally bring Mylo, but . . ." Finola cringes slightly. ". . . I don't know. It's fine. I mean, it's totally your call, but . . . y'know, whatever you want, whatever you think works."

Lu has to practically clamp down on her lids to keep the deep eye roll from escaping. There are many things on the list of human inadequacies that Lu can simply brush away, but the mealy-mouth, passive-aggressive habit that women all too often employ—not saying what they mean for fear of being branded unlikeable—irks her down to her toes. She catches Finola's obvious drift and gently leads Mylo back inside.

"So, what's all this? What's going on?" Lu says, climbing into the passenger seat nice and easy. It was always Lu's intention to never find herself in any part of this ridiculous buggy. Its color alone—sage green—annoys her. But, here she is, perched on the edge of the saddle-brown cushioned seats like this was fated. Finola reaches down to turn on the sound system—a saccharine coffeehouse love song on low—and Lu is about to throw herself out the side of the non-door opening. She buckles her seat belt instead.

They head off down the Barlows' driveway. "Margot called as soon as I left, so I kind of invited her to come walk with us. She was totally game, but then she started talking some more and it was clear that she was upset. Not hysterical, but definitely not in a good space."

"Is she OK?"

"She's fine, like, she's not physically hurt or anything. Ah, I should maybe let her tell you what's going on, but . . . well, OK, just so you're not going in completely blank . . ." Finola says. She turns the music off completely now. "She was pretty upset. In between her sobs and swears—like, *lots* of swears—the basic story I gathered is, Graybeard's in deep shit."

"Wait, Graybeard—is that a yacht?"

"Sorry; Mac. Graybeard is his nickname because, well, as you know, there's quite an age gap between him and Margot. I guess his actual *gray beard* is part of it too."

"Right . . ." Lu says, smirking. "So, what brand of deep shit are we talking about?"

The golf cart picks up speed as the women cut a sharp turn, zipping by a few of the larger waterfront properties bordering Partridge Hollow's expansive beach. The crisp, briny air fills Lu's nostrils and for a minute she allows herself to go with it, to float outside of herself unfettered and follow the path of the breeze over to the shore, skimming along the cold, murky waters. It's another moderate swerve of the cart that pulls Lu down from her free float back to the cushioned seat and, thankfully, taut lap belt.

"Promise you'll act like this is brand-new information if she tells you?" Finola says. Lu nods. "OK, it's super hush-hush, but there've been insider trading accusations swirling around Mac for months."

Is everyone in this town up to no good? "Oh, shit."

"*Oh, shit* is exactly right! According to my source—"

"Annabelle Dupree," Lu mutters to herself.

"—Mac's on very thin ice. And between us, they might axe him, like, *soon*."

"Wow, that is pretty major," Lu says. "Is the insider trading thing true?" *Of course it is!* "I mean, is Mac capable of doing something like that?" *Also yes!*

"Mac's a good guy. You saw how he is, charismatic, funny," Finola says. "Always there with a word of advice. Kind of like your favorite uncle. But then again, I've only known him a year, so . . ." She shrugs. "Hell, we're all capable of doing bad things, right?"

"True." Lu keeps her voice even and eyes on the road ahead when she says this.

They turn the last corner, moving with even more haste toward the Pearson residence. "I really feel for Margot in all of this," Finola says, whispering. "All those rumors about Mac, must be horrible. Margot puts on a good front, but she's got to be coming apart at the seams."

As distant as Lu likes to keep things between her and this group of rich housewives, hearing about Margot's troubles does get under her armor. She likes Margot, from arm's length anyway. And despite the woman's old-money background and pronounced privilege, strangely Lu still wants Margot to win. Or at least for her to be able to have a laugh about all of it.

"It's good of you to head over and check on her. Thanks for bringing me along," Lu says.

"Ah, if Harry were in trouble, I know she'd do the same for—"

Finola's phone lets out back-to-back-to-back chime notifications. They are stopped at the entrance of the Pearsons' gently sloping U-shaped driveway. Finola mutters, fishing around her leather pouch until she finds her device. "Jesus, Mary, and Joseph!" shoots out like a sneeze.

"You good?"

"Yeah—it's the twins," Finola says, and roughly zips up her quilted puffer jacket right under her chin. "They got caught using a chatbot or something for a history assignment—I don't even understand it. But it looks like I'll have go up to their school to deal with this mess. I swear, it's never just one of them, always both, collaborating toward chaos, colluding to drive me crazy!" Finola steps on the gas, sending the golf cart jutting forward, a zippy beeline to Margot's three-car garage. "Meanwhile Matty is relaxing in HK like some pretend, TV dad. Father of two angels, for all he knows."

"Yes, the mental load of motherhood, they're calling it now . . ."

"Plus, Evangeline's back," Finola continues, somehow sounding even more frazzled. "For the gala. And Didi just asked me stop by to help with some last-minutes."

"Meaning, *after* we leave Margot's . . . ?"

Finola looks up from her phone, trading a series of fraught glares between Lu and Margot's front door. "Don't hate me."

"No, no, no—"

"I'll be back—"

"Back?"

"I'm sorry!" Finola squawks.

"No, seriously. I'm not good with this—I don't even know Margot like that."

"She loves you! Like, maybe even a bit obsessed. And you're such a good listener too," Finola says, her attention back to her phone.

"OK . . . sure." Lu, still thrown by everything she's just learned, unbuckles herself in a hurry and climbs out of the golf cart. "Uh . . . good luck with your kids."

"Thanks," Finola says, already beginning to reverse. "So sorry! I gotta go. But I'll keep you posted." Her words trail behind her as she speeds off.

Lu turns and takes in the grandeur of the Mediterranean-style villa she had previously looked into online, with its eleven rooms and seven thousand square feet, not including the dreamy terrace partially overlooking the golf course. The same home that Margot had the nerve to refer to as the ghetto of Partridge Hollow. Even the gardens wrapping the house feel lifted from an old-world, European time and place. The deep-pink roses off to the side of the house summon her. Pretty and peaceful. Lu takes a few more steps toward the blooms and snaps a photo. She hears a distinct *psst* coming from over her shoulder.

There's a petite, middle-age Latina woman in a chambray shirt, black slacks, and comfortable black shoes, reminiscent of Miss Goodwin's, with her salt-and-pepper hair pulled up into a high bun, waving Lu over to the side door toward the backyard. Lu squints at her, confused, which only increases the fervor of the lady's waving. Lu low-jogs over to meet her.

"You crazy?" the woman says in a hushed bark, her accented English crisp.

"No . . . ?" Lu says, jokingly stretching the ellipsis in her reply.

"So why you do this crazy stuff? And you late!" the woman says with a huff. She grabs Lu gently by the forearm and pulls her along to follow closely behind her into the back laundry area, bright and roomy with a deep, long sink, giant white side-by-side washer-dryer, and more than enough cerulean-painted cabinets. "You only use *this* one," she says, releasing her grip on Lu and pointing at the door beside them. "Mr. Mac and Miss Margot, yeah, they nice in general but they don't like stuff like that, us using the front door. No, no, no. Only this one." She scans Lu's workout attire and makes a face. "And where is your uniform? My God, you just start and you trying to get fired already?"

"Oh, uh . . . no—"

"It's OK, this time. I have extra top just in case I spill or something like that. The shirt, you can put it over your shirt. Is gonna be big up here"—the woman gestures at her own ample bosom—"because you don't have too much."

"I mean, they're fine. A good mouthful," Lu says, cupping a hand over her breast.

Her wit seems to translate as the woman cracks her first short smile.

"Yes, they good," she says, winking. "But you have to be here on time. No, be *early*. And bring your uniform. Everybody is like this right now"—she makes her hands flitter and shoulders jitter—"because the bad people, they coming to this town and, I don't know, maybe they do the house invasion. They watching everything close now to make sure."

"Oh, really?"

"Yeah. They watching, they watching. They nervous," the woman says. "And a new girl like you; you not white"—she whispers that last part—"and if you want keep the job, you need to be on time and not sneaking around doors you not supposed to be, OK?"

"Wait, what's your name?"

"Mariana."

"OK, Mariana, I'm Lu . . . so, look, there's been a little misunderstanding here. I'm not—"

Margot comes through the archway already talking. "On second thought, let's do coffee, Mariana. Although, they might want lattes. Let's wait and see—Barlow? What are you doing in here, lady?" Margot walks over to Lu, clearly bemused but covering it well with pleasant surprise. “Did Mariana let you in . . . but I didn’t even hear the doorbell?” She makes a show of looking around the room. “Is tiny Grey hiding in the washing machine or something?”

Mariana turns to Lu, shock pushing aside her confusion. Her face registers her mistake and the unfortunate fallout she believes is about to occur because of it.

Lu gives the woman her most reassuring look and the slightest nod. “Mariana did let me in, but through the back,” Lu says, smiling at both women. “I was taking a picture of those rose bushes at the side. Didn’t know roses lasted this long into the fall.”

“Oh, my God, yes. They’re Double Knock Out. I demanded that those shrubs be planted,” Margot says. “They are my absolute favorites. I’ll send you our landscaping company’s info. Ballinger’s. They’re excellent. Anyway.” Margot gestures with a head tilt for Lu to follow her out of the laundry room. “Let’s go sit.”

“Sure.” Lu starts walking with her, but drops a step behind and turns to quickly send Mariana another trust-me nod.

“So, Grey just dropped you off on the doorstep like a newspaper and left?” Margot says, shaking her head as she leads Lu through the kitchen.

“Yeah, she had to deal with something at her daughters’ school.”

“What is it this time—the girls need more Boll & Branch bed sheets? Another pair of equestrian helmets?” Margot says, rolling her eyes. “Honestly, I’ve seen those girls maybe twice. They’re fine. But their mom? Ugh.” Margot continues firing shots at Finola, but Lu has already tuned out. Instead, she is scanning the Pearsons’ superb kitchen, a perfect representation of old meeting new, and noting some of its finer details; things that the dated photos online did not do justice. Like the antiqued beamed ceilings and massive fire-engine-red AGA stove, the funky mix of exposed brick and patterned tile, ensuring every inch of the room exudes warmth with a rustic finish. Unlike the other PH2 homes, this one feels like love lives here too. An affection that seems soaked through every wall and surface. The other thing reflected throughout the house: Cormac. From the giant "Big Daidí" coffee mug by the kitchen sink to the stubby half-smoked cigar resting in the groove of the heavy blown-glass ashtray on a side table near a patio door, his literal fingerprints are everywhere. By the time the women reach the palatial living room, Lu is about ready to implode. The man's DNA is laid out for the taking, yet here she is without a single tool from her dark arts bag. This missed opportunity is making Lu's skin crawl.

"Anyway, enough about Grey. How are *you* doing? I mean, you look good. As usual."

Lu gathers her wits in time to respond without a hitch in her tone. "I'm about ninety-eight-point-five-six-two percent."

"Don't make me do math right now!" Margot says, laughing. "I'm just glad you're better. And perfect timing for the gala."

If I hear this one more goddamn time . . . "Yes, the gala is indeed happening."

Lu's noncommittal response zips by Margot as she is frowning again, clearly in her head about something. "Still can't believe Grey just dropped you off like that!"

"It's fine."

"It's not fine, actually," Margot snaps, her usual playful, bubbly disposition cleared. "She thinks I don't know why she's avoiding me. I'm sure she's told you about Cormie and these insider trading claims or whatever." Margot doesn't wait for Lu's answer.

She shoots up from her cozy sofa post. "Bullshit! Bullshit and slander." She stomps over to a neat storage cabinet by the wall. On top of it, a polished tray with a covered ice bucket, a short pitcher of water with cucumber slices floating on top, highball glasses, and several cans of Diet Coke. Margot slides open one of the tiny square drawers and pulls out a dainty pillbox. She opens it, takes out a mix of pills from the many sections, cracks open a can, spills out pebbled ice high into a glass, and pours the soda over it, while popping the pills into her mouth like breath mints. She does all of this in mere seconds, a flawless choreographed dance apparently living deep in her muscle memory. She turns to Lu, as if remembering she is actually hosting a person and not ranting in the room alone. "I'm sorry to be spewing all of this crap at you. I just . . . I'm just . . ." The tears practically race to fill her eyes, then slide down her face. "This is a lot. It's *been* a lot. This whole fucking year . . . it's too much."

"Aw, man." Lu joins Margot on the sofa and, after a stuttering hand hovers over the woman's shoulder, eases her palm down at the top of her back, adding a few soft pats. "I'm sorry you're going through it."

"Thanks," Margot says, sniffling. "But, really, you don't need to hear any of this shit."

"It's fine. I'm here."

She turns her body awkwardly and gives Lu a clumsy hug. Lu tenses. "Sorry," Margot says with a chuckle and sniffle. "I don't even know if you're a hugger . . ."

The answer is a committed no, although there are exceptions. Two, to be exact. Lu adores hugs from Solomon and Harry. End of list.

"It's OK," Lu says, softly, and slings her arm around Margot to return the embrace, albeit stiffly, then eases out of the bend just as quick. Receiving a few annoying hugs, dishing out lukewarm ones, small price to pay for getting vital information about these corrupt weirdos in this one-horse town. Lu is used to working a lot harder to gather intel.

"No, really, thanks for having an actual heart," Margot says, attempting to daintily dab at her wet face and clean up her smeared mascara with the pads of her fingers. Lu gives her a kind smile and some space, moving back around the coffee table to her single chair. "The others . . . I don't know, they act like fucking machines. Everything perfect, everything good," Margot continues, tilting her head side to side and taking on a mocking robotic voice. "Like they've never encountered a real-life problem."

"That stinks, man," Lu says. "I guess the only thing we can do is give ourselves permission to feel our way through things—the good and the bad."

"So true. But, with those ladies, it's like it does not compute." Margot sniffs. "Do you know what Didi said to me after I came home from . . ." She casts her eyes down and lets out a heavy sigh. "After I came home from the hospital . . . ? Four years ago, I had some work done in Denver after we decided that Declan was going to be our last baby." Margot lifts her head and turns her attention back to Lu. "It was botched."

"Shit. That sounds traumatic."

She gives Lu an appreciative nod. "So, last year, I went to a different surgeon in the city to get all of the mistakes fixed and things redone right. And they did it—Dr. Aldridge is called the best of the best for a reason. It was maybe my second day back into regular life here, off of bed rest, and to my face, Didi said, 'We're so glad that all the king's horses and all the king's men put you back together again.' Can you believe that shit? Who says that to someone? To your close friend?"

"Wow. That's some nasty work. Just vile."

"And in the group chat, she kept referring to me as HD. For *months*. Humpty fucking Dumpty." Margot scoffs. "I'm sure I'm still HD in her phone."

What the fuck is wrong with these people, Lu thinks. They show up as their worst possible selves at every turn. "That's messed up! Seriously, Margot. You don't deserve that."

"She knew how sensitive I was about that whole ordeal. They all knew."

"Sometimes when you brush up against another person's vulnerable underside, the soft spot beneath their hard shell, it scares them and they react by baring their teeth and swiping at you. My guess is, Didi's shitty treatment of you during that rough time was a weak attempt to conceal her own insecurity and bitterness. It's been my experience that jealousy doesn't leave room for kindness."

"So *true*!" Margot shakes her head, flopping back in her seat. "Or maybe the real explanation is, Didi's just a mean bitch."

"Yeah . . . that's probably it."

Margot's smile signals the return of her brighter disposition. Lu responds in kind with her own warm, genuine grin while quietly adding Cormac's misdemeanors to her growing-thicker file on Kastille's top row.

CHAPTER NINETEEN

"What's behind all this, dove? You're not a worrier. Not your style," Harry says. He is sat on the footboard bench in their room, leaning back on the bed, waiting for Lu to exit her closet for good this time and finally be ready to leave. He dusts the arm of his black wool suit jacket folded neatly beside him.

Each time she comes out with the latest adjustment to her attire, she finds something else that isn't quite right and slinks back to her closet to fix it.

"Is this about Olivia again? Look, I trust Rochelle; she's the best assistant in the entire company. Best I've ever worked with. She's always raving about her kids, but especially her Olivia. The girl's got a good head on her, Loubie. Like I said, responsible, adores children—camp counselor for years, a maths and science tutor—and I know I told you the girl's a junior at Harvard, but did I tell you what she's studying there?" Harry says, when Lu asks him to zip up the back of her floor-sweeping lace-panel tulle gown. "Astrophysics! She wants to work at NASA," he says, beaming.

Lu spins around to face him while adjusting the cap sleeves on her dress. "So, basically, Solomon's marrying the new babysitter?"

"Exactly. Maybe even by next week . . ." Harry pauses to take in his wife's final look, hopefully. His giddiness about Solomon and the babysitter is gone as his grin melts into something lustful and wicked. He sits up straighter. "Jesus, Loubie." He rests his hands on the low sides of her hips and softly tugs her into him. "You are resplendent."

This pulls her out of the fidgeting and smoothing of the gown. She rests her open palm along his jaw and looks down at him, so tempted to kiss his soft, waiting lips deeply, push him to his back on the bed gently and press her chest into his with all her brawn and craving. Instead, she must add the finishing touches to her outfit and go to the ridiculous masquerade ball—to try to gather even the tiniest bit of intel about Kastille. If she had it her way, this assignment would be already over. Harry would be protected, unharmed by her action, and none the wiser. They would just be going to a gala, dressed like royalty, ready to dance and drink and dine and laugh, as if everything were good and normal. If she had it her way, they would skip it altogether and instead strip out of these clothes, let the babysitter know they'll be otherwise occupied for the next two hours and to order a pizza for herself and Solomon.

But if Lu truly had it her way, she and her family would still be in Brooklyn, far removed from this company and its expanding chaos, and her box of sin would be burned and trashed, her deceit buried, and ties to The Atlas severed completely.

Lu pulls her head out of the smog of these fantasies, dragging herself back down to the cold reality of the situation. The sooner she can be through with this the better. *Get in, get out, get on with my real life.*

She reconnects with Harry, still staring up at her, his warm eyes like waxing moons. "And you are so British," Lu tells him, teasingly, and takes a short step back from him. "Resplendent? *Bruv . . .*"

"Never mind the cheek, are you ready or what?" Harry says. He swats at her bum as she heads back to her closet.

"Just about. For real this time," she says. "In fact, I'm so almost-ready, you can even put your jacket back on. I'll meet you downstairs in six minutes." Lu had read somewhere years ago that people respond better to specific time increments over generic ones like two, five, or ten minutes. Six minutes implies that one has a thought-out time goal.

"Don't mess about, woman," Harry calls out to her from the bedroom. "I'm timing you."

Lu waits in the farthest corner of her closet, listening for Harry's footsteps to fade. Once he's gone, she hustles back to her secret box of tricks and tools partially covered by her bathrobe. She grabs the last few items that could come in handy tonight. Her Fenty Beauty makeup compact dupe—actually an electromagnetic pulse generator—is stuffed into the cutaway section of her black evening clutch along with her microfiber gloves, the pen camera with Wi-Fi, the mini forensic-grade silicone print casting kit, and a backup-backup burner phone, the one preloaded with spyware and cloning applications. She also grabs Jonathan's flash drive. It's a stretch, but Lu is holding on to the thin idea that an impromptu plan for getting the drive back into his home safe might just present itself at this masquerade ball. She is about to close up the burn box and leave when, on second thought, she reaches back inside and pulls out the once treasured vintage pilot watch and tosses it into the bag on top of her regular lipstick and cell phone before closing up the box and stowing it properly.

She collects the black Venetian masks—his a sleek gladiator style, hers with shimmering gold glitter by the eyes—and stops by the giant mirror for last looks. The dress still fits her perfectly—a ten-year-old custom masterpiece from then-emerging designer Rina Ramsay, whose first atelier was only a few doors down from Lu's studio in Brooklyn. On her feet, classic black patent So Kate red bottoms. She kind of forgot how weirdly comfortable the nearly five-inch heels are—99 percent ankle be damned. All of it has Lu resembling a lavish princess or a celebrity who plays one on TV. She gives her reflection another quick up-down scan, pausing for a beat to stare at the West Indian bangles on her wrist. Though she hasn't worn them in nearly twenty-five years, something about the start of this final assignment for The Atlas is making Lu oddly wistful, launching her unexpectedly back in time to when her life was simple and her future was more than just bright, it was assured.

With just about a minute to spare out of the promised six, Lu moves expeditiously to the island of drawers containing her few accessories and jewelry pieces and pulls out the red gift box Mr. V recently gave her with the new bracelet and stealthy flash drive charm still inside. Lu slaps the glimmering thing onto the same wrist as the bangles and dashes out of the room before she can think better of it. As she rounds the corner right outside of the closet she is halted by Solomon standing there.

"Oh! Sweet pea! What are you—how long have you been there?" Lu says. Seemingly at the sound of her voice, Mylo comes trotting around the corner to join them.

Solomon shrugs. Even with Mylo plopped by his feet, the boy's face is sullen.

"What's happening, you all right?"

Another shrug.

"Honey, you have to use your words so I can understand. Are you not feeling well?" *Not another fever. God, please.* She presses the back of her hand to his forehead. He's fine.

Solomon reaches up and spins Lu's bangle around her wrist. His face brightens a little with recognition. "You're wearing the key bracelets."

Lu's head tilts as a twitch runs through her entire face. *He's been in the box.* She makes a point of keeping her voice leveled while her eyes peer, softly, at her son. "What do you mean?"

"Those bracelets," he says, pointing at them even with Lu trying to hide them behind her gown's full fabric. "If you undo the little bean things on the skinnier bracelet, they connect and make a key."

"How do you know that?"

His expression morphs from slightly gloomy to clearly guilty. "You're gonna be mad."

"No . . . never." Lu stoops down to be in his eyeline. "Tell me."

"OK . . . I wanted to have something to remember our old house in Brooklyn. The doorknob in my room, the one that looks like a globe. I was going to bring it with me here. But I needed a screwdriver to take it off. I couldn't find Dad's yellow toolbox anywhere. Everything was already packed up—almost everything. You said the movers would be there any minute now. So, I went to see if the toolbox was in one of the big boxes in your room. But I never found it. There was just this other box with a lot of stuff inside and then a small red box. That's where the bracelets were . . ."

"What other stuff was in the box?"

"I don't know. Tools, weird-looking ones—definitely no screwdriver. There was also some broken phones and pretend passports in different colors for different countries, and also some fake money in stacks, really straight and stiff. But the bracelets were the coolest thing in there. I just liked how they looked—the scratch marks on the sides, it's kinda like ancient writing or something. And I liked how the beans felt in my fingers. I just kept fiddling with it and then it came apart. I thought I broke it. When I tried to put it back together, it turned into a key!"

"Then what did you do?"

"I got scared. I knew I was going be in trouble," Solomon says, his eyes wide and brows raised to their highest pitch on his forehead. "I just put it back with all the weird tools and phones and fake money. And then I put *that* box in the bigger moving box and ran back to my room hoping you wouldn't notice."

Lu's throat goes bone dry and her struggling gulps get louder, making her ears pop with each hard swallow.

The boy seems to notice the shift in Lu's demeanor. He leans into her, a pronounced fretfulness covering his small face. "I'm sorry, Mom. I know that was bad and hiding it was even worse. I know better, I do."

Lu gives him a smile, though it is weak and quivering at the corners, and runs her hand from the top of his close-cropped curly Afro down the side of his face, cupping his jaw and chin in her palm, though it's starting to get clammy. "It's OK, sweet pea, but I need to ask a favor of you. Just like with my friend's shiny necklace"—she whispers the last two words—"I need us to keep this between us. That box has a lot of Mom's old stuff from another time. A time that I don't like to think about a lot, so I put it all in the box to help me put it out of mind."

"Like when Dad put that plant over the big black burn stain that he made on the chopping block island with the crazy hot pot lid in the old kitchen?"

Lu forces a chuckle; it sprays from her mouth like a mist as she uses the wall to pull herself up to standing. "Yes, just like that." She can hear Harry's footsteps, heavy even in socks, approaching. And by the way that Solomon's ears pitch behind him, he hears it too.

Harry pops his head in, raising his hand up and looking down at his watch with exaggeration. "Loubie, does six minutes mean something different in America?" He stretches the same arm over to palm the back of Solomon's head. "Ah, Boxer, are you the one keeping your mum stalled here?"

Solomon turns to look up at his father. "No, we're talking about her—" Lu's eyes flicker at the child ever slightly, but somehow he receives the transmission and interprets exactly what she means. ". . . about her dress and how beautiful she looks tonight for the Halloween party."

"It's a masquerade ball, big man," Harry says, laughing. "But I suppose we are in costume, and Halloween's just 'round the corner, innit? You're not all that wrong." He playfully pulls Solomon back into him for an embrace. "Lu, really now, are you ready to go? Or shall I just change into the ol' PJs, call it a night?"

Still rendered speechless by the perceptiveness of an eight-year-old, it takes Lu a breath to untangle her words. She finds her snark somehow and pulls out a Roadman accent to properly tease Harry. "Don't rush the peng, bruv. Especially if mandem want me to come through looking fresh still, yeah? 'Low it, bruv. Calm."

"Please don't start that." Harry laughs and shakes his head. "Do you think you can quit the *jokes ting, bruv*, and focus on getting out the door in the next two minutes?"

"Indeed. I believe in me."

"I do too, Mom!"

She rests her hand on Solomon's cheek again, re-centering herself. "All right, funny guy. We're going to head out. You're going to be good to Olivia . . . not a suggestion, my man."

"Yeah," he says, smiling up at her. "I'm going to wait up for you tonight. Not a suggestion, my lady!"

"Well, we'll see what Mylo says about that plan." Lu kisses his forehead and then gently wipes away the red lipstick mark with her thumb. "We'll be sure to take lots of good pics."

This settles the boy's expression. His sweetness returns as he sails a wide smile at his father, who turns to lead the way out. As they round the corner from the bedroom, moving in a near straight line across the landing toward the staircase, Solomon falls back to walk close by his mother's side. Lu feels him looking up at her and she drops her head to meet his twinkling gaze.

"I know you're going to have a good night, my sweet potato," she says.

"You will too, my broccoli," Solomon replies, and runs a single finger halfway around the thinner bangle on Lu's wrist. He notices the new bracelet slung between the West Indian bangles; his smooth brows knit together as he narrows his eyes at the unique lock charm on the wrap chain. His frown unfurls as his eyes glide up to Lu's once again, but now with an added glint of recognition—or maybe it's suspicion. He smiles and takes that same finger that had been tracing the bangle's curve and brings it to the center of his lips. *Shh.* A nod and knowing look follow, a tacit agreement between mother and son.

He can see her, clearly, and is assuring her that, although he knows secrets are not safe, hers will be, with him. And she, in turn, sees him, but in a light too intense for the moment. Her vision, temporarily clouded by floaters, flashes of herself reflected in him; those same parts—astute, keenly observant, a talent for stealth—that Mr. V had spotted in Lu when she was barely out of childhood herself.

She had been living under Mr. V's roof again—this time at the age of majority, according to the state of New York. Barely four months into it, he had asked her to accompany him on "an excursion," he had said. Her yes came fast and with alacrity. The trip was to the Metropolitan Museum of Art, and for it Lu was gifted a stylish but subdued all-black outfit, complete with a French beret. She was also given succinct instructions to purloin a small glimmering brooch on display there. But she didn't take it. For young Lu, having had only seen the brooch once in a catalogue, recognized that the gemmed pin beneath the glass display at the Met was a fake. This would earn Lu her first success and an eager invitation to join The Atlas.

Although Solomon has always been wise for his young years, right now he's moved beyond even that to a liminal state that Lu cannot process. She remains shaken by the very real possibility that genetics have loaded the gun and the boy has inherited her strange talent for stealth and deception. Now, she must do everything in her power to make sure that his environment doesn't pull the trigger.

CHAPTER TWENTY

Majestic. The single word echoes in Lu's head as she and Harry approach the lit-up Marwood Manor, one of four mansions spread across the illustrious and historic Strathmore Estate. It looks like something preserved from the Gilded Age. The Tudor-style castle, with its granite-and-limestone exterior and forty rooms inside, once served as the summer residence for renowned mining heir and art collector Benedict Arthur Strathmore and his family. Today, the fifty-thousand-square-foot, three-story mansion is Partridge Hollow's premier event space.

The slow drive through the main gates and the couple's even slower walk up the short steps to the carved wooden door leaves Lu's mouth ajar. Even standing in the center of the fifty-foot-tall entry foyer with the vaulted ceilings snatches Lu's breath clean away. So awed, her head on a swivel, she doesn't even hear Harry's question the first time.

"I said, do you want me to see if I can find someone to make you some tea and meet you in the ballroom with it? Your teeth are practically chattering," Harry says.

"I'm fine," she says.

"Maybe we should get you something to eat, then. I spot some people with trays moving into the ballroom. I can grab something for you while you check the coats . . ."

"Really. I'm good, H," she says, but this is nowhere near true. That Solomon's been inside the box has her deeply rattled. He's noticing things and asking pointed questions—the necklace, Codename Celeste, the bangles, her odd middle-of-the-night dog walk—and his heightened senses are evolving by the day. And Lu can't do anything to slow it down.

Harry doesn't buy it. He signals for a young man working the event to come over and hands him their two coats along with a crisply folded twenty-dollar bill. "Appreciate you," he tells the worker before guiding Lu away from the snaking line near the walnut-paneled library and toward the ballroom. "We are getting some food in you this minute," Harry tells her.

Inside the grand ballroom, even after being practically force-fed rosemary marinated feta cubes and deviled egg crisps by her husband, Lu's stomach has hardly settled. Still, she takes a long beat to admire the palatial room. As expected, every fine detail is pristine. It feels as if they are standing in the middle of an enchanted fairy tale and any minute now the chandeliers might animate and break into a rousing, rhyming musical number.

Harry gently runs his hand along her bare arm. "Darling, you are freezing. Gooseflesh all up and down. Come here." He starts unbuttoning his suit jacket.

Lu stops him. "I'll warm up once we start moving around. Promise."

"I suppose if you get desperate and you're absolutely frozen, you could always tuck into one of those *capes* the men in the coat check line were wearing," he says, his mask covering half of his snickering expression.

"Proudly in their *Eyes Wide Shut* era." She wants to appear light and playful, but her insides are swirling and her mask is scratchy and irritating her face. She's just trying not to gnash her teeth. She scans the bustling space, casually keeping track of the main players.

On the other side of the room, Didi, wearing a metallic strapless column gown, seems busy if not overwhelmed. She is talking *at* two women dressed in black uniforms, both gripping tablets and nodding along to whatever Didi is dictating to them.

Standing near that trio at a high table, sipping from champagne flutes, are the Blooms. This is first time Lu is seeing Evangeline in the flesh. She's much prettier in person than in any of the photos of her online. Unfortunately, her white, high-neck, sleeveless silk gown is surprisingly unflattering, and paired with her bad updo, the usually chic notable is rendered plain and matronly. Ward wears a black tux and a simple dark mask that obscures his eyes, but his head keeps turning like an old-school sprinkler, looking over his shoulder to sneak glances at Calista, a vision in white. Her stretch-sable gown with a deep plunging bodice and high side slit is arresting, and her gold mask with green rhinestones shimmers as she dances, albeit a little clumsily, with Finola. Each bounce and wiggle from Calista draws Ward's lusting eyes to her. Evangeline, her handheld stick mask resting on the table, is also sending Calista looks, but there is nothing soft or swooning about her glare. She is incensed, that is clear, and from the hunched way she's standing, it's possible that she's also uncomfortable in her dress.

Finola looks beautiful as well. More notably, she seems happy, grinning wide, wearing a rich royal-blue organza halter gown and glittery black eye mask with a vibrant side peacock feather. She laughs out loud at something Calista says, tossing her head back and catching Lu's eye in the process. She sends her friend a cute wave. Lu nods and returns a weak smile.

Margot is playfully dragging Cormac away from a small crowd of men—looking like a colony of penguins with their matching masks and near-identical tuxes—talking and laughing almost in unison. Cormac seems all too happy to follow his wife wherever she leads him. His portly posture, fitted mask, and obvious jocularity combine in a way that makes him look like a friendly cartoon owl slowly waddling his way down some magical path. Margot is wearing a strapless crepe gown in a rich chocolate brown and a Venetian mask with gold scrollwork and silver glitter around the eyes. There is not a hair or stitch out of place. The undone version of her from the other day apparently melted away and gone. She slips her arm from Cormac's and says something to him while gesturing at Lu.

She's coming over here. "I'll be right back," Lu whispers quickly to Harry. "Bathroom."

Lu doesn't even know where the closest restrooms are and doesn't bother asking anyone. Maybe if she just waits here by this roped-off section near the darkened hallway, she can catch herself, she figures, and wait out the Margot Tornado.

Leaned against high-polished dark wood wall, she allows herself a few more breaths before starting back toward the main ballroom.

"Hiding or seeking?" a man says.

Lu isn't jolted by the intrusion. For the last month, she's been in a steady state of bracing for what is surely coming next.

She calmly turns around to greet the voice. It's Jonathan, maskless and smirking in his perfectly fit tux like he's the man from U.N.C.L.E.

"What . . . ?"

"Hide-and-seek—which one are you?" He chuckles as he unbuttons his jacket.

"Neither. I'm just minding my business." Lu keeps her expression stern. She's not impressed by him and wants him to know it.

Jonathan raises his left brow slightly and glances down at Lu's middle, grinning as he drags his eyes back up along Lu's torso to her face and slowly reconnects with her stiff glare. The look is dirty and leering and obvious, and she is instantly repulsed and uncomfortable. There's also something frenetic building in his eye. Lu chalks it up to his having probably done a bump in the car before handing the keys to the valet. She holds her stare, unwilling to be the first to blink in this odd game of chicken.

He breaks. "Actually, while I have you," he says, seemingly unphased by Lu's frost and grimace, "I've been meaning to talk to you and H-man. One of my neighbors—Warnock, Jack—mentioned that he saw a woman, Black . . . or *African American* . . . poking around our boxwoods at the side of the house a couple weeks back. He figured it was one of the staff girls out with the dogs or something. I told him we didn't have anyone like that here. Most of the girls working for us are from South America—Colombian, mainly, one or two Brazilians in there." He pauses, tilting his head, and stares at Lu. She makes her most determined effort to keep her expression dispassionate as he talks about his support staff like a can of mixed nuts. "I wanted to bring it to your attention in case you—"

"In case what?" Lu drops all decorum and forged consideration. "In case Harry and I—the only African Americans in this town—might just know who some random *maybe*-Black person your neighbor Jack *maybe* saw slinking around your mansion in the middle of the night is?"

"I didn't say it was the middle of the night . . ."

Lu's stomach drops. "So, now I'm making things up? Look, it's fine. Harry and I know how it goes in these towns."

"Hey, hey—" He reaches for the side of her arm. "It's not like that. Just a heads-up in case you get the *Beacon* text—our little neighborhood watch system—and feel a little concerned about the safety levels here. That's all."

The Beacon? Annabelle didn't mention that, Lu thinks. Neither did Finola. "Well, thanks for the hot tip, then," she tells him.

His smarmy grin returns. "Of course. Guess I'll see you in there," he says, lightly gesturing at the main ballroom beside them. "We'll raise a glass. Toast to friendly neighbors, yes?" He gives Lu a firm nod, then breezes by, making sure to brush his shoulder against hers.

"WHAT IS GOING on? Why are you still covered in goose flesh, Loubie?" Harry says, as he leads his wife into a graceful half twirl on the ballroom floor.

"Might be an allergic reaction to the gold crumbs on those beef tartare bites," Lu says, and melts back into his waiting arms. Although they haven't found the time to do much of it since embarking on parenthood, dancing with Harry is still one of Lu's all-time favorite things. They never practiced it or took any kind of formal lessons; the two were just naturally in sync from their first pairing and continue to be dashing on any and every dance floor, with an enviable delight in each other always on full display.

"Fucking gold crumbs on food! Jesus wept . . ." Harry says, with a snort. "There's spending money, then there's dashing it straight away into the wind."

"And in the cocktai—" Lu's eyes fall on Jonathan standing straight ahead of her across the room, staring. He raises a glass in the air at her and she turns away, pretending not to have seen him, but the idea has already rooted in Lu's brain. Now it's just to carry it out.

"Exactly, and in the cocktails!" Harry finishes the line, shaking his head and chuckling.

"Speaking of . . . I'll get us a couple," she says, tapping his shoulder. "I'll surprise you."

Harry kisses her temple and stays close, his cheek pressed to hers, talking softly in Lu's ear. "After this dance, darling. . . . Thank you for putting up with all of this pomp and piss."

"I'm here with you. All that matters," she says, and means it—mostly.

Harry pulls her body even closer and nuzzles her ear. It tickles, as intended, and Lu gives him a light, teasing nudge with her shoulder. Harry separates from Lu and sends her off on another effortless turn, their corresponding arms stretched and fingertips kissing. As Lu coils back to him, she allows the buzzy charm of the moment to take over. A giggle springs from her open-mouth grin and she lets the heaviness that is pressing down on her slide off her shoulders—if just for a breath—as she quicksteps and twirls with her loving man across the stately ballroom.

"You OK?" Harry says, craning his neck back to look at her face.

"Yeah . . . just catching my breath, dancing machine." She slides off her mask. "I'll get us some punch."

"Or perhaps grab yourself some Bengay to rub on those rickety knees, milady."

"Look who's talking, oldster," Lu says, with a light, playful punch to Harry's shoulder, before heading off to the champagne tower by the bar near where Jonathan stands.

As Lu gets closer to the still-maskless Jonathan, his smile broadens. "I feel like we need a take two," she says and uses her free hand against her loaded clutch as a pretend clapperboard.

"Mmm," he offers, still grinning.

"My apologies. I sometimes get a little overwhelmed around crowds of virtual strangers."

"I get it," Jonathan says, with an indulgent bow of his head.

"Do you, though?" Lu gives him a teasing look.

"No, not really," he says, chuckling. "I'm just glad your mood has improved."

"Thanks for the understanding. Now, what about that friendly neighbor toast?"

"Ah, yes, let's do it. What can I get you?"

"And Harry . . . can't forget H-man," she says.

"Of course. I love H-man." He shoots a squinting glance at Harry across the way, chatting with a small group. "So, two glasses of . . . ?"

"What are you having?" Lu says, jutting her chin toward Jonathan's rocks glass with a neat, heavy pour of caramel-colored liquid.

"This here is off-menu," he says, sounding almost bashful. "From my private batch." Jonathan opens the left side of his tux jacket and flashes a monogrammed, leather-wrapped glass flask tucked only partly inside his inner pocket. "Didi hates that I sneak in my own stash—even though she gave me the fucking flask to begin with." He shakes his head and it seems to chase away the annoyance that was beginning to rush in. "Any interest?"

Though Lu planned to stay sober tonight, only a few performative sips of ginger ale poured into a flute—a discreet favor done by a gracious waiter—she happily accepts Jonathan's offer. "Definitely!"

"I'll scare up a couple glasses at the bar and—"

"And I'll wait here, with your flask," Lu says, adding quickly, "I've been looking for one for Harry, and that one is perfect."

"Uh . . . sure." He furtively pulls it out, laying the navy-blue leather thing on the side of Lu's evening clutch in her cupped palms. "Just don't—"

"Didi won't know a thing," Lu says, her smile sweet and steady. "Trust me."

"Us being the only two people here not wearing masks, I kinda trust you already."

Jonathan barely takes three clean steps away before Lu gets to work. In one swift but graceful move, she snatches a cloth napkin from a passing server's tray and slides behind the impressive champagne tower. She loosely swaddles the flask in the napkin, tucking it between her breast and armpit, while also reaching into her clutch for the fingerprint kit. With one hand, she carefully peels off a clear silicone strip and wraps it in a small semi-circle around the part of the flask peeking out from its cloth napkin sheath. She begins her silent timer—*one Mississippi, two Mississippi*—as the print sets, then peeks between the stacked flutes of the tower to track, as she best she can, Jonathan . . . who is on his way back, walking at a fast clip. To Lu's dismay, not a single Kastille striver has slowed him, hoping to bend his ear.

Just one ass-kisser, please.

"Hey, who are we hiding from?" Finola says, leaning too close to Lu's ear.

Despite the startle, Lu makes quick work of removing the duped print from the flask and stuffing all evidence of this sin into her bag. "Clearly my hiding spot is a bust," Lu says, smiling.

"Wait." Finola glances down at the flask in Lu's hand, reading the monogram. "That's Jonathan Killigrew's. Why do you have that?"

"Well, don't tell Didi, but he's giving Harry and me a sample of his—"

A boom of high-pitched shouting cuts Lu off. The clamor is coming from the other end of the ballroom. Lu and Finola hustle toward the tumult. They arrive to find Calista and Evangeline yelling in each other's faces. Didi, looking flushed and panicked, is beside them trying to pull Evangeline—the more aggressive of the two friends—away. Margot, off to the side, is tucked behind Cormac, who looks to be shielding his wife from the melee. While Ward is nowhere to be found, Jonathan swoops in, pushing through the sloppy circle of guests watching the fight in stunned silence, and gets right in the middle of the two women. He doesn't even notice that he roughly elbowed his own wife in the gut in the process.

"You knew the rules!" Evangeline shrieks, trying to claw out of Jonathan's soft hold. "We were all clear about the rules!"

"We didn't plan this," Calista says, sniveling, her eye makeup a smudged mess. She's halfway falling out of her sexy gown. "You have to believe that. We didn't mean to hurt—"

"Don't you dare! You didn't want to hurt me? What part of falling in love with my fucking husband wouldn't hurt me, you fat bitch!"

Audible gasps followed by a wave of whispers engulf the room. The onlooking crowd has quadrupled in size.

Didi's eyes are as wide as her open mouth. Her arms fall away from embracing her so-called best friend. "Don't do this," she hisses. "Not here."

Calista stuffs her partially exposed breast back inside her gown. "And to think I told Ward that you'd try to understand," she says. "But he knew you're way too heartless, frigid, obnoxious, and self-seeking to understand shit!"

The hum of hard breaths rises and joins with the growing chatter, expanding into a full rumble of loud opinions and let-loose judgments. Even Jonathan looks bowled over by the murky stew that has just been spilled.

Lu scans the crowd, looking for Harry. Nothing. Just a sea of white men in black tuxes, standing next to their partners, nearly all masks off.

Evangeline appears as if she were just slapped across the face.

"Calista!" Didi barks, clutching at her stomach, pained from either Jonathan's elbow or the ugly turn of this night or both.

"What? Am I lying?" Calista says, gawking at Didi. "You're going to pretend that you don't think your 'best friend' is a stone-cold bitch?"

"And you're an evil cunt!" Evangeline spits back at Calista.

"Evangeline!" Didi shouts, and claps her hands loudly like a school teacher. "What's wrong with you? Why would you do this?!"

"Oh, my God," Finola whispers to Lu, leaning so close she could nibble her ear. "She means, why would you do this to *me*.

Whoa. That is fucked up." Finola is still sporting her Venetian mask, but her eyes remain glued to the live stage play before them.

Finally, a gaggle of men file in, rejoining the happenings inside. Ward steps in first, a burnt-out cigar stub jutting out from his puckered lips. The room drops silent with all eyes on him.

Calista, sobbing now, is the first to speak. "I'm sorry, Ward. It's a mess." She storms out.

"What the hell happened?" Ward says, and moves to go after her, but Cormac shakes his head and puts his arm up to gently block him.

"You were going to chase after her? Really, Ward? *Really?*" Evangeline says. The bitterness and hurt in her voice swirl together and push Ward backward like an angry gale.

"Evangeline, it's not . . . we didn't . . ." Ward stammers, looking between his wife and, strangely, Harry standing next to him.

The room becomes a tennis match, a Grand Slam, with everyone's head vacillating between Evangeline at the baseline and Ward scrambling all over the box.

"I—I—what—this is . . . look, we have rules," a bumbling Ward says halfway under his breath as he starts over to Evangeline.

The murmuring starts rising again. Lu gives Harry an unmistakable "these people crazy" look and he responds by mouthing the words, *Let's go!*

She nods energetically and starts over Harry's way. The idea to leave is not exclusive to the Barlows; other couples are making their exit, too, using whatever door is closest.

"Let's all take a deep breath," Jonathan bellows to those still lingering. "I think we need a deep breath here."

Margot rushes over to Lu, cutting the woman's path to Harry. Her arms are out, the hug fully loaded and inescapable. Lu acquiesces.

"Sorry about all this, Barlow," Margot says, quietly, as they embrace. "Your first Secret Garden Gala turned into the Secret Garden of Sneaky Shit."

"Good title for a thriller," Lu says.

"Always hilarious, even in the face of crazy drama." Margot laughs.

"FKT—foster kid tactic," Lu says, surprised at how easily this truth slipped out. When it comes to a question of background and family history, Lu finds a way to skirt the topic or, when pressed, create a hazy, shapeless fiction that fades just as easily as she made it appear. A magic trick she'd pull out of her hat, especially in her early twenties. Back then, Lu was building a reputation for herself at The Atlas, traveling the world, embarking on the unthinkable heist and getting away clean, and thus could be anyone she damn well pleased. But now, standing in the middle of a ballroom turned circus act, the urge to share some truths about her real life eclipses her usual sagacious approach. Lu allows herself to loosen at least the top button to the vest that holds everything tight against her chest.

Margot's face sinks into pity, and she takes easy steps over to Lu like a teen boy on TV preparing to take his shot at kissing *the* girl. "Oh, my God, I didn't know you were a—"

"It's fine," Lu says. "Came away with a carbon steel spirit and wit sharper than a katana, so I'm good. I landed on the bright side."

"You are *extraordinary.* Seriously." Margot beams. "Let's talk more tomorrow, OK?" She squeezes Lu's arm and returns to a waiting Cormac.

Lu's quickened walk toward Harry is interrupted once more, this time by Finola. Her new habit of sidling up to Lu's ear like a hissing snake is already the most annoying thing about her.

"Wild! Can you believe this?" Finola says, walking alongside Lu. She sends a friendly wave at Harry, who is now holding his wife's coat, clearly ready to exit this colosseum.

"I don't even know what to say about this Jerry Springer muddle."

"Right? Very Jerry Springer," Finola says. "I don't think the PH2 is going to ever recover. Didi's absolutely destroyed. Look at her."

Lu sneaks a glance. In addition to Evangeline and Didi, there are a handful of other women crying too. Solidarity tears, perhaps, Lu thinks. She notices Jonathan at the same time he spots her. He's patting his wife's back like she's a baby who needs to burp. He sends a what-are-you-gonna-do shrug over to Lu.

"What's the deal with you and Jonathan?" Finola says. "He's giving you a *look.*"

Jesus. Don't start. "I ended up stuck holding his precious booze," Lu says, dryly. She wags the flask in his eyeline. "He probably thinks I'm going to steal it. He already warned us about Black people *lurking in the night.*"

Finola frowns. "Oh, yeah . . . the *Beacon* thing."

Now she mentions it?

". . . I don't think it's a big deal," Finola continues. "Like I said, it's so safe here—"

"Hey, do you mind giving this back to Jonathan?" Lu hands over the flask, unwilling to take no for an answer. "Harry is anxious to get out of here—me too. A lot to process."

"Of course," Finola says, smiling brightly. "We can debrief tomorrow on a walk."

"Not gonna fall for the banana in the tailpipe this time, lady. These walks are a ruse!"

"No! Not a ruse. Promise." Finola laughs. "I'll call you."

"Sure, Jan."

"Hope you had a good night here—despite everything."

Lu squeezes her loaded clutch against her chest. "Definitely."

CHAPTER TWENTY-ONE

"This was so good," Harry says pouring the leftover fish tea into a deep, round glass food storage container. His sleeves are rolled up and he's wearing one of Lu's floral aprons as he usually does for his kitchen cleanup duty, with a tea towel draped over his shoulder. "What inspired you to even make it? Been a long time. Too long."

This is true. Lu has not even so much as thought about the fragrant fish soup in well over a year. The spicy seafood soup, a Jamaican go-to comfort dish, was one of Mr. V's specialties. Traditionally, the light broth loaded with veggies, potatoes, and a mix of shrimp and mild white fish can take several hours to prepare, but Mr. V taught teenage Lu how to make a quicker, less spicy version, and the two would occasionally dine on it on particularly wintery Sundays. As to why Lu decided to make it for her family tonight, she's not quite sure. Could be the choppy wind that picked up force on this fall evening that made her think of the instant "chest warmer," as Mr. V would call it. Or maybe her old mentor figured out a way to enter through the back door of her thoughts, sneak up on her, and be slow to leave. Either way, the dish went down well, and making good food for Harry and Solomon always warms her chest.

"Glad you liked it," Lu says, and wipes down the countertop. "Moreover, I'm really glad Solomon liked it."

"He didn't even blink twice about it being called *fish tea*. Think Boxer's starting to develop his palate." He laughs. "Speaking of discerning tastes, you get a look at the book he's reading? *Operation Midnight: A Spy in Moscow*. It was curled up under the covers with him."

"Oh . . . ?" Lu stalls, putting away the broom in the hall closet, her back turned to Harry as she steadies her breath. "I didn't see any books when I tucked him in."

"Yeah, got it at the school library, judging from the stamps. So, guess it's age appropriate . . . ? But then that boy's always reading beyond his years. Maybe he's developing a new interest in spies and double agents. Maybe now I can get him to watch some Bond films with me. Ha! He also borrowed a thick space atlas. More up his lane, I'd say—"

Harry's phone, usually kept on silent deep in his work bag stashed in the den, lets out a series of loud chimes. Internal chat notifications. It startles them both, and he takes quick steps over to it. Meanwhile, Lu moves to the edge of the kitchen and closer to the den with a damp cloth in hand, wiping at an invisible stain on the archway. She can hear Harry cursing under his breath. He storms out and back toward the kitchen, almost catching Lu spying on him.

"These men are trying to cause me a fucking stroke!" Harry says, scrolling and tapping the phone's screen hard as he stomps on by her and starts pacing between the breakfast nook and the back door. "Are my words just worthless bits floating in the ether? The fucking nerve of these blokes. I've told them, this is not the way, man. First and flawed is not the way."

"What's going on?"

He rubs the back of his head and sighs. "Lu . . . I can't . . . Let's just leave it out, all right? I'm sorry for all this heat and fuss. It's all right."

"Jesus! Just tell me what's going on, H. I'm here. Tell me what's got you so pissed. Are they throwing you under the bus or something?"

Harry stops moving and stares out the windows to the yard, still gripping his phone like it's a stone he's ready to pelt out there. "I've told them. It's documented. We can't move forward yet. The code, it's not ready. I've been the lead on this from almost the beginning; I know what I'm talking about! Kastille has the opportunity to do something truly revolutionary, but if we rush through, we end up being the next Theranos. I can't stand by and let that happen."

"What are you going to do?" Lu doesn't go to him to hug or comfort or calm. She knows that when Harry's like this, prickly and indignant, what he needs most is space.

"I have to process my next steps. Sort this out in my head," he says, and roughly removes the apron, tossing it on the back of the nearest chair. "Gonna have a hot shower and then bed. I've got to come at this fresh and leveled. You OK to lock up?"

"Of course. Do your thing."

"I don't mean to get you tangled in all this. I'm sorry to bring it home." Harry pats his hand over his heart as he sends Lu a soft apologetic look. "Good night, love."

"Good night."

Lu joins Harry in bed shortly after finishing the cleanup. He's turned away from her and on the very edge of his side of their king size, dead to the world save for some light snoring. On his nightstand rests one of their crystal rocks glasses with a giant, clear ice cube halfway melted into the last sip of his brown liquor. *At least he remembered to use a coaster,* she thinks. She tips out of bed, walks around to his side, and searches the rest of the bedside table for his phone, but it's not there. It's just the glass, his watch, and a stress ball shaped like the Greek evil eye—a Secret Santa gift he received from Niko Pateras, his friend and former colleague at the old job where he first started working on the nanocode with a small team. She's about to lean in and kiss him, but stops short when she spots his ultraslim laptop wedged halfway under his pillow. Not Harry's style. He rarely brings home his laptop, but here it is, in their bed. Lu silently curses at the ceiling, then does the thing she doesn't want to do but can't afford not to: eases the laptop out from under him and slinks off to her closet.

With his usual passcodes—Solomon's birthday and their wedding anniversary written out in words—not flying, Lu is now left with no choice but to try using some tools from the box. Problem. For one, the bulk of her tools are made for cracking into safes, doors, locks, not laptops. The other hitch is simple but deep: This is Harry. She never imagined a day where she would be trying to break into her husband's anything.

"Lu?" says Harry, voice groggy.

She spins around on the floor, sliding the opened box behind a pair of flopped-over boots. Harry is standing at the closet's edge; his pajama bottoms are twisted and he's slightly wobbling in place. "Oh, hon, did I wake you?" Lu pops up, kicks the box farther behind the boots, and hustles over to him in the dim. She drapes as much of herself as possible over the squinting man.

"What are you doing in there in the dark?" he whispers.

Lu tries to gently turn him around and guide him back to bed. "It's Finola—*again*," she says with an exasperated sigh. "She's still in London visiting Matty and they got into an argument." The first part of this is true. Finola canceled their most recent walk-and-talk, as predicted, but her reasons this time were at least justifiable. Her absentee husband, Matthew Grey, was in London on an unexpected work trip. Five days alone with her man, whom she basically only sees on Zoom screens, got an immediate "all good" text from Lu.

Harry follows Lu to the bed as if pulled by a string through a cloud. He might not even realize he's awake, Lu hopes, as she attempts to tuck him in. "But . . ." He rolls his head to look right at her now. "Why do you have my laptop?"

Shit. "Oh, that . . . you fell asleep on it, H. Which is . . . like, what the hell, oldster?"

"Did I?"

"Yep. I was just moving it downstairs when Finola pinged me." Lu again pulls the thick covers up over him, rolling him to his side. She can't bring herself to look in his face any longer.

"Right . . . thanks, dove. Tell Finola to work it out, yeah? Come back to bed," he grumbles. "And leave your phone downstairs."

"Of course," Lu whispers and slips back into the closet to reset the box and grab the laptop. She continues her tip-toe all the way downstairs, trying to make as little noise as possible despite her heart pounding in her ears. By the time she reaches the living room, where she plans to dump the laptop, Lu is a trembling mess. She's about to follow Harry's directive and actually leave her phone on the table too when it buzzes. *If this is Finola . . .*

It's not. Nor is it an area code or number she recognizes.

"Yes?" she whispers sharply into the phone.

"It's me," Mr. V says. "We need to meet. It's important."

"When?"

"Right away."

"I . . . can't do that. I'm busy."

"You must," he says. "I'll respect your wishes and not come to the house. Meet me by the beach, at the food stand. You must come. No delay."

"Hello? *Hello?*" Lu knows he hung up, but doesn't want to believe it. Still, she maps out her quickest route to the local beach on foot.

Back in her closet, she gets dressed in her skulking uniform to the sound of Harry snoring. She loads her small backpack with an array of tools, just in case, and eases out of the bedroom, sliding in socked feet down the hall. She debates for a slip of a moment on whether to check on Solomon before she goes, make sure he's as sound asleep as his father. And if he's not? A chance Lu can't afford to take. Instead, she cracks the boy's bedroom door open but doesn't go inside. With her eyes closed and head bowed, she listens to his low-pitched light wheezing for a beat, then pulls his door closed, gently, and continues creeping toward the stairs to begin her hustle over to the beach, bracing for what new nonsense she'll find there.

CHAPTER TWENTY-TWO

Racing across the six consecutive, shadowy tennis courts toward the beachy area of the famous park, Lu's mind is struggling to focus. What more could this man want from her? What new, impossible add-on will The Atlas introduce to this already impossible assignment? The sweat is making her leather gloves feel squishy inside and the rolled-up wool balaclava atop her head isn't helping either.

As she hits the sand, Lu slows her run to a brisk walk with long strides. Despite her internal fire, the chilly night air is causing her cheeks to sting a little from windburn and the tip of her nose is damp. She wipes at it with the back of her gloved hand before reaching into her pocket again for her flashlight. The beach is dark, but the radiant Hunter's Moon offers some assistance. For added good measure, she goes back into the bag for her Taser. People can be weird and unpredictable under a full moon.

Lu stops completely to gather her bearings and sweep the slim torch around her. "So, this is it," she whispers. Harbor Crest. She's never been to the town-operated beach, not properly anyway. She saw it while skimming the "recreation" section of the Partridge Hollow official website back when Harry first talked about the job offer. Lu shakes her head again, this time from fresh anger and affront at how naïve and foolish she had been, believing that the job and move were real, that it was a path to freedom, not an extension of the leash The Atlas has around her neck.

With the next sweep, Lu turns her body along with the flashlight, taking in what she can of the darkened vista. Under normal circumstances—whatever those are—this beach would be the perfect place for a peaceful respite. Somewhere for her to breathe in the heady mix of salt and fresh waters, lulled by the thwack of the tides under the indigo sky. But that doesn't seem to be in the cards for Lu. Not tonight at least.

She continues moving forward as her flashlight picks up a large wood board with a property map and two signs, one above the other, with arrows pointing out the direction of some of the park's features: Buccaneer Bay, the pirate-ship-shaped play-ground, and a fit trail are straight ahead while the bathhouse and Tide & Table are over to her left. Lu picks up her pace, marching toward the concession stand to meet Mr. V as instructed. Even though she knows that he's already there, wait-ing, a curious wave of nerves washes over Lu, like a stark cold shower. Is this a setup? Maybe The Atlas thinks she's come to the end of her rope and it needs to cut her loose. She's been trained to stay ready, always prepared for the unexpected, but there's something else at play tonight—a harbinger she cannot see, but definitely feels, that is walking close behind, ready to pounce on her back and drag her to the ground in a vicious fit.

She spots the rustic sign for Tide & Table just ahead. A deep breath in, a forceful exhale, and Lu is steady, ready.

A swooshing sound, a rustling of fabric, spins Lu around with a start. She whips her light along with her head to the right. It's Mr. V in a dark windbreaker and newsboy cap, leaned against a white wooden lifeguard tower.

"Jesus! What are you doing here?" Lu shouts, gripping both the Taser and flashlight tighter in hand.

"Meeting you," he says, plainly.

"Yeah, but you're supposed to be down *there*." She roughly pokes her light in the direction of the concession stand, wiggling the beam around the now-illuminated Tide & Table sign. They both clock it at the same time, with Mr. V only coughing out a half syllable of caution before Lu quickly cuts the power to her flashlight and lowers her voice. She starts again, stepping in close to him and whispering, "You clearly said to meet you over there."

"But I'm here," he says. "And now so are you. Nothing to fret over, my yout."

"Stop calling me that," Lu snaps. "I'm a grown woman. *Hardback*, as you like to say."

"Hardback yet still acting like a child."

Lu narrows her eyes at him, seething. "The hell's that supposed to mean?"

"There's no time to explain, Twenty-two. I've led you as far as I can. Now, you need to think for your—"

Lu takes a hard step even closer to him. "Here's what I *am* thinking," she barks, spittle from her frozen lips sprays into the biting air. "I think that you will never let me go. The Atlas will never let me be free. And all of this is just a game to you, to them. This was just a scheme, this idea that one last job is all it takes. You hung the glimmer of my freedom over my head like a fucking carrot, and I snapped at it right away."

She's not able to see Mr. V's face all that clearly, but can make out his gloomy stare resting on her. She imagines that he's doing his usual slow blink.

"Hm," he says.

Unsure if that was a groan, a low belch, or actual acknowledgment, Lu is livid. "*Hmm* . . . ? That's what you have to say?!"

"In this world, I believe a man has his word and not much else," he says. "I taught you at least that, Lu. I taught you the virtues of living by a code."

"I'm not up for the goddamn riddles, man." Lu takes a few steps back away from him, exasperated, her head to the blackened heavens. "You want to talk about codes and honor. Look at me." She glares in his direction. "Look at what you've done to me. You've forced me into a horrendous corner, pushing me to betray my husband so I can finally take back my life. What part of the code is that? What about the virtues of honoring my vows to Harry?"

"You're not listening."

"Good Christ!" Lu breaks away from the shelter and shadow of the tower, stomping around in the sand, her voice loud and reckless. "I'm listening, I'm listening! That's all I've ever done, listen to you. But you're not saying *anything*! Just say something real. Something I can use. Something to help me."

"I gave you my word, and you gave me yours," Mr. V says, still cool and even. He moves over to Lu, practically gliding, standing close enough that she can now see his face better. He does not look like himself. More, he does not look well. His face is sallow and his breath metallic. She halfway wishes she could offer him a chair, a bench, a shoulder, something to lean on and rest for a moment. But this makes no sense. This is Vincent King. A mountain in the shape of a man. Lu believes, even now, that he will figure a way to live forever.

She thinks to ask if he's OK but shakes away all glimpses of concern or sympathy. No space for it. Lu is backed against a wall, hindered by time and circumstance. She needs him, still, despite everything. She needs his help to complete the mission if she has any hope of finally walking free.

Lu swallows hard, quickly tempers her gall, and lowers her head, her softened voice aimed at the steel toes of his heavy black boots. "Yes, you gave me your word and I gave you mine. Somehow that still means something, between us."

"Correct. I will hold my end," he says.

"And I will hold mine, sir. It's just . . . Kastille is complicated. There are more tentacles attached to this thing than originally thought. This town, the people, all wrapped up in the web of it too." Lu scoffs. "I've been basically dropped into the middle of *The Real Housewives of the American Psychos* . . ."

"That's not the reason I called you here. You need—"

"I need more time to get into Kastille and do this properly," she says.

She can hear him draw a deep breath. "Denied," Mr. V says.

Lu's face twists into an indignant knot. "Wha—denied? *Denied?* In thirty years, I've never once asked for more time."

"No, you've just taken it," Mr. V says. He sounds like he's in the midst of a yawn—or is that a wince?

"I've never—"

"The Neapolitan piece. The file remained opened for weeks past its contact date."

Lu shakes her head in disbelief, annoyed and huffing loudly. "Are you kidding me? That's because I was in the middle of what I thought was a life-changing move. A move that turned out to be a *setup*! And despite that utter bombshell, I still delivered the piece before the final deadline."

Mr. V comes out of his sleepy lean and zips up his swishy jacket all the way to his chin. At once, he's gone from looking clammy and gray to chilled through and shaky. He's still trying to hold it together, though it seems to be taking every ounce of his energy to do so.

"I can't give you more time because I don't have it. At this point, your only option is to follow through. Now more than ever before, you must keep your word, Twenty-two. It is paramount." He gives her a weak half-nod, turns his body toward the bathhouse and concession stand behind Lu, and begins to push off to walk that way.

In two swift, long steps, Lu is in front of him, blocking his path, her fists clenched, bracing to physically stop this man from moving forward if it comes to it. "You have the power to do whatever the hell you want. You're the inimitable Seven. You *are* the fucking Atlas. You can get me more time, if you wanted to. You just need to want to."

Mr. V stops moving but keeps his face forward, staring off just over Lu's head. He takes a breath; it's labored. And for the first time ever, she sees his shoulders slump down as if a literal ton of bricks were dropped on them. His usually tight jaw is slack and his lips have turned a deep purple hue, almost blue-black. Lu juts her own face forward in the vicinity of his chest for a closer whiff of the tangy odor emanating from inside his zipped-up-tight jacket.

It's perspiration. Again, something Lu has never once smelled on him.

"You of all people should know . . . not everything is as it seems. Your whole life is an illusion," he says, his tone quiet and doleful. He takes another ragged breath and, at last, casts his softened glare down to look right at her. "One would only need to ask your brilliant husband or your darling Solomon. He looks just like you, Lucille. Especially the eyes. I saw it right away."

Hearing her child's name on this man's lips is the tripwire. Realizing that Mr. V has been close enough to Solomon to see his sweet, bright eyes is the dragged boot over the taut line. Lu explodes in Vincent's face, ignoring the twitch pulling at his right cheek, and unloads thirty years of suppressed anger and opposition on him.

"This is my life you're fucking with, you goddamn heartless demon!" she snarls. "My *real* life, not some illusion. How dare you? Everything that I am that is broken and sick and corrupt is because of you. You made me like this. *You* did this!" Lu pounds a fist to her chest. "You knew I hung on your every word, put my life, my entire *being* on the line every fucking time just for an ounce of your approval. You were supposed to protect me, but you killed me. You snatched my life away like it was nothing. You couldn't give a shit how I felt about any of it. And now that I've built something for me, an existence, a family that is all mine, you want to call it an illusion? You want to force me to choose between you and them? The choice is clear, *Vincent.* I am doing this to be done with this."

"You're not listening, girl," he hisses. "You're doing this, seeing it through, in order to save Solomon."

"I already told you," Lu says, her lips curled and voice gathering force from the pit of her burning gut. "Keep my family's name out your fucking mouth!" With the boom of that final word, Lu's balled hands raise up at once—the left still holding the Taser gun tight—and she violently shoves Vincent.

He stumbles backward but remains on his feet—barely. He's staggering, slightly swaying side to side, unable to catch himself, like a discombobulated lush roused from a drunken stupor. Lu, stunned, watches his torso flop from one side to the next. It sounds like he's gasping for air—*no*—it's gurgling, like he's drowning. She drops the Taser. A mix of confusion and horror causes Lu's limbs to lock up. In her mind she's rushing over to him, trying to help, but her body refuses to move. His legs give way and Vincent crumples, flopping flat onto his back in the sand. His raised hand, feebly waving her over, finally unfreezes Lu's body. She races to him. He often cautioned Lu about the dangers of not knowing her own strength, but this . . . this cannot be real.

"Sir?! Sir!" She roughly unzips his jacket to free the space around his neck, get him some air. With her other hand, Lu dumps out her bag beside her, rooting around her work tools, hoping to pull out something, anything that could work double-time to help him with whatever this is. Did the accidental jolt from the Taser induce a heart attack? Did her furious fists dislodge something in his chest wall? Is this that rare heart condition she once read about in *The New Yorker* . . . commotio cordis? A collapsed lung? "You're OK, you're OK . . .

it's—it's—your heart, I think . . . or your lung. I—I—I don't know, I don't know . . ." Lu leans down, putting her ear to his chest, but all she hears are her own panicked exhales and the easy waves lapping on the shore beside them. "Just breathe . . . breathe," she tells him, her face close to his now. Even in the dim of night, she can see that Vincent's eyes are glassy. She pulls away, diving back into the pile from her emptied bag. "I'll call it in," Lu says, rummaging through it all for her Atlas phone. "I know the protocol!"

Though she's never had to call in a medical 9-1-1 on an assignment, Lu had heard rumors about the black-and-red van belonging to Atlas Ventures International, the *dust management company*, that would find its way to you, equipped with all manner of cleaning chemicals, oversize bins, plastic bags and coverings, and long rolls of industrial carpeting.

Vincent shakes his head and wraps his free and working hand around Lu's arm, yanking her back down so that the side of her face is again close to his mouth. He's trying to whisper, but no formed words make it out, just shallow tones and groans.

"Don't talk, it's OK," she says, her voice catching. "Let me call it in. They'll get here. They'll fix it." Vincent shakes his head once more, harder this time, with might and main. "*Yes* . . . they'll come. They have to!" The snot and tears come together, pooling first in the divot under Lu's nose, then sliding over her lips into her mouth hanging ajar. She attempts to quickly wipe her face with her knuckles but only further smears the mess with her stiff, cold glove. Lu looks down at him, her hand resting on his slow-rising barrel chest, and strangely her fear and trembling begin to level off. He's fading. The foggy light in his eyes grows dimmer. She swallows hard and thinks of what to say. Something sincere and meaningful because Lu knows that these are probably the last words they'll share. But what could she say to her mentor turned tormentor? What string of words would carry enough weight to pardon any of this, as he lies on his back, weak and withering, knowing that she put him there? *Sorry? Forgive me?*

Vincent turns his head toward her, his face pallid and slick with sweat. His eyes widen for a handful of seconds, his lips part, and then he says it, loud and clear. "Your word."

A rush of air, a deep sigh, immediately expels from his slack mouth. The tension in his eyelids releases and his inky orbs remain frozen there, looking at nothing. His limbs flop down flat like a wet string mop. And that is it. Vincent King is gone.

Lu, still gripping the special phone, stares at him, unable to breathe or blink. She forces herself to move, stretching her hand and pressing her coupled fingers to his neck, checking for a pulse that she knows is not there. She sits back on her knees, a queasy swirl climbing up her chest and rushing into her throat. Lu turns her head away from his dead body, her mouth opening, ready for the vomit to spew, but instead what comes is a sickened, guttural sob.

"*I'msorryI'msorry*," she chokes out between snorts and sniffles. "I didn't mean it. This is not what I wanted to happen. I'm sorry. I'm—sor—"

Lu's squeezed-shut, tear-soaked eyes fly open and her bobbing head pops up at the realization of two key facts. One, she is sat, crying over a dead body—a *stranger*, as it were—at a public beach in the middle of the night. And two, on a more important, deeper level, she is sat, dressed in head-to-toe black, wearing gloves, and crying over a dead body. She hops up to her feet. There's no way she can call this in now. There are too many unmatched pieces, too many Q's and no A's, and there's no mission code to file. The third realization hits the top of Lu's head like an anvil. She will need to get rid of the body on her own—and do it right this minute.

She shovels the contents of her bag back inside of it along with what feels like a bucket of sand. Next, Lu looks around the immediate surroundings for rocks, driftwood, a random but highly convenient tire and tire iron. Anything with some weight to add to his body when she pushes him out into the mopey waves of Long Island Sound. She knows enough about human biology to count on his lungs filling with water and then the corpse will sink fairly quickly, even without a heavy boulder stuffed into his windbreaker. It's a rushed plan, but she really has no choices here.

Lu reaches into the man's coat and pant pockets, searching for any identifying pieces. But all he's carrying is a thin phone that she stuffs into her tote along with her own. She removes her coat as well as anything else on her person—keys, lip balm, fountain pen, even the watch—that could possibly become loose, unfastened, or otherwise fall from her pockets while she's dragging the corpse to the shore. *Leave no crumbs*, Lu reminds herself. She stashes the bulging backpack beside the wide leg of the lifeguard tower, kicking a little sand over it as camouflage. Lu pushes up the sleeve on her left arm and is about to do the same to the right, when she distinctly hears rustling coming from the direction of the bathhouse behind her. In one clean motion, Lu drags her ski mask over her face and lunges for the backpack. Her fight or flight reflex ignited, Lu snaps up like a track star out of the blocks, ready to bolt . . . until a familiar voice—though shrill and frightened—calls out.

"*Lu?* What are you doing out here?" Finola squawks. "What is that—oh, my God!" she screams at the sight of Vincent's body.

Lu spins around, making sure to first free her face from the mask, quickly sliding the soaked thing down the waistband of the back of her pants. She raises both hands next, palms exposed, and speaks to her friend, slow and steady. "OK, hear me out . . . this is not how it looks."

CHAPTER TWENTY-THREE

"Is that man . . . *dead*?" Finola yelps, craning her neck around Lu to get an unobstructed look at Vincent. "Is he . . . ? Is he dead? Oh, my God! Jesus, Mary, and Joseph!" Her face is red and painted in terror. "We have to call the—did you find him like this? Oh, my Godddd!" She claps her gloved hand over her mouth, muffling her coughing sobs.

"*Shh . . . shh* . . . it's OK, it's OK." Lu eases closer to her, like a zookeeper approaching a chimpanzee outside of its enclosure. "Let's just take a breath . . . let's take a *deep* breath, Finola, OK?" Lu moves her hands slowly toward Finola to rest them on her trembling shoulders to ground her, not shake her, as she wails like it's an Italian funeral.

"Holy fuck! What happened? How did this happen? Did he . . . attack you?" she cries.

Lu slings an arm around Finola and gently angles her away from the scene, slowly leading her toward the bathhouse again. With each hiccup Finola utters, Lu pats her shoulder, adding a soft and comforting *shush*. When the two women reach the closest bench, Lu sets Finola down to sit. She, on the other hand, needs to keep moving in order to kick up a story that is halfway believable that might just stall the unraveled woman from calling the police. But Finola's hysterics are wildly distracting. If she can talk her way out of this one, Lu reasons, she'll buy herself a thick-ass cheeseburger and a Birkin.

"What happened? Who is that? Who is that man?" Finola manages to say. "I can't believe this! Where did he come from? We should call Harry or the police or something!"

Lu stops her quick-step pacing long enough to say, in her most calm and reassuring voice, "Slow down. I can explain."

This does nothing to calm or reassure Finola as she breaks into a fresh sob, throwing her hands over her face again and shaking. Lu stares at the top of her bowed head, wishing she could see what's going on inside the woman's brain, try to forestall her next move, especially if it's calling the police. It's then that she notices Finola's black leather gloves for the first time. They are near identical to her own.

As Lu takes a small step closer to her, peering at the gloves to gather more detail, another thought arrives, landing in her already frantic mind with a heavy thud: Finola's supposed to be in London. How is she just showing up here now, out of nowhere, on the beach alone in the middle of the night? Before the odd observations can fully unfurl, Lu notices something else. Finola's sniveling, it sounds different, it's changed. It almost seems like—

Finola's sobs melt completely into an undeniable chuckle. She peels away her hand and raises her head to reveal a new countenance, cold and devilish. It's still blushed, but she is undoubtedly laughing.

Lu's face crumples up. She goes to speak, but not even a stuttered syllable makes it out.

"I would love to hear how you explain this one, Twenty-two," Finola says after a giddy sigh. Her American accent has fallen away, replaced by a strange and melodic Dublin cadence. She leans back into the bench, her posture cocksure and relaxed. "You're good. I mean, really fuckin' good. I'm honestly kind of starstruck, so . . . definitely want to hear how you work your way out of this." This New Finola tilts her head, gesturing roughly at Mr. V's dead body. "Oh, and don't worry; it weren't your big, angry shove that did him. His lungs were done; they took him. Ah, that's not all the true. I should come clean: It was the fizzy drink and Nexatrin that I put *in* his lungs that killed him. But potato, *potahto*—he's dead either way, right? Right."

"What the fuc—you're working for them?"

"I prefer to say *with*. I've got an enviable collaborative spirit, as my mentor put it."

"Who are you?"

"Come on, Lu. That information is highly classified," Finola says. "You know that." She claps her hands together. "Ah! I'll throw you a little something, since I do honestly like you. Just a few bits and then we're on to the next."

Lu, aghast, stares at this new character—this alien—sitting before her, unable to properly communicate with it beyond wide-eyed blinks.

"Jesus, the puss on you. Look like you're watchin' a ghost, Lu," Finola says, grinning easy. "All right. Here's the quick. Maybe it can quiet your spinnin' brain for a minute. I've been here, in position for a year, waitin' for you. Do you know how much shite I had to eat for a solid year from those four clueless cunts just so that they would trust me and, by extension, trust you when you got here?" she scoffs. "Work grumbles, *amirite*? Anyhows, essentially, I'm with a new-ish department at The Atlas. Call it People Management. Making sure folks do as instructed, and in a timely manner."

"What, so, like, deadly HR?"

"Uh . . . you know what? Yeah. That's kind of it." Finola leans over and reaches into the pocket of her long belted trench coat. Lu flinches, but it's unwarranted. Instead of a weapon, the petite woman pulls out a sleek, shimmering vape pen. Lu takes a beat to regard her, head to toe, trying to figure out how she missed this. How she allowed herself to be stabbed, slowly and surely, in the back by this woman earmarked to be a potential true friend.

"Is Matty working for them too?"

"Oh, dear. There is no Matty. Not really. There's a man who gets paid to sometimes come 'round wearing a wedding band, but there's nothing real there."

"What . . . are your kids real?"

"Yeah . . . well, by surrogate. But I'm raising 'em as their proper Mam. I do sometimes wish they were fake, if I'm honest," Finola says, with a coy shrug and slight grimace. "But that's enough of all that." She hits the vape and follows that with a long exhale, giving Lu a slow, sweeping look. "Do you know what they call you out in the field?" Finola says. "Black Viper. I know, on the nose and a tad problematic, but it's fittin'. Sleek as a snake, clean as a whistle on jobs—in and out, pristine. No blood, no blunders. I've been hearin' about you for ages, Lu. What is it—you came on the scene as a teenager, fresh out of secondary school or something mad like that?" Finola chuckles, shaking her head. "And he brought you in, right?" She points over to the corpse.

"The fuck is wrong with you people?" Lu squawks. She glances ever briefly at the body. "Why did you do him? He's top brass."

"Unlike you, hon, I do as I'm told. I don't ask follow-ups. I am here to—how do they say it?—bat cleanup. No, wait, that's not right. I'm a *closer*, yeah, I think that's right. Jesus, I never fully understood feckin' baseball; I was trying to stretch there. Point is, I am here to make sure the door gets closed on this project and that it's done on time. Which is a perfect lead-in to the next matter." Finola slaps her thighs and pops up to standing, the vape momentarily clenched between her teeth. "Time. You came here to ask him for more of it and he denied you because he didn't have any to give. You stalled long enough and your oul man was stalling for you further. There's no space for that. Not anymore."

A soft pang hits Lu's chest at the mention of Mr. V and his trying to help her from behind the scenes. Like always. Hard shell, soft underbelly, with a tucked-away, warm, oversize heart. And now, just a cold cadaver laid flat on the soggy sand. "No one is stalling," Lu snaps. "I work how I work. I'm *Black Viper*, or whatever the fuck. I don't need a coach from the sidelines." Another stab in her chest, this one sharper, comes from just looking at Finola. All the curious little mysteries about her coming together at once as clues. Albeit much too late.

"Well, hon, you'll need to work faster," Finola says. "Keep your eyes on the clock, because know that there are a lot of eyes on you."

"How many others like you are here?"

"Like *us*, you mean," Finola says, smirking. "I'm the only embedded. Everyone else here is gen pop. That much I can share with you. But you know how they work. They don't need a whole team clocking your every move. They're more . . . how do you call it? They're like an omniscient narrator in your favorite story. For you, this one reads more like a horror, *amirite*?"

Lu scoffs. "That's the realest thing you've said in this whole thing. Fucking nightmare." The reality behind this grisly, trust-no-one revelation bores through Lu's gut like a hot poker. Finola says there are no other plants in Partridge Hollow, but that too could be a lie. Another artful head fake. The last-ditch escape plan that Lu never wanted to consider is bubbling to the surface as a bleak but honest refrain begins to sound off in her mind.

"I like this, us commiseratin' like oul comrades, but we gotta cut it. Once again, you've gotta work faster here. First order? Getting rid of *that*." Finola points her a stiff finger gun over at Vincent's body. "Not to sound like a *coach from the sidelines*, but you best think of something fast to fix your fixer. Calling this in is not an option. I mean, maybe you could say this whole thing falls under the death by misadventure category . . . ah, nah. It's too tangled for that, to be perfectly honest."

"*Death by misadven*—you killed him, you fucking sociopath!"

"If we want to be technical, this has nothing to do with me. The Mighty Seven had been compromising himself for a while protecting you. This . . . this was inevitable."

"You didn't have to kill him."

"Not your call, I'm afraid," Finola says, cringing. "Or mine, really. This job came from an even higher power than yours. But, alas . . . you need to make a move with haste, my friend. Thing is, I'm not even here, as it were. I'm in London with my Matty with all manner of receipts lined up to prove that I was indeed there. And still am. So, if you were to initiate the 9-1-1 process and that black-and-red van were to come screeching 'round now, you're the one in bits, hon. They'd haul you right quick away; and that corpse is the most damning evidence, I'm afraid."

"Jesus Christ . . ."

"I know, it's tangled, like I said. But I believe you'll make a good choice here." Finola switches back to her practiced American accent. "You totally got this, girl."

Lu slowly turns her head to glare at her, calculating the pros and cons of punching Finola square in the throat. The odds are not in her favor, though, so Lu decides to not quite skip the uppercut but more postpone it. She paces for a few steps, then approaches Finola, standing close enough to smell the overly chemical, fruity stink of her vape smoke. And for the first time since revealing her dark second self, Finola looks skittish, her eyes wide and chest rising and falling quickly, as if bracing for a fight she knows she'll lose.

"Two questions," Lu says, plainly, her heated stare unwavering.

"All right."

"What happens if I don't complete the assignment on time? Am I the next one to get your toxic fizzy cocktail?"

"You?" Finola says, squinting and pursing her lips. "No . . . were those your two questions, because those *were* two questions, if I'm being an actual arsehole about—"

"*Second* question . . ." Lu continues, ignoring Finola's wicked grin. She steps away and pads over to Mr. V, forcing herself to look down at him, at the bones in his face protruding, the gray skin already sagging, his dull eyes like an expired fish partly shielded by the heavy drape of his lids. He looks so cold, frozen even, with the death chill progressing as it will. She lets out a loud, heavy sigh next before turning to look over at Finola. "Could you *not* be an actual arsehole, and help me get rid of the body?"

Finola's half grin quickly spreads into a broad, almost charming smile. "Of course. I'm actually not a monster."

Lu drops her backpack by the lifeguard tower again and pushes the back of her wig further beneath the heavy wool ski mask. "*Potato-potahto*," she hisses at Finola, and rolls the mask down over her scowl.

* * *

VINCENT KING WAS a mystery to Lu in many ways. However, over their thirty-year relationship, she managed to gather a few key truths about him from both studied evidence and refined conjecture. The most irrefutable fact being that the man was rooted in honor. Integrity, character, was everything, possibly the only thing.

She knew that as a very young man he became a proud member of the Royal Navy. She discovered this after stumbling upon, and later actively searching for, a small collection of photographs from that time that he had carefully hidden alongside a polished wood box with the Distinguished Service Cross and other sterling medals.

Lu quietly wished she could have had something—one small piece—from Mr. V's distinguished naval career to include with him as he was laid to rest tonight. Instead, he was bound, weighted down, wrapped in a weather-beaten tarp, and quickly pushed out into Long Island Sound like some unsung, blighted vagrant. A John Doe to be later washed ashore and found bloated and putrefied by some hapless beach jogger.

Nothing honorable about this, Lu mumbles to herself as she backs away from the shore, her private farewell to Mr. V quick, quiet, and unremarkable.

Finola, who had offered her a moment alone on the beach after they dumped the body, waves Lu over to meet at the signpost near the park's entrance.

"You OK?" Finola says, so easily returned to her American friendly neighbor cosplay.

"What do you think?" Lu snaps, and keeps walking, stomping forward, roughly butting Finola's shoulder as she passes her.

"Uh . . . we should go over some rules, friend," Finola softly calls out to her. "Think a few guardrails are needed for everyone's safety."

Lu whips around and rushes back, stopping in front of Finola, standing almost nose to nose with The Atlas's special operative. "Stay away from me . . . that's the only rule you need."

"Doesn't work like that," she says with a sigh. "You know that it doesn't. But just so we're clear . . ." Finola pulls out her phone—the company-issued one—and taps at the screen, unbothered by Lu's hot breath scratching at her forehead. "Staying away from me, bringing any unwanted attention to me, stalling on the assignment, or flat-out sabotaging it would be a grave error. You should know that the consequences for deviating from the explicit script in any way will be dire." She turns her phone toward Lu. A compilation of video clips starring Solomon, bright and in full color, pop up in different corners of the screen like a videogame. In one, he is playing fetch and catch with Mylo in their backyard. In another, he's excitedly hopping into the back of Harry's car with his mini portable telescope in hand. And another clip, from just this morning, he is hugging Lu goodbye at the bus stop as he heads off to school. The video even zooms in on the child as he plops down in his seat and turns to wave at his mother through the window. "The price is steep."

Lu doesn't think, she just acts. Quickly enough, she unleashes the first punch, connecting with Finola's jaw. She is on the ground before she can fully register her next move, straddling Finola with her fist balled, arm drawn back like a bow, ready to unleash another wallop.

Finola presents her chin to Lu, teeth clenched, as if daring Lu to try that shit again. Though her eyes are watery, she isn't flinching. "Think about it," Finola says, slow and soft, blood and saliva beginning to pool by her gumline. "Look, I know . . . I know this is fucked up. No denying that. But you need to think about it, Twenty-two. You know exactly who you're dealing with here. I'm just the messenger, a small part in the larger wheel. But you know how it works: Do away with me and there's another cog coming to take my place, keep the wheel rolling, and do as we're told."

The phone, knocked from the blow a good arm-stretch away, is face up and still on. The video of her joyful, sinless son continues playing on loop; it catches the corner of Lu's eye. Although she has never incurred the full ire of The Atlas, never felt the inevitable impact of being on its wrong side, Lu knows that Finola is right. Whatever it takes to get the job done is what will happen. Neutralizing interference does not get a second's thought. Perhaps this is what Mr. V was trying to tell her with his last breaths. More important than the retirement, if Lu truly wants to protect her family, then she must see this through. She must keep her word.

With her fiery fists re-racked, Lu peels herself off of Finola and stands. She goes one further and offers her pretend friend a hand up.

"Nice," Finola says. She winces and starts gently massaging her obviously wounded cheek. Even in the dimness of the park's lamppost lights, the purpling bruise is visible.

The two women start walking, both of them winded and wobbly. Lu is focused on the ground just ahead of her, trying to put one foot in front of the other and stay upright despite the weight of this new reality pressing down on her. She sighs and it sounds like a windstorm. This is the definition of insanity, the fact that she actually expected a different result. But once again The Atlas showed her the truth with a swift, rough yank of her leash. Worse, they've strapped a shock collar around her neck now too. From here on, every one of her moves needs to be prudent and precise.

"You know . . . I didn't want it like this," American Finola says, glancing over at Lu. "Meeting you. I didn't want it to be like this. When they told me that I'd be working with you, I thought . . . ugh. I don't know what I thought, really. I just didn't think it would be like this. Same team but not teammates, you know? Just regular old adversaries." Finola turns to look at Lu, again, letting her eyes linger on her stern profile. "I'm sorry about—"

"Are you fucking serious?" Lu snaps, halting in place. She turns and glowers at Finola, again ready to throw hands. Instead, she gets quiet, her angry words slithering out of her clenched teeth. "You threatened my son. He's eight. A child. Children should never have any part in this shit. *Never.* This is how they're making the new operatives these days? Where is your code, your honor?" Lu begins to storm off but only makes it a couple of vexed steps before stopping again. She walks back the few paces to cut Finola's slowed path. "You killed my mentor like it was nothing. Like he was nothing."

"Lu . . ." Finola starts, but seems unable to properly meet her angry, devastated eyes. "There's more to it than that. I—"

"Don't care," Lu says, sharply. "You know what I do? I lift things from here and drop them off over there. For thirty years, lift and drop. No murder. No threats on innocents. On *kids*. I don't poison people. I don't dump bodies in the goddamn drink." She roughly points over Finola's shoulder at the beach. "And now you want to talk about apologies and adversaries? About how you wanted things to be different? What the fuck are you made of? What kind of animal are you?"

"I'm just following—"

"Keep all that shit." Lu says. "I'll do my part, exactly as expected. But when it's over and done"—she turns hard on her heels and starts marching, tossing the last cruel words behind her like a pulled grenade—"watch your fucking back."

CHAPTER TWENTY-FOUR

The sound of the doorbell is unexpected, but no longer does it startle Lu. At this point, there's nothing that would surprise her more than what has already unfurled before her in the last two days. Mr. V is dead, his body wrapped up like days-old fish and shoved out to sea, possibly making its way to the surface of the water within the next week. Finola is an undercover devil. Everything that wicked sprite has ever said to Lu has a giant asterisk beside it, footnoted as LIES. And adding more crap croutons to the shit salad she's been eating basically since setting foot in this ridiculous town, Harry has been in a foul mood, acting very outside of himself and going to bed earlier and earlier, barely saying good night to his wife. Also not helping matters, Solomon still hates his school, complaining almost nightly about it while loudly wishing "we never moved to this place."

Lu doesn't bother checking the security video panel. Nor does she hustle to stash her work materials back into the box in her closet. She just ambles downstairs to answer the door.

"Hey, neighbor," Finola says, her smile annoyingly bright as she cheerfully waves.

Lu's bares her teeth like a wild canine and takes a hard step toward her. "What the hell are you—"

"Hi, Lu," Calista says, sheepish and taking her time walking over from Finola's car.

"Oh, hey, lady . . . I didn't see you there."

"Yeah, that's kind of been my default thing lately—being hidden away," she says. Her underlook and slumped shoulders are beyond pitiful. She's wearing a black oversize jogger set with the hoodie pulled all the way up, covering her hair, which is already in a ponytail tucked under a hat.

You fucked your friend's husband, not butcher an embarrassment of pandas, Lu wants to say, but opts for something much softer with, "Looks like the band's back together; that's good!"

"Not even close," Calista says. "Didi hasn't spoken to me since . . . And Margot reached out twice, but she's dealing with her own stuff. Evangeline's in New York and then on to Italy. Finola's the only one." She rubs Finola's arm. "She's been a good friend through all of this."

Lu cannot bring herself to look at the devil, not even a side eye.

"She's always checking in. She practically dragged me out of my dungeon today. Said your house would be a nice place to land. I mean, that is if I'm still welcome here."

"Oh, behave. Of course you're welcome here, Calista," Lu chirps. "Come on in. I was just doing my Connections and Wordle and shit."

She leads the women to the kitchen, offering them coffee and pumpkin-maple quick bread from the Pour House Café that Annabelle dropped off yesterday along with intel that *The Beacon*, largely idle for the last three years, has spontaneously reactivated with recent reports—and possible footage—of someone suspicious milling around neighbors' backyards.

"So, Didi's still pissed?" Lu asks, her eyes on Calista, and Calista only.

"I don't blame her. It's all so messy . . ." she says, and peels off the hat to smooth a hand over her head. "Ward is staying at a hotel. We've only spoken a handful of times by phone. Trying to give it all some space."

Finola, licking the loaf's sticky, sweet frosting off of her fingers, chimes in. "Space sounds smart right now. Everyone just needs to be able to process all of this stuff. Right?" She tosses to Lu, looking over at her, innocent and true.

But there; right there! A flicker of something mocking and mean crosses Finola's eye. Lu still cannot believe how she missed it before, these tiny red flags being waved less than an inch from her face.

"Yeah, space is smart. We all need to process," Lu says, pursing her lips ever so slightly as she looks directly back at Finola, acutely aware that she is being tested, determined to clear the hurdle without a moment's doubt.

"Ashley is crushed. He's trying to be civil, but I think he's going to extend his time in Europe—again—and just avoid me forever. Ugh, it's so complicated," Calista says, her shoulders dropping further. "My stomach's a mess. I can hardly keep anything down."

Out of reflex, Finola and Lu give each other the same look.

"No! I'm not pregnant," Calista shrieks. "Ward got snipped two years ago and my IUD is *firmly* in place, thank you very much . . . God! I'm so embarrassed. I look like some dumb whore. We didn't mean for any of this to happen. Was just this fun thing, you know?"

"We are not here to judge you," Finola says. "We all make mistakes in the name of *sounds like a good idea at the time.* It's called being human, Calista. We get it. Didi and everyone else will come around."

"As simple as that is, it actually makes me feel better just hearing it out loud. Thanks, girlie." Calista's face perks up and she slices a small bite of the loaf with her fork. "Who knew Finola Grey was so wise!"

"None taken!" Finola says with a playful pout.

"Oh! I didn't mean it like *that.* It's just that you're always so quiet and hanging back, kind of taking in our whole toxic craziness. You need to share some of your good advice more."

"Honestly? It's all Lu. We've gotten close and she is always coming up with the gems. Making me see situations for what they are."

"Totally! Lu, what were we doing without you?" Calista says, glowing at Lu too.

Jesus, I'm the Magical Negro now? The Oracle, or maybe Bagger Vance. "Enough with the smoke!" Lu says, waving off the empty praise. "Can I get you some water? We also have that crisp apple seltzer that everyone's snatching up at Whole Foods."

"Oh, Lonie, our fabulous house manager, got some cases too. It's so good! Instantly makes me think of fall and Halloween," Calista says, passing on the drink with a polite little headshake and wave.

Lu doesn't extend the offer to Finola. She doesn't even let her eyes rest on the fabulist.

"I'll pass on the seltzer too, Lu, thanks," Finola says anyway. "Speaking of Halloween, have you seen the decorations over by the golf course? It's like, whoa!"

"Maybe Partridge Hollow goes a *little* overboard on Halloween, but it's super cute and the kids love it," Calista says. "There are hayrides, carving contests, a mini parade for the littles, and, of course, Bennett Carlyle brings out his giant projector to show clips of scary movies, but like, kid-scary. No gore. And then, the very best part? At nine eleven PM on the dot, he shows the *Thriller* video, and the whole group does the dance. It sounds corny by it's so, so fun!"

"We missed that last year," Finola says. "We were visiting Matty's family in Boston."

Lu slightly grits her teeth at the mention of the imaginary husband.

"I refuse to miss it! And with everything going on right now, the Avery family needs some fun. Less than a week away!"

"Sounds like a good time," Lu says. "I've never been big into Halloween—"

"Because of the foster home?" Finola interjects. A soft, surprised "oh" falls from Calista's mouth as she looks over at Lu. "Sorry—was that a secret? Annabelle mentioned."

"It's fine," Lu says, aware that the pint-sized fraud probably already knew this bio fact, culled from her Atlas file. "I'm not big on it," she continues, unperturbed, "but Harry and Solomon love it. They go all out—elaborate matching costumes and all. I hang back and hand out candy."

"How sweet. Truly phenomenal. A phenomenal woman," Calista says, her voice already changed to something lighter and pitying to accommodate the poor Black girl from foster care.

From Bagger Vance to Maya Angelou—perfect. "Yeah, I like watching other people enjoying the moment," Lu says.

"Oh, my God, speaking of watching people, did you guys see the urgent text from *The Beacon*?" Calista says. "There's like, a *prowler*?"

"Prowler? I wouldn't go that far," Finola says. "More like Jack and Beverly Warnock being super annoying. Those two are always on high alert for possible 'deplorables' casing the goddamn neighborhood."

Calista chuckles. "Well, we shall see. I think there's footage of the prowler—or *whatever*—which is kind of scary."

"More coffee anyone?" Lu says.

"Thanks, but I should probably head back home. Ashley and I have a prelim phone meeting scheduled with a new therapist in about an hour to see if she's a good fit." Calista slowly puts her thin disguise back together, starting with the ball cap. "Thanks for the ear and the coffee, Lu. It's like, *really* good coffee. I might have to come back!"

"You're always welcome," Lu says. "And, honestly, let yourself off the hook, girl. The things we do don't define who we are. Just honor your heart; can't go wrong with that."

Calista, tearing up, nods softly.

"See?" Finola says, draining one last sip from her mug. "Lu somehow knows the right thing to say. And the mellow voice is like . . . I would totally listen to that podcast."

"You do have a great voice," Calista adds, dabbing her ring fingers along her lash line.

"All right, all right, already. Gassing me up . . ."

After offering to help Lu clean up their coffee break service at least three different ways, the two women finally relent and gather their things to leave. The goodbyes don't linger too long and Lu is able to maintain a sugary smile and pleasant demeanor despite the fawning hugs and arm rubs. She's about to close the door on the final "thanks again," when Finola doubles back.

"I'll be quick," she shouts over to Calista, who has already climbed into the SUV with haste lest any of the neighbors happen to see her in blink-of-an-eye passing. "Sorry, I just need to pee," Finola says, trotting over to Lu. "My bladder was basically obliterated by the twins."

"Sure thing," Lu says, kindly, adding a gentle *après-vous* gesture toward the open door.

The two are barely inside before they simultaneously drop their respective acts.

"Are we good?" Finola says, peering at Lu. "Because it felt a wee bit chilly between us."

"Oh, whatever . . . can you just go now?"

"Ah, but I'm going to need a verbal commit, my friend. Are. We. Good."

A flash of Mr. V's corpse, stiff as timber and bound up in a tarp, skitters across Lu's mind. She doesn't take a full breath before responding. "Yeah, we're good, *friend*."

"Great," Finola says, cheerful again. "And your plan, ready to launch?"

"Indeed," Lu deadpans.

"Oh! Burying the lede here. You'll need this." Finola pulls a small, flat, square compact from her pouch and shoves it at Lu. "Vera Touch. State-of-the-art fingerprint duplicator."

"I'm all set on that, thanks."

"Not quite." The ebullience is wiped from Finola's face in half a breath. "Kastille's security is particular. It uses biometrics. To get in, you'll need a print that can pass body temp analysis. This gets you there," Finola says. "The one print you took from Jonathan or Cormac or whoever, won't work."

"This information would've been useful weeks ago!"

"I just found out myself. Normally your principal would have brought this to light, but he's, uh, not exactly *in the light* anymore. So, now you know. It'll be easier this way. Just climb on top of that hot husband of yours, get his heart rate up, and—"

"You need to watch your fucking mouth," Lu snaps. "I'm not using Harry or his print!"

"Fine, fine," Finola says, sighing. "Get the print when *whoever*'s heart rate has been boosted. The Vera Touch will replicate it."

"Jesus Christ," Lu hisses. "Is there anything else I should know?"

"No . . . just that you need to get this done ASAP—but I think you already know that part, mate." Finola gives Lu a thumbs-up, turns, and is out the door, walking jauntily to a waiting Calista, slumped down in the passenger seat of the car, then tosses a breezy wave behind her. "Thanks for everything, Lu!"

CHAPTER TWENTY-FIVE

Lu opted to sleep in a guest room last night. She needed the space to think through her next steps without guilt rearing its many heads like a Hydra every time she glanced over at a snoozing Harry. "Scratchy throat, sinus pressure," she had told him before dinner, then called it a very early night. He blew her a kiss from a great distance in response and offered to handle Solomon bedtime duty and the get-ready school rush in the morning.

This, of course, didn't help the case of Lu vs. the Venomous Guilt Serpent. In fact, never has Lu been so tempted to tell Harry the full truth.

The last time she felt this kind of pull toward honesty was more than a decade ago, almost nine months into their relationship. Lu was in the UK on a deux or, as she often called it, a two-fer. First, artnapping five pieces, including C. Montague's "Ephemeral Sonata," collectively valued at £133 million, from the Windsor Merrilon Gallery in Central London. The second charge was acquiring the contents of two very important safe deposit boxes deep in the belly of Northam Bank in Chelsea. In between successfully completing the two jobs, Lu also met Harry's moribund father for the first time. The heaviness of seeing the senior Barlow—a man she had imagined to be stately and stalwart like Mr. V—rendered feeble and bedridden stirred up something unexpected and uneasy in Lu. Soon, she had found herself actually answering Harry's questions, telling him about her humble early days in foster care. No real names. No solid details. No whole truths. But it didn't matter because Harry empathized immediately. He listened and understood. And, most important, he loved her, still.

Maybe he would do that again, love her despite the deception and dark dealings.

Maybe.

Lu lets go of this wishful thinking and focuses on that which she knows for sure. As much as it sickens her, she will have to use Harry, specifically his hot fingerprint, to get this job done. Short of challenging Old Man Pearson to a 5K race or grappling with Jonathan in a fursuit, she has no choice. It's Harry's heart rate she must manipulate and his fingerprint she must duplicate. But she's determined to find a way to keep him protected, to shield him from the toxic ash that will surely rain down when this bomb goes off.

With Harry and Solomon gone for the morning, Lu gets ready to make her way to Porterfield Art Museum in Elmwood Hills, a town forty-five minutes north of home. There she will meet Nine, her new principal, the new Mr. V, and arriving early feels even more important now than it did with him.

Lu knows nothing about this person—he, she, or they; young or old; normal and personable or hardcore and stern. Although the help-desk request came from Lu, The Atlas sent careful instructions for the clandestine meet. And Lu follows each step precisely, including:

1. Buy two tickets for admission at the fourth self-serve kiosk.
2. Leave extra ticket by red bench in solarium adjacent to the museum's café.

On the second floor of Porterfield, by the farthest corner without widows, there's a small group of people gathered around a large-scale painting of a woman in a field. Lu analyzes each person as they gawk at the piece. One by one, and also by two, the people disperse. Lu sits on the adjacent bench, on close standby, watching. She feels an arm brush lightly against hers. It's the sign she's been waiting for. Nine. She smells the person before she even begins to turn and glance their way. A warm and sweet honeyed tobacco.

"There's a brilliant Elizabeth Catlett exhibit on the first level," Lu says, sneaking a peek to her left at this mystery beside her.

The striking woman is tall, even seated, and lithe. Her features, in profile, are delicate but also sharp. She is notably pale and, besides visible fine lines around her eyes, her complexion is smooth with a shimmery rose blush blended into her already pronounced cheekbones. Her short brown hair is cut close on the side that Lu can see and the top is piled high in an airy pompadour.

"Yes, I saw it earlier," she says, her voice deep and raspy with a hint of an accent that Lu can't immediately place. "But it's a small portion of her vast works. I've only seen nine pieces myself." She turns and looks at Lu directly now. The principal is not wearing any visible jewelry and is generally unadorned except for the fact that she is handsome while also being pretty with red, pouty lips.

"That's a good start," Lu says, taking in as much detail about the woman's countenance and comportment as possible.

"Royce," she says. "Figured a name sounds better than a number."

"Oh, OK . . . Lu," she says. "But you probably already knew that."

"I did," Royce says, with a soft smile. "You need help, I'm told."

Lu leaps right to it. "Yes . . . I need to protect my husband." Royce's easy smile wanes. "I mean, this next job, he's tied in tight, as you know, but I need to make sure there's no blowback on him." She pauses for less than a blink before pushing out the rest. "For my cover . . . I need him to be in the clear to keep my cover intact."

Royce raises a brow, seemingly considering the different prongs to the predicament. "How do you see this working, this help?"

"It's two-fold. I need a way to scramble the log-in info. Erase his print after I use it, maybe? And two, when the job's complete, I need help casting suspicion far away from him."

The brow is pitched again, but the expression behind it is different. It's less ponder and more wonder with a thick undercurrent of skepticism. Lu would know immediately what this look meant had Mr. V dispensed it. With Royce, it's a grasp, a guess, a gut feeling.

"Isn't this what they pay you to figure out?" she says, coldly.

Lu wants to tell this stranger a few curse words, but biting the hand that could pull you up from a deep, dark pit is never a good idea. "Yeah, it's a straight input-output dilemma. I just don't have resources to build this. I need more people on it."

"Very astute, knowing your limitations. Do you have the start of a plan at least? Or do we need to come in to do a full build?"

"I do," Lu says. "I have some fall guys teed up, all C-suite. The grime on them is straightforward and locked in. But I'll need an assist to diffuse it." Royce parts her lips to speak, but Lu keeps going. "Above all this, I need to know the price. What will this help cost me?"

Royce gets up and straightens her tie, then buttons her jacket. She's wearing a finely tailored navy suit beneath her slim dark-gray trench. "The so-called 'retirement plan,' for one," she says, using loose rabbit ears and hardly trying to cover her sneer. "That ship is sunk. *Titanic*. You'll be back in play. I'm talking regular rotation and quick turnarounds on jobs."

Lu also gets up from the bench, making sure to keep an aloof air about her despite the utter devastation taking to her bones. "Figured as much," she says, and quickly masks her grimace. Although Lu had arrived at this fact on her own last night—that she will have to attach The Atlas's leash to her collar once again—it doesn't make it any easier to bear.

"You should note: Unlike old man Seven—may he rest—I stay on top of my numbers." Royce casts her eyes down to focus on buttoning her trench. She's no longer looking at Lu, but definitely still talking to her. "I don't operate like he did. My blood is thin, my heart is cold; I don't tolerate much of anything. We're not friends or even acquaintances. There are no special requests or easy let-downs with me."

"Clear," Lu says, feeling strangely relieved for the hard boundaries. She buttons up her own lightweight black wool coat and takes a beat, staring over at the painting of the pensive woman in the grassy field. "Here's what you should know about me: I don't give a fuck about your heart or your blood or how you operate. Doesn't matter. My husband's name gets cleared before even a whisper of new coordinates comes my way."

"Fair enough," Royce says. "Anything else?"

"Yeah . . ." Lu swallows hard. Despite the rumination and torment, she is resolved about this final decision. With no real options, Lu's next course of action felt preordained. All she could do was follow it through. Still, she has to coax the words out to let the full measure of her gut-wrenching plan hit the open air. "Once this job is completed and I'm fully back on the books, it's just me. I'm a total island. I'm leaving my family behind," Lu says, her gaze steely. "This means my husband, my kid, they no longer exist to any of you. No surveillance, no phone taps, no secret video recordings, no underground operatives checking in on them. It's guaranteed no contact with them or this doesn't go."

Royce tilts her head slightly, pursing her red overlined lips for a moment, then gives Lu a firm nod. "Well, I better go check out the rest of that Catlett exhibit, right?" she says, louder and with obvious brightness. "Always a pleasure meeting new art lovers."

Instead of watching Nine leave, Lu returns to her seat on the bench, admiring the finer features of the woman in the giant canvas before her.

ONCE AGAIN, DINNER is a hit at the Barlow home. And once again, Lu found herself making a dish from *back a yard,* another Mr. V favorite. Brown stew chicken with rice and peas and a hearty green salad. She followed all of his steps to the letter from the show-and-tell recipe committed to memory. With this dish, he would sometimes serve festival on the side, sweet and fried to crisp perfection, but only on Sundays. He took pride and pleasure in cooking traditional Jamaican fare. She could tell by how content he would look while doing it: even dicing onions the man would have a gladness about him, far removed from his usual stern comportment. And though he never said it outright, Mr. V relished in the fact that Lu liked the food he made. She also liked sneaking looks at his face beaming—his slight version of it at least—as he watched her eat, so quiet she would be, so focused on her plate, but still minding the table manners he had taught her.

Although both Harry and Solomon clearly enjoyed every bite of the savory dish, joyfully declaring their compliments to the chef, Lu couldn't quite rouse an appetite. Too busy running through the steps of her midnight plan. "I taste-tested too much while cooking!" was her excuse.

Solomon went to bed earlier than usual, only requiring one very short story read to him by his dad, because tonight was special. Tonight, as a treat for his three consecutive "good effort days" at Maple Grove, Mylo was allowed to sleep in Solomon's bed with him. His parents' immediate and unified *yes* brought Solomon immense joy. He was unable to contain it. Infectious and adorable, to be sure, but it still made Lu feel a way, caught in a whirling mix of guilt and sadness. Although the boy had earned the treat outright—he had been trying really hard not to complain about anything Maple Grove–related and was fully participating in class, highlighted in a glowing email from his teacher—Lu's reasons for happily agreeing to the doggy sleepover were not as honest or pure. She was proud of her boy, of course, and made a show of praising him for his improved mood and good-foot approach to the week at school, but Lu was also thankful for the timing of Solomon's ask as it lined up with her bigger scheme that required concentration and alone time.

"You've been operating on a higher level, darling. Honestly," Harry says, his voice slightly hoarse and sleepy. He pulls himself up to seated in the bed, leaning his shirtless back against the thick pillows behind him, eyes set to high twinkle, as he watches his wife softly pulling her hair into a loose top bun. "I'm not just talking about the meals either—which have been five-star. It's more than that. You seem focused on, I don't know, being happy here . . . ?"

Lu gives him a demure smile and nod then slips out of her silky robe to reveal her red short pajama set. The shorties, as he calls them. This is Harry's second favorite of her sleepwear; the first being a tie between her ratty, double-XL *The Low End Theory* album cover T-shirt and completely nude. She makes sure to look back at him, sly and flirty, before she playfully tosses the robe over to the ottoman. Lu knows what she's doing to him, and from the way Harry's slinky smile is moving up the side of his face, he's clear about what he wants to be doing to her.

He rolls back the fluffy duvet for her, and Lu crawls in toward him, straddling him before slowly spreading her lower body over his. Harry palms one side of her bum, rubbing it like it's a crystal ball while using the other hand to slide up her back, along the side of her ribs, over her shoulder, across her collar bone, and then gently wrapping his fingers around her neck.

The kiss is hot and hungry, but still sweet. Lu begins to lose herself in it, the groping and stroking, nibbles and nuzzles, allowing herself to feel every inch of every heated thing her man is bringing to her. That this is part of a different agenda, phase one of an intricate process, is a fact easily pushed aside, just like the crotch of her pajama bottoms right now. But Lu's qualms about manipulating her husband like this are far less pliable. Using sex as a pacifier for him is not something she ever envisioned having to do, but then that particular How Did We Get Here column seems to be widening every day.

As usual, Harry ravishes her, working up a thorough sweat, moving her from one position to another with a craving—Lu on top, Lu on her side, Lu on her knees, Lu's leg over his shoulder, Lu's sweetest part sat square on his face and him lapping up every drop of her melted essence with raw thirst.

Breathless, Harry collapses on Lu's back not with a sweaty thud but rather a gentle crumbling. She can feel his heart beating out of his chest against her. He coughs out a chuckle; it sounds like a mix of relief and bliss. Her own body is vibrating, knees trembling as she tries to slow her pulse with deep breaths and wrap her head around this level of yearning for each other. More than a decade together and the desire between them is stronger now than on that very first chance run-in.

Harry rolls off of Lu and pulls her into him, tucking her under his strong arm. "I love you, dove," he whispers into the back of her neck. Lu squeezes his hand three times, a wordless

I love you. It's all she can manage as tears roll across the bridge of her nose and the side of her face, soaking into the pillow.

Now, she waits.

For Harry to quickly fall asleep, as usual.

To peel herself out from his warm, heavy hold.

To ease his hand open, palm exposed.

To remove the stashed Vera Touch device from her nightstand.

To get his print copied, carefully, quietly.

And then figure out how she might crawl back into bed beside him without spilling the contents of her sickened stomach.

CHAPTER TWENTY-SIX

Harry, dressed in a vintage-style NASA flight suit, is trying to coax Mylo over to him with a fake treat, but the dog is hip to the old trick and continues to escape him, the small wheels on the back of his high-effort Mars rover costume whirring behind him as he zooms from one side to the next about the family room.

"Come on, mate! This won't hurt you," Harry says, trotting after Mylo with the dog's little antennae headpiece in hand. "This completes the look, man." His own retro mission control headset mic bobbing in front of his mouth as he moves.

Lu watches them, her heart shattered. She wants to pull Harry and the dog into her, squeezing them so close and tight they might gasp for their next breath. Walking away from this, from them, will destroy her, Lu knows, but staying and putting them in harm's way—she could never forgive it.

She dumps the last three full-size chocolate bars into the big orange bowl fashioned like a menacing jack-o'-lantern and heads off to find Solomon. The two nearly collide at the bottom of the stairs. The boy is all smiles and ready for spacewalks in his white astronaut suit with helmet and backpack covered in pristine badges. Barring the final remnants of his little-kid pot belly, Solomon looks official, and should; Harry ordered the costume directly from the Shop NASA website a month ago. He and Solomon work on their Halloween theme from early in the summer. The ideas usually center around the nerdy duo's interests—mad scientist and mini lab assistant, solar system and Nicolaus Copernicus, George Washington Carver and the world's most adorable peanut toddler—with Lu cheering them from the sidelines.

"You all ready, sweet pea?" she says, her voice thin and unsteady.

"Mom, I'm not sweet pea today!" Solomon points at his call sign badge embossed on his suit. **Comet One.**

"Of course. Beg your pardon, Comet One, sir," Lu says, beaming at this sweet kid.

"Wait," Solomon says, scanning his mother's all-black attire, "what are you this year? Where's your witch's hat?"

"Oh, you know, I couldn't find it. Think we left it back in Brooklyn. I think I'm going to be—what was that chemical super black . . . ? Vantablack. That's me."

"That's a good one, Mom!" he says. "Or maybe you could take something from your secret box. Be a spy, be Codename Celeste again."

Lu is unable to catch her falling face in time to fix it. She is frozen, her immediate words tangle together at the base of her throat. Harry comes in to find them with Mylo in hand, the tiny antennae headpiece finally secured. Both he and the dog look even brighter and happier the minute they see Solomon, who is himself too giddy to recognize the gut punch he just landed on his mother. Harry whoops and pumps his fist in the air, telling the boy that his costume is perfect, prize-worthy, and possibly their best creation yet, while Lu stays stuck, struggling to form intelligible words or even make a sound. All she can do is let her stunned eyes trace lines from patch to patch on the boy's flight suit. Shuttle Program patch, the NASA Commander patch, the USA Flag patch, and Solomon's unabashed favorite, the NASA Meatball patch.

"You all right, Loubie?" Harry puts Mylo down.

She nods and gives Harry a slanted grin.

"I know . . . it's happening so fast. In two blinks this young man will be sixteen, then twenty-three, and on and on," Harry says, shaking his head.

"Mm-hmm." She keeps her eyes on the dog, pretending to look closely at the details of his shimmery outfit.

"You sure you're OK?" Harry moves toward her.

"Yes," she tells him, and averts his touch by stooping down next to Mylo to fiddle with one of the wheels on the costume. "Always."

"Mom, you can still come trick-or-treating with us. You don't have to be all alone here." Saying this, Solomon sounds almost sorry for Lu. Poor Mom is missing the best parts of life.

"Oh, thanks, sweet—uh, Comet One. I'll be fine. Plus, I like seeing the kids' costumes."

"You can always join us later for the *Thriller* portion." Harry makes a snarky face.

"Yeah, I'm all set on that. But you two should get going!" she says, gently shooing them along. "I'll see you later tonight, rocket men. Have fun for me, OK?"

"Copy!" Solomon cheers. "I'll also make sure to save you your favorite—"

"Reese's Peanut Butter Cup!" mother and son say in unison.

"Aw. Looking out for your mama's RPB fix. Thanks, hon." Lu's chin begins to quiver, but she pulls it together before all the seams tear open. "All right, get out there."

Lu sends her little family off with a kiss, a salute to high-five, and an under the chin tickle for Harry, Solomon, and Mylo, respectively. She follows the trio out to the garage and keeps waving, gaily, even as Harry has completely reversed down to the end of the driveway and his car is turned, ready to take off into the dusk. She remains there outside, standing on the top step of the side door for a few minutes more, breathing in the night's crisp air. The sediments from the jolt a moment ago slosh around the bottom of her heart. Another deep inhale, staring out at nothing, Lu feels it building before she can properly claim it. Heavy as wet wool, it's something greater than sorrow and more far-reaching than remorse. She is regretting everything, even that which she has yet to do later tonight. They deserve better, she chides herself. Right down to the dog, they all deserve better.

* * *

EVEN THOUGH IT adds nine minutes to the trip, Lu still takes the byway to the checkpoint in the smaller neighboring town of Millstone. Driving along dark twisty two-way and some single-lane back roads, she avoids other cars as well as heedless pedestrians meandering from house to house on local streets looking for more sweet treats. In turn, they also avoid seeing her, out dodging people with her car when she should be home handing out candy. The bowl she left out on the front step full of treats is surely empty or nearly so by now. Doesn't matter how big or clever her **Take One Pls**. sign is, she knows that kids hopped on sugar are well into DGAF mode and live for moments like this when they can just be rude gluttons—their parents too, sadly.

She's wearing her usual black night crawler attire, with a few new pieces. She added extra padding to her shoulders and around her torso to throw off how her build might appear on a random security camera capture or to a passing eyewitness, and switched to a pair of sized-up black Reebok men's leather sneakers, as they are lightweight but also so common that it would be hard to trace any footprint impression left behind. The thicker sole also boosts her height a couple inches. There's a dishwater-blond long mullet wig and a Ghostface character mask stuffed into the wide front pocket of her new black drawstring satchel. She had picked up these last items at the dollar store four towns over, way north of—and a very different world from—Partridge Hollow, along with a small assortment of Halloween decorations, paying cash, of course, while wearing a different wig and hat combo than the one right now.

There is a smaller car, a gray MINI Cooper, parked as promised near an old diner, across from a tire shop and mailbox shipping store. The instructions from The Atlas last night were brief but clear. Park her own vehicle by the tire shop and use the supplied car to drive the rest of the way to Kastille's office. On the return trip, she is to stash the MINI Cooper directly behind the shipping store, leaving the fingerprint duplicate in the glove box and the windows to the car rolled all the way down.

Lu moves swiftly, being sure to stay alert with every step. Both the mailbox and tire stores are closed and in complete darkness, not even a set of dim security lights shining behind their glass windows and doors. At the diner, there are three other vehicles in spaced-out parking spots, all older models and slightly beat-up. The diner's folksy white curtains are drawn, but Lu can pick out the silhouettes of five patrons seated inside. She still makes quiet haste in getting over to the company car, using an app on her work phone to unlock and, in a moment, start its engine too. Exactly as The Atlas's coded message mapped out, inside the glove box Lu finds the sealed clear pouch with a vial containing a nanocode replica. Lu has no idea if this forgery is a close approximation or a shoddy, obvious dupe. And there's no time to research it either. Lu just slips it into her bag and starts making her way over to the Kastille offices.

She parks the car just outside of the back lots. There are two utility trucks lined up near a row of miniature silos. Bending down as low as possible in front of the car, she suits up—mask down, gloves on—and positions the tools on her person depending on when she'll need to use them and how accessible they need to be. Lu pulls out the clunkiest of her devices last, but must use it immediately to disable the cameras and scramble the security system's signals. The first attempt fails and for an instant she wonders if she herself is being set up to fail, but when it works the second time, she lets go of that fear. Besides, the short delay has only set Lu back four minutes. Not too bad, especially when every second counts here. Lu has done the calculations and considered the permutations and landed on twenty-two minutes. She's giving herself twenty minutes to get this whole thing done. That means she'll need to scale the low barrier to her left, sprint the quarter-mile across the parking lot, enter the building, run the stairs to the third floor and break into the locked case to swap out the vial containing the precious nanocode with the decoy, plant the dirty leave-behind virus in the central system, reset the fingerprint log, and reverse her way out of there, all without a single hitch. She sets her goggles—night vision not yet activated—on top of her masked head and stretches her legs like a runner before a race. Lu checks her watch next, staring down at it, waiting for the sweep hand to round to the twelve.

The watch strikes the number, and now it's time to press play.

All that's left for her to do is take the deep, shoulder-shrugging, ready-breath like a top girl preparing to be launched into the next gravity-defying cheerleader's stunt.

By the time Lu gets to the second floor, she is slick with sweat, her uniform clinging to her with every move. Even with her disloyal ankle now throbbing, her boggy under-boob, drenched wig cap, and marshy crotch, it's the cheap rubber of the scary mask that is proving to be the most egregious offender. Although she can already feel hives beginning to sprout all over her face from the scratchy, crappy mask, Lu is still focused. And the fact that she's barely ninety seconds off schedule is helping her push through the marked discomfort.

She hits the third floor at last and uses the Harry fingerprint dupe to gain access. Just like the others downstairs, the doors pop open easy, emitting the softest chime and flashing green light. Lu beelines to the northwest corner toward the secured suite.

She gets all the way into the vault with ease, but needs a minute—or two—to study the locked case. It's slightly different than what she was told to expect, and again Lu's mind races to her earlier thought: *I'm being set up.* She shakes away the notion, dismissing it again as nerves and self-imposed pressure, because this job has to work. For all parties involved. She lays down a drop cloth and sits for a soggy beat to think. It takes Lu another full minute and a half of complete focus to figure an efficient way into the case and, using a secondary laser tool, she is successful. She makes the careful switch, returning the case, vault, and suite to the way she found it. The last part—loading the virus into the company's system—is a bit of scramble but happens without complication, and Lu finally breathes. She's only six minutes over her limit with apparently no further stumbling blocks on the horizon.

Lu practically flies down the staircase, ignoring her pulsating ankle. She's ready to burst through the back warehouse doors and take off running toward the low barrier near the field, rip off this mask and wig, and take in fresher air. But once outside, she notices that one of the parked utility trucks has moved. It's now over by the annex where security is housed. Squinting, she can see that there are two figures seated in the truck and exhaust coming from the tailpipe too.

Please be could-give-a-shit, oblivious cogs. Please don't be hard-working heroes.

She's off like a shot, burning a path toward the field, which, thankfully, is in the complete other direction of the annex and the truck. Lu throws herself into the MINI Cooper, ducking down as she scrambles to get her phone out of her pocket and the bulky signal scrambler from the bag. She yanks off her glove with her teeth and taps her trembling fingers on the device to unblock the security feed. She has to load a different program to reset the access log, and it is taking its goddamn time booting up. Lu starts the car in the meantime, pulling off slowly, hardly controlling the steering wheel but keeping her eyes sliding between the slow-load reset program on the device wedged into the gear shift and the annex across the way, trying to gauge whether the truck has moved at all or, worse, if it looks like it's about to head her way. The program barely comes into full focus before Lu jumps in and pounds the keystrokes launching the reset. She tosses the device onto the passenger's seat and gently presses the gas, picking up even more speed while staying slumped down in her seat.

Once on the main road and with no signs of a tail in the rearview, Lu turns on the headlights and cranks the speedometer up to fifty and then sixty-five. Her breath is ragged and hot, and her heart feels like it's seconds away from leaping out of her chest. Lu peels off the mask and the wig in one go, then runs her palm along the same path, wiping away the sweat and wet from her face into her damp nylon cap. She runs through each of her steps on this job, saying them out loud as she drives, and over again from the top. She needs to be sure that she didn't forget anything back there. She needs to be sure that this ominous feeling taking over her entire spirit is just nerves or residual panic from the potential close call with the utility truck. She just needs to be sure.

* * *

IT'S LATE, AND many of the houses in Partridge Hollow have turned out the front door lights, signaling the end of the tricks and treats. Judging from Harry's status report text—"**boy's having an absolute blast, wish you could see it. got video**"—and the fact that she can almost see her house from this distance at the bottom of the gradual hill, Lu estimates that she'll make it home just before her family does with maybe enough time to drag a bathrobe and bonnet over herself and shove her wet grimy clothes somewhere in a back corner of her closet. She can do a proper cleanup, pack up her tools, and then take a Silkwood shower after everyone's gone to bed.

Lu hears and feels the vibrating buzz from her phone and glances down at her lit-up device in her lap. A text from Harry with a video attachment. She picks up the phone, her thumb hovering over the missive, then quickly glances up at the road in front of her. There's a person. THERE'S A PERSON WALKING!

She slams on the brakes. Everything from the passenger's seat takes flight and lands on the rubber floor mats with a clanking thud. Lu throws the car in park and jumps out, hobbling over ready to apologize to the sauntering stranger.

"I'm so, so sorry! I almost didn't see—"

"Hey, neighbor," Finola says as she steps farther into the streetlamp's beam. "Goodness, you almost ran me over! Hope that wasn't planned."

"Jesus. What the fuck are you doing out here?"

"Just coming from your house, actually. Your little candy bowl is empty, by the way," she says. Lu scoffs and starts back to her car. Finola trails her. "I've been pulled."

Lu steps back from the car door, the pucker in her brow taking over her face. She turns, only slightly, in Finola's direction. "Why?"

"My service is *needed elsewhere*," she says, imitating the notorious wooden tone of The Atlas handlers. "SF for a bit, then a longer thing in HK."

Lu deepens her frown, an effort to disguise the relief spilling across her face. But she can't help it. Her little family will be free from Finola and her malicious surveillance. Royce is still a mystery to Lu, but at least this is proof that she keeps her word. And for a moment—the length of a meaningful exhale—Lu considers not keeping her own promise and instead staying put, with her two loves, and finding a way to manage her two lives. But one glance at Finola roughly pulls Lu out of this reverie and back into reality: Leaving is the only recourse, the only way for her family to be free. She purses her lips and sneers at Finola. "Finally, you can spend time with your *Matty*," Lu says, and continues on to the car.

"Funny, that's what I told Didi and the gang—moving to be with him. Day after tomorrow. The girls will stay at the boarding school, finish the semester, then maybe I'll move 'em back home to Ireland—"

"Do I look like I give a shit about your maybe-could-be-kids?" Lu whips open the door.

Finola, standing too close as usual, catches glimpse of Lu's wig partially covered by a damning pile of proof on the passenger side floor. "Ah . . . maybe this is why I've been pulled," she smirks. "Mission complete, Twenty-two?"

"Is there a potion I can pour on you to make you fuck off?" Lu hisses, shoving her out of the way and roughly getting into the driver's seat. When she goes to pull the door closed, Finola grabs at it.

"So . . . this means you're done? Heard talk that you were hanging it up after this—which everyone in my department thinks is pure fiction, a fairy tale." She drapes herself over the open door, resting her chin on her clasped hands. "But then again, stealing from your *actual* husband, maybe torching his career, his life? Jesus, Mary, and Joseph, how does one move on from that?"

The sting of this truth is sharp, but breaking down in front of Finola cannot happen. "You have a good night—and a safe flight, doll." Lu yanks the door out of her grip and scratches off up the hill for home.

Through her tears, Lu can see the entrance to her driveway in the short distance. She accelerates, speed bumps be damned. But there's another person in the middle of the street ambling toward her. As she gets closer she sees that it's Jonathan. "Come on, ref!"

He waves her down. She wipes her face and drags an innocent expression across it.

"Hey," she says, rolling down the window. "What's going on?"

"Needed some air," he says, and starts moving closer to Lu and the car. Lu hops out and meets him before he can reach the car and glimpse what's inside.

"Ah. Almost didn't see you, man. In those dark clothes."

"I could say the same . . ." He gestures with this chin at Lu's all-black outfit.

Lu shrugs it off. "Had to get Tums from the store. All that candy. Fun-size can add up."

"That's not the truth," he says, shaking his head. Lu freezes. "I'm not out here getting air. I came out for a smoke." He pulls out a stubby, perfectly rolled, unlit spliff from his pocket. "A night with all those fucking kids. Needed to level off, you know? Don't tell Didi." He laughs, but then pulls it back. "No, seriously. She's already pissed at me. This would send her over a cliff."

"Of course. I'll keep it under my wig."

"Heh. *Under my wig.* Funny." He smirks and those piercing eyes seem to get brighter even in the darkness. Standing close to Lu now, he puts the joint to his lips and lights it, taking a long drag before offering it to her. She declines with a polite wave. "Your turn."

"None for me," she says, repeating the wave but this time with more emphasis.

"Not talking about this," he says, his grin vanished. "I mean, it's your turn to tell the truth. Don't you think?"

Lu's sigh is long and low. Her energy gauge had shifted to E miles ago. She doesn't even have fumes to work with to keep up her expansive front. She steps even closer to Jonathan, keeping her eyes locked on his. "What is it you want me to say right now?"

The man refuses to flinch. "That maybe you're the one who's been sneaking around our yards, casing our homes for what you can peddle at pawn shops," he says, slightly angling his face to exhale his joint smoke while maintaining his stare.

Pawn shops? Is this guy from fucking 1982? Lu slowly shakes her head at the absurd chasm between the accusation and the reality. Also, his rich white guy is showing and it's not cute. "Ah, so we're just stripping down to it, huh?" she says, keeping her frosty gaze on him too. "Racism untucked and out in the open?"

"It's not about that," he snaps. "Harry checks out. He's flown at this altitude before—nice English chap. He knows how to act. But you . . . some random foster kid from who knows where. I looked into you. You're not accustomed to all of this."

"Is this the coke talking? You sound ridiculous." She turns to leave, but he cuts her path.

"This town, we're a family," Jonathan says, his pungent breath hitting Lu's nose like a punch. "We look out for each other. So, just watch your step, know your place, Lucille *Doctor*, and you'll do well for yourself here. Clear?"

She has to actively bite her tongue to refrain from laughing in his face. The temptation to expose all she knows about his furry, dirty secrets is making Lu physically itch and twitch. She nods, slowly, and offers him her best Mona Lisa smile. "Crystal," she says, and side-steps the man, calmly climbs into her car, and drives straight home, sending out a quiet but desperate entreaty to whomever is holding on so tightly to her voodoo doll to please let go.

CHAPTER TWENTY-SEVEN

She expected to feel some brand of relief after clearing the Kastille hurdle, but the only thing Lu feels is disquiet. Even now, three days later, with Finola officially gone and no apparent fallout from the nanocode swap or the virus she planted, Lu can't help but to think there's a mighty aftershock rearing to rock her already fragile world.

Meanwhile, everyone else around Lu is back to normal, or close to it. The PH2's golf cart is mostly back on course. According to Calista's most recent call with Lu, the quad has been dissolved, but Avery is pushing for a trial separation. And she and Evangeline will start the work of healing their friendship "as soon as she's back from Italy in two weeks."

With the fun of Halloween over, Solomon is back to complaining about hating his school. And Harry is busier, and seemingly crankier, than ever, coming home late from work.

And Lu, stuck in panic mode, unable to draw a clean breath, is seated alone at a dingy coffee shop an hour's drive from home in a lonely town called Brookhaven, waiting for her nameless connect to arrive in order to make the nanocode drop.

As instructed, she's sat at the second-to-last four-top table by the large window with a slice of pumpkin pie—despite being utterly grossed out by it—and a cup of black coffee, both lined up precisely to her left. The nanocode is secure in its baggie inside a folded copy of today's newspaper—the science section, not so ironically—laid on the inside edge of the table.

She's wearing colored contacts, heavy-framed glasses, fake face piercings, and an old, itchy wig—a quick dollar store buy after burning the one she wore on that horrible Halloween night. She points and flexes her toes under the table, trying to work her re-injured ankle that is discreetly bandaged beneath thick, fuzzy socks, and then does a sweep of the room again. Another gander at the few patrons in the coffee shop along with her. Although each of these people has a sad, forsaken look about them, they all seem legitimate, real, like they are meant to be there. None of them strikes her as undercover. But then, Lu remembers with a wince, she also took Finola as legitimate and real, meant to be there, so really, what does she know?

Lu checks her personal phone. The connect is late. They are never late.

She scans the small group of customers again. Did she miss something? Someone? Is Finola 2.0 going to pop out from behind the loud espresso machine to reveal that Lu's family is in fresh danger? Maybe the sick feeling that's recently come over her isn't paranoia but instead a premonition, and The Atlas is indeed trying to set her up. Is this nasty pumpkin slop on crust her last meal, Lu wonders, as her nervous jumping knee beneath the slanted table causes the teaspoon to rattle against the pie plate, calling unwanted attention to herself. She pulls out her phone again and scrolls for today's Wordle. She hasn't played in weeks. Lu types her first word:

CRIME

Then deletes it.

~~CRIME~~

She gives up and goes back to what she's been doing for the last two days: scrolling the news sites and hitting the refresh button on them like it's a Las Vegas slot machine, but instead of every hard tap releasing dopamine, she's getting a double boost of cortisol. It was only yesterday that she saw a troubling update on the necklace heist.

Breakthrough in Hell's Kitchen Jewelry Heist as Key Evidence Surfaces

After weeks with no new leads, detectives in the Hell's Kitchen warehouse jewelry heist have confirmed a pivotal breakthrough in the case. Nearly two months after a team of thieves made off with a priceless necklace from a rarely displayed Neapolitan collection, investigators revealed they've found a critical piece of evidence left behind by one of the suspects. Authorities remain tight-lipped about its nature, saying only that it could help "close in" on the culprits.

Sloppy. She shakes her head, annoyed and appalled, then moves her internal police scanner to social media, Facebook specifically. She set up a sham profile about fifteen years ago,

Julia "Jules" Townsend, that she updates as needed, depending on where she—or, moreover, her pseudo self—is in life. As it stands on the platform right now, Jules Townsend is a charmingly down-to-earth, slightly scatterbrained *Mom to three wonderful kids, wife to my best friend, soccer chauffeur, and CEO of DIY! Raised in the Midwest, now living life one day at a time in Connecticut.* The picture of suburban normalcy. Even her profile pic is perfect—a white lady with a warm smile, wearing a cozy sweater and holding a mug with the words "Mom Fuel" in a crafty, cursive font. Jules is currently a member of Neighbor & Friends, Town Hall, and Police Department pages for a few towns that surround Partridge Hollow (PHPD, Lu discovered shortly after moving there, would not deign to broadcast official town business on something as plebian as Facebook).

There's a post from this morning on the Millstone Police Department's page about a suspicious car fire in the parking lot of the Pak-Mail shipping store and ProFinish Auto Solutions on East Farms Road. *Burnt down beyond the frame* was the description Captain Nate Kessler, Head of Arson Investigation Division, gave.

A man with two kids bursts through the coffee shop's doors, ushering in chaos behind them. The younger child, no more than three years old, is calling out his order to the man on a loud loop. *Chocolate chip muffin! Hot chocolate alotta white cream! Bagel bread and butter! But only melted butter!* The other child, a girl who looks to be about four, is singing and dancing along to a video playing on her iPad. The girl's giant over-the-ear headphones appear to be working well, as she cannot hear the strength of her own voice, which is amping up the deeper the trio moves into the space. The man, who looks like an enlarged copy of the boy, is frazzled but is still managing to keep the lid on. They order at the counter and make their way, rolling like a ball of confusion, toward Lu.

"Sorry about all this," the man says as they ease by Lu, balancing mugs and to-go cups and straws and napkins and plastic cutlery.

"Sure," Lu says, in a quick, low chirp.

They settle in at the table right behind her. He plops down in the seat directly backing hers. She pushes in her chair even closer to her table despite there being enough room for him to maneuver. He manages to get the kids situated fairly quickly and the noise they've introduced has simmered to a murmur.

"My wife's traveling and naturally the sitter is sick today," the man says, turning his head slightly to talk to Lu's back. "I was supposed to be here alone." He lowers voice. "You won't say anything to them, will you?"

Lu shoots up out of her slump, her back straight and stiff as a board. She turns her head an inch and barely dips her chin in a nod to show the man—the surprise connect—that she heard him and agrees to leave out the part about his bringing the kids to work. She keeps her ear primed, waiting for the flustered man to feed her the required line. It needs to be the next thing out of his mouth, otherwise she'll have to get up, hurry out the door without looking back, and immediately call in the infraction to The Atlas. From there, she can only hope that the man—and those kids!—won't meet a horrific end. Only once Lu has heard tell of a wily infiltrator from a rival French organization who attempted to hijack a drop by posing as the connect in Luxembourg back in the early nineties. The story was never fully confirmed—or denied—but it's always in the back of Lu's mind during these carefully orchestrated meets.

She clears her throat and moves the cup to her mouth, hoping the man will say what he needs to say and not force her to go through with playacting sipping this horrible brew.

"Sorry to bother you, ma'am, but are you done with that paper?" he says, finally. "There's a story in the science section that I wanted to finish reading."

Again she angles her head, moving her chin slightly toward her shoulder. "About the maglev trains on page . . . ?"

"Page twelve," he says. "That's the one! Can't believe the maintenance costs are thirty-seven percent lower than with those old track trains."

"Fewer moving parts," she says, and rests the cup down next to her plate with the barely touched slice of pie, then pushes back from the table. "Go right ahead. I'm all set." She moves the newspaper toward the edge of her table, just within his casual reach once turned around, and calmly stands and walks out, holding her breath with each unhurried stride until she is outside only steps away from her car.

She starts the vehicle and cruises off. It takes ten miles before she is able to set her shoulders back in the driver's seat. She pulls off her wig, tempted to toss it straight out the window, but opts to chuck it to the floor on the passenger's side. Her personal cell gets pulled out of her pocket next and connects to her car's Bluetooth; she needs music. Definitely something stirring and strong, so she can feel something other than her heart pounding in her chest. She fiddles with the sound system buttons on the dash before mashing the OFF button and sitting in aching silence. For Lu knows what comes next. She knows that in a matter of days she will be gone. Abandoning her family, throwing herself overboard so that Harry and Solomon don't drown. This silence, helping to grind the shards of her heart to dust, is what she deserves.

But then the first *ding* sounds and it seems to unlatch the barrage in her phone's notifications.

Message from Harry Honey
Message from Harry Honey
Message from Annabelle Dupree
Message from Harry Honey
Message from Harry Honey

It's ping after ping, forcing Lu to pull over. That's when a call comes through. It's Harry's special ringtone. He rarely calls, preferring the efficiency of texts.

"H? You good?" she says, her voice shrill and fretful.

"Jesus fucking Christ, Lu! The nanocode . . . it's a fucking bust. Not working. All the data is scrambled and it's failed every single test. Everyone's looking to me for answers and I've got fuck all to say about. Nish."

Lu's stomach leaps into the back of her mouth. She can taste something like bile starting to coat her tongue. "I—I—"

"Lucille, are you there? Can you hear me? Lucille??"

"I—I—I'm here. I—what—what happened?"

"I have no fucking idea, I just said! Are you not hearing me?" he shouts.

"I hear you, I'm hearing you!"

"This is absolutely fucking mad. It was in check last week, now it's cracked?"

The echo and staticky whoosh of feedback lets her know that he's driving with all the windows down. A thing Harry does, no matter the weather, when he needs "the rush of wind to knock some sense into me." Lu almost moves to put all her windows down too. Why didn't she think about this part? So wrapped up in keeping her family safe, Lu didn't account for the section of this where Harry falls apart when his life's work falls apart.

"Where are you? I—I can meet you," she says.

"Uh . . . I don't know. I've been driving in a daze. Had to get out of there. I think I'm in Millstone." Lu hears him slam his fist down on the steering wheel. "How is this happening?"

"Harry, it's OK. We can figure it out."

"Figure it out how, Lu? It's not fucking working." Harry takes a deep breath. "Change of plans. I need to think. I'll just meet you at home later, all right?"

"I get it, I get. I'll just see you later. And, H . . . I love you."

"All right, later," he says, curtly, and disconnects.

Lu stays unblinking, staring at the dashboard for a long beat, then cranks open the car door and vomits.

CHAPTER TWENTY-EIGHT

"Preeee occupied," Solomon says. "That doesn't really make sense, Mom. Pre means before, so you're saying you're *before* busy, or is it *previously* busy?" He uses his fork to shove his mashed potatoes into two separate, small mounds that he's created on his plate. "A better word would be, like, *spacewalking*. So, you would've said, '*I'm sorry, pumpkin, I didn't hear you, I'm kinda spacewalking*,' and I would instantly know what you mean. That you're kinda floating around in your brain. Don't you think that's better?"

Lu pulls herself back down to earth, to the kitchen island where she's seated next to the boy as he plays with his requested bedtime snack of re-warmed mashed potatoes and gravy—"on the side only"—from tonight's dinner. Harry is still out driving. Not a word of check-in from him either. Not since this afternoon when this giant sinkhole—one that Lu didn't fully realize she had created—opened up in the middle of his world and everything that he's worked hard for these many years plummeted right through the center of it.

She feels sick; her throat is raw. And trying to hold it together in front of the boy is a losing game. Lu has apologized for not listening well and for her attention being elsewhere so much in the last hour alone that the child is now trying to analyze the meaning and etymology of the word she keeps using to excuse her brooding behavior. He does have a point, Lu thinks, hearing him in full this time. *Spacewalking* is better than *preoccupied*.

Lu looks down at Solomon's plate, tuning in to the fact that he's not really eating the mashed potatoes that he called for; she's not sure he's even had a single bite. It all looks pushed around and played with at this point.

"Wait a good gosh minute here, young sir," she says, forcing levity into her tone and comportment, placing her hands dramatically on her hips. "Is this whole mash potatoes thing a bit of a stall tactic?" She leans into him, so close that her nose is a kiss away from his temple.

Solomon, trying his hardest to keep a straight face, moves only his eyes to the side to catch a peek at his mother. "Uhhh, if I say yes, will I get in trouble?"

"No . . ."

"OK, then, yes," he says. His chest caves as if he finally let free a long-held breath. "I wasn't even hungry. Sorry, Mom."

"Well, thank you for being honest." Lu gets up and clears the plate of butter-yellow mush mountains. "I'll add this to the dishwasher and finish up down here. You start getting ready for bed, get your bath going." She pushes a soft finger into his cheek.

Solomon's frown is instant and sharp. "Argh. Do I have to?"

"Bathe? Of course. Every day, like you've been doing since you were a baby. And soon, when you get older and a start smelling a little ripe, you might even start doing two-a-days."

His pout only gets heavier. "Not the bath. I like baths. I mean, getting ready for bed. It's the beginning of having to get up tomorrow and go to school. School's the worst. It's so crappy."

"Hey!"

"Sorry, but I'm not allowed to say any of the other words! And crappy doesn't have four letters. Only six."

"Maple Grove is a top-tier school, hon. What makes you say it's so crappy?"

"Wait, can *I* say crappy?"

"No."

"Drats."

"Focus, pumpkin." Lu directs him to hop off the chair. She rests her hand high on his back, gently guiding him toward the stairs as they talk. "If you could list all the things that you don't like about this school, what goes in slots one and two? Just those two."

"Easy." The boy clears his throat dramatically, then takes on a high-pitched, nasally voice, his impression of his favorite ESPN sportscaster. "All right, folks, buckle up, because we're diving into the dark side of Maple Grove Academy. We've seen some incredible performances this season, but not every play can make it to the top. Today, we're counting down the *bottom* of the barrel—the top two worst things about Maple Grove. Let's get riiiiight into it."

As if on cue, Mylo comes trotting around the corner to boost the cute factor of all of it.

Solomon returns to his natural voice. "In slot two, we have the teachers. They are . . . um . . . not good. All of them except my language arts teacher, Ms. Tully. She listens to me and smiles a lot. She does these funny voices when she reads stuff too. She likes comic books—collects them. And I don't know why, but it feels like she *really* loves being a teacher."

"That's very sweet, hon. She probably does really love it." Lu grabs a fluffy sky-blue towel from the linen closet in the hall and hands it to the child while still ushering him toward his bathroom, the puppy dutifully following each step. "And the fact that you can sense that, see it from just the way she acts, is really special, you know that? You're always paying close attention to other people, looking at them in full—their behavior, how they might be feeling deep down inside. It's called being empathetic, and that's a good thing."

"It is?"

"Oh, big time. You can see the human part—the humanity—in other people, and at just eight years old."

"Eight and a half, Mom!"

"I stand corrected, Your Honor. I meant, at almost nine years old. How's that?"

"I'll allow it." Solomon uses the nearby tube of bubblegum toothpaste as a pretend gavel and taps it hard once against the bathroom counter.

"Easy now," she says with a laugh. "Back to the countdown. Hit me with slot number one."

His gavel turns into a microphone gripped in hand and he turns to the mirror to finish his performance from earlier with sportscaster voice pitched up even higher. "The number one thing that makes Maple Grove Academy so crap—*crazy* annoying"—a quick cringe as he checks the mirror for his mother's reaction to the near flub—"is that it's boring. Boring—all caps, folks."

Lu gives him a side-eye and hands him a matching blue washcloth. "Boring is boring, babes. Boring is gonna happen in life, no matter your age or stage. No matter who you are or what you're doing, whether it's school or work or—"

"What you do isn't boring," he says, putting down his partially squished tube of toothpaste and still looking at Lu through the mirror's reflection.

Lu sits on the edge of the tub, keeping her expression pleasant and her tone even and patient, shrouding her quickening pulse and trembling core. She looks back at her son through the mirror with an easy smile. "And what is it that I do, sweetheart?"

The boy takes a long beat before answering, but calmly maintains eye contact with his mother as he seems to consider his best response. "You pretend."

"Pretend? . . . Like in what way?"

Solomon takes off his shirt and rolls it up inside the towel like a sushi chef, casting his eyes down as speaks. "You have all these wigs and glasses and props and stuff in that secret box. And back in Brooklyn you used to go to a studio a lot and go on trips . . . oh, I remember what it's called now—improv! You do improv. Or . . . you're a spy. Both of those sound fun."

Lu's concaved body, perched on the edge of the tub, is ready to completely crumble to dust, her melting mind scrambling for what to say.

"*Improv?* You are so silly, pumpkin," Lu says, ignoring the spy talk. She forces a laugh, making it sound as natural as she can muster. "I'm a Pilates instructor, you know that. In my past lives I've had a range of jobs and adventures, and that box is just the leftover pieces of that." Lu gives the tub a quick rinse and uses the time turned away from the boy to piece her composure back together. "But anyway," she says talking into the tub, her voice slightly raised above the *shoosh* of the faucet, "I'm getting rid of that box. Those adventures are over and done, and so is that old life. OK." A kneeling Lu turns to him, her comportment partially readjusted. "Let's get that bath rockin' and rollin'. It's getting late."

"It's so dark out," he says, slowly removing his socks and rolling them into neat balls. "Wait . . . is Dad sleeping over at work? Can he even do that?"

Lu goes back to dealing with the tub, overly fusses with getting the bath water going now. "Your dad is definitely busy with work, but he'll be home soon. I guarantee it. Now, for this bathwater, sir, would we prefer bubbling or still?"

"Bubbles, please. And could I have the squishy pillow too? And also the table thing you use to watch that show on your iPad . . . *Gold and Grandmas—*"

"Uh, you mean *Golden Girls*—how dare you?" Lu says, clutching her invisible pearls. "No iPads after five PM, you know that. And definitely no iPads during bathtime."

"No, I want to use the table thing to read. I have this big book on dark matter I want to flip through and I don't want to get it wet."

"Ah, OK. Sure, I'll set it up."

"One more thing?" he says, with a light grimace. "Can Mylo hang out in here while I have my bath? He won't lick the water this time! He doesn't like the taste of the soap and bubbles." Mylo wags his tail enthusiastically, leaving Lu briefly wondering how much this paid actor is earning for his part in this well-crafted production.

Lu closes the bathroom door halfway behind her, leaving it ajar enough to keep an ear out for Solomon as she quickly hustles back to the kitchen to grab her phone. She's hoping to see that Harry reached out to let her know he's on his way home.

But there's nothing from him. Still. Only a text from a local number she doesn't recognize. Her mind leaps to Mr. V, posing as some sham company again in order to organize a meet to discuss the latest tumult.

But, Lu reminds herself, Mr. V is dead.

Back upstairs, she cruises by Solomon's bathroom door en route to her closet, quietly chanting the same two words over and again: *another way, another way, another way.* There's got to be another way for her to stay here with her family but still keep them safe, keep them protected from the long, severe reach of The Atlas. There's got to be a way to fix things for Harry without her tracking more mud through his pristine career. A way for her to pay off this debt owed without sacrificing her own free life lived.

Once installed in her corner office, Lu rummages through the box for the company phone. She's not even sure what she wants to ask Royce but starts dialing into the answering service anyway. On the second ring, Lu hangs up. The reality of it all stares her raw in the face. More than selfish, staying here with them is dangerous. Solomon is much too bright and this brand of work too dark. Maybe, after a year or two, if the world finally spins her way, she will be able to quit this crooked life and return unburdened to her real one, the good one. And by then, maybe Solomon won't hate her. Maybe Harry will be able forgive her. Maybe she might too. Maybe.

Maybe.

"MOM, CAN YOU come back in here?" Solomon calls out to Lu from his darkened bedroom. "It's important." His face looks obviously sleepy when Lu turns on his soft lamp, and his voice is a little froggy. Clearly, he had already started dozing off before a last thought roused him awake.

Lu pads over to the cushy bench at the foot of his bed. She doesn't want to get too close for fear that the boy will see her flushed, damp face and red, teary eyes. She's expecting a second bedtime story request or at least a last flip-through of one of his jumbo, high-def photo books on space as she curls up beside him, looking on in genuine wonder. He'll be more focused on the book and story than her weepy face, she tells herself. "Hey, sweets. What's up? You OK?"

"Yeah," he says through a yawn. "I just want to tell you something."

"Tell me," she says, resting a hand on his foot poking out from under the thick duvet.

"OK, remember at bathtime when I said that my number one reason for hating Maple Grove is that it's boring? Can I change that?"

"Sure. If there's something that plucks your nerves more . . ."

"Boring is still on the list; let's not get too confident here. But I'm moving it to the number three reason."

"So, what's the top reason?"

"The real number one thing is the other kids." His eyes go from drowsy to indignant, then sad. Watching him deflate ruins Lu further. "Everyone in my class acts like I'm an alien. Like I'm speaking a different language that they've never even heard of before. I told you; Declan and Asher are the only ones who don't act like I'm some little weird nerd boy."

"Little weird nerd boy? *Honey* . . . you are not any of those things. Not even a little bit." Lu moves closer to him, scooching over on the side of the bed, no longer concerned about her tearstained face. "I know it's going to sound like something moms are supposed to say, but I want you to really listen to me, Solomon. You are the most captivating person I've ever met—no question. I have learned something utterly spellbinding from you each of the three thousand, one hundred and two-and-a-half days that you have blessed me with your being here . . . including how to calculate eight-and-a-half years into days."

He smiles, and it's real and sugary and infectious. The shine in his eye sparks up again too, though it's just a gleam for now, but Lu will take it. She presses her hand against his soft cheek and leans even closer to look into her child's doleful eyes. "I'm so happy that you were honest with me about the things that make Maple Grove crappy—"

"Mom! You said we shouldn't say—"

"Shh-shh, I know what I said; we'll both allow it this last time." His grin is darling but small, as the tiredness slides back into his face. He looks cozy and tucked-in, ready for sleep to come back to him. But Lu has something more to say while she still has his attention. It's something she knows that she must say, right this minute, because the countdown clock has already started for her. She heard the thing click on in the very moment she agreed to relinquish her dream of retirement and was reinstated at The Atlas. "I want to be honest too, and tell you something," Lu says, moving her hand from cradling the side of the boy's face to rest on his chest, right over his heart. "Do you know what the word exponentially means? You've heard it before, right?"

"Mm-hmm. When I learned about the Big Bang and cosmic inflation; Dad explained it."

"Good. Well, the thing is, Solomon, you've changed my whole world. From the day you were born, my life got exponentially better. It improved by leaps and bounds, all because of you. And I consider myself truly lucky to have you, *specifically* you, as my child. To be exposed to your big brain and even bigger heart, to feel your love, your brilliance and energy every single day—it's a life force that makes my heart swell with pride and real joy." Both Lu and the boy's eyes are twinkling now with tears, though he is trying his hardest to be steady about it, blinking rapidly and nibbling the side of his bottom lip. "I know you're tired and I'm saying a lot at once, but if you remember anything from all of this honesty and tender hearts, I hope it's this: You are exceptional, Solomon Ali Barlow, and the very best thing I have every had a hand in creating."

A single tear escapes the boy's eye, tracing a clear line along his right cheek, but then quickly disappears into the curl of his lip as it pulls his smile wider. "Mom," he whispers. "You make everything better."

Lu knows her voice is about to break along with everything else in her chest held together by the flimsiest string now. She swallows the grainy lump in her throat and fixes Solomon's bed linens, folding down here and gathering there. He reaches a hand out from beneath the taut covers and places it on the inside of her forearm, catching her in the midst of the fluttering. She stops moving and he keeps his hand resting on her through the pause, as if he can sense that she needs to be told, even wordlessly, to take the breath, that it's OK, and that he understands.

CHAPTER TWENTY-NINE

Harry arrives home at exactly 2:16 AM. Not a single text sent regarding his whereabouts. His phone died, Lu had reassured herself a few times, as she sat on the literal edge of her seat in the family room waiting for him. Her dry, strained eyes had been glued to the hallway that starts at the side door, watching to see that he arrived in one piece. She figured he had been out somewhere drinking, alone or with newfound "friendlies," as he liked to call the inebriated people one meets in bars after the witching hour has arrived and the tab is as long as a human arm. When he crosses the swath of rug over hardwood that ran in front of the family room, it's clear that he had hit the bottles hard. His long stride—a swagger that usually teetered perfectly between self-possessed and stately with a just-right dash of arrogance and sex—has turned into a sloppy stagger toward the stairs. He only notices Lu sitting in the dim room after Mylo and his clinking collar tags trotted across his path.

"Hey," he says, gruffly, then gives his wife a slack salute from the distance. No approach. No kiss. No draping hug. Not even a slinky grope of her breast or bum, as the man was known to do after a few Negronis. "Heading up. Talk about it tomorrow." This isn't a question and so Harry doesn't wait for her response before continuing to lurch over to the stairs and on to their bedroom.

As much as Mr. V exalted her preternatural aptitude for this brand of work over these many years—*one of one*—Lu has always thought it was mostly a case of luck being on her side. That, plus her ability to look beyond the first layer of what is being presented. Sometimes this homing in came from a simple tilt of her head for a new perspective, but usually it was the result of her sitting still long enough for an alternative, an escape route, a solution to materialize. But sat here, in a room almost the size of their last apartment, with the two biggest parts of her beating heart asleep upstairs, Lu must reconcile with what has been laid bare. They don't deserve this, and, more importantly, she doesn't deserve them. Luck has left her. Now, she must face what her dirty dealings have wrought.

When Lu finally arrives upstairs, he's already peeled out of his hand-tailored pinstripe suit, leaving it rolled up halfway underneath the armoire and stripped down to his boxers, having obviously forgone a shower—an absolute anomaly for Harrison Barlow. He is stretched out diagonally across their king-size bed, lightly snoring. She nudges him gently at first, then with more weight. He rolls his head toward her. The gravity of her expression jolting him fully awake.

"What's wrong?" he says, his eyes red and wide. "Solomon?"

Lu shakes her head. "I . . ." This is as far as she got in thinking about what to tell Harry, how to tell him that she's leaving him and Solomon behind not because she wants to, but because there is no other choice.

Harry gets up from the bed and goes for his pants on the floor. The sound of him roughly pushing his legs, left then right, into each pantleg sounds as loud as thunder in the awful silence of the room. "Is this about the box?" he says, and zips the fly piece, leaving the side tab undone.

Lu exhales and her chest sinks. Her body tilts back the two inches to meet the wall behind her, knocked over by Harry's words. "What?"

"Solomon, he told me. Yesterday. You have a secret box in there"—he motions over to her closet with a slight nod—"*with props*, as he called it. I pressed him—he didn't want to say. Didn't want break his promise to you. His *promise*," Harry says, glowering at Lu. "He said it's wigs in this hidden box, and money and passports and—and—and a bloody diamond necklace from a friend or something. What the fuck, Lu? Is there someone else? You making that boy keep your secrets?" His brows are knitted tightly together and his jaw is practically locked in place as he waits with literal bated breath for Lu's response.

"No, no . . . it's not like that, it's, it's . . . complicated."

"I would imagine it is," he snaps.

Lu forces herself to maintain eye contact. "It's a debt—kind of—that I have to clear for my guardian, Vincent."

"Your what?"

"Guardian . . . foster parent, father . . . *ish* figure—"

"You said that you had no family," Harry says. "An orphan. No ties to anyone, but now there's guardian, Victor?"

"Vincent," she whispers.

"Vincent, Victor, whatever! The fact is you've never mentioned this man to me, not once in a fucking decade. And now you're paying off his debts?"

"He was my longest and most stable foster parent, and then when I turned eighteen, he became . . . my mentor."

"Mentor in what? Pilates? Breathwork? Mindful fucking stretching?" Harry's eyes are red and bulging. It's obvious he wants to roar and howl, but a sleeping Solomon at the end of the hall and Mylo downstairs in his cushy crate successfully hold him back.

And Lu wants nothing more than to collapse through the floor, let her whole body shatter to shards and dust against the hard basement tile, if that will make this nightmare end. She works to keep her voice down too, for Solomon's sake, yes, but also to maintain a leveled tone and to avoid devolving into a mewling mess. "He was part of a crime organization and got up to a lot of bad things—"

"Is this man a fucking mobster?! Are you about to sit there and tell me that your fake father of the last *thirty-odd years* is running around murdering people, cutting off horses' heads like he's bleedin' Don Corleone?"

"Not murder . . . just other things."

"Oh, assorted crimes, then. Right. That's better."

"Harry, please. I know it's a lot and it's shocking and horrible, but this is important. Just hear me out, OK?"

He bows his head, pinching the bridge of his nose with his thumb and middle finger. "All right," he says, the words tumble out reluctantly. "Go on, then."

She takes a shallow breath. "He had a hand in a lot of different things, and I'm caught in the middle of some of that . . . because of him. And now I need to clear this debt."

"You? Why doesn't he deal with his own dirt?"

"Because he's dead, Harry."

His head pops up. "What . . . ? Jesus, was he . . . killed?" For the first time since this torturous talk began, there's real terror moving across Harry's face "Lucille, are you in danger? Are *we*?"

"It's . . . it's not black-and-white like that."

"Are you mad?" he spits. "Not black-and-white? Either we are in danger or we're not. Do we need to go to the police?"

Lu springs out of her defeated lean, her arms extended and palms exposed as she takes a few easy steps toward a shaken Harry. "No, no, no . . . no police. That will make it much, much worse. This organization is not a game. Its reach is long and sweeping."

"So what are you telling me? We just sit around waiting for a might-be-deadly crime syndicate to possibly come in here and slit our three throats in the night?"

"No, that's not what they . . . that's not going to happen." Lu leans back on the vanity.

"Tell me then. What *is* going to happen?"

Lu's stomach sinks further to her knees. "Harry, I need to get this all settled and—"

"This mysterious debt?"

"Yes," she whispers.

"How? How, Lu? How are you—a mum from fucking Partridge Hollow by way of Brooklyn—going to match wits with some crazy crime org? We need to go to the police."

She scuttles over to him, grabbing his arm before he can take another step forward. "We can't! You have to just trust me, H." Lu is looking right at him, staring directly into his eyes, imploring him to listen this last time.

"Trust you?" he scoffs. "Why would I do that?"

"Because you love me and I love you and we are real. This family is real. And we both know that we would lay down our full lives to protect that boy."

Lu's words penetrate Harry's irritated skin. He concedes with a nod and rests back on his heels. He brings his hand behind his head, interlocking his fingers as he looks up to the dim light and slowly walks around in a loose circle. He stops after the third rotation and, with a loud exhale, looks sharply at Lu. "So, what now?"

"I will fix this, but . . . I can't do that with you, with *him*, here." Lu shakes her head. "I can work this through—but I have to leave." Her eyes well up right as she readies to tell him the most concocted part. ". . . just for a little while."

Harry makes his way over to her, now standing arm's-length from his wife. "You promise me right fucking now, Lu. No harm's coming to that boy. Promise me," he hisses.

"I promise," she says, but it's half-swallowed. She stares back at him, repeating it, strong and resolute. "I promise you. He's safe."

Harry's eyes are lined with water as he glares at Lu. "Then, yes," he says, calmly. "You need to leave. Whatever *this* is, I don't want it anywhere near that boy."

Lu's face melts behind a rush of tears; her mouth is open but only a hollow choking sound escapes as her body buckles in place. Harry, his expression like stone, steps back from her as if she were a ticking bomb on the last set of digits.

"I—I'm so sorry," she says, sobbing, the few words trickling out before the rush of everything breaks through the dam, a choppy reservoir sending Lu pitching forward.

Harry, naturally, lunges to catch her. And does what he promised, twelve years ago, that he'd always do: be there, stand with, support, love. *Ever and a day.*

He's angry—Lu can feel the heat of that burning through his skin—but also patently destroyed by what has come to pass. "Jesus Christ," he mutters into the top of Lu's head. "This is going to crush every chamber of that boy's heart to wake up and find you gone."

Lu is fighting for her life trying to keep from crumbling into a soggy, howling disaster. She buries her wet face into Harry's bare chest. "Tell him that my brain is sick, that I've unraveled and needed to go get better . . . or that I'm helping a friend who needs me more than both of you right now. Whatever it is, he has to know that it's not his fault I left," she pleads. "It's not because of anything he did or didn't do. Make sure, Harrison. Please. Tell him this has nothing to do with him. Convince him. He must know that he is good and perfect."

This seems to pierce Harry's cold front and he wraps himself tighter around Lu, gripping the back of her shirt as if letting go would mean falling to his death. "It's just for a little while," he whispers, his voice reedy and wounded.

Lu nods, though she is not agreeing with his affirmation. She has no clear idea on how long she will have to keep working to settle up with The Atlas. Helping her to keep Harry's name free and clear while tossing other plausible culprits under the fast-moving bus could have Lu on the line for eight months or eight years. Royce doesn't even believe retirement is a real thing for their kind. What Lu does know, assuredly, is that she will be living a life deep in the shadows, heartsick and ruined, only able to watch Harry and Solomon from far enough away. That she will never be able to forgive herself for destroying the one thing she's wanted the most ever since her very first breath: a family.

She manages to pin all of this havoc back behind her chest and look up, sweetly, at her remarkable husband. She's ever grateful that he doesn't recoil or shove her away in this strained moment. He's not smiling but the rage and resentment behind his eyes have dimmed as traces of warmth, and maybe even love, begin to dawn. She wants to kiss him, deep, long, and with everything moving through her trembling body, to climb on top of him one more time, one last time, and proclaim the obvious.

I love you.

Ever and a day. The last four words of their wedding vows.

But that is too much, too soon. Instead Lu chooses another four words, saying them to Harry gently. "For a little while."

CHAPTER THIRTY

COPENHAGEN. DECEMBER.

"What, you don't like oysters?" Evelyn Royce says before tossing her head back and slurping down her tenth briny mollusk. Her hair, still cropped short on the sides, is now an icy platinum blond and the pompadour is deconstructed into a sleek, side-swept bang. Everything else about her is the same, although her matte red lipstick does appear brighter, possibly a throw to the holiday decorations surrounding them at the well-regarded seafood spot, Blue Wave Bistro.

"Too slimy," Lu says, swallowing a yawn. She reaches over her own artfully plated but untouched food—sea bass in a Barolo sauce, ordered for her in advance by Royce—and grabs her shot glass with a heavy pour of aquavit and downs it. Alcohol has been her one saving grace.

"Fair, but slimy ain't always bad, right?"

Lu nods and grunts out a couple of barely intelligible words. This is the third meeting like this that she's had with Royce since arriving in Denmark a month ago. The confabs consist of Royce gorging on food while urging Lu to "live a little," as far as her palate is concerned, and a recounting of how well Lu's last jobs have gone.

The two women are seated in the restaurant's moody private room adorned with rich, velvety upholstery, ornate chandeliers, and more candles than a Catholic cathedral.

"Did you receive the updated dossier on the Venezia collection?" Royce asks, digging into her elaborate bouillabaisse. "The client has extended the ask. It'll mean an extra day for you in Naples to organize and time code the second site."

"What's the additional?" Lu says.

"They want the Masquerade Gems too," Royce says between slurps. "Those hideous masks with the overdone diamonds and rubies . . . but who am I to judge? They ask, we get it."

The masquerade mention pulls Lu's mind away from the depressing table and sends her back a short distance in time to the infamous Secret Garden Gala two months ago. She makes a point of not thinking about Partridge Hollow much. It's dangerous, and leaves her barely able to function. But she lets it come this time, the musing, thinking about the opulence of the event, the gowns, the food . . . dancing with Harry that night.

Harrison. His name alone brings an ache to her body. She was practically comatose for two days after accidentally hearing part of a new voicemail from him on her old phone. He was struggling to find the words to fill the hard silences as he told Lu of his new job. After a "fluke" computer glitch was discovered as the reason for the failed nanocode tests, Harry had said, he decided to continue his telomeres work, but as the head of R&D

at a government-funded, highly respected lab based in Queens—a position Lu knew that he landed all on his own. No assist from The Atlas. He and Solomon had already moved back to Brooklyn, he added. She was happy to hear it but couldn't bear to at the same time. When she recovered from listening to the missive, Lu made sure to destroy her personal cell phone in the back of a lonely limo while heading to yet another airport. Before wrecking the phone, though, she re-read the news stories about Partridge Hollow's troubles. The Atlas arranged the anonymous release of Jonathan's blackmail video and exposed Ward's shady dealings trying to save his soon-to-be ex-wife's failing business. The subsequent investigations into their personal woes spilled over to Kastille, with authorities taking a closer look at the company's innerworkings, which kicked over the powder keg containing Mac Pearson's insider trading troubles, and overnight, the biotech giant became a veritable sinking ship. She also finally read the missed message from Annabelle from that fateful afternoon of the nanocode meltdown.

No surprise, the power house Realtor's text was a tea-spill, this time about Finola "nearabout running off to Asia in the middle of night," and about her having multiple offers on the Greys' house practically overnight.

Lu still had a burning rage in her gut knowing that Finola never got her comeuppance. Mr. V, for all of his flaws, deserved a better end than that.

She has recently found herself dreaming about Mr. V, once or twice, in the midst of her tortured sleeps. Mostly replays of things he'd told her, echoes of his proverbs for living an honorable life, and she wonders what he might say if he were to see her now, hollowed out and disassociated—that is, when she's not drowned in alcohol and sweaty, fighting her burly demons.

Lu reaches for her other glass now—this one filled with straight vodka—and takes a strong sip. But it does nothing to guard against what's already stirring in her belly. It always begins in her belly and surges straight to her brain. She's never prepared for it. They rush in like a tsunami, thoughts of Solomon. When it happens, usually in the middle of the night, Lu lets it engulf her, and she sobs and pushes her face deep into her pillow until she is struggling to breathe. Why it's happening now, in the middle of this gaudy restaurant while Royce prattles on about bejeweled masks and time codes and oysters, is baffling. Maybe it's because Solomon's ninth birthday is in a couple of weeks, Christmas Day.

The boy will always be the best gift she has ever received.

Lu has three massive bags filled with gifts for him back at her all-cash luxury rental. Every day this week, she has ventured out with the full intention of shipping the parcels off to him. But each day she begs off and carries it all back to her place, vowing to try tomorrow.

"I have to tell you," Royce says, interrupting Lu's off-balance reverie. "I wasn't keen on you at first. Thought you'd be a lot of work. Prima donna. But you've been excellent. File on time. No hassles. No attitude. Think I've heard ten words out of you since you landed here."

"OK," Lu says, looking back at her blankly.

"Make that eleven words," Royce says, chuckling to herself. "Anyway, could be the holidays getting to me, but just want to say, this has been good so far. I'm glad they changed the plan." She returns to sopping up the last bits of sauce from her shallow bowl with the end piece of some crusty bread.

Lu tilts her head. "The plan?"

Royce stops mid-chew, and Lu can see the mushy piece of wet bread rolling over her tongue. "Ah . . . think I got too comfortable there, Twenty-two. Disregard."

Lu squints at the woman, locking in on her eyes. Royce, a mostly cool customer, is now slightly shifty, her gaze bouncing between Lu and the bottle of sparking water between them.

"What plan?" Lu says, her tone sharpened.

Royce pulls the white linen napkin up from her lap and dabs it over her full mouth. "OK . . . you're an adult, you can handle it. In the original script, you were getting killed off."

"What?"

"Too many strikes."

"Strikes."

"Yeah. You were real late with the Neapolitan necklace drop, that's one. Then there was a chance that you left a paw print on that security guard's face when you two scrapped it out. That turned out to be a bust, but they still had to look into possibly cleaning that up for you. That's strike two. But it was that last job in Connecticut that sealed it. You became a liability. So, the plan was whether you succeeded or not, they were not moving forward with you. Your old guy, Seven, went in for all the marbles to protect you, and you saw where that got him. But . . . it also made them take a second look at you, as an asset, and then you called for help. Perfect timing, I guess. What did that famous economist say? *There are no solutions, only trade-offs.*" Royce goes back to picking at the scraps on her many plates scattered around her. She catches Lu's disconcerted, distant stare. "Hey . . . they changed their mind. That's a *good* thing. Everybody won. Balance restored."

"Right," Lu says, nodding. She drags an easy smile across her face while beneath the calm surface, all the pieces begin to click loudly into place. The clarity on what she needs to do next is brighter than the Hope Diamond. She whispers a classic Vincent King epigram to herself, even invoking his crisp Jamaican accent in her head: *When yuh dig fowl, yuh dig up duppy.*

He had told Lu this gem a handful of times when she was in her very early twenties and still bitter, angry about not knowing who her mother was or where her real roots began. Back then, Lu would often think up schemes, ways she might disrupt the faulty foster care system from the inside, hack into its databases and wipe them clean or divert the government's funding to go directly to the suffering kids. The few times that she relaxed enough to share her revenge fantasy with him, he would listen in full to her short but heartfelt rants, and then counter with the colorful phrase. At first she didn't understand, but he slowed it all down once—the last time he told her this—and explained what the warning meant.

"When you seek to bring someone harm," he had said, "you might just unearth bigger problems and bring a new world of trouble onto yourself."

But Lu is ready to dig things up. The Atlas had fucked around, and now it's time for them to find out.

CHAPTER THIRTY-ONE

BERLIN. SEPTEMBER.

Lu has plotted out this course six times over and has done the run-through at least twenty. With each rehearsal—both on her video rendering and live in the miniature replica that she built in an abandoned barn—she has been able to shave off an additional three-point-two seconds. And now, as she crouches beside a fleet of silver Mercedes-Benz panel vans at the end of the lot, preparing to run the mission for real, she feels exceedingly confident about pulling this off. She'll be able to get into the site and out in eighteen minutes.

She is dressed in all new black attire. Each piece of the upgraded uniform is the more aerodynamic and souped-up version than the previous one, and her ski mask is so thin and breathable, it feels like there's nothing there at all. Her night goggles are streamlined as well and look like a regular pair of spectacles with a slightly thicker prescription. She can wear them the whole time, from the dim parking lot to inside the brightest server room, as the state-of-the-art glasses have an improved sensor that detects even the slightest light change in any environment.

The only possible hitch, her chronically sore, permanently wrecked ankle, is taped and bandaged tight, wedged into her lightweight but ultra-sturdy boots.

Lu has envisioned this moment so many times, it's practically etched on the inside of her eyelids. But she is ready, almost excited to get to it.

She reaches up and lightly rests her gloved hand against her chest, just below the jugular notch, to touch the pendant hanging there from the delicate gold chain beneath her heat-tech neoprene jacket and Teflon-coated bodysuit. The chain is the same one Harry gave her the morning after Solomon was born. She replaced the original pendant—a darling, gold disc that used an original, vintage fiscal school year letterpress calendar featuring the month of December with a small perfect diamond marking the date of the twenty-fifth—with something that she had custom made in London back in the spring. The new charm, a fresh ode to her boy, is a tiny glass vial pendant with a swirling design of deep blue, black, and silver flecks, resembling a mini galaxy. It has been her amulet since the moment she strung it onto the chain, and she couldn't imagine attempting this specific job without it. She looks down at her watch next—once again held as prized and lucky—and waits for the sweep hand to round up to the twelve before she takes off sprinting toward the darkened, featureless building in the short distance.

Once inside and with her tools neatly stowed on her person—no more weighty rucksacks or totes—Lu continues to flow through each studied move methodically, with the exactness of an atomic clock. She goes directly to the server room on the main floor, encased in a temperature-controlled, all-glass room resembling a greenhouse, but instead with icy, negative degrees inside. After hacking the main digital security panel to the room, she's inside in fifteen seconds flat. Her heat-tech gear activates from head to toe to maintain her body temperature at 97.6 degrees while she moves slowly through the freezing space. She slides through the narrow passageway between each of the silent servers until she gets to the third one from the front, where the bulk of The Atlas's encrypted operational blueprints are kept, namely, the active—and more important—upcoming mission files. She unlatches her glove attachment, reaching into her cuff to her special gold bangle, near identical to the piece Mr. V gifted her decades ago. With this new version, which Lu had purchased for herself on New Year's Day, she is able to download files via Bluetooth with just a steady wrist held up close to the server port.

She finishes up in the glass box, then reverses each step and makes her way out of there, clean. Lu finds herself down by the side doors of The Atlas's deeply undercover secondary headquarters without even so much as a hurried breath or an anxious trot—and with forty-two seconds to spare. Still, she sprints back across the lot to her waiting BMW motorcycle, lying on its side tucked beneath the underbrush, her black helmet wedged beside the front wheel. She peels the ski mask up past her mouth, just enough to breathe in the fresh, cool air, and hops onto her bike. Lu pulls the clutch in and puts the gear shifter into neutral, rolling the bike forward while on her tiptoes. When she gets close to the portion of the back fence with the huge hole that she had cut open herself ninety minutes ago, she starts the engine.

Lu jets off into the night, her wicked grin stretching wider with each kilometer climbed on the speedometer and the façade of The Atlas's modest building growing darker and more distant in her side-view mirror. By the time she is a quarter of the way from her hotel, Lu is practically laughing aloud, her face bright and alive. This is the first step toward her real future. The is the first step toward reclaiming her life, reclaiming her true loves.

For she is the duppy they dug up.

And she is bringing a whole galaxy of trouble right to their front door.

The End

ACKNOWLEDGMENTS

This story has lived in different parts of my brain for more than a decade. To see it now, at last a book out in the real world, is exhilarating. Honestly, I don't have the words to describe this brand of joy. Know that my heart is full.

I want to start by thanking you, the readers. Domestic thriller is a new genre for me. It's been (let the pun be!) a thrilling adventure, and I'm so honored to have you here, riding along with me at every turn.

Thank you to my literary agents Carolyn Forde and Lisa Rambert. Your dedication, thoughtful guidance and endless support is a true blessing. Having fellow Canadians in my corner is perfect, sweet icing on the cake.

To my editors Rebecca Nelson and Marcia Markland, cover designer Heedayah Lockman, and the entire Crooked Lane team, thank you for all the hard work and care you've poured into this novel. I feel so fortunate to work alongside folks who consider collaboration a key ingredient for success.

Big, hollering thank-you to Estelle Laure, for the smart questions, kind heart, and expert edits, forcing me to dig deeper while also keeping my voice centered. You're a gift.

To my ever-smart film co-agents Sanjana Seelam and Mary Pender at WME, thanks for your instant enthusiasm and sharp vision for the WILTY universe.

Thanks to my family, who continue to keep me afloat with their love, laughter, and eternal support. I'm so grateful for my parents, Maureen and Tony Blades, and my *sestras*, Yvette and Nailah. Sending more love and thanks to my brother Sean, brothers-in-law Everton and Monté, and sister-in-law Faye. Big, tight hugs and kisses to my sweet nieces-pieces Ebonie, Tishana, Symone, Nina, and Zoë, and the best nephew ever, Jackson. Thank you to the Burton family especially my big-hearted, deeply missed, late mother-in-law, Janet Burton.

The list of dear friends and colleagues who continue to support me through my entire career is as long as an elephant's trunk. I am forever grateful to have you all in my life. I do want to highlight a few folks whose pep talks, advice, valuable two cents, needed reminders, early draft reads, and endless cheers were instrumental in getting this book to the finish line: Sadeqa Johnson, Colleen Oakley, Karma Brown, Amy Reichert, Saada Branker, Laura Dave, Barney Bishop, Ravi Howard, Lloyd Boston, and Todd Wilson.

Thank you for the very kind words, Attica Locke, Emily Carpenter, Hank Phillipi Ryan, Sandra Block, Amity Gaige, and the other fabulous, rock-star writers who offered advanced praise for this book. You've made my entire year!

Sweet Murphy, thanks for being a good-good boy and constant, lightly-snoring, ever-snuggly companion through every step of writing this book.

And, of course, thank you to my extraordinary Quinn. You remain the very best thing I've ever had a hand in creating.

To Scott: For all of the love, encouragement, kindness, and care you show me—across two decades and counting—the words thank-you will never be enough. You have my heart, completely, and continue to treat it as a precious gem. I love you. Like, a lot.